ELENA'S EYES WERE TIGHTLY SHUT. IF THIS WAS A DREAM, IT HAD ALL THE TEXTURE OF REALITY.

She felt the forest floor beneath her feet. Stiff, starched clothing enclosed her from head to toe. And in her hand was something small and solid and cold. Its icy surface pulsed in her grip, writhing to be free.

Then the sounds began. The screams and cries were distant at first, but they grew louder. A nameless fear spread through this strange new body that Elena found herself possessed of.

Her eyes snapped open. She was surrounded by a frenzied mob, all in old-fashioned clothes. Torchlight was reflected on their contorted faces. And looming over her was a man. He had been handsome—once. The corpselike pallor, the blank eyes, the slack jaw with torn bits of dirt and weeds clinging to the teeth...

It was the face of a dead man. The corpse clutched blindly at her hands, trying with soulless desperation to pry open her fingers, to reach the icy talisman.

Also by
GENE DeWEESE

The Wanting Factor

A DIFFERENT DARKNESS

GENE DeWEESE

PLAYBOY
PAPERBACKS

A DIFFERENT DARKNESS

Copyright © 1982 by Gene DeWeese

Cover illustration copyright © 1982 by PBJ Books, Inc., formerly PEI Books, Inc.

All rights reserved. No part of this book may be reproduced, stored in a retrieval system or transmitted in any form by an electronic, mechanical, photocopying, recording means or otherwise without prior written permission of the author.

Published simultaneously in the United States and Canada by PBJ Books, Inc., formerly PEI Books, Inc., 200 Madison Avenue, New York, New York 10016. Printed in the United States of America. Library of Congress Catalog Card Number: 82-81381.

ISBN: 0-867-21201-2

First printing November 1982

For Carl Brill and the Trinity Trio, Pat Cameron, Beth Weber, and Joyce Harling, whose help in finding out what really *happens to dead bodies was invaluable.*

AUTUMN, 1910

On the tenth night, when he could resist her call no longer, Henry Winton returned to his sister's unmarked grave.

The first leaves of autumn crackled beneath the worn soles of his plow shoes as he moved determinedly through the shadows of the towering oaks and ghostly white birches that covered the hills behind the scorched remains of the Reimann mansion. Only occasional drops of moonlight reached soundlessly to the ground as the dry north wind shivered through the branches and worked its way through his heavy flannel shirt and work-worn overalls. Behind him, the jagged walls of the mansion, a massive skeleton of what once had been, loomed dark against the midnight sky. The bitter, metallic stench of sodden ashes still filled the air and scraped at his lungs. From the darkness ahead came the distant splashing of the creek as it tumbled over the series of shallow, rocky falls and into the shrub-filled ravine that slashed through the woods a hundred yards beyond the grave. But Henry Winton barely heard it.

Abruptly, he stumbled to a halt. Without looking down, listening only to the wordless voice that whispered coldly in his mind, he knew that he had reached his goal. In his mind's eye he could see the mass of dead branches and leaves spread over the mound of raw earth at his feet. His hands, callused from a full summer in the fields, were clenched around the spade; and his wiry young body trembled with each shuddering breath.

Finally, he was able to move again, to look down at what he knew was there. His sister's face, like a mirror image of his own agonized soul, joined the whispering voice to beckon from the darkness at his feet.

In a spasm of motion, he kicked and scraped at the tangled branches and matted leaves until the irregular mound of dirt lay bare. The dozens of footprints that had been stamped into the soil with such fear and fury were already eroding and fading. Another rain, like the sudden downpour that had quenched the burning mansion and drenched the departing mob, would easily complete the process.

Still trembling stiffly, Henry Winton positioned the spade at the center of the dark oval mound and brought his right foot down hard on the top of the blade, driving it into the soil almost to the handle. It would go quickly at the start, he thought gratefully as he pried up the clods of dirt and heaved them to one side. For the first foot or two, he could use all his strength, letting the physical exertion warm him and mask the icy core of fear within. But soon he would not dare to thrust the spade blindly into the earth but would be forced to feel his way cautiously, an inch at a time.

As he rammed the spade into the ground once more, he felt his stomach twist; his mind conjured up grisly images at the thought that the grave was shallower than he had remembered. But he would take no chances. Even if it meant scraping through a foot of the gummy clay with his bare hands, he would take no chances. Jessica had suffered enough, at his own hands and at the hands of others, without having to undergo this final horror.

At a little over two feet, the odor began.

Gasping and then holding his breath, he scrambled out of the hole. Shuddering, he stumbled through the woods to the creek, where he soaked his huge cotton bandanna and tied the now-icy cloth over his mouth and nose like an outlaw's mask. It helped a little, but the pungent odor still filled his nostrils as he lowered himself once more into the pit.

As he forced himself to pick up the spade, he could think of nothing but the time, a dozen years before, when a dog had burrowed its way under the family's house to die. It had been found only because of the smell, and Henry, the only male member of the Winton family small enough, had had to wriggle in and drag the body out. His nightmares had lasted over a month, nightmares in which the foul odor almost suffocated him, nightmares in which the dog howled piteously as Henry dragged its disintegrating but still twitching carcass through the narrow, filthy crawl space.

Soon, as the odor grew steadily more stomach-wrenching, he put the spade aside and dropped to his hands and knees. He tried to breathe only through his mouth, but the odor was so thick that it filled the air like a haze and formed a slimy coat on his teeth and tongue.

Warily, fighting back nausea with every motion, he began to work with his fingers. Compared to its original hard-packed state, the clay was soft despite the efforts of the dozen people who had filled the grave and tamped it down. Even so, his hands were raw and his nails torn and broken when his fingers finally touched the filth-encrusted cloth of her sleeve.

In that instant of contact, his hand jerked back as if the cloth were a red-hot stove lid. His body lurched sideways, his shoulder gouging into the jagged wall of earth. For a moment the darkness swirled around him, and it seemed that he could see the outline of her entire body stretched out beneath him, but he knew that it could only be illusion, fostered by the constant whisper of her voice as it wordlessly urged him on.

But she *was* there. Her body, hidden now by no more than a few inches of earth, was not an illusion.

And the talisman was there.

And as long as it remained, she could have no peace.

He could have no peace.

Ignoring the stench and blotting out the pain in his torn fingers, he took the dirt, handful by trembling handful, and flung it from the grave. Gradually, her arm, still encased in the heavily bloused sleeve, was uncovered.

And then her hand.

He shuddered anew as the hand appeared, giving visible body to the odor of rot and decay that almost smothered him. It was no longer Jessica's hand but a blackened caricature, closed tightly into a shriveled fist and pressed hard against her sunken stomach.

Slowly, with a soft moan escaping through clenched teeth, he turned the hand over and began to pry open the fingers. He could feel their leathery texture beneath the slimy coating of clay, and he prayed that they would not crumble.

Reluctantly, with a soft popping sound, her dead fingers yielded and opened.

The talisman lay in her palm, a seven-sided pool of darkness that seemed to drain even the faint starlight from the air. He could see where, in her last moments, her bone-cracking grip had forced the edges of the talisman's metallic frame deep into her flesh. The chain, broken when she had torn it from Marcus Reimann's neck, was still tangled around her fingers.

For a long time Henry Winton could not force himself to move, desite the wordless pleas that whispered ever more urgently in his mind. But he knew he must. Jessica could not be free until the thing was destroyed. His sister could not be free, and he could not be free. Her call, still burning in his mind, repeated that simple fact again and again.

His hand shaking, he took the chain in his bleeding fingers and pulled. Her hand, her entire arm, was lifted. The sounds of the dislodged dirt falling into the hollow where her arm had been were loud in his ears, but they were drowned by the sudden resurgence of her voice. No longer was it a distant, wordless whisper. Each syllable was now crystal clear, but the language was not of this earth.

There was a desperate urgency as her bodiless voice echoed through his mind, the same urgency that had brought him to the grave, but multiplied a hundredfold.

Unable to help himself, he began to speak, his lips and tongue contorted to form the guttural, alien sounds.

As he spoke, the pool of darkness in her hand seemed to shimmer like a tiny black sun. Even the spots of moonlight visible here and there between the trees faded as if something were feeding on the energy of the light itself. The wind, now coming at him from every direction, grew colder, penetrating the sweat-soaked flannel of his shirt like tissue paper and raising an icy blanket of gooseflesh wherever it touched.

He tried to stop, but he could not. Her voice urged him on, repeating the impossible sounds again and again like a senseless litany. He could not stop even though his teeth chattered from the cold and his eyes ached from staring unblinkingly into the tiny pool of pulsing darkness. In the pool, as the alien wind grew stronger, images began to form and flicker in time with the pulsing blackness.

Images of Marcus Reimann and a hundred others, dead for centuries, for millennia. Images that were human and yet radiated the same aura of unearthliness as the pool of darkness in which they appeared.

And behind them all, lurking in the depths of the talisman's nightmarish world—

Abruptly, Winton became aware of another sound. It was the same sound, he realized, that his own hands had made as they clawed through the wet clay. But now it was muffled, barely audible in the patches of silence that marked his pauses for breath. Muffled, as if the sounds were being made not by something scraping at the surface of the ground but by something burrowing molelike in the darkness beneath.

But still he could not stop mouthing the litany of alien sounds, nor could he move from where he crouched within the frigid confines of the grave. Even as the sound grew louder and he could feel the earth shifting beneath his knees, he remained frozen except for his lips and throat. Even as some still-rational corner of his mind screamed at him to flee before the corpse of Marcus Reimann—whose body had preceded Jessica's into the open grave on that terrible night— could break free of the earth that imprisoned it, Henry Winton remained rooted to the spot, repeatedly spewing out the guttural syllables that were being forced again and again into his mind.

Then, abruptly, the earth beside his sister's body was forced upward into an irregular, crumbling mound. Sucking in his breath with gasping suddenness, he felt the bandanna, long since dried and useless against the thickening odor of putrefaction, plastering itself tightly over his mouth and nose and cutting off his breath.

With a moan, he ripped the cloth from his face, but then he froze as a hand erupted from the growing mound.

It was the hand of Marcus Reimann, he knew. It was beginning to discolor, but the deterioration—retarded or even reversed by the power of the talisman?—was obviously less advanced than it was in Jessica.

Blindly, the hand clawed at the air, and then, with a lurch

that sent clods of earth tumbling, its fingers closed around Henry Winton's wrist.

Winton screamed, and the sound echoed from the hills and the shell of the mansion. Jessica's pleading voice and the tiny pool of darkness were both driven from his mind by the horror of that slimy grip.

He wrenched his hand away, feeling the dead nails gouging into his living flesh. He lurched backward, falling against the edge of the pit as the hand and lower arm, clothed in a dirt-encrusted broadcloth sleeve, twisted and searched for another hold.

Half screaming, half gasping, Winton managed to scramble out of the grave. With his hands, he began desperately flinging the loose dirt back into the pit. Finally, he remembered the spade, and he scrabbled through the darkness until he found it.

As he threw the first spadeful of dirt, his sister's body began to move, sitting slowly up as it was lifted from below. The caked earth fell from her lifeless breast and then from her face. Even in the darkness, he could see that it was as blackened and shriveled as her hand. Where her nose had been, there was now only a ragged cavity. A ghastly pale slug writhed where her lips had been.

Winton stood frozen as Jessica's upper body lurched sideways, falling against the wall of earth as Marcus Reimann's body, dirt crumbling and falling from its ravaged face and hollow sightless eyes, struggled to raise itself. One hand clawed at the ground only inches from Winton's feet while the other tried blindly to push the other body to one side. There were sounds: soft popping noises as the dead flesh flexed and moved; gargling whispers as the movements forced the trapped gases of decay out of the lifeless lungs and stomach; ragged, angry moans as something in the body tried to make use of the rotting vocal cords.

Then it touched him.

The dead hand that had clamped itself to his wrist now clutched at his leg, sliding from his overalls, slippery with wet clay, to his shoe.

Jerking as if the touch had brought him back to life, Winton raised the spade above his head and brought it down with all his strength. The flat of the blade smashed against the creature's head. He could hear and feel the bones of the skull splinter as they were driven into the pulpy mass beneath.

But still it moved, its hands clutching spasmodically over the rim of the grave toward him.

Gasping for breath as the stench of decay enveloped him anew, he raised the spade again, and again he brought it down with shuddering strength. Again. Again.

At last, with a final, bubbling exhalation, the lifeless body, its head and face crushed beyond recognition, collapsed backward into the grave. Jessica's body, no longer supported, fell backward, too, with the talisman's chain still firmly clutched in one clawlike hand.

Whimpering, his tears turning to mud on his cheeks, Henry Winton kicked and shoved at the motionless bodies until they again lay flat in the bottom of the grave. Slowly, methodically, he began to shovel the dirt back over them.

As he worked, he realized that the voice was gone from his mind. He did not know whether it was because his sister, his twin, was at last free despite the shimmering fragment of icy darkness still pressed to her decaying breast or because he no longer allowed himself to hear her cries.

He only knew that whether he had failed or succeeded, he could never bring himself to return to this place again.

AUTUMN, 1975

Day One

Elena March blinked and shook her head sharply, forcing her tired eyes to focus on the pale oasis of light that skidded along the winding, tar-patched highway ahead of her and brushed fleetingly at the nearly leafless trees and brush-filled ditches on either side.

Taking one cramped hand from the wheel of her boxy sedan, she raked her fingers through tightly curling dark brown hair and harshly massaged the flesh at the back of her neck beneath the collar of her utilitarian flannel shirt. For a moment, alertness returned. The craggy New England hills—mountains to her Indiana flatlander's way of thinking—sprang into sharp, moonlit focus. Every sound that darted out of the shadowy forest, every cricket and owl and frog, stood out sharply against the hypnotic background of the motor's uneven hum and the *hiss-slap* of the tires. The chilly night air pounding through the open wing vent seemed suddenly filled with mossy forest smells; the sharp scent of pine mixed with the damp fragrance of decaying bark and leaves.

But then the moment was gone, and as she replaced her big-boned hand on the wheel, fatigue closed in again, almost like a physical presence. Her other arm trembled slightly as she moved to close the vent partially. Suddenly she realized that the car had drifted onto the road's faded center line.

A shot of adrenaline jolted through her, and she jerked the wheel sharply, sending the car back into its own lane, almost overshooting onto the narrow berm that separated it from the ditch. Trembling, though not from fatigue, she lifted her foot from the accelerator and let the car coast to a stop. One highway death, even that of an ex-husband, was more than enough for one family in one year.

"Where are we, Mommy?"

Beth's five-year-old voice came sleepily from the floor of the Checker's huge rear seat, where she had spent most of the more than three hours since sunset. One of Elena's bulky cardigans was wrapped around her, while another was rolled into a passable but lumpy pillow beneath her head.

"I don't know, honey, not exactly," Elena said, managing to keep the tremble out of her husky, contralto voice.

"Are we lost?" Beth's slender, freckled face—an inheritance from her father—appeared over the back of the seat, one tiny hand knuckling away the sleep while the other curled around the metal support of the headrest to steady her as she stood up. Her hair, a curling tangle like her mother's but several shades lighter, like her father's, was in even worse disarray than usual, and her pullover sweater and jeans were rumpled and twisted from the hours of off-and-on sleep.

Elena smiled and shook her head. "No, we're not lost. We're in Vermont." She added a silent "I think" as she reached back to take her daughter's hand.

"Oh." The child nodded, sleepiness and curiosity fighting for possession of her features. "That's okay, then," she finished, apparently satisfied.

Elena pressed her lips together to keep from laughing and then leaned across the seat back and kissed her daughter on the cheek. "Just go back to sleep, hon," she said. "We'll be stopping pretty soon, and you can get into a real bed."

But the words were unnecessary. Even as Elena spoke, sleepiness triumphed over curiosity, and the child's face began to sink below the seat back. Releasing her hand, Elena let her drop to her makeshift bed. There were times when she envied children. Beth was probably asleep by the time she hit the floor and wouldn't wake up until she felt the car stopping again, or maybe not until morning. Elena wished she herself could be reassured as easily.

But she couldn't.

After five days—or was it six?—of aimless driving that had taken them through Ohio, Pennsylvania, and much of upstate New York, she was beginning to doubt the wisdom of this impulsive odyssey. There were even moments, particularly when she awakened in a strange motel room, not sure what state, let alone what town, she was in, when she had fleeting doubts about her sanity, wondering whether her in-laws, Gerald's parents, might not be right, after all. Maybe Beth would be better off with them. If money and creature comforts were any criteria, she certainly would be. There was nothing Davis and Miriam Grantland couldn't buy for her: toys, trips, the best private schools and tutors, perhaps even friends and playmates.

Shaking her head irritably, Elena started the car moving again. The relative merits of herself and the parents of her late ex-husband were irrelevant at this late date. Things had gone too far for any kind of reconciliation. The Grantlands had been against the marriage from the start and had finally succeeded in breaking it up. After the divorce, they had been perfectly content to let her take Beth. They had even condescended to pay a healthy lump sum to Elena to guarantee that there would be no more need for contact between her and Gerald. He had, as far as they were concerned, "gotten over all that rebellious nonsense" when he had finally capitulated and agreed to take his proper place in the Grantland business empire, a chain of discount department stores that spread throughout four states. They had wanted to be positive that he wouldn't suffer any relapses. They had been willing—eager, even—for Elena to legally resume her own name of March, as if by so doing she would wipe out the final evidence of their son's five-year folly.

But that all changed when, late one Saturday night, Gerald smashed his brand-new sports car—a final-decree gift from his father—into the rear end of a semi that had been slowing for a highway intersection. He was their only child, and Beth was their only grandchild; suddenly, she was the only grandchild they could ever have. They decided that they wanted her. To them, particularly to Davis Grantland, who thought of himself as a small-town Daddy Warbucks who could do no wrong and to whom nothing could reasonably be denied, it was simply a matter of reclaiming their temporarily pawned property.

First they offered to adopt the child, an eminently practical and charitable action from their point of view, considering that they could "give the child all the advantages the mother couldn't." When Elena refused, they dropped the idea of formal adoption but expanded their offer to include Elena herself, proposing to take her in and treat her like their own daughter, a laughable concept considering the bitter antagonism they had displayed toward her for nearly five years.

Then the offers of money started. If they couldn't reclaim or adopt their property, they would buy it.

When the ante had been raised for the third time by one of their increasingly patronizing attorneys, Elena had decided she had to get away, at least for a while. She converted a few thousand from her savings account—still fat from the lump-sum payment of several months before—into traveler's checks and took off, telling no one but her family and a couple of close friends. She could imagine her father-in-law screaming "Kidnaping!" at the top of his lungs when he discovered her departure, but she didn't think he could do anything, not legally at least, unless he could buy a judge. But he could make a lot of noise and a lot of trouble.

It might not be, as Grantland's attorneys so patiently and repeatedly pointed out, best for Elena and her daughter to give in, but it would certainly be easiest. On the road she was free of them, but she would have to stop her directionless tour some time. And when she did, when she returned home or when Grantland found her at some new home, it would start all over again.

A distant light glinting through the sparsely leafed trees somewhere ahead and to the right brought her attention back to the deserted highway. A headlight? she wondered as it vanished a second later. It was certainly about time. Any highway, even a narrow two-lane one like this, should have more than one car every ten miles.

If I'm still on a highway at all, that is, she thought with a sudden sinking feeling. It would have been easy to miss a sign and let the highway curve off to one side unnoticed while she traveled straight ahead onto an unmarked secondary road. The road did seem to have narrowed and deteriorated in the last few miles.

Why, she wondered, hadn't she stopped fifty or a hundred miles ago, when she had been skirting Albany and Troy?

There had been acres of motels, and the sun had already touched the horizon. Other days she had stopped at five or six, after a leisurely eight- or ten-hour mixture of driving and sightseeing. But tonight it had been different somehow. Each time she thought of turning in at one of the flickering "Vacancy" signs, she changed her mind at the last minute and drove on, meandering in a generally northeast direction. They stopped for a snack and at a service station for gas, but that was all.

And now, more than three hours after sunset, she hadn't seen a motel for the last twenty miles and no other cars for the last five or ten.

She squinted, trying to locate the light again. At least, she thought, the gas tank was nearly full.

As she looked, the road twisted and turned upward. Ahead, far up a hill, a bare bulb burned in the darkness, starkly illuminating a roadside sign. Slowing the car, Elena watched the sign as if afraid that it might vanish if she looked away.

Newly painted with black letters on a stark white background, the sign thrust its way out of the brush that lined the road. "Groves Lodge," it said, and in smaller letters at the bottom, "Rooms by Day or Week." A small rectangle filled with a blunt-tipped arrow pointing to the right hung from the bottom of the sign.

Fifty yards beyond, an intersecting road angled sharply to the right. The road to Groves Lodge? She thought for a moment of passing it by, but at the last second she cut the wheel sharply and made the turn. The trees, their few remaining leaves rusty and brown in her headlights, met over the narrow road, giving her the feeling of moving down a wavering tunnel. Remnants of vines and bushes, some with shriveled berries still clinging to them, pushed close to the edge of the road, making her wonder what on earth Groves Lodge might be, existing on a road like this. Perhaps it was closed for the season, like so many other tourist-area motels, but someone had forgotten to turn off the light over the sign.

But then, as she reached the crest of a low but steep hill, another light appeared less than a hundred yards ahead. A mixture of relief and a strange, tingling anticipation swept through her. It was the same kind of feeling, she realized, that had been touching her lightly since the beginning of the trip, but stronger. She liked to explore, had always liked it and had probably inherited that tendency from her parents. She remembered that the high points of their cross-country vacation drives in the late 1950s and early 1960s had not been the usual tourist attractions but the back-road routes they often took from one town to the next. Not that what they found on those roads was any prettier or more spectacular than what was in the guidebooks; it was simply unknown, unexpected, and always a surprise.

And Groves Lodge, whatever it turned out to be, was certainly an unknown.

The second light, she soon saw, was mounted over a sign that was a twin to the one on the highway. It jutted out from a wall of evergreens on the left side of the road. It was only when Elena was nearly abreast of it that she saw that it was suspended from one of a pair of polygonal concrete and stone pillars that flanked a gravel drive.

A moment later, the faint tingle of anticipation that had been playing along Elena's spine became an icy blanket that wrapped itself shudderingly around her as her eyes were drawn to the tops of the pillars.

Snouted, bat-eared faces thrust themselves toward her out of the shadows, and it took her a full, frightening second to realize that the gargoylelike creatures were lifeless stone and not a pair of grotesque beasts about to leap from their perches. But then common sense prevailed, and with a shiver of relief she saw that it was only the shifting shadows cast by her headlights that had created the illusion of motion, that and her hyperactive imagination.

Even so, Elena brought the car to a full stop, pulled in a deep breath, and spent several seconds working her shoulders in a circular, shrugging motion in an attempt to rid herself of the chill that had set her heart pounding. Finally she looked up at the forms again. They were no prettier, but they were obviously motionless. She smiled ruefully.

"Quaint," she said in an almost inaudible whisper, "very quaint."

Then, nodding a mock greeting to the two monstrosities, she released the brakes and guided the boxy car between the pillars, with the gravel crunching loudly under the tires. Within a dozen yards, the drive opened out on the right into a narrow parking area. There was room for more than a dozen cars to angle park, but only two—a beginning-to-rust sedan a few years old and a slightly more recent subcompact—huddled together at the far end, nosed up against a chain-link fence that apparently formed the boundary of the lot. A single unfrosted bulb, mounted high on a wooden post beyond the cars, cast a thin, brittle light over everything.

At least it's open, she thought as she eased the car to a stop next to the sedan and shut off the lights and engine, and it's certainly not full up.

For a long moment she sat silently, idly wondering why Beth hadn't popped up the second the car had stopped. But it was just as well. With any luck, Elena might be able to get the sleeping child out of the car and into bed without awakening her. Despite the tingle that still played over her back, the fatigue she had felt the last hundred miles was stronger than ever. She would feel a lot more like giving cheerful answers to her daughter's often impossible questions in the morning, after a good night's sleep.

Directly in front of her, beyond the chain-link fence, were more trees, stretching as far back as the light from the single bulb could reach. Somber elms and oaks towered in the foreground, and farther back, grayish-white birches hovered like forest spirits. The few leaves that remained moved slowly in an invisible wind, the sound of their rustling gradually penetrating the silence of the car. Even as she watched, a leaf from an oak, jagged and brownish in the dim light, slid from a branch and wavered toward the ground. From somewhere in the distance, so faint as to be almost lost in the light movement of the air, came the splashing of a stream as it flowed through the night.

Her hand moved toward the door handle, and Elena realized, curiously, that it was as if she were moving in slow motion, the way you sometimes do in dreams. Or when you're so tired that you don't know whether you're dreaming or not, she told herself sharply.

Shaking her head briskly, she snatched open the door and slid off the high seat. Beth, she saw, was still curled up on the floor in the back. Wrapped cocoonlike in the cardigan, the five-year-old showed no signs of stirring. Easing the door shut as silently as she could, Elena turned away from the car.

As she turned, she realized that until that instant, she had somehow avoided looking at Groves Lodge itself. As she drove in, her eyes had remained fixed on the two cars and the trees beyond the fence. Only now, as she stood next to the car, one hand still resting on the door handle, did she see the building, set back a good thirty yards from the drive on the opposite side from the parking area.

The tingle of anticipation strengthened, almost driving out the fatigue. Groves Lodge, easily visible through the branches of a dozen nearly bare trees, was square and blocky with wide steps leading up to a massive front door. A pair of imitation columns, not standing separately but built into the wall itself, flanked the door. Two rows of windows stretched out in either direction, and above the upper row a half dozen archaic-looking gables jutted into the darkness. Only a few of the windows, all on the first floor, showed any light. A frosted bulb of no great brilliance was mounted directly over the door, and a small sign was set in the center of the door itself. A concrete walkway, swept clear of the leaves that carpeted the grass on either side, made a meandering path to the bottom of the steps.

Well, it is different, she thought as she left the car and moved along the walkway. I just hope the desk clerk, assuming they have one, doesn't look like Morticia or Gomez. Or worse, Tony Perkins.

The sign on the door said simply "Open, Walk in." She did, and she smiled as the door opened silently, with no creaking or grating, and she found herself in a small entryway, facing another door. The second door was of more normal proportions, with a curtained window in the upper half. It, too, was relatively noiseless as she pushed through.

She blinked as she looked around. The room she had entered took up the entire central section of the building, extending all the way from the front door to what must have been the back wall. At least twenty feet above her head were the wooden beams that marked the ceiling. The room was a good twenty-five feet wide, and a balcony ran the full length of each of the sidewalls at the second-floor level. The only openings in the walls were four doors, two in each wall, one directly above the other, one on the ground floor level and the other leading off the balcony. She assumed they led to halls, so that each floor of the house was divided into quarters.

But the most surprising feature was the staircase. Directly in front of her, in the center of the open area, was a totally enclosed spiral staircase. The structure went completely to the roof, and she wondered whether a third floor existed beyond the beamed ceiling. At the second-floor level, a pair of what could only be called walkways or bridges connected the enclosed staircase to the balconies at the points at which the hallways emerged. The outer wall of the staircase was of plain, dark wood, and, Elena noticed with a puzzled frown, it was seven-sided.

Almost as an afterthought, she looked at the chairs and couches that were distributed along the walls and the innocuous landscapes and still lifes that hung over them. A large television console, its back against one of the seven sides of the staircase, looked oddly out of place.

Immediately to the right of the entryway, where Elena was still standing, was a counter that served as registration desk. A ledger rather than the usual four-by-six cards lay open on the counter, and a dozen or more keys hung on the wall behind it. A small ring-for-service bell sat near the register, and next to it, almost curled around it, lay a small, yellow-orange, very long-haired cat.

Elena was reaching out cautiously to stroke the animal's head, when a voice startled her into whirling abruptly.

"May I help you?"

The voice was soft, with none of the twang or harshness she associated with New England accents. A woman, slender and several inches shorter than Elena's five foot eight and probably a few years younger than her twenty-nine, was coming from the ground-floor hall on the right. She wore dark slacks and an everyday long-sleeved blouse, and her hair, a brown a few shades darker than Elena's curling mass, was pulled back in a loose bun.

"If you have a room to rent for tonight, you certainly may," Elena said. "For two, my daughter and myself."

"Odd you should ask," the woman said with a warm smile as she hurried to the registration desk. "We just happen to have one. Or a dozen, if you'd care to really spread out."

"One will do nicely, I'm afraid," Elena said, returning the smile.

The woman shrugged as she slipped behind the counter, slid the yawning cat to one side, and moved the registration ledger closer to Elena. "Can't hurt to ask," she said, cocking her head at an angle to watch as Elena wrote. " 'Elena and Beth March,' " she read. "You're Elena?"

Elena nodded. "Beth's my daughter. She's five, and she's still sound alseep in the car."

"I'm Mattie—short for Madeline—Groves," the woman said as she turned the ledger around to look at it right side up. "I'm roughly one-third, speaking weightwise, of the 'Groves' on the sign. The other two-thirds is my husband, John. If you need any help with your daughter or your bags—anything heavy, I mean—I can roust him out."

Elena shook her head. "I can manage. We just have a suitcase and a few odds and ends."

"I'll give you a hand, then," Mattie said. She glanced at the register again. "Just tonight? Or could we interest you in our weekly rate?"

"Just tonight, I think. However," Elena added, glancing at the cat, who was watching them both sleepily, "I may have a problem on my hands dragging my daughter away from your friend there. It's been a week since she's seen any animals close up, and I think she's coming close to having withdrawal symptoms."

"Her name's Buttercup," Mattie said, scratching the cat behind the ears. It stood up, arching its back and rubbing against her arm. "B.C. for short. You have cats at home?"

"My mother does. She and my brother live on a farm, and we spend a fair amount of time there. Beth has adopted most of their cats and dogs and even a chicken or two."

"Sounds familiar. I grew up on a farm in Ohio. Everyone and his brother was always dumping animals, it seemed." A harsh tone had entered her voice, but then it lightened again. "We had a reputation, I guess. Or an animal aura or something, which maybe I still have. B.C. here just showed up on our doorstep two or three months ago. But back to business. Are you in the market for breakfast in the morning?"

Elena glanced round. "You have a restaurant?"

"No, not really. What we have is a large kitchen table. Or a medium-sized dining room table, depending on the number of guests. Normally I just throw on a few extra slices of bacon or whatever and pour some extra juice when I fix breakfast for John and me. Very informal."

"What about cereals? I'm afraid Beth—"

"No problem. We keep a supply of the standard sugar-coated tooth destroyers and a few more wholesome items if you feel experimental. And plenty of milk."

Elena hesitated only a second. The prospect of a breakfast—or any meal—that didn't have to be driven to or picked from a menu was, after a week on the road, virtually irresistible. And Madeline Groves herself—whose pixieish features, ready smile, and pleasant blue-green eyes went much better with Mattie than with the more formal Madeline—radiated an easygoing, contagious informality.

And, she thought with another glance at the registration desk, there was B.C., who would undoubtedly entrance Beth. The main problem would be convincing the child that the cat couldn't come with them when they left.

"All right," she said. "Breakfast it is. What time?"

"Sometime between seven-thirty and eight, if that isn't too early. John has to be at school—he teaches English and history—a little after eight-thirty."

"That's fine. I like to get an early start even if we don't have any particular destination in mind."

"All settled, then. Good. Now for your room. Would you like the isolation ward?" She gestured toward the door to the far hallway. "Or the family quarters, so to speak?" She nodded toward the other hallway, the one from which she had emerged a few minutes before. "The kitchen and the rooms John and I use are down there, along with a few to rent out."

"Same price?"

"Same price. And quite reasonable, I might add."

"I don't feel very isolationist, somehow," Elena said. "So if it's all right with you and your husband . . ."

Mattie made a quick mark on the register. "Perfectly," she said, and then named a price. "That includes breakfast for the two of you. You can take a look at the cereals tonight and pick out what you want for your daughter."

Mattie insisted on going to the car with Elena to help bring Beth and the suitcase in, and in a few minutes they were settled in their room, with Beth curled up on one of the twin beds with Elena's cardigan still wrapped around her. Aside from a few muffled murmurs, the child hadn't made a sound as Elena carried her in, still sound asleep.

"How about a snack tonight?" Mattie asked as she stood in the door of the room. "No extra charge."

Elena started to shake her head but changed her mind. She normally indulged in late-night snacks, and she had been missing them on the road. Going out to a restaurant was too much trouble once they were settled in for the night at a motel, and the kinds of things you could carry with you in the car and take into the room with you weren't really the same.

"Sure," she said, "if it's not too much trouble. And if you don't mind if I take a hot bath first. I'm feeling more than a little gritty at the moment."

"No trouble at all. I usually heat up something for John and me, and we just happen to have some leftovers we've been trying to get rid of the last three or four days. With your help, we might just make it tonight. And your bath will give me time to get them warmed up. I'll give you a knock when things are ready."

With Mattie gone, Elena looked around the room, taking it in fully for the first time. Except for the TV set, a small portable black and white rather than the usual nailed-to-the-floor, out-of-adjustment color sets she had been treated to the last few nights, the furnishings were standard: twin beds with green bedspreads with only one or two cigarette burns in each, easy chair, scuffed but clean bureau and writing desk, and three more of the same bland landscapes that dotted the lobby. Beyond those items, however, the room was no more standard than the lobby. For one thing, it was twice as large as any hotel or motel room she had ever stayed in. For another, the ceilings were well over eight feet high, and the one huge window, stretching from almost the floor to within inches of the ceiling, was covered not with a curtain or some variety of mechanical blinds but with floor-length, deep red drapes. They looked even older than the furniture, but still there was an air of richness about them. And the closet! There would have been room for everything she owned, not just what she had brought with her.

Even the bathroom had the same air of bygone luxury about it. A huge washbasin, as large as some kitchen sinks she had seen, complete with old-fashioned ornamental faucets, was opposite an ancient tub that was equally large. It was, she noted with pleasure, more than long enough for her to take a bath without having to subject herself to all kinds of contortions to get both her shoulders and knees under water at the same time. And she was, she realized, developing a downright sybaritic urge to simply stretch out and soak and relax.

Turning on the tub's faucets, she paused only long enough to make sure that the sudden rush of water didn't awaken Beth. Stuffing her dirty clothes in the laundry bag she had brought along for that purpose, she quickly stripped and climbed into the tub. Lowering herself slowly into the steaming water, she luxuriated in the warmth as it flowed around her body and quickly penetrated her flesh, softening her muscles, easing out the tensions, and dissolving the stiffness that had grown steadily throughout a long day behind the wheel.

With the water almost up to her neck, Elena stretched and reveled in the feeling and then leaned her head back against the lip of the tub. A smile spread across her face as she discovered that the lip of the tub, instead of being straight across, held a softly curved niche, carved just in the center. Her head rested in it easily, comfortably, as if it had been made for her.

Perfect, she thought, wriggling her toes and closing her eyes. Just perfect.

For the first time in she didn't know how many weeks, her mind was fully occupied with her own comfort and nothing else. She was totally submerged in a languorous sensuality. Beneath the water, she felt her hands move slowly down her body, over her generous breasts, her not-quite-flat stomach, her rounded hips. It was not quite a caress but more than a simple touch, almost as if the hands had a life of their own. She felt moisture beading on her face from the warmth of the water, but she didn't wipe it away. Somehow it was part of the feeling, part of the total relaxation.

She closed her eyes, letting the real world fade out of existence.

Slowly, aimlessly, she drifted toward a twilight region that was not quite sleep and yet not quite wakefulness. A vague knowledge of where she was remained, but it was submerged in a warm, glowing cloud, just as her body was submerged in the water. Her mind floated gently and contentedly, not caring where it was or where it was going.

For a time she drifted, feeling only the warmth as it soaked through to her very bones. She analyzed no thoughts, recalled no bitter memories, worried over no quarrelsome futures. She simply existed, alone in her immeasurably comfortable, self-sufficient universe.

But then, slowly, over a period that could have been seconds or minutes or even hours, the realization crept over her that she was not, after all, alone.

But the thought did not disturb her. Rather, in her lethargic, drowsy state, she accepted it. It seemed natural.

It was natural that she should not be alone.

It was natural that something should exist in this universe of her mind: something distant, beyond the golden haze, beyond the warmth and the comfort.

Something dark and indistinct, something hidden in a world of shadows that brushed at the edges of her mind and yet remained elusively beyond her grasp.

And then, ever so gradually, she felt herself retreating even farther from the external world. But it was not the same aimless drifting it had been before. Now there was a direction. It was as if she were being tugged by a gentle current, farther and ever farther until finally she could no longer feel the water touching her body, could no longer feel the perspiration streaking her face, could no longer hear the distant leaves as the wind brushed them against the frosted window.

Yet still it all seemed quite natural. No pinprick of fear punctured the bubble her mind floated in.

Gently but relentlessly, she was drawn farther and farther from the physical realities around her, until at last all sensation was gone and she floated in a silent, featureless ocean of darkness. This must be what it's like to sleep in space, she thought as her mind seemed to roam idly: no weight, no pressure, no heat or cold, no sound, nothing but her own consciousness.

But then, slowly, her senses began to return, and with them came a growing uneasiness.

The first sense to return was touch.

She could feel pressure on the soles of her feet. It was a sharp, uneven pressure, and the image of the rough ground of a forest floor touched her mind.

She could feel the clothes on her body. From neck to toe they enclosed her, stiff and starched, scratching at her shoulders and neck. About her waist there was something so tight and constricting that it took a conscious effort to breathe.

She could feel an object in her hands, something small and solid and cold. It seemed to have a life of its own, yet she knew that it could not be alive. Its icy, slippery surface pulsed in her grip, writhing to be free, yet she knew that it was a lifeless thing that could not move. Her hands ached from the effort of holding it. Her mind shrank from it, and yet she knew she dared not release it.

And the wind . . .

From all directions, as if she were standing at the center of a vortex, an icy wind struck at her, pressing against her face, her back, every side of her body.

Then the sounds began, the screams and cries, faint and distant at first but gradually growing louder and nearer until their chaos surrounded her like the invisible wind.

But standing out from the background din was a single voice, and only slowly did she realize that it was her own. It was impossibly harsh and, like the others, came cascading out of the darkness around her. She felt her lips move in unison with the sounds, felt her throat ache and burn from the effort. Her mouth was dry as bone as the sounds—senseless, jumbled gibberish—emerged.

The feeling that all this was normal and natural had already been strained to the breaking point, and now it suddenly vanished, leaving her gripped by shivering terror. A nameless fear spread through this strange new body she found herself possessed of, spreading from the unearthly thing gripped painfully in those hands, flowing up that other woman's arms and through her body like ice water slithering through her veins.

Behind it all, in the tiny, observing corner of her mind that was still Elena March, another independent feeling of terror was growing. Where am I? it screamed silently, even as the other voice, the voice that she knew was that of her nightmare self, continued its shrieking, repeating the same impossible sounds again and again.

Then, for just an instant, there was sight. Only for an instant, as if a circuit breaker somewhere in her mind had been tripped by the first touch of vision.

But in that instant the scene was etched in her brain with fingers of ice.

Trees, great towering skeletons, were all about her. It was night, and heavy clouds hung low, but still there was light, an ominous flamelike flickering from beyond the trees.

And people, dozens of people, all in strange, old-fashioned clothes, from starched and ruffled shirts to the coarsest of work shirts, surrounded her. The screams and shouts, still cloaked in unreality, were tearing from their throats and contorted faces.

Closer than all the rest, looming over her in the flickering light, was a man's face. It had once been a handsome face, but now it was smeared with mud and grass. Hair fell over the forehead in a matted tangle. Even in the faint, unsteady light—from a fire, she realized distractedly—a bloodless pallor was obvious. The eyes were blank and staring, the pupils were dilated until the irises were almost invisible, and a dull, lifeless film covered iris and pupil alike, reflecting nothing, not even the flames that were leaping ever higher behind her. The lips, as mud-smeared as the rest of the face, were parted slightly, the jaw was hanging slack, and she could see dirt and torn bits of grass and weed clinging to the teeth.

It was the face of a corpse.

A corpse that stretched out its arms and clutched blindly at the hands of Elena's nightmare self, trying with soulless desperation to pry her fingers open and grasp the thing in her hands.

In a nursing home a hundred miles away, an old man cried out in his sleep.

Deborah Harris, the attendant on duty after visiting hours ended at nine, looked up from her paperback romance and hastily checked the call board. There were no lights, but that didn't mean that no one needed help. Half the time they were unable to reach the buttons.

Her heart beating faster and her stomach knotting, Deborah got to her feet in the cramped office. Swallowing heavily, she pulled in a deep breath and hurried into the hallway that ran the length of the U-shaped, single-floor building. Her footsteps, even in crepe-soled shoes, were loud on the uncarpeted floor.

She listened, waiting for another cry, but there was none. From a room on the right came the feeble snoring of Jennie Barton, and from a room near the corner came the mumbles of Vern Alderton, once again carrying on a one-sided conversation with whoever he thought was in the room with him.

That was all.

Suppressing a shudder, Deborah started down the hall. She would have to check every room. Those were the standing orders. If there were any unexplained noises, whether a human cry or something crashing to the floor, she had to check until she found the cause and then, if she thought it necessary, notify whatever doctor was on call for the night.

She hated the job at times like this. During the days it was bad enough, feeding and cleaning and giving medication, listening to endlessly repeated stories and querulous questions and laments about ungrateful, forgetful children. And watching the visitors when they did occasionally come to the spartan rooms to try vainly to engage in small talk with someone—a mother, a father, a grandmother—with whom they no longer had anything in common. It had to be the most depressing job in the state of Massachusetts.

And now, in the middle of the night, searching from room to room to see who had cried out. God knew what she would find: someone who had soiled himself, a nightmare, a stroke or heart attack, or simply one more pathetic bid for attention.

She was almost to the first turn in the corridor when she heard the buzzer in the office. Gratefully, she hurried back. Whoever had cried out apparently was at least able to operate the call button, and she wouldn't have to search every room, after all.

The light was on for room 17. She breathed a sigh of relief. It wasn't anything serious, just old Willie Braman. Every couple of weeks he would, he said, have a bad dream, but what he really wanted was for someone to come and sit with him for a few minutes. Sit with him and listen to a vivid retelling of the dream, which usually turned out to be not so terrible after all and which, more often than not, bore a suspicious resemblance to bits and pieces of TV shows from the last few weeks. Then he would go peacefully back to sleep, and that would be it for another few days.

Resetting the light on the board, Deborah returned to the dimly lit, echoing hallway. Would she end up in a place like this in another fifty or sixty years? she wondered uneasily. Not if she had anything to say about it, she wouldn't. But that was the trouble. Most of the people here didn't have anything to say about it. Without the ability to care for themselves and without the money to pay someone else to do it—and without relatives willing to do it—most of them didn't have much of a choice.

As she rounded the corner and neared room 17, she noticed that the room was still dark. Odd. Willie usually had the light on and was propped up on his rickety elbows, waiting for whoever answered his buzzer.

She quickened her pace. Maybe this time there was really

something wrong. Maybe for once it was more than a bad dream or a late-night urge for company.

Flipping on the dim, overhead light, she stepped into the room. "Willie?"

But Willie, his parchment-pale hands resting easily on top of the blanket, was motionless and silent. For an instant she thought that he might be dead, but then she saw the covers on his chest moving ever so slightly and his fingers shifting on the blanket.

"Miss?"

Gasping, Deborah spun around to face the other bed. Its occupant, an ancient shriveled man who had once been broad and tall, was sitting with one emaciated hand clutching the railing that guarded the side of the bed away from the wall.

"Did you press the buzzer?" she asked, knowing that he couldn't have. She didn't remember his name, but he was almost ninety, and so far as she knew, he hadn't spoken a word in the six months since the stroke that had put him here. He simply ate, slept, and eliminated waste, an ancient automaton with a digestive tract.

"Yes, I did." The voice was cracked and unsteady, as much from six months of disuse as from age. His jaw was grizzled, with three or four days' growth of stubble, since his weekly shave wasn't due for another couple of days. His face turned toward the other bed and the shared nightstand, bare of everything but a small vase of plastic flowers. "Where am I? How long have I been here?"

"This is Parkside Manor," she said. "Are you feeling all right? Is there something I can do for you?"

The old man swallowed, his Adam's apple bobbing like a wrinkled yo-yo. "Yes, there is. You can tell me how long I have been here." His voice seemed to gain strength with each word.

"I couldn't tell you, sir. I'd have to look it up in the records. But it might be better if you would just lie down and try to sleep. It's late and—"

"My nephew, I have to talk to my nephew. I have to get out of here."

"I'm sorry, but it's really very late. We can call your nephew in the morning."

He shook his head, and his eyes went to the nightstand again, as if searching for a phone. His hands gripped the railing at the edge of the bed and tugged at it, trying to dislodge it.

"Please, sir!" Deborah caught his hands and tried to remove them from the railing, but they clung tightly. "Please, sir! It's all right. If you will just lie down, I will get in touch with Dr. Edwards, and you can talk to him."

"My nephew," the old man persisted. "Not a doctor, my nephew!"

"Please, you mustn't get yourself worked up. I— If you will just lie back and rest, I'll see what I can do."

"My nephew! My nephew!"

"Your nephew, yes. Whatever you say."

Abruptly, the strength went out of the frail arms, and the old man slumped back onto the bed. "Go," he said, his voice fading. "Go."

Her heart was pounding as she stepped back from the bed, bumping her shoulder against the door frame. He seemed to be calm now, although it might simply be exhaustion. And at his age, after half a year of total inactivity, both mental and physical . . .

Abruptly, she turned and hurried down the hall to the office. A quick check of the file gave her the man's name and the name of the nephew who, as the old man had said, had brought him here after the time in the hospital recovering from the stroke.

She picked up the phone and dialed Dr. Edwards's number. A sleepy voice answered on the fourth ring. "Yes? What is it?"

"Dr. Edwards? This is Deborah Harris at Parkside. It's about one of the patients—"

"What happened?" All traces of sleepiness were gone in an instant.

"One of the patients, one who's been totally unresponsive ever since he was admitted, woke up. And he insists on talking to his nephew. He was very agitated, tried to get out of bed by himself."

"You were right to call me. I'll be there in ten minutes.

34 GENE DeWEESE

Try to keep him calmed down in the meantime, all right? Who is it?"

She glanced at the folder on the desk in front of her. "His name is Henry Winton."

Every muscle and joint in Henry Winton's stick-thin, eighty-seven-year-old body ached as he lay exhausted, listening to the nurse's hurried steps recede down the echoing hall. But it was not the physical discomfort that occupied his whirling thoughts. It was not even the fear and confusion of suddenly awakening and finding himself in totally new and strange surroundings without the faintest idea where he was, how he had gotten there, or how long he had been there. Instead, it was the suddenly resurrected memory of that nightmarish time an eternity ago and the terrifying realization that his sister, now almost seventy years dead, was calling to him once again, begging him wordlessly to return and complete what he had failed to do so long ago.

But gradually, as the silence of the barren room settled over him, rationality returned. Irrational actions—even actions that appeared irrational—would not help him answer that call. He could not, as he had then, simply strike out in the night toward where he knew she lay waiting. Except for the meaningless words the girl had spoken—Parkside Manor, whatever that was—he still didn't know where he was, although it was obviously a nursing home of some kind. Something had happened to put him here. A stroke? He had had a minor one a dozen years before, but he had, he thought, recovered fully. But whatever it was, how serious was his condition? How long had he been here? Could he get out? And even if he could get out, would he be able to get around on his own? And money—how could he manage to get his hands on the money he would need? He had turned over everything he had left to Donald and his wife to help with the down payment on their house when they had agreed to take him in. And the few dollars he made from occasional neighborhood baby-sitting jobs . . .

He tried to remember what he had had in his bureau drawer, but he could not. It couldn't have been more than five or ten; it never was. No, he had nothing, and he could not see how he could get enough to do him any good. Even if he did get out of here, and even if he was able to go back to baby-sitting, it would be weeks before he could save up enough. And he certainly couldn't ask Donald or his wife. They would want to know why he wanted it, and he couldn't tell them, couldn't tell anyone. No, it was impossible, utterly impossible.

But it had to be possible! He could not fail her again, not again! Somehow, even if he had to beg or steal, he would not fail. By the time the attendant returned apprehensively to the room, he knew what he had to do.

Abruptly, Elena March came awake. The nightmare images, the sounds, the screaming terror—all were gone, and she was lying once more in the tub, the once hot bath water now gooseflesh cool.

But her body was still tense, every muscle stretched taut, her fingers curled so tightly that except for her short fingernails, her palms would have been bloody. Her throat felt raspy and dry, as though she had screamed those guttural nonsense syllables in unison with her nightmare self.

Slowly, despite the chill of the water, she relaxed, and the same odd calmness she had felt at the start reasserted itself. Everything was all right. It was just a bad dream, inspired by the long hours on the road and the strange new surroundings and perhaps those hideous little gargoyles crouching atop their pillars at the end of the drive.

She stood up, toweling herself briskly and bringing a momentary flush to her skin. Stepping out of the bathroom, she saw that Beth was still sound asleep. Whatever I did in the nightmare, Elena thought gratefully, I must not have been very noisy about it.

Taking a clean pair of panties, another pair of slacks, and a comfortable, dark-green blouse from her suitcase, she dressed quickly. Another couple of days, she thought, and she would have to find a laundromat somewhere. She and Beth were both down to another two or three days of clean clothes.

Closing the suitcase and sliding it into the huge closet, she crossed the room to the hall door. Her hand on the knob, she paused to look back at the room, at Beth still asleep and thoroughly tangled now in both Elena's sweater and the bedspread.

For an instant, as she turned, an odd sense of disorientation settled over her. She blinked, shaking her head. She realized as she looked again around the room that something looked wrong.

But what? Nothing had changed. Everything was the same. Yet it didn't look right.

She frowned, trying to analyze the feeling. It was not déjà vu, which she had experienced often in the past. It was not a feeling that she had seen the room before, at some other time and in some other place. If anything, it was the opposite. It was the feeling she occasionally got when she entered a familiar room and knew instinctively that something had changed and yet could not for the life of her put her finger on the difference.

Shaking her head sharply, she jerked open the door. This was getting ridiculous. First a nightmare before she had even gone to bed and now this. She would be jumping at her own shadow next.

As Elena turned irritably from the open door, the petite form of Mattie Groves appeared in the door to a room at the end of the hall. She waved as she came toward Elena.

"All cleaned up and ready for that snack?"

Elena nodded, glad for the interruption to her thoughts. "Very much so," she said, and then inclined her head toward the door to her room. "Beth's still asleep, so I'll leave the door open. So I can hear her if she wakes up."

"I can do better than that," Mattie said, grinning. "Come on."

She led the way back to Elena's room, went quietly to the heavy night table between the two beds, reached underneath, twisted at something, and stood up. Holding her fingers to her lips, she returned to the hall.

"An intercom," she said when they were safely out of earshot of Beth. "Not sure who put it in or when, but it still works. Every room in the place is hooked in. I suppose it's a primitive substitute for room telephones, which, you may have noticed, we do not have. And which," she added, "helps explain our low rates, along with the black and white televisions. When you want to turn the intercom off, just turn that little knob. You saw where I was reaching for it, didn't you?"

Elena nodded. "I'll find it."

"What brings you to Wertham?" Mattie asked as they neared the end of the hall.

"Wertham?"

Mattie laughed. "Wertham, Vermont. Population approximately six thousand, tourist attractions approximately zero. You didn't know you were a couple of miles outside that sterling community?"

"To tell the truth, I didn't. I was just driving and wondering if I'd mislaid the highway when I saw your sign."

"You did. Mislay the highway, I mean. The main one, anyway. Out there, where you saw our sign," Mattie said, "is what used to be the highway until they built a bypass around metropolitan Wertham a few years ago. Quite a few, and hardly worth the trouble, especially since 91 bypasses the bypass now, so to speak. But I guess the state got some highway money it didn't know what else to do with. Or so the locals tell me." She shrugged. "Besides, even if Wertham were the tourist mecca of New England, we'd get beat out by the chain motels. Name recognition, you know. And tourist lodges are a dying breed, anyway, by all indications."

"I'm sorry," Elena said, sensing an undercurrent of resentment beneath the flip monologue, but Mattie brushed it off, shrugging again.

"John inherited the damn place from some relative we didn't know we had until he kicked off last spring. We came out from Cleveland just to look the place over and see about selling it. It had been closed down for God knows how long, a real white elephant, the local real estate agent told us. And then John decided he liked it, and then he lucked out and stumbled into an unexpected opening at the local high school. And here we are," Mattie shrugged broadly. "It's a place to live, and the taxes are certainly low. But that's not your problem, sorry. Anyway, here's the kitchen."

Mattie waved Elena through the door before turning toward a door back down the hall. "I'll get John."

Halfway to the other door, she hesitated and turned back to Elena. "I should warn you about one thing, though. John may—in fact, I can almost guarantee that he will—want to hear all about your dreams."

Elena blinked. "My dreams?"

Mattie nodded, looking vaguely embarrassed. "He's had this thing about dreams ever since we came here. It's nothing to worry about, but I just thought I should warn you. And don't be bashful about telling him it's none of his damned business."

Suddenly Elena grinned and shook her head. "On the contrary, I think I'd welcome the chance to talk about it. You won't believe this, but just now I dozed off in the bathtub, and I had the damndest dream—nightmare, really."

Mattie was silent a moment, and then she sighed. "You'll make his evening for him," she said. "You're the first one who's had one before even going to bed."

"But I don't understand. Why is he—"

Mattie shook her head and interrupted. "Best thing you can do, if you're really interested, is talk to John. I have a couple of theories, but he doesn't like them, to put it mildly."

Turning, she knocked on one of the doors and then pushed it open. "Snack time," she said, leaning inside, "and I think I have a live one for you out here."

There was a mumbled response, and a few seconds later a man in his thirties, barely taller than Elena's five foot eight, with a dirty-blond beard, emerged from the room. His broad forehead and tired eyes were set in a scowl, and his straight, blond hair, relatively short but brushing at his collar in the back, showed signs of repeated finger combing. He wore a light blue dress shirt open at the collar, with the sleeves rolled up to just below the elbows.

"John, this is Elena March," Mattie said. "Her daughter, Beth, is asleep in their room. Elena, this is my husband, John. As I think I already told you, in what passes for real life around here, he teaches English and history at Wertham High, which accounts for his general surliness."

"Glad to meet you," Elena said, taking the offered hand and finding it tentative and limp. "I can sympathize with your feelings. I taught English for a couple of years myself, back in Indiana. What years do you teach?"

The beginnings of a genuine smile crossed his face, but it turned quickly to a grimace. "Freshman," he said, "except for a few errant sophomores and juniors in history." He turned to Mattie. "What was it you said about having a live one?"

"A volunteer for your dream survey," she said, nodding at Elena. "But let's get in to where the food is. You can exchange nightmares while you nibble."

She herded them forcefully into the kitchen, where she handed out paper plates and, pointing at a baking dish half full of an unidentifiable variety of casserole, told Elena to spoon out whatever she wanted.

"And don't be bashful about making a face after the first taste," she added. "It's my own personal and unpredictable mixture, guaranteed not for all palates. And if you feel the need to kill the taste, there's a limited variety of soft and hard drinks, including some fair to middling wine. Not to mention such gourmet dessert items as Twinkies if you go in for that sort of thing."

John, barely able to restrain his nervous impatience, remained relatively silent until everyone had a suitably filled plate and Elena had commented favorably on the casserole, which turned out to be a Mexican meatloaf by virtue of Mattie's addition of taco sauce. But then, before touching any of his own, he asked, "What did Mattie mean, a volunteer for my survey, as she calls it?"

"All she did was warn me that you might ask me about my dreams, and I told her I didn't mind at all, especially after the humdinger I just had." She shivered illustratively as she downed another forkful of the casserole.

"Here? In the lodge?"

She nodded, still eating.

"But I don't understand. You just arrived. Didn't you?"

"She fell asleep in the tub," Mattie said.

"That's right," Elena said. "It was so comfortable, I just

dozed off. But is something wrong? Don't they count unless I have them while I'm in bed?"

Mattie let out a brief snort of laughter, drawing a flustered scowl from her husband.

"Of course it counts," he said, turning back to Elena. "You don't mind talking about it?"

She shook her head. "Not at all. But I'm curious. Why are you interested?"

"It's a long story," he said hesitantly.

"He thinks the place is haunted," Mattie said lightly when he didn't continue.

"Madeline!" His irritation was evident in his tone as well as in his use of her full name, but he pulled in a deep breath and turned back to Elena.

"The building is not haunted, as she so melodramatically puts it," he said, "certainly not in the conventional sense. There are no ghostly moans or clanking chains, no ectoplasmic displays or poltergeist phenomena, none of the standard bump-in-the-night manifestations."

"But?" Elena prompted when he fell silent.

"People dream," he said, studiedly avoiding looking at his wife. "When they stay here, they dream, even if they never dreamed before in their lives."

"And you think there's a reason?" Elena asked, beginning to feel uneasy.

Groves shook his head. "I don't know. But I assume there must be. I don't see how it could possibly be coincidence. In any event, coincidence or not, I'm intrigued. So what I've been doing is collecting the dreams our guests have, the ones they'll tell me about, anyway. Some day, perhaps I'll write a scholarly little article for some parapsychological journal. But whether I ever do or not, it's still an interesting phenomenon. Or a statistical anomaly. I hope you won't mind helping out."

As he spoke, Elena's uneasiness grew. "Does everyone dream? Everyone who stays here—even you?" She gestured at the married couple.

"No," said John flatly. "Not everyone."

The same icy fear settled over Elena once again, making

her shiver and stiffen in the chair. Then the feeling that had preceded the dream, the feeling that someone or something lurked in the shadows of her own mind, also returned and was intensified. Even though she was fully awake this time, fully alert to her surroundings, she could feel it. There was something nearby, she knew. It was the same feeling she had often had as a child when, alone in her room after reading a ghost story and turning out the light, she had been absolutely positive that if only her eyes could pierce the darkness, a horde of invisible phantoms would be revealed.

But then, as before, that icy chill subsided and was replaced by an irrational calmness. It was as if, no matter what logic told her, it was perfectly natural for something to share her mind this way. It was certainly nothing to worry about.

"All right," she said abruptly, realizing that both Mattie and her husband had been looking at her with increasing concern throughout her lengthy silence.

Then, pulling in a get-yourself-together breath, she began. As she spoke, recreating the nightmare in her own faltering words, it became more vivid with every phrase that passed her lips. It was as if, by the telling, it was being transformed from dream to reality. The grotesque, mud-smeared face and grasping hands of the zombielike creature lost the facade of horror-movie caricature. She could feel its cold, clawing hands, slimy with the wet clay that coated them. She could hear the guttural, mindless croak that scraped from its throat. She could smell the sickly-sweet stench of sudden death that rolled over her like an invisible, cloying fog and even now threatened to choke off her breath.

But most real of all was the object her dream self had clutched so tightly in her hands. She could feel its edges— seven, she realized with a start—biting into the flesh. She could feel the force it somehow exerted, a force that, like an unearthly magnetic field that grasped at living flesh rather than metal, permeated her entire body, pulling and writhing like a pulsating demon struggling to be free. She could feel the slippery ice-cavern coldness it held about itself like a piece of some alien, lightless universe.

She could feel it touching the mind of that other, nameless

woman and, through her, touching Elena herself. Touching her and saying, in a thousand different voices crying out of the alien darkness at its center: "It is finished. It is finished. It is finished."

Shaking her head sharply, Elena brought her account to an abrupt halt, trying deliberately to bring her mind back to the here and now. Blinking, she looked at Groves and his wife. Both were listening intently, but Mattie was frowning uncertainly, while Groves was leaning forward over the table, his blue eyes bright and excited.

"Flames," he said. "You mentioned seeing flames. What was burning?"

"I don't know," she said, drawing back from his intensity. "It was beyond the trees. Besides, it was only for a second, and I couldn't really see."

"But it was something large?"

She nodded. "It must have been."

"A building? A house?"

"It could have been."

"And the clothes—you said they looked old-fashioned? How old-fashioned? Fifty years? A hundred? Two hundred?"

"Sorry. I'm no expert on the history of clothing styles."

"But you must have some idea."

She shrugged. "A hundred maybe, but don't quote me. There weren't any knee breeches or armor or togas or anything like that. And there were a couple of handlebar mustaches in the crowd, I think."

"The trees. What kind of trees did you see?"

"I don't know that, either," she said, beginning to feel more annoyed than uneasy at his brusque tone and rapid-fire questions. "For one thing, it was dark. For another, even in broad daylight I wouldn't recognize anything more exotic than an oak or a weeping willow. But look, I've told you all I can about what I dreamed. Now it's your turn. What kind of dreams have your other guests had?"

Groves was silent for a long moment, and then he nodded reluctantly. "You're right, of course. I'm sorry. It's just that yours was so different and so vivid."

"Vivid, yes. But how was it different?"

He hesitated again as if considering his words carefully. "Yours," he said finally, "is the first outright nightmare. Not that the others have been overly pleasant, but no one has mentioned anything remotely like yours. You said you were terrified in yours, but the others— Well, one said he was the owner of a ship, a sailing ship, on its way from Africa to America. A slaver most likely, and either fairly rich or soon to be rich. Another said he was the master of a castle somewhere in Europe, apparently during the Dark Ages. One was a sheik sometime around the time of Mohammed. All powerful people in one way or another, certainly none afraid for their lives."

Suddenly Mattie snapped her fingers. "I've got it," she said, grinning. "I didn't realize it until I heard you going through your list like that, but it's obvious what we've got here."

Groves turned on her with a renewed scowl. "If it's so obvious, then what is it? I would really like to know."

"Reincarnation, of course," she said, and went on in response to his blank look. "Don't you see? Those dreams are just our guests' former lives, that's all. This place is like the grotto at Lourdes, only instead of healing people, it puts them in touch with their past lives. Probably enhances their psychic powers all around, too."

Groves's scowl deepened, but he only shook his head with a mixture of anger and sadness.

"We could start New England's first reincarnation spa," Mattie went on. "Just think about it. We might actually be able to make a little money out of this white elephant."

Abruptly, Groves let his breath out in a sigh. Slapping his hands palm down on the table, he stood up.

"Very well," he said, "I see it is impossible to talk intelligently about this subject." He looked down at Elena. "I'm sorry, Ms. March. I thank you very much for your cooperation, and if, despite what has happened, you are willing to continue that cooperation should you have another dream tonight, I would appreciate it even more."

When she gave him an uncertain nod, he hurried from the room and returned a few seconds later to lay a miniature cassette recorder, barely as big as a cigarette pack, on the table next to her plate.

"You can use this to record them when you wake up, while they're still fresh in your memory," he said. "Just press this button and this one." He demonstrated. "The microphone is here," he added, pointing.

Swiftly, he turned and left. A few seconds later, Elena heard the door to his study close softly. She looked back at Mattie uncomfortably. If there was anything she hated, it was getting involved in the family squabbles of strangers. Mattie was eyeing Elena speculatively now, her teeth worrying at her lower lip.

"You're not a ringer, are you?" Mattie asked abruptly.

"A ringer? I don't understand."

"I mean, John didn't put you up to this, did he? You're not a friend of a friend or anything like that, are you?"

"Sorry but no," Elena said a little stiffly. "I'd never seen or heard of either of you until I came here an hour or two ago."

"Then you really did dream those things you told us about?"

"Unfortunately, yes."

Mattie watched her silently for another several seconds, her teeth still worrying her lip, her blue-green eyes still narrowed in speculation. Finally she sighed gustily. "I guess I owe you an apology, then. I'm sorry. It's just that, well, your little nightmare was pretty impressive, particularly for a spur-of-the-moment doze in the bathtub. Forgive me?"

Gradually Elena relaxed. "I'd probably be suspicious, too," she said. "In fact, if you want the truth, I've been having a few suspicious thoughts about the two of you, too."

"No wonder," Mattie said with a sheepish grin. "We must've sounded like a couple of fugitives from *Who's Afraid of Virginia Woolf.*"

"Yes, I was wondering about that. But if you thought I was part of a practical joke—" Elena found herself laughing, and all the tensions were suddenly gone once again, almost as if they had never existed.

*   *   *

"Damn," John Groves muttered under his breath as he dropped angrily into the office chair in his study. "Damn! Damn! Damn!"

The casserole he had eaten lay like a lump of lead in his stomach, and the underarms of his shirt were dark with the uncomfortable wetness of nervous perspiration.

When would he learn? When the hell would he ever learn? Rational discussion of the dreams with Mattie was simply impossible. He had thought, since she had brought up the subject herself this time, that it might be different with this woman. But it had been worse. Mattie hadn't even waited until they were alone to start her wiseass cracks. "Reincarnation spa," for God's sake. He was surprised the woman hadn't demanded her money back then and there, packed her bags, and left. He could imagine how she felt, getting caught in the middle of someone else's family squabble.

He stared balefully at the pile in front of him. He still had the rest of these damned papers to get through. And in his present state, he'd be more inclined to rip them to shreds than grade them.

He thought for a moment of the bottle he had been keeping in one of the desk drawers in recent weeks, but he pushed the thought away. He would pass out before he could drink enough to relax.

Closing his eyes, he leaned back and gripped the arms of the chair, purposely tensing every muscle in his body, making them strain against each other until they trembled. Then, abruptly, he released them, letting himself go limp. Old Mr. Carver, the civics and health studies teacher, had told him about this method of relaxing, and it seemed to work. It had gotten him to sleep a half dozen times when he had been sure he was going to lie awake all night. Now, as he repeated it a second and third time, it seemed to be working on his waking tension and anger as well. At least the knot in his stomach was slightly looser, even if it wasn't unraveling totally. The ache at the base of his skull was already beginning to recede.

After a minute, he straightened in the chair and looked at the papers on the desk. For the most part, they were the same kind of crap he'd seen a thousand times before, first in

Toledo and then in Cleveland. It was no wonder the national test averages were going down every year, no wonder more and more colleges were having to institute remedial English classes for incoming freshmen.

With a grimace, he forced himself to start reading the paper he had been about to start when Mattie had interrupted him. It was, like all the others, an outside reading report. He had given them their head in picking what books to read, as long as there was at least one novel and one nonfiction title included in the four required for the semester. Arthur Corman, a hulking brute with all the imagination of a concrete slab, had apparently decided to get the nonfiction requirement out of the way at the start, and he was doing it with *Conspiracy of Silence: The Truth Behind the Government's UFO Coverup*, a sensationalistic paperback barely a step above the *National Enquirer*. But even that, Groves realized before he had read through even the first paragraph, had apparently been too much for Arthur.

"This is a very interesting book," the report began, "and I enjoyed it very much." But then it launched into something obviously copied directly from an advertising blurb. "The UFO Age began in 1947, and since then the entire subject of flying saucers has been hopelessly bogged down in a morass of lies, rumors, half-truths, wild theories and just plain hallucinations. Now this noted author has produced a book that has been hailed as a major breakthrough in UFO research."

Not bothering to read any further, Groves scrawled a huge red F at the top of the paper, adding, "If you would care to tell me what you think of the book rather than what the publisher or some ad agency thinks, I might raise this to a passing grade." Or I might not, you stupid bastard, he added to himself.

The things they thought they could get away with, particularly those clowns on the football team, like Corman. With Coach Radford to run interference for them—"I'll make sure he makes it up, don't you worry. But for right now, if you don't up that grade a notch, he's out of the game Friday. You know how it is."—they thought they couldn't be touched. And that weasel of a principal, Showalter, was no better:

"I'm aware there are problems, of course. But perhaps a little individual attention is all that is needed. We can't be too hasty, you know, not when our star players are involved."

Groves had been teaching at Wertham High a little over a month, but already he had begun to hate the job in a way he never had in Cleveland or Toledo. Or at least he couldn't remember hating it this much, although for the life of him he couldn't think why not. At least here in Wertham he hadn't been physically threatened or assaulted yet. Not that it was impossible or even unlikely. There were at least a half a dozen, including Corman, who very well could. The hulking six footers towered over Groves by four or five inches and outweighed him by as much as fifty pounds in a couple of cases. And they certainly wanted to give him a pounding. He could see it in their eyes every time he reprimanded one of them for a wrong answer or a neglected assignment. It was the same sullen, get-off-my-back glare he had seen on the Carstairs boy two years ago in Cleveland the day before two tires were slashed and the windshield covered with spray paint. He would doubtless see it again tomorrow when he handed the papers back.

Briefly a puzzled frown wrinkled his forehead, and he wondered, Why is it so much worse now? Last spring, when he and Mattie had first come out to look over his unexpected inheritance and he had discovered that against all odds there would be an opening on the Wertham faculty in the fall, he had been elated. A small town, not unlike the one he had grown up in in eastern Ohio. None of the hard-core, big-city delinquents like Carstairs and his vicious friends. Scenic New England countryside all around. Just what he had always dreamed about, and yet he hated it here. There was more tension in his classes. He didn't get along with the few parents he had met. Most of the faculty, particularly the coach and principal, were, to put it charitably, getting on his nerves. He was even fighting with Mattie, and that was something he had never done. Like this spat tonight, in front of a perfect stranger, too. And all because of a couple of cracks Mattie had made.

He shook his head. Although it was hard to believe, the

way he felt now, he knew that a year ago he would never have lost his temper the way he had tonight. They had had hundreds of bantering exchanges, each poking fun at the other, during the six years they had been married. Their shared sense of humor had been one of the things that had drawn them together.

But now . . .

God, it was a good thing she didn't know the whole story. It was bad enough as it was, as this evening had clearly illustrated. If she knew that he had been listening to local superstitions, even doing his damndest to confirm them, it would be intolerable. He couldn't count how many hours he had spent searching through the files of the Register of Deeds and the microfilms of the Wertham *Gazette*, talking to people at the local historical society, even roaming through weed-grown cemeteries, reading tombstones. But however many hours he had spent, she would consider them totally wasted.

To make matters worse, he couldn't rationally justify a single one of his actions. He could never explain it to Mattie or to anyone else, not in a thousand years. Hell, he couldn't even explain it to himself. At least a dozen times he had come to the point of heaping more ridicule on himself than Mattie or anyone else ever could, but each time either a new dream had come or some new piece of confirming evidence had popped up: a brief item in an 1889 *Gazette* mentioning the seemingly miraculous cure of a young boy, a 1930s headline about a suicide. But most often it would be a new dream, and he would awaken, trembling and sweating, staring into the darkness and thinking: What if it is true? What if the Reimanns truly did have some kind of power? And what if the source of that power is still out there, just waiting for someone to find and claim it?

What if . . . ?

With a grimace of disgust, as much at himself for indulging in such fantasies as at the prospect of another hour of semiliterate book reports, he leaned forward and pulled the next paper from the ungraded stack.

With some relief, Mattie watched while Elena March entered her room and pulled the door shut behind her. Despite a couple of shaky minutes when John had stalked out of the kitchen, things had not turned out too badly. She and Elena had talked for a good half hour, although Elena had said little about herself, just that she was divorced and that her ex-husband had since died. Still, they had seemed to be friends by the time Elena got up from the table to return to her room. It was just lucky, Mattie supposed, that Elena was a fairly easygoing type and hadn't been too upset by the brief domestic strife. The appearance of an inquisitive and soon purring B.C. hadn't hurt.

Turning back to the kitchen and putting the empty casserole dish into the sink to soak, she sighed. John was definitely getting touchier by the day. This was the first time he had blown up in front of a guest. She was going to have to be more careful, that was all there was to it. But it was so damned hard to have to watch practically every word she said. And so different, so damned different. Five years ago, even five months ago, he would have taken her reincarnation spa remark as the joke it was meant to be, and he probably would have topped it with one of his own. They both would have been laughing instead of scowling and snarling at each other.

If she didn't know better, she would think he was going through male menopause, but he was obviously too young for that, only thirty-two. But what was it, then? Was he worrying about making a go of the lodge? Not likely, since they had known from the start that it was going to be little more than a relatively cheap place to live, certainly not something to make themselves rich on. They might, if they were very lucky, break even during a couple of the summer months, but that was the best they could hope for.

She had for the first month or so pushed pretty hard to get him to sell the place, no matter how little they could get for it, but she had given that up once it became clear just how set he was on staying. She might not like the relative isolation—she'd gotten enough of that on the farm growing up—but with occasional guests like Elena March to talk to, she could survive. Soon, though, they would have to close for the winter, and then she wouldn't be stuck out here waiting for nonexistent guests to arrive. She hoped to join a local drama group that would be putting on a play in the high school auditorium in a couple of months. Once the lodge was closed for the season, she could go to their meetings. She was even thinking of volunteering the lodge with its huge lobby as a rehearsal hall. If, she thought, John didn't lose his temper the first time he saw them. With his increasingly short fuse these last few weeks, it was possible if not probable.

Was he having problems at school? Was that the reason for his fits of temper? He did bitch more often and more bitterly than ever before, but his problems in Wertham seemed minor compared to the ones he had contended with in Cleveland and Toledo. Besides, his surliness had started well before the beginning of the fall term.

Or was it possible that she herself was at the root of the problem? She had changed, she knew. Her remarks were a little more cutting, a little more serious than they used to be. But any such changes in herself were results, not causes, damn it. Results of his withdrawal from her, of his inability to take or return a joke anymore, of their gone-to-hell sex life.

She shook her head, trying to remember when they had last made love. A month? Could it have been as long as a month? When they had first been married, if they ever went longer than two or three days—

Abruptly, a reason flashed through her mind, a reason that sent a sick shudder through her body. Could he be having an affair? Was that why they made love so rarely, why he was so tense and defensive about everything? He had never strayed before, but there was always a first time. A couple of the single teachers at the school certainly were attractive enough. He was sometimes late coming home from school, and a couple of Saturdays he had gone on errands he had never really explained.

Damn, she thought as she put the last of the silverware in the dish drainer and turned toward the hall. Could it be something as simple and mundane and unpleasant as an affair? Should she ask him point blank? No, that would only make matters worse, particularly if he wasn't having one.

Somehow she still couldn't bring herself to believe that he was.

But it had to be something.

And there had to be something she could do about it while there was still a chance. Another month or two like this and they wouldn't even be speaking.

Day Two

Gratefully, John Groves put the last of the papers on the graded stack and slipped them into the folder. Thank God, he was finished for another day. He couldn't have taken many more misspelled variations of "I enjoyed this book because . . ."

He glanced at his watch. It was after midnight already. He had heard their guest walk down the hall past the study door almost an hour ago and had heard nothing since.

Stretching, he stood up, releasing the yawn that had been building up through the last half dozen papers. Mattie was probably reading or watching the late show on TV. These days she almost always waited until she was sure he was asleep before coming to bed. As if, he thought with sudden bitterness, she was afraid that something might happen if she showed up while he was still awake. Not likely, not the way things had been going between them the last few months.

In the bathroom, he brushed his teeth and, noticing an uneven spot in his beard, located a small pair of scissors in the medicine chest and did his best to hack it back to the level of the rest. Frowning as he finished, he peered more closely at his image in the mirror, tilting his face to try to remove the shadows. Except, he realized after a few seconds of looking this way and that, they weren't all shadows. The darkness under his eyes was real, not the result of bad lighting. Shaking his head irritably, he ran his fingers through his dishwater blond hair and stepped back from the mirror, glancing sideways as he did. Shit! He would have to get a haircut soon, too, he realized, and get the beard trimmed a little more neatly while he was at it. He started feeling uncomfortably self-conscious about his appearance.

And that damned barber would surely want to know, the very first thing, "Any good dreams lately?" Groves had made the mistake of talking about the dreams the first time he had gone to the man, just a few days after moving to Wertham, and he hadn't been able to avoid the subject since. On the other hand, if the barber, a chatty old-timer named Cecil, hadn't insisted on telling Groves the entire history of the land the lodge was built on, he probably never would have made the connection between his dreams and reality.

At the thought of the dreams, his heart beat a little faster, a little harder. Would there be another tonight? There had been none last night or the night before, but that didn't mean anything. He had sometimes gone as long as a week without one, and there was nothing he could do about it. They either came or they didn't.

It was the same with the guests as far as he could tell. There was simply no logic to it. Some dreamed and some didn't, and that was that. Some, of course, did dream but denied it. From the embarrassed look, the irritable or sheepish shaking of a head, he knew that much. Not that he could blame them for holding back; he probably would have done the same himself under similar circumstances. He had suspected that he was receiving censored versions now and then almost from the start, but his suspicions had changed to near certainty the morning a meek, balding little man named Willick had admitted hesitantly to a dream about a victory celebration held in a huge gray castle in some other country or century. A little questioning—What kind of food? Did anyone have any names? What did the room look like?—convinced Groves that what the man was telling him was a skeletal, G-rated version of the same dream Groves himself had experienced a few days before. The victory celebration had been, literally, an orgy, directed and fully participated in by his dream self, a feudal lord in medieval Europe.

Although that was the only one that came close to duplicating one of his own dreams, a little reading between the lines revealed that every single dream, including those of the women, was an ego or power trip of some kind, whether the power manifested itself in sex or in other, less savory ways.

Except for the one this evening.

He grimaced, remembering Elena's vivid description. It was totally different from all the others. It was the only one in which the dreamer had been in any kind of danger or had not been in complete charge of the situation. It was also the only one in which the dreamer experienced any kind of fear associated with the seven-sided object, the talisman, as he had come to think of it. In all the other dreams in which it had appeared, it was an object of power, something the dreamer would sooner die than part with.

And suddenly Groves wondered: Could the woman be part of a setup? Some friend of his wife's who had been put up to it? The way Mattie ridiculed him for his obsession with the dreams, it wouldn't surprise him. He would have to remember to check the woman's car before she left in the morning, just to see whether the license plates were really from— where had she said? Indiana?

As he moved down the broad hall from the bathroom to the bedroom, he was tempted to slip out now to check, but he decided against it. Mattie was probably in the living room, and it had windows that looked out on the parking area. She would see him and realize that he had tumbled to the joke, if joke it was. It would be better if he checked it discreetly in the morning as he went out to his own car to drive to school.

Irritably, he jerked open the door to the bedroom. Inside, he lurched to a startled halt. The small table lamp next to the bed was on, switched to its lowest setting.

Mattie wasn't in the living room, reading. She was in bed, half propped up by at least two pillows. From the bare shoulders and arms that were visible, she obviously wasn't wearing her usual nightgown. If he didn't know better, he'd think she was naked beneath the covers. Her hair was loosened from its usual bun and fell loosely over her shoulders. Her pixieish features were set in a faint, slightly uneasy smile.

For a moment he wondered: Is this part of the joke, too? And if so, what the hell is the punch line going to be?

She beckoned to him, moving only her fingers. "It's been a long time," she said softly.

He nodded but came no closer. "It has," he said.

Despite his misgivings, despite the anger he still felt, despite the strong suspicion that he was about to be the butt of a practical joke, he felt a sudden desire. He felt an erection beginning.

Then she was shifting, sitting up, letting the covers slide down. Her breasts, small and firm, the nipples partially erect, seemed to quiver as the sheet slipped down. And farther down, across her stomach, still lean and flat, to where her generous patch of pubic hair began. Her fingers touched it lightly as she looked up at him.

"Now, isn't this more interesting than all those dreams?"

Abruptly, anger erupted within him again, as it had a hundred times in the last dozen weeks, and he started to turn away, swearing under his breath. Another putdown. Another goddamn fucking putdown!

But then he stopped. All right, he thought coldly. All right, if that's the way she wants it, that's the way it will be.

He turned back to the bed. Her smile was fading into the beginnings of an apologetic frown, but the smile quickly returned, although now it was even more uncertain than before.

"It'll do," he said expressionlessly as he removed his shirt and dropped it carelessly on the floor.

He kicked off his shoes and pulled off his socks and then, purposely standing facing her, loosened his pants and slid them off. As he lowered his shorts, his erection, held partially in check by the clothing, completed itself. For a moment he stood silently, one remote corner of his mind marveling at his actions. Only rarely had they even made love with the lights on, and never had he stripped this way, in full view of her, as if throwing down some kind of macho challenge.

But even as those thoughts ran through that one corner of his mind, he found himself slowly crossing the few feet to the side of the bed. Mattie drew back slightly as he stopped, his erection only inches from her face. He thrust his pelvis forward, bringing the tip of his erection almost to her lips, which now were unsmiling and nervous.

"John?" The word was as nervous as her expression, almost plaintive. Her hands had started to pull the covers back up. "Are you all right?"

He laughed, a short, harsh sound. "Of course. Never

better. And as you said, it has been a long time." He barely recognized his own voice.

"You've never—" she began, but he cut her off.

"There's a first time for everything," he said, his eyes still on hers, which alternated nervously between his unsmiling face and the erection so close to her own face.

Then he heard himself laughing again, saw himself reaching down and grasping the covers, throwing them roughly to one side. For an instant he hesitated, that corner of his mind still bewildered at his actions, but then he shoved those thoughts aside. He dropped onto the bed, pushing her slender body toward the center. Wordlessly, he rolled on top of her, forcing her legs apart.

With no preliminaries, he thrust at her roughly, bringing gasps of shock or pain instead of pleasure from her. As much in self-defense as anything else, she reached down to guide him. Then he was inside her, still thrusting violently, doing none of the little things, making none of the moves that he knew had always given her little spurts of special pleasure. He was, that corner of his mind realized with shock, doing nothing more than masturbating within her, but still he didn't stop. If anything, he increased the tempo and violence of his single-minded pumping, and in little more than a minute it was over in a brief, explosive orgasm, his first in more than a month.

Still wordlessly, he withdrew, even before his erection had faded, and rolled to one side, pulling the tangled covers over himself.

"Don't go away," he heard himself saying, almost as if he were observing another of his dreams rather than participating in reality. "I may want a second helping after a while."

Stunned, feeling as if she had been run through a wringer, Mattie lay quietly, a mixture of fear and anger filling her. She had realized, the instant the words were out of her mouth and she saw the tightening of his lips, that it had been a mistake to mention the dreams. But he had seemed so cold standing there, so totally unresponsive to her invitation, that the words had just popped out, a desperation bid to get his attention when it seemed painfully obvious that her naked body was not doing the trick by itself.

But then he had turned back to her, his face tense and grim. What had followed was closer to punishment than sex, closer to rape than love.

Uneasily, she turned her face toward him. Already he was asleep, and that, too, was totally unlike him. But at least the grim scowl present throughout the entire affair except for the brief, shuddering moment of orgasm was fading; his entire face was relaxing and taking on the smoother lines she was familiar with, or had been familiar with until the last few months. She hadn't seen much of that face recently.

But there had never been anything like tonight, not anything remotely approaching it. Over the months he had grown increasingly withdrawn, increasingly irritable, increasingly sensitive to the slightest joke directed at him. But this was a different order of magnitude. It was as if he had suddenly become a stranger, even an enemy.

It was then, with a start, that she remembered Doris Hershman. Doris had been her roommate for one semester at Ohio State a decade ago. Doris had come back from the Christmas break that year almost in tears. Her father was in the hospital, she said, to have a brain tumor removed. It turned out to be benign, as they discovered when they removed it two days later, but the only thing that Mattie remembered now was what Doris had said about the effects the tumor had on her father.

"He isn't the same person," she had said. "When I was home for Thanksgiving, he was like a stranger."

Was that what was happening to John? Was that the reason for his erratic behavior?

A new kind of fear, not for herself but for her husband, settled over Mattie.

Despite the uneasiness that John Groves's ideas about the dreams had raised in her, Elena March found herself drifting toward sleep as quickly and easily as she had earlier in the tub. For an instant, that uneasiness caught up with her, and her eyes blinked open, as if expecting to see the images of her nightmare in the darkness around her.

But there was nothing, only the dim outline of the ceiling-high window across the room and the tiny bulge that the still-sleeping Beth made in the other bed a few feet away.

Then, without really remembering closing her eyes or rolling onto her side, she was sliding toward sleep once again.

But she was not alone.

That same presence, that same indefinable something, lurked once more just beyond the reach of her fading senses. Once more she accepted it.

And waited.

Gradually it began. As it had the time before, the sense of touch was the first to return. Again there was the feeling of stiff and starched clothes from neck to toe.

But this time there was also a feeling of motion: rough, bumpy, uneven motion. And the feel of a hard, wooden seat beneath her as she jolted against it. Beneath her feet was another hard, jolting surface.

Then came sight and sound.

She was seated on a farm wagon, a rectangular box on huge, wooden-spoked wheels. The seat was little more than a wide plank fastened near the front, across the top of the box.

A team of horses—one brown, the other spotted gray, both heavy and broad—lumbered ahead, pulling the wagon along a narrow, rocky road. Trees, mostly birches and elms with the ever-present oaks in the background, lined both sides of the road. Unknown bushes and vines filled the gaps between the trees so that the wagon seemed to move down a green-walled corridor.

What little of the sky that could be seen directly overhead between the rows of trees was dotted with clouds, dark on one side and tinged purple and red from the setting sun on the other.

Seated next to her on the wooden plank was a man, the reins in his hands. His clothes, a grayish, checked flannel shirt and dark gray pants with suspenders, were coarse and heavy. His face, square and expressionless, had a drooping mustache and a two- or three-day stubble of beard. A crumpled cap was pulled low on his forehead. His hands, rough and weathered, the knuckles prominent and bony, held the reins loosely.

All these things Elena noticed. She saw them through the eyes of the girl who sat on the wagon as it jounced toward its unknown destination.

The girl herself, through whose eyes Elena looked out at this strange world, in whose mind she hovered like a ghost, saw none of it. She was oblivious to her surroundings except to realize that her hundred-mile journey was nearing an end. Her mind was a stew of emotions, her stomach a quivering knot, and she found it almost impossible to remain seated and not leap down from the wagon and run ahead of the plodding horses.

The wraithlike presence that was still Elena March looked into that mind and saw fear and desperation. As the wagon jolted slowly onward, memories bubbled to the surface of the cauldron that was this girl's mind.

The memories, this avalanche of dream memories, became Elena's. She knew and felt them just as this girl did, and yet she remained above them, almost like someone observing the action in a play, while she tried to arrange them into a coherent whole.

Her name was Jessica Reimann, although a part of her would always think of herself as Jessica Winton. Her husband, although she had not seen him for more than three months, was Marcus Reimann.

She and Henry, her twin brother, had grown up on a small farm nearby. Despite parental admonitions, she had often taken long detours on the way home from school in Wertham to look in at the huge gates of the Reimann estate. One did not disturb the Reimanns, she was told repeatedly. They were, after all, known not only for their seemingly limitless wealth but for a never-ending stream of good works, not only in Wertham but in surrounding communities. Orphanages, humane societies, scholarship funds, and a dozen other charities were supported almost single-handedly by them, and they certainly deserved their privacy. There were also rumors—gossip as far as Jessica's parents were concerned—that they had the power to heal the sick as well as to destroy their enemies. "Money is the power," her father often said, "and the likes of us should stay clear of it."

But Jessica persisted, not really knowing why she ignored

the dozens of lectures and punishments designed to keep her from invading the Reimanns' privacy. She often saw Marcus, the only son of Ben and Sarah Reimann, during those first years before he was sent away to school. He was only a few years older than Jessica, and when he returned, she herself was out of high school, a fully grown young lady. He recognized her instantly as "that funny little girl I always saw hanging around our gates."

They were married within a year, to the very mixed feelings of her parents, who thought she had been shamelessly forward. They spent most of their first year together traveling, although their official residence was the west wing of the mansion.

But then Sarah Reimann died, and everything changed. They had been at home little more than a week, when, in the middle of the night, a grim-faced Marcus stormed into their bedroom and ordered her to pack. They were gone before dawn. Marcus never explained his reasons beyond a strained "family differences," but whatever the differences were, he refused to ever return to the mansion as long as his father lived.

In the two years that followed, Marcus performed real physical labor for the first time in his life, supporting himself and Jessica by a series of unskilled jobs. The money his father sent unsolicited was left untouched in a bank.

Then, a little more than three months ago, they had received word that Ben Reimann had died. Vowing to be gone only long enough to claim his inheritance and set in motion the machinery to sell everything, he went to Wertham.

He did not return.

There were no replies to Jessica's increasingly urgent letters. Even letters to her own family, who still lived on the same farm near Wertham, went unanswered. It was as if the entire community of Wertham had dropped out of the world altogether.

But then, finally, word had come. The summer was gone, fading into a New England autumn that seemed to have lost all the color and briskness of past autumns and instead seemed only dark and frightening to her. The note itself was short, less than a page of his characteristic scrawl. Had she not been so familiar with his handwriting, she would not have believed that it had come from him.

The note was formal. The greeting, "Dearest Jessica," was the closest approach to feeling revealed anywhere in it. "I shall never return to you, and you are not welcome here," it said, and went on to advise her to begin divorce proceedings, something that would have been unthinkable to him only weeks before and was still unthinkable to Jessica. He would not contest it, he said, and would, in order to spare her as much of the inevitable shame as possible, admit to anything she cared to accuse him of.

The only other communication was a letter to a nearby bank, instructing it to open an account in Jessica's name and providing a single deposit large enough to support her in moderate comfort for the rest of her life.

Further letters and telegrams went unanswered and unacknowledged.

What had happened? He had been as vehemently positive about his intention to simply dispose of the estate and return to her as he had been about leaving Wertham two years before and as determinedly closed-mouthed about his reasons. If he had been able to stick to that earlier decision, able to resist the temptation—even her own puzzled urgings—to touch the money that had been sent him those first months, then how could he have failed now?

She could not imagine a reason for him to desert her, particularly not in this strange, almost cowardly way. He loved her, of that she was as positive as she was of anything in this world or the next. He would not simply walk away from her. He could not; it was not in his nature.

And yet it had happened.

She had to know the truth. She had to confront him or whoever was in control and speaking for him and ask the questions. She knew that she might be turned away at the door by servants. She knew that she was risking the loss of the money that he had already given her, for it could be taken back as easily as it had been given. She knew that she was risking losing the easy divorce he had promised, for witnesses against her could be purchased for far less than he had at his disposal.

In her darker moments, she even feared that she might be risking her very life if Marcus was dead and someone had taken illegal control of the estate.

But soon she would know. No matter what happened, she would find a way to learn the truth. Now that she was here, she would find a way.

With a conscious effort that Elena, still a separate observer in Jessica's troubled mind, could feel as a tightening and strengthening of that mind, the girl focused her attention on her surroundings, on the rutted road, the trees, the sky that was now swiftly darkening as night approached.

Ahead, standing out from the ten-foot wall of evergreen shrubs that lined one side of the road, a pair of massive pillars appeared to mark the entrance to the Reimann estate.

Until that instant, Elena had felt the same irrational calmness she had experienced during the first dream. Even the impossible fact that her dreaming self realized that it was a dream had not disturbed her.

But now, at the sight of the pillars, all of Elena's calm aloofness vanished, and a touch of the terror her earlier dream self had felt returned.

The pillars, Elena realized, were the same pillars that still stood at the entrance to what had been the Reimann estate.

The entrance to what was now Groves Lodge.

With that realization came the irrational but totally unshakable conviction that what she was experiencing was not a dream. Jessica Reimann was not a dream. She had existed. Marcus Reimann had existed. The mansion which she now approached had existed. In her mind there was no doubt.

That other dream, that nightmare of terror and death—that, too, was real. It had happened—would soon happen—to Jessica Reimann, to *this* Jessica Reimann. In a few days, a few weeks ago at most, this young woman, so determined to learn the truth at any price, would pay that price. She would find herself in the midst of a living nightmare.

No, the Elena March presence in the girl's mind screamed. No! Stop! Turn back!

But the wagon moved on, the sky growing ever darker as night approached. The first stars were already appearing in the rifts between the clouds.

Creaking, the wagon turned down the drive between the seven-sided pillars and the hideous statues that peered down from their tops like a pair of grotesque sentries. They had been erected, Jessica had been told by her parents, by the first Reimanns to own the land more than a hundred years before.

Beyond the pillars, Jessica at first saw nothing, only the drive as it started to wind its way through the trees. Then, on the right, the carriage house appeared. The parking area, Elena managed to think as they drew abreast of it. That's where the parking area is—will be—for the lodge.

Then the drive turned left, and the mansion itself loomed up against the darkening sky, half hidden by massive oaks and elms and willows. Here and there the glimmer of a lighted window showed. For an instant, like a pair of pictures projected together onto a screen, the building was overlaid by the image of Groves Lodge in her mind. Except for the mansion's greater size, the two were nearly identical. Where the lodge's columns were merely carved in relief on either side of the front door, the mansion had huge, freestanding columns flanking the steps that led up to a door that must have been at least nine feet tall.

Then the wagon was crunching and creaking to a stop only yards from the steps. Jessica climbed down slowly. The driver made no effort to help her or even to look at her, although he had known her from the day she was born. He only reached silently behind the plank seat, picked up her luggage, and dropped it to the ground at her feet. Without waiting to see if anyone came out to meet her, he flipped at the reins and started the horses at a hurried pace back down the shadowy drive.

For a long minute, Jessica stood at the foot of the steps, shivering and working up the courage to take the last dozen steps of her journey.

Elena, still present, tried to speak, tried to shout, tried to force the girl to turn her back on the house and run after the wagon.

But she could not. It was as if she didn't exist.

And, Elena thought in a sudden moment of lucidity, she didn't exist!

She was here as an observer, not a participant. She had been brought here to watch, not to act.

These events had occurred—the numbers popped unbidden into her mind—well over half a century ago. They *had* occurred. Her being here now, whether it was reality or dream, could not affect what was happening. The nightmare Elena had already seen lay in Jessica's future, but it could not be delayed or halted.

The door opened then. Slowly, ponderously, it swung back, releasing a widening swath of shadowy light that rippled down the steps.

Marcus Reimann stood silently in the opening, as Elena had known he would. His face, as she had known it would be, was the face from her nightmare. The eyes were still alive; the features were clean-shaven, not smeared with the mud and filth of a hastily dug grave, but the face was the same.

Jessica resisted her first impulse to dash up the steps and throw herself into his arms. Instead, she stood waiting at the foot of the steps, gradually taking in the shocking changes that leaped out at her from his face.

His features were thin and drawn. His complexion, once a healthy tan, was pale, as if he had not seen the sun in months. His forehead, once smooth and untroubled even during their worst trials, was creased in an angry frown. His lips, which had smiled encouragingly at her when she had last seen them, were pressed tightly together, little more than thin lines only slightly less pale than the face that surrounded them.

For a full two minutes they stood like that, only yards apart.

Finally he smiled, but the smile was no more inviting than the frown it had replaced. He held out his hands.

Slowly, as if approaching a stranger, Jessica moved up the steps.

And as she did, Elena watched—and saw.

If there had been even the slightest doubt in her dreaming mind before, now there was none. The final link between the two dreams was there, suspended from a slender chain about his neck, visible where his ruffled shirt was parted below his throat. The final link, the object she had clutched with skin-piercing strength, the object that had been the most real, the most terrifying of all in that other nightmare: the tiny, seven sided pool of glinting blackness.

Abruptly, as if someone had pulled an electrical plug from a socket, the images were gone, and Elena March was half sitting up in bed, her heart pounding so heavily she was sure that the front of her pajamas was pulsing in time with its beat. Every muscle in her body was wire-tight; her fingers dug into the mattress on either side. It was only after several seconds that she realized she was holding her breath.

With an effort at silence, she let her breath out. In the near darkness—a trace of moonlight entered between the parted drapes—she could see the small form of her daughter, half out from under the covers. She turned as Elena watched, and then she quieted.

At least, Elena thought gratefully, she's not being affected by whatever insanity has gotten a hold on me.

It was beginning to look as if Groves were right, she thought with an attempt at ruefulness. She had never had dreams like this before. Nightmares, yes, but none so vivid, none so well remembered, none that had such a feeling of realism. Even now, after she was awake, it seemed more like a memory of an actual happening than a dream.

Thank God she was getting out of here in the morning. Many more nights like this and she would be a nervous wreck.

Forcing as many muscles to relax as she could, Elena lowered her head onto the pillow and pulled the covers up over her shoulders. The warmth of her body trapped beneath the blanket felt good, comforting. Then she remembered the miniature recorder Groves had given her. It still lay within easy reach on the table between the beds, but she didn't turn toward it. Recording the dream would only make it more vivid, and that was the last thing she needed. Besides, the sound of her voice could easily awaken Beth. If she had to try to explain to a five-year-old why she was talking into a little machine in the middle of the night, she would never get back to sleep. If Groves asked about the dreams in the morning, she would—out of hearing of Beth—tell him. There was damned little danger that she would forget it in another four or five hours.

Or in four or five years, she thought uneasily.

Finally, hoping that the show was over for the night, Elena closed her eyes.

When Elena awakened, sunlight rather than moonlight filtered through the narrow opening between the heavy drapes, and Beth was snuggled in bed next to her. There apparently had been no more dreams, at least none that she could remember and certainly none that had disturbed Beth.

The little girl's eyes popped open with her mother's first movement. She looked a little dazed, as she always did the first few seconds after awakening, but then she blinked, and her eyes widened as the huge room came into focus around her.

"Is this Vermont, Mommie?"

Elena stifled a laugh as she realized that for her daughter, the last ten or twelve hours didn't exist. To her, it was just a few minutes since she had awakened briefly in the car.

"Yes, this is Vermont," Elena said, reaching out and hugging the girl under the covers. "And it's time we were getting outside and seeing some of it. But first some breakfast. And a bath for you."

Beth shook her head without lifting it from the pillow. "I'm not dirty," she said matter-of-factly.

"And you're not going to be, either." Elena released the girl and pushed back the covers. "Now let's get on with it. For that matter, you owe me a toothbrushing, too. You missed last night. I almost forgot."

"Oh, Mommie!"

Once Beth saw the huge tub, however, all protests were forgotten, especially when Elena let her brush her teeth between splashes in the tub. To her, the tub was large enough to be a swimming pool with soap, and she was totally absorbed in it for the few minutes the procedure took.

Later, decked out in their next-to-last fresh sets of jeans and pullovers, they made their way down the hall to the kitchen. Beth looked around in wonderment at the high ceilings and huge paintings that were scattered along the walls. As they entered the kitchen, her eyes widened even more.

"Wow! Vermont is really neat," she said, making use of two of her currently favorite words in the same breath. "Can we stay here?"

"No, honey, this is a hotel. We couldn't—"

"It is?" Her eyes widened even more as she looked around. John Groves, seemingly totally absorbed in a plate of eggs and sausage, sat across the table from Mattie. "No, it isn't," Beth said excitedly.

"Yes, it is, honey. It's different from the ones we've been staying in the last few days, that's all."

The little girl shook her head. "This is a house," she said in a tone that brooked no argument. Then she seemed to notice Groves. "Do you live here, too?"

"That's right," Mattie said. She was smiling at the girl, but there was an unexpected stiffness in her voice, although Elena doubted that Beth would notice. "My name is Mattie, and this is John."

John Groves nodded stiffly and gave Beth a sideways glance but said nothing. Another family squabble, Elena wondered, or just the leftovers from the night before?

"Are you mad at me?" Beth asked, her eyes still on Groves.

"Beth!" Elena took her hand and started to turn her away, but a laugh from Mattie stopped her.

"That's all right," Mattie said. "He just looks that way in the morning."

"Oh." The little girl nodded solemnly. "Daddy used to look like that. But he went away. Are you going away?"

"That's enough, Beth," Elena said firmly. Then she said to Groves, "I'm sorry." She hesitated uncomfortably, resisting the impulse to add the usual, "You know how children her age are."

"That's all right," he said. Then, glancing self-consciously at his watch, he pushed himself back from the table. "I have to be going." And with a sideways glance at his wife, he was gone.

Well, so much for his interest in the nightmares, Elena thought.

"What would you like?" Mattie spoke quickly into the silence. "There are plenty of eggs and sausage and the cereals I showed you last night." She seemed more relaxed now that her husband had left.

"We'll take the eggs and sausage," Elena replied, looking down at Beth. "Won't we, young lady?"

Beth's freckled face looked uncertain. "Do I like them?"

"I'm sure I don't know. I guess we'll just have to find out, now, won't we."

"I didn't like what you made me eat yesterday." The child's blue eyes almost disappeared as she squinched her face in remembrance. "Is it anything like that?"

"Nothing like that," Elena said, and then turned to Mattie. "We had a breakfast special at one of those MacDonald imitators. I didn't much care for it, either."

Mattie, trim in green slacks and gray blouse, the bun of hair pulled back in early-morning tightness, motioned for them to sit down as she lifted the foil covering from the platter in the center of the table. "Sit down and dig in. And if it's not hot enough, just yell. Now, you also have your choice of orange or tomato juice. Or milk."

"Orange juice, orange juice," Beth insisted. And then, as Mattie opened the refrigerator, the little girl pointed at it triumphantly. "See? This *is* a house. Hotels don't have 'frigerators."

When the cat, even yellower and fluffier than it had seemed the night before on the registration desk, meandered in a few minutes later, looking for a supplement to its own earlier breakfast, Beth was even more loudly positive that this was a house. With both a refrigerator and a kitty, it couldn't possibly be anything else.

Dr. Victor Edwards, still disheveled and unshaven at nine in the morning, looked speculatively at Donald and Edith Winton, the old man's grandnephew and his wife. Winton, fortyish and balding, wore a dark suit and blue-striped tie, while his wife, a few years younger and considerably more slender, wore a conservative tan pants suit. Both looked decidedly uneasy, even apprehensive.

It had been a hectic night for Edwards. After being awakened from an unplanned nap in his den at home, he had hurried down to Parkside to find that Miss Harris had not been exaggerating. The old man, Henry Winton, was not only in remarkably and unexpectedly good shape but had also been, as she had said, attempting to leave Parkside on his own. After talking to Winton and explaining the situation to him as best he could, Edwards had, despite the hour, given him as thorough a physical as he could under the circumstances. It had only confirmed his first impression, but there was nothing to indicate what could have prompted such a sudden switch from vegetablelike passivity to full alertness and nervous impatience. All the examination told him was that the old man was in surprisingly good shape for one who had been confined to bed for several months after a stroke at age eighty-seven. He could even, to Dr. Edwards's amazement, stand unsupported and walk, though with a slow, shuffling gate. All traces of the stroke were just that: traces. It was as if, during the past six months, the old man had simply turned himself off to allow the healing to proceed; now that it was completed, he had somehow turned himself back on.

Finally, once Edwards had convinced the old man to sleep for at least a couple of hours, he called the nephew and his wife, who now stood stiffly in front of his desk, waiting nervously.

"You're telling us," Donald Winton said in a puzzled voice, "that we should take him home with us? Is that it?"

Edwards shrugged his narrow shoulders. "I am merely explaining the situation to you. Any action you may take is, of course, entirely up to you."

"But you're recommending that we take him."

"I can only repeat what I said before. As far as I can tell, your uncle is in excellent health, all things considered. However, when it comes to the mind, we can only make guesses. I don't know why he suddenly awakened, so to speak. I don't know why it happened now rather than last week or next week. And I don't know how long this lucid period will last. It could be very short-lived, or it could last until the end of his life. However, the one thing I am reasonably sure of is this: For anyone in his condition, the probability of a relapse is significantly lowered if the individual is in familiar surroundings, looked after by people who know him and care for him." Edwards's tone, as it had before, plainly added the unspoken, "You do care for him, I assume."

There was a long pause, and then the sound of Donald Winton's breath easing out in a resigned sigh. "Very well. You seem to leave us little choice."

"On the contrary, it's your choice entirely."

Winton grimaced. "Very well, you've made your point. When will you release him?"

"I was thinking of, oh, say ten or fifteen minutes from now. As soon as he can get dressed. He is very anxious to be out of here."

"But I assumed— Look, there must be some papers to sign, forms to fill out, red tape to get through. There was certainly enough when he came here."

"Yes, there are a few forms to be processed, of course. However, as you say, they are little more than red tape. They can be taken care of later. The important thing is your uncle's recovery."

Winton blinked as Edwards, who had been rising and moving out from behind his desk as he spoke, hurried from the room, leaving them once again to wait.

"Donald," his wife began in icy tones as soon as the door closed behind Edwards, "I will have you know that I do not appreciate this one little bit. I am the one who will have to look after him, not you."

"What the hell was I supposed to do? You heard the doctor."

"I heard him very well. He is obviously an expert in making people feel guilty."

"Edith, for God's sake! We owe the poor old bastard a little something, don't you think? That money he gave us for the house, for one thing—"

"Little enough for five years' free room and board."

Winton shook his head angrily. "Perhaps, if that were all there was to it. But what about his being a live-in baby-sitter for Nickie for five years? Don't tell me that doesn't count for anything."

"Of course it does! I never denied it. But the situation is different now, don't you see? No matter how healthy your

Dr. Edwards says he is right this minute, there is no getting around the truth. And the truth is, he had a stroke, a serious one. And there is no telling when he'll have another."

"If he has another or he gets to be too much trouble, I'll make other arrangements."

"If he has another! Do you have any doubt at all that he will? He's almost ninety years old, Donald! Don't you understand that? Ninety years old."

"Is that what's got you in an uproar? You're afraid he's going to have the nerve to die right there in front of you?"

"Yes, damn it! Yes! That scares the hell out of me. You weren't there the last time, so what would you know about it? I had to take care of everything. I had to call the hospital. I had to stand there, afraid to move him, afraid to touch him, afraid to do anything. And it will be the same next time, you mark my words." Her knuckles were white as she gripped her purse tightly in her lap, as if trying to crush it. "I'm still not convinced he even is your uncle," she went on in an almost hysterical voice. "Where was he all those sixty years?"

"You knew very well where he was. On a farm in Ohio."

"So he said. But why? Why didn't he ever tell anyone where he was? Why, after sixty years, did he suddenly decide to find his family?"

"Keep your voice down! Do you want everyone in the building to hear you? Besides, there is no point to this hysterical nonsense. We've been over it until I'm sick of hearing it. He *is* my uncle, no matter what wild fantasies you care to dream up. And even if he weren't, we owe him a little consideration for the last five years. The matter is settled. Period!"

Folding his arms, Winton turned his face away from her and toward the nearly bare trees visible through the window behind the desk. In icy silence, they waited for Dr. Edwards to return.

For the first time in the six weeks he had been teaching at Wertham, John Groves came back to the lodge just before noon, ostensibly for lunch. As Mattie, taken completely by surprise, put together sandwiches for them both, he paced nervously behind her, saying nothing, just as he had said nothing when he had gotten up that morning. It was as if last night had not occurred. But finally, as she was finishing, she felt his hands touch her shoulders. Involuntarily, she stiffened.

But his voice was a hesitant whisper, his words as tentative as his touch. "I'm sorry," he said. "I don't know what got into me last night."

Relief washed over her. She had been vainly wondering how to approach the subject.

"I know," she said, turning toward him.

"It was just that crack you made, about the dreams. It got to me. I wasn't thinking straight. I wasn't thinking at all." He shook his head miserably. "You know I wouldn't hurt you for anything in the world."

"I know you wouldn't." Tentatively, she put a hand on his arm. She could feel it trembling under her touch.

"I couldn't. I couldn't hurt you." He seemed to be talking to himself as much as to her. "It's those dreams, those goddamn dreams. They're driving me up the wall."

"Perhaps you should see a doctor," she said, speaking rapidly and nervously.

"A doctor? A psychiatrist, you mean?"

"No, a doctor."

"But why?"

"There might be something physical that's causing the dreams and everything."

She felt him stiffen. "Something physical . . ."

Then, suddenly, he laughed. His fingers closed more tightly on her arms, and he leaned down and kissed her. His bearded face was split in a wide grin as he pulled back. "Something physical. I'll be damned. You're probably right. I don't know why I didn't think of it myself. Too close, I suppose. Couldn't see the forest for the trees and all that proverbial nonsense. But you're right. I'll just bet you're right."

Releasing her, he looked at his watch. "Not quite twelve. Everyone will probably be out for lunch, but—" He broke off. "I'll go back to town right now and stop at that clinic on Jefferson and see if someone can work me in today."

He leaned down and kissed her again and then snatched up one of the sandwiches as he hurried from the room. From the hall, Mattie heard him call back, "I'll call you this afternoon, let you know what happens."

As he hurried to his five-year-old Ford, a mixture of emotions boiled within him. Until Mattie had mentioned it, the possibility of a physical explanation for what had been happening to him had not even crossed his mind, although now he could not imagine why it hadn't. For weeks—months—thoughts of hallucinations and insanity had plagued him, but that was all. That the dreams and his increasing irritability might have a medical rather than a psychological cause had never once occurred to him. Even his compulsion to question the lodge's increasingly rare guests about their dreams had not suggested it to him. Nor even had his unforgivable performance last night, when he had gone beyond hallucinations and actually acted out the grotesque fantasies.

He could remember—could not keep from remembering, even for a second—every word, every movement, every thought. And they had been *his* thoughts; that was the most frightening part of all. Although some small part of him had held itself aloof and merely watched, they had been his thoughts, not the product of the sick mind of some medieval warlord but his own, John Groves's. Despite that tiny, aloof corner of his mind, *he* had done it, and *he* had felt good about doing it. If he could act that way, if he could attack his own wife without the slightest hesitation, what else was he capable of?

Shivering, he climbed into the car and, tires spitting gravel, pulled out and onto the road. But if it was something physical—a hormone imbalance or something like that, even a tumor—it was a whole new ball game. That was at least something that could be dealt with, here and now. It was something he could get help for, effective medical help, not some psychiatric mumbo-jumbo that had as much chance of harming as helping. Pills, shots, even an operation: the possibilities were endless.

If it was something physical.

If . . .

Beth, although she wasn't outright cranky, was far from being on her best behavior. From the moment she realized they were definitely leaving the house she had apparently set her heart on staying in, she had worn a glum face and had reminded her mother every few minutes how nice the kitty had been. She also displayed an instant dislike—or indifference at best—to practically everything. Spectacular views on the highway, the same kind that had been greeted with enthusiasm and dozens of questions only the day before, were ignored or dismissed with a simple, "It was prettier around the house." The occasional wildlife that appeared in the trees and fields along the road were not pettable and therefore not in the same league as "that nice kitty." The usual highway games—spotting different colored cars and different types of houses, even singing songs— were entered into only desultorily. Even her current favorite food, a chili dog, was pronounced "not as good as what I had at the house," despite the fact that aside from the orange juice, Beth hadn't seemed at the time to particularly like anything she had for breakfast.

By late afternoon, however, faced with the prospect of looking for another motel for the night, Elena began to wonder whether Beth didn't have the right idea, after all. Aside from the bad dreams—and that's all they were, she told herself firmly, just dreams—and despite Mr. Groves's short temper, the lodge had been the most comfortable and relaxing place she had stayed at recently, including her own apartment. Besides, six days in a car—or was it seven now?—was more than enough, particularly for a five-year-old who, Elena realized now that she took the time to think about it objectively, had held up very well under very trying conditions. Elena hadn't been able to tell the child where they were going or even why, just that they were "taking a trip, going away for a while." And six days for a five-year-old was roughly the equivalent of six months for an adult. Elena wasn't sure how well she herself, at a few days under thirty, would have held up under similar circumstances.

Thus it was a pleasant surprise for them both when, checking the map at the next town they came to, Elena discovered that, unknown to her, they had taken a roughly circular route most of the day and were within fifteen miles of Wertham and Groves Lodge.

* * *

Angrily, John Groves shoved through the door and out of the spartan concrete building that housed the Jefferson Street Clinic: two doctors, a dentist, and a pediatrician. Why the hell had he come? There was nothing wrong with him. He had known that from the start, or he should have. He didn't need any damned doctor to tell him that.

"I wouldn't worry about it," the doctor, a grumpily no-nonsense type named Seth Laird, had said after what struck Groves as a very superficial examination. "If you really want me to, I can set it up for you to have some special tests at the hospital—electrolyte imbalance, that kind of esoterica—even recommend a psychologist if you think it would help. But I don't think the tests would tell us anything that the routine tests on the blood we've already taken won't tell us, and I don't think you're anywhere near needing any kind of psychiatric help. Frankly, your dreams—or nightmares, if you want to call them that—and the irritability and all the rest is, in my opinion, just the result of the stress you're under. New job. New part of the country. Living in that mausoleum out there and having to rent rooms and share meals with complete strangers. Your subconscious is probably overreacting, that's all. As for your interest in other people's dreams, it seems a natural enough subject for breakfast conversation with strangers, particularly if a lot of them have dreams, too, as you say they do."

For a moment, Groves had been tempted to say that it was not just an interest in other people's dreams but that, at times, it was an obsession. Luckily he had resisted the temptation. Nor had he given in to the proddings of his guilty conscience to tell Laird about his near attack on Mattie the night before. He knew that anything he said to a doctor was supposed to be confidential, but Groves really didn't know Laird. What he did know was that Laird's son, who occasionally put in an appearance at school, was rapidly turning into one of its biggest problems. Skipping school was the least of the boy's offenses. He'd been picked up for reckless driving at least once, and rumor had it that he'd been drunk, or more likely on drugs, at the time. With a son like that, Laird did not inspire great confidence; and Groves knew that it would take nothing more than a chance remark from father to son for Groves's personal problems—sexual problems at that—to end up as locker-room gossip at school. That would be all some of those bastards would need. He had enough trouble keeping them off his back as it was.

Why the hell had he listened to Mattie in the first place? "Maybe it's something physical," he mimicked silently.

"Sure," he should have said. "Sure it's something physical. One piece of ass in five weeks is what's physically wrong." What did she expect?

And why was he always worrying about cracking up? Now that he thought about it, in spite of the harassment he had been putting up with all day at school, in spite of all the whining about grades, he felt better than he had in weeks. He was just angry, and why shouldn't he be? Between the shit he had to take at school and the putdowns he got at home, it was no wonder. Anyone subjected to the kinds of pressure that had been squeezing him dry the last few weeks and months would be irritable. There was nothing wrong with him.

And the dreams. Instead of wasting time trying to wish them away, he should damned well simply acknowledge their reality and try to find out what was causing them.

Find it and use it, the way the Reimanns had.

When, five minutes later, he pulled into the lodge parking area, he was pleasantly surprised to see Elena March's boxy blue sedan. He had not talked to her at breakfast, but he had a feeling, a very strong feeling, particularly after thinking about that first spectacular dream she had had, that if anyone could help him get to the bottom of what was going on around here, she could. The mere fact that she was still at the lodge despite the nightmare and the bickering was proof in itself. Something was keeping her here, and that something, he was sure, was related to the dreams. And to the talisman.

Perhaps, he thought eagerly as he climbed out of the car, his luck was changing at last.

Mattie, seeing the car as it turned into the lodge grounds, hastily finished peeling and slicing the last of the frying potatoes for supper. By the time she heard John coming down the hall and going into his den next to the kitchen, she was drying her hands on a paper towel and hurrying into the hall.

He was standing with his back to the door, leaning over his desk, when she entered.

"Well?" she said even before the door clicked shut behind her. "What did the doctor say?"

It seemed to take him a second to realize what she was asking about, but then he grinned as he pulled a fistful of papers from his briefcase and dropped them on the desk. His teeth showed whitely through his beard.

"What the doctor said was that there's nothing wrong," Groves said. "Not a thing except a case of nerves. You know, moving to a new part of the country, getting a new job, having to get used to a new batch of problems at school, moving into a new house, if you can call this a house. I guess it was getting to me more than I realized, that's all."

Relief flooded through her. "You're all right, then?"

"Physically, apparently I am. As all right as I've ever been, anyway. Blood pressure a hair on the high side but not out of limits or anything like that. And even that's probably just from the nerves."

"You sound better. And look better."

He shrugged. "Just relieved, I suppose. And now that I've got an idea of what's been making me act the way I've been acting, I think I can do something about it." He took her hands in his. "I'm sorry about last night and about a lot of other nights."

She hugged him impulsively. For an instant a one-liner about his preoccupation with the dreams darted through her mind, but she pushed it firmly away, making sure it didn't get transformed into spoken words.

"Don't worry about it," she said instead. "I understand."

"I know," he said, "and you've put up with quite a bit. But now that I've gotten a handle on it, as they say, things are going to get better, much better. You can count on it."

"Can I talk to Uncle Bill? Can I? Please?"

Beth stood eagerly next to the phone at the end of the couch in the living room while Elena lowered herself onto the cushions. Mattie and her husband, who had been on their best and most cheerful behavior throughout supper, had retreated to some other part of the building to give her "privacy" for her call, although she had insisted that there was no need. She was, after all, only calling her mother and younger brother to let them know where she was and that nothing disastrous had befallen either her or Beth during their week on the road.

"All right," Elena said to her daughter, "but just for a minute, when I'm finished." Carefully, she dialed and waited through the interminable series of clicks and buzzes that apparently indicated that the connection was being made. At last the ringing began.

"Hello?" An unfamiliar male voice had answered.

"Bill?" she asked uncertainly. "Is that you?"

"No, it isn't. Who is this?"

"This is Wilma March's residence, isn't it?"

A brief hesitation and then, "That's right. Who is this?"

Apprehension grabbed queasily at her stomach. "This is her daughter. Now what's going on there? Is something wrong?"

"Ellie?" Surprise and relief filled the voice. "Where the blue blazes are you?"

"New England. Now who is this? And where's my mother?"

"Oh, I'm sorry, Ellie, it's just that . . . this is Charlie Wallace. And your mom's right here. Just hang on a sec."

"Charlie, wait a minute!" But he was gone before she could ask him anything else, and then there was the sound of the receiver being shuffled around.

"Ellie, darling." Her mother's voice had come on the line. "We've been worried. Where are you? Are you all right?"

"Beth and I are fine. And we're in Vermont. Now what's going on back there? Why did Charlie answer the phone?"

"He's an old friend and a good neighbor. Why shouldn't he be here?"

"Mother! You've never been any good at lying. Now please, tell me what's going on? Nothing's happened to Bill, has it?"

"No, of course not. He's right here, and he's fine."

"Then what? Come on, Mother, I know something's wrong. Now what is it? Have my ex-in-laws been causing trouble?"

There were more phone-shifting sounds and muffled voices, and then her brother's distinctive drawl came on the line. "Hi, Sis, nice to hear from you. Charlie says you're all the way out in Vermont."

Elena let her breath out in an explosive sigh. "That's right, but come on, Bill. Will you tell me what's going on before you give me an ulcer?"

"It's nothing for you to worry about, Sis. Just your esteemed ex-father-in-law making a pest of himself, that's all."

"A pest? How? I suppose he wants to know where I am."

"To put it mildly, yes, that's about the size of it. That creepy lawyer of his—Morton or something like that—has been calling a couple times a day, making little sugar-coated threats. A total idiot, that man."

"Threats? What sort of threats?"

"Like I said, nothing to worry about, they're so ridiculous. Having you charged with child abduction, for instance."

"What? My God! Look, I'd better come back there and—"

"I told you, it's nothing to worry about. After the second or third call, I talked to Chief Travers, and he says Grantland's just making noise. There's not a darned thing he can do, not a thing in the world. He never had any rights in this thing to begin with, and even if he did, he and your late ex signed them all away."

"I know, but—"

"Hold it a minute, will you, Sis?" Her brother's voice became muffled as he apparently turned away from the phone. "Mom, we're just about out of coffee. Why don't you put some more on?"

After some unintelligible background voices, he was back. His voice was lower now, and he spoke faster.

"Look, Sis, what I said was true. There's not a darned thing Grantland or any of his high-powered lawyers can do. Look, I didn't tell Mom—that's why I chased her out to the kitchen just now—but I talked to Grantland's wife, Miriam, a couple of days ago. She's on our side, more or less. Grantland's just ticked off because you defied him, she says. She figures he'll eventually come to his senses if we give him enough time. Another week or two, or something like that."

"From what I saw of her while I was married to her son,

Miriam went along with whatever Davis said, no questions asked."

"Don't let her public face fool you. That's what I thought, too, until I talked to her. She's pretty tough in her own way. She'd have to be to live with Grantland all these years without cracking up. Anyway, she thinks she'll have him calmed down in another week or two if nothing new comes along to stir him up. And she's got a couple of people—her own lawyer, for one—working on him, trying to point out the legal error of his ways. So don't worry. It'll all work itself out if you give it a little more time."

"If you say so. But if he's causing you and Mom all this trouble, and Charlie's getting dragged in—"

"It's just a couple of phone calls a day, that's all. They only came in person once. And you know Charlie. He's been sweet on Mom ever since his Millie died. This business just gives him a good excuse to hang around here and protect her. I'll bet he tries to make it permanent one of these days." There was a slight fading as he turned from the phone again. "Right, Charlie?"

There was a mumbled "Smart aleck kids!" in the background but no denial.

"See? I told you. Now, you just relax and enjoy yourself on old Grantland's money a while longer. When you come back, everything will be all taken care of." A light chuckle. "You might even have a new stepfather."

"You're positive about this?"

"About Charlie? Well—"

"You know what I mean."

"Sure, I'm positive it's best for you to stay away for a while more. Grantland may be self-righteous and conceited and mad as a wet hen, but he's not stupid. If enough people—lawyers, for instance—tell him often enough that he doesn't have a legal leg to stand on, he'll settle down. And once that's happened, he'll probably turn into a devoted grandfather and start showering her with gifts, which I hope you will not be too self-righteous to let her keep."

"I guess I'll have to take your word for it.'

"Was I ever wrong?"

"More often than I care to think about. You're the one

whose first car broke down before you even got home with it."

"I'm a bad judge of machines but a good judge of people. Now, Mom should be back any second. Don't tell her any of this, at least not the part about me talking to Miriam. That would be consorting with the enemy, and it'd just upset her."

"All right, little brother. But if anything comes up, anything at all, you be sure to let me know. We could leave the car here and fly back if we had to. You promise you'll call?"

"I promise," he said with exaggerated resignation in his voice. "That is, I'd promise if I knew how to reach you. Unless you don't know where you're going to be and you just want to check in yourself every night."

She hesitated a moment, glancing around the room at Beth, whose eagerness had turned to anxious fidgeting. "I think I'll stay here another day or so. Beth seems to like the place, which may be the understatement of the decade. She's attached herself to a cat, and you know how she is with animals. And the place is pleasant. It's sort of an old-fashioned boardinghouse in a way."

"I didn't think those things existed anymore. I suppose it's priced out of sight."

"Just the opposite. It's called Groves Lodge, and it's a mile or two outside a little town called Wertham, not much bigger than Greenville," she said, and went on to give him the phone number.

"Let me know if you decide to move on," he said as he copied the number.

"I will, don't worry. In fact, I'll probably check in with you every day if I don't hear from you first. I know you're probably right about Grantland, but I can't help but worry a little."

"Don't. As long as you're a thousand miles away, there's no problem. Like I said, just give him time to cool down and come to his senses."

She was silent a moment, remembering similar words from Gerald himself when they had first been married: "Dad will calm down and accept our marriage once he's had time to think about it."

But he never had. For five years he had carried on his

sometimes subtle, sometimes not so subtle campaign, until Gerald had finally folded. But she was no Gerald, she told herself, and Grantland knew it. He knew that the kind of pressure that had eventually worn her late ex-husband down wouldn't work on her.

"All right," she said, "I'll just have to take your word for it. But right now your number-one fan is standing here threatening to have a fit if I don't let her talk to you."

She held the receiver out to Beth, who grabbed it instantly and held it, two-handed, in the general vicinity of her mouth and right ear. "Uncle Bill? This is me."

Barely pausing for any replies, Beth ran through a quick quiz on the condition of the livestock, particularly the cats and dogs and the chicken she had adopted during her frequent visits to the farmhouse. Then she dashed through a high-pitched and slightly garbled version of their trip so far, ending with an account of the "wonderful great big house" they were staying at now and a glowing description of "the nice, new kittycat." Finally she came to an uneven stop and then held the receiver out to her mother.

"Grandma wants to talk to you," she said glumly.

"Thank you, honey," Elena said solemnly. "You can talk to Uncle Bill again tomorrow if you want to."

Most of the glumness disappeared, and the child started toward the door. "I'm going to find the kittycat," she said.

Which wouldn't, Elena was sure, bother the kittycat. B.C. seemed to enjoy being petted as much as Beth loved to do the petting.

"Ellie?" Her mother was back on the line.

"Hello, Mother. Bill was telling me about the trouble Grantland's been causing. But I don't think there's anything to worry about. Just let Bill and Charlie take care of everything. It'll all iron itself out."

"I suppose you're right. I know that's what they keep telling me all the time. But when will you be coming back? It strikes me that so much driving might upset Beth. Five-year-olds aren't like grown-ups, you know."

"I know, Mother. Don't worry. She was getting a little cranky, but we're staying in one place for a few days now, and she really likes it here. She even has a cat to play with."

"But when—"

"We'll be back in a week or two."

A pause, and then her mother said, "I suppose we should tell Mr. Grantland that we've heard from you."

"Why don't you talk to Bill about that? He didn't seem to think it would be a very good idea. Everything will sort itself out if you just let him and Charlie handle things. How is Charlie, by the way? I understand he's spending a lot of time with you."

"He's quite all right," Wilma replied with a touch of embarrassed stiffness in her voice. "You'd think the man didn't have a home of his own these last few days."

A distant laugh, probably Bill's, filtered through the line.

"He's a pretty nice man, Mother. You could do worse."

There was only a flustered silence, which was what Elena had hoped for. She, being an even less skillful liar than her mother, hadn't wanted to have to answer any questions about what her brother had told her.

After a second she went on: "I gave Bill my number, so you can get in touch if anything comes up, all right? And we'll be back in a week or two. In the meantime, give my best to Charlie."

Hastily, she hung up.

In the abandoned farmhouse a quarter of a mile north along the gravel road past Wilma March's house, a third listener put down his earphone as the sound-activated tape recorder clicked off. In the darkened room, shielded from the outside by makeshift cardboard shades, a tiny flashlight flickered on, and the sound of the dial of a portable phone echoed from the cracked and dusty plaster.

He had barely finished dialing when a tense voice answered sharply. "Yes?"

"I know where she and the child are."

"Well?" the voice snapped. "Where?"

"Just outside Wertham, a small town in Vermont. They're planning to stay there a few more days."

"Good work. Get someone out there by morning at the latest."

"All we agreed to do was locate—"

"I don't give a good goddamn what you think we did or didn't agree to. I said, get someone out there. Now!"

"But, sir, I've explained the legal aspects of this matter, and I really think—"

"I would prefer not to speak in clichés, but I am not paying you to think. And if you want any more business of mine—or if you want to stay in business at all—get someone out there! Do you understand?"

Nervously, the man wet his lips and swallowed. "Very well. You're paying the bills. But I hope you're willing to pay bail and attorneys' fees if it comes to that."

There was a click and then silence. Sighing and wondering once again why he had let himself get involved in this affair, the man hung up and sat for several minutes in the musty darkness before reluctantly stirring himself.

The evening went remarkably well in Groves Lodge. When John Groves, still on his best behavior, retired to the den to grade more papers, Mattie delighted Beth by offering a guided tour of the rest of the lodge. The five-year-old poked in every corner and behind every door, but what sent her into absolute ecstasy and even made her forget the kittycat for a few minutes were the enclosed spiral staircase in the middle of the lobby and the "bridges"— almost catwalks—that connected the second-floor hallways to the staircase. Luckily, the railings were nearly as tall as Beth and quite sturdy, and so there was no danger of her falling, but it was almost impossible to get her to return to the ground floor, particularly after Mattie, pretending not to know that Beth was up there, walked beneath the bridge while Beth peeked through the openings in the railing and made believe she was hiding, although her loud giggles would have given her away to anyone anywhere in the building. To Elena's surprise, however, the child was yawningly ready for bed only a few minutes after her normal at-home bedtime. All the exploring and giggling must have tired her, Elena thought as she tucked her in, although the fact that B.C. was snuggled on the covers next to her stomach probably had something to do with it as well. The tucking in completed and the intercom again turned on, Elena made her way to join Mattie in the living room, where the news was about to start on one of the local channels.

When the news was finishing, John, looking as disheveled but not nearly as grumpy as the night before, came in from the hall. "Anything new in the outside world?" he asked as he dropped into the recliner chair next to the couch.

"Slow news day, as they say," Mattie said. "Biggest story was President Ford stubbing his toe on something."

Groves laughed, shaking his head. "There are times when I think Nixon and Agnew were right about the press. Jerry just better watch out or someone'll try to make clumsiness an impeachable offense." He turned to Mattie. "Any coffee hot?"

She stood up abruptly. "It won't take a second. Elena, how about you?"

Elena hesitated a second, glancing at the two of them before answering. "If you're going to have some, sure. That would be nice."

When his wife had left, Groves turned to Elena, still seated near one end of the couch. "I didn't get a chance to talk to you this morning," he said. "Any more dreams?"

Abruptly, her almost euphoric mood evaporated. The dreams—nightmares—had been pushed entirely out of her mind, but now, with only his question as a trigger, they blossomed out to dominate her thoughts. She wondered sharply whether returning here had been such a good idea after all.

"Something wrong?" he asked, apparently seeing her change of expression.

She shook her head, forcing a slight smile. "No, nothing. But I did have another dream."

"Like the first?"

"Not as bad, but similar."

"Would you mind telling me about it?"

She hesitated, while the sound of the TV set, now running through sports scores, faded into the background. "Tell me," she said, "do you really think there's something supernatural about them?"

He shrugged with a lightness totally unlike his approach the night before. "Who knows? There are times when I think there must be and others when I'm just as convinced it's imagination or coincidence."

"Your wife doesn't seem to share your ambivalence."

He smiled and shrugged again, although this time there was a hint of strain in his face. "She's never experienced one of them, that's all. But tell me, what do *you* think?"

She shook her head. "I don't know. I really don't. Last night, even after I woke up, I was convinced it was as real as could be. I just knew I was being shown these events that happened to a girl named Jessica Reimann. But now—"

"Jessica Reimann? Was that your name in the dream?" He was suddenly tensely alert, almost the way he had been the night before.

"It was and it wasn't," she said. "That is, well, it was the strangest dream I've ever had. And so unlike any other."

"Unlike? In what way?"

"For one thing, it was incredibly detailed. And I could remember it so well. This person, this Jessica, she was a totally different person, not just me with a different name, not just some anonymous fantasy character my subconscious dreamed up. She had a whole life history, a whole different personality, everything. But I wasn't really her. I was just watching her, but from inside her mind." She stopped, shivering. "It was as if *I* were the ghost, if you can imagine something like that."

"But you're positive about the name? Jessica Reimann?"

"Yes. Does it mean something?"

"It might. You mentioned that the people in your first dream were dressed in old-fashioned clothes? Was it the same in this one?"

She nodded and then remembered the number that had popped unexpectedly into her mind in the middle of the second dream. What had it been? Sixty years? Seventy?

"It was," she said. "I think it was around the turn of the century or a little after." As she went on to explain, he seemed to be hanging on her every word.

"But this new dream—what was it about?" he asked when she finished. "What was this girl doing?"

As briefly as she could, Elena recounted the dream, ending with the belief that she had held so strongly the night before but that now seemed so impossible, the belief that the two dreams were two different episodes from the other girl's life.

"I know logically that it makes no sense, but that's the feeling I had," she finished, but before Groves could question her further, Mattie returned to inform them that the coffee and a snack were ready if they cared to repair to the kitchen.

Groves carefully avoided any further talk of dreams or nightmares, but when Elena returned to her room a half hour later, she was still uneasy, lost somewhere between the matter-of-fact acceptance that had overwhelmed her during the actual dreams and the total disbelief that common sense and logic dictated. For more than an hour she sat, the lampshade tilted to keep the direct light from Beth's sleeping face, trying to read one of the detective novels she had brought with her but failing miserably.

Finally, after what could have been ten minutes or a hundred, she gave up, having no idea what, if anything, she had read during that period. The unfinished mystery of her own life, she decided with a self-conscious grimace at the mental wordplay, had too strong a grip on her to let her concentrate on fictional mysteries. In order to turn the page, all she had to do was go to sleep. The next episode, real or imagined, was awaiting her arrival. She had already tried the logical alternative, to leave Groves Lodge and never come back, and it hadn't worked. Therefore, logical or not, the only course left open to her was simply to let the next page be turned, whether by her own hyperactive imagination, stirred to a boil by John Groves's nonsensical theories, or by something that would prove those theories to be not so nonsensical, after all.

With deliberate movements, Elena rose from the easy chair, straightened the shade on the lamp, kissed Beth lightly on the forehead, took the quilted robe off her unstylish but warm flannel pajamas, and climbed into bed.

Sleep was slow to come despite a drowsiness that flowed aggressively over her the instant she pulled the covers over her shoulders, but eventually it did come.

Eventually sleep came, and when it did . . .

Her first death that night was on the jagged rocks at the base of a moldering castle wall.

Storm clouds boiled across a darkening sky. The rain had

not yet begun, but lightning already flickered from the depths of the clouds.

But she would not, she knew, survive to feel the first chilling drops. It was only a miracle that life and consciousness had persisted even these few moments.

With an effort that sent pain lancing through the entire twisted length of her body, she turned her head until she could see the weatherworn stones of the castle wall towering above her. A dozen yards up was the featureless opening from which she had been thrown. No one looked out, and no one would.

Above that, high above, were the fading outlines of the towers and battlements that had withstood a hundred sieges.

And the face.

On a banner unfurled defiantly above the highest tower was emblazoned the bestial, gargoylelike face she had seen a hundred times before, in a hundred different lives, at a hundred different deaths. The same twisted face that, some isolated corner of her mind realized, was duplicated with uncanny accuracy in the sentinel-like statues that stood on their seven-sided pedestals only yards from where her body—her twentieth-century body—lay engulfed in sleep and nightmare.

She had lost.

Once again she had lost, and the face of the repellent creature once again mocked her in the final moments of her life, mocked her not only with impending death but with the terrible knowledge that because of her failure, it would be enabled to live on through yet another generation or another hundred, leaving in its wake yet another century or another millennium of horror.

She had failed as she had failed a hundred times before, and she was dying as she had died a hundred times before.

Slowly, the storm clouds fused into a single mass of blackness that reached down to enfold her, and the pain faded from her shattered body.

But her death was not the end. It had not been the end then, and it was not the end now.

Another death was waiting and yet another. And with each death waited that same bestial face, mocking her in its repeated victories, its continued survival.

In one, drawn out for what seemed like an eternity, she felt a painful poison burning through her veins while she lay helpless and paralyzed in an opulently furnished mansion looking out over a medieval, plague-ridden village. Across the room, visible in the fading light of an agony-filled dusk, hung an ancient tapestry with the creature's hideous face woven into its very fabric like an obscene Shroud of Turin.

For yet another eternity, the face stared blindly at her from a witch doctor's mask on the dirt floor of a hut, while her life drained from the untended spear wound in her side.

Even in the scorching sands of an endless desert it confronted her. As she lay half conscious, her tongue swollen and parched, her exposed skin burned raw by a sun that seemed forever lodged at its zenith, her own dying mind conjured up the triumphant features in a swirling dust devil that shimmered across the barren dunes.

There were more deaths, dozens more, in every corner of the world, in every era of time. She died a dozen times and then a dozen times again, each death watched and mocked by those gargoylelike features in an infinite variety of forms.

Finally, when she thought she could stand it no more, the visions of death slowed and stopped, and she found herself once again looking out through the eyes of Jessica Reimann.

But it was not finished even yet, that remote, observing part of her mind realized instantly. She had yet one more death to die, one final death, the prelude to which she already knew, had already experienced.

Once more the Reimann mansion loomed above her in the gathering dusk. It had been nearly a month, she knew, since Jessica had returned, uninvited, to the mansion, returned and been turned away.

As she had climbed the broad steps to Marcus's waiting arms, she had been convinced, despite the pallid face and stiff, unwelcoming smile, that all would be as it had been before.

But that illusion had lasted only moments, until instead of enclosing her in his arms, he grasped her shoulders in a bruising, trembling grip. For a long moment the only sound was his labored breathing. Then, almost spasmodically, he turned her and forced her awkwardly down the steps.

"I told you," he said, his voice grating and his lips barely parting, "you are not welcome here."

Releasing her with a shove toward her luggage, still on the gravel drive, he moved quickly back up the steps. Pausing only for a brief, hard glance over his shoulder, he moved back inside, swinging the huge door solidly shut behind him.

Up the drive, unbidden, came the same wagon that had delivered her here, its driver carefully avoiding her gaze as the horses came to a whinnying halt. Reluctantly, she heaved the pieces of luggage and then herself onto the wagon.

In the weeks that followed, she stayed with her family on their small farm not far away. The letters she had written to them the last three months had not been received, they said, and she had no reason to disbelieve them. Marcus, they told her, had stopped briefly at their farm the day he had returned, telling them, as he had previously told Jessica, of his intention to dispose of the estate as quickly as possible and turn the bulk of it over to the charities it was already contributing heavily to. He had already, he said, dismissed the servants with generous severance allowances and letters of recommendation. In another day, two at the most, he would return to Jessica.

That was the last they or anyone else had seen of him.

The estate was not put up for sale. Attorneys, appearing for appointments arranged during that first day, were confronted with locked doors and were totally ignored. Townspeople calling to express condolences fared no better, whether they were businessmen who had dealt with Ben Reimann, clergymen, or even the mayor. Food, the simplest of canned goods, was ordered by phone and delivered once a week. Even the clerk who took them to the mansion, although he always returned to the store with more than enough money in payment, could not remember Marcus Reimann either taking the merchandise from him or giving him money.

And so it had gone until the evening of Jessica's arrival. She was the first to set eyes on him in nearly three months. And after that one brief meeting, she saw him no more than did anyone else. She returned to the mansion day after day, only to find the doors locked, no sound coming from within, no answer to her repeated pounding at every door and window she could reach. Once, she thought she caught a glimpse of his face at one of the upper windows, but that was all.

And now, at last, it was to be over, one way or the other. She and her twin brother, Henry Winton, moved slowly up the drive in a wagon not unlike the one in which she had made the first trip. She was dressed in the same starched, confining clothing she had worn then and—that corner of Elena's mind told her—would still be wearing at her death. Her brother, in bib overalls and heavy plow shoes, sat worriedly beside her on the plank seat. His hands gripped the reins so tightly that his tension seemed transmitted through the lengths of worn leather to the horses themselves as they continually snorted and flared their nostrils at every sound, even the rattles and creaks of the wagon itself.

At the looping end of the drive, within yards of the broad steps and massive columns, he brought the wagon to a halt. The horses, normally placid as they pulled a double-bitted plow or dragged a harrow or disk across a field, switched their tails and scraped at the gravel with their unshod hooves.

"Jessie," the brother began, but she cut him off sharply.

"With or without you, Henry, I am getting in there. He could be dead for all you know."

For a moment she watched him, blond strands of his lanky, bowl-cut hair hanging limply over his frown-creased forehead. Then, without another word, she climbed down from the wagon, using the large metal-rimmed wheel and then its protruding hub as steps.

Dropping the reins, he hurried after her, catching her only as she reached the door at the top of the steps. As before, her repeated pounding brought no response, nor did his more violent raps and door-rattling kicks.

While he still pounded at the door, Jessica moved down the steps and back to the wagon. Stepping up on the hub of the back wheel, she reached over the side and into the bed of the wagon. A moment later, she lowered herself to the gravel again, but now she held, clublike in one hand, a wooden singletree, the metal harness hooks rattling on each end as she moved.

"Jessie, wait," Henry Winton called as he turned and saw

her advancing, not toward the door but toward one of the many windows that lined the front of the mansion.

Before he could reach her, she was beneath one of the windows, its bottom more than a foot above her head. Shielding her face with one arm, she swung the singletree like a tennis player making a serve. The glass shattered, and most of the shards collapsed inward, although a few showered down on her and onto the ground at her feet.

"If you'll back the wagon up to the window, it will be easy to get in," she said matter-of-factly, although in truth her entire body was trembling.

He stood, his long arms dangling, watching her openmouthed, but all he could do was repeat an almost plaintive, "Jessie!" Finally, apparently resigning himself to his sister's blind and unstoppable determination, he turned toward the wagon. The horses, startled by the shattering glass, shied but did not run.

He was clambering aboard the wagon when the massive door at the head of the stairs swung open. Marcus Reimann stood in the fading twilight, looking down at them.

Both Jessica and her brother gasped. The change, the deterioration she had seen in Marcus only weeks before had obviously accelerated rapidly during those weeks. Several days' stubble darkened his normally clean-shaven jaw and cheeks. His clothes, expensive trousers and a tailor-made silk shirt she remembered from the first days of their marriage, were stained and wrinkled, as if they had been worn without interruption for days or even weeks. His jet-black hair, normally well trimmed and neatly groomed, was an impossible tangle that had not felt scissors or comb for as long. His eyes were hollow, his cheeks approaching gauntness.

"What do you want?" His voice cracked as if long unused and no longer able to function properly.

Winton, struck speechless by Marcus's haggard appearance and by twenty years of ingrained deference to the Reimann name, said nothing, but Jessica, with the singletree still gripped tightly in her hand, took a trembling step toward Marcus.

"We want to know," she said in a voice almost lost in a sudden gust of wind, "what has happened to you."

For just an instant, something glimmered in his sunken

eyes, something faint and distant that reminded her of the Marcus she had known and lived with for nearly three years. But then, with a shiver that might have been the result of another gust of the dry, chilly wind, it was gone, leaving only grim lifelessness inhabiting the face.

"Nothing has happened to me," he said in that same unsteady voice, "unless you count that act of senseless vandalism you yourself just committed." His dead-alive eyes flicked sideways toward the shattered window.

"Jessie only wants to help you," Winton said, his voice high-pitched with nervousness.

"I neither need nor desire your so-called help!" Marcus said with harshness entering his tone despite the weakness of his voice. "I would appreciate it greatly if you would simply leave."

"I'm sorry, Marcus," Jessica said, "but I cannot."

Then, despite the suppressed trembling that shivered through her entire body, she began to move up the steps toward him.

"I told you, stay away. Both of you."

And with those words from the shell of Marcus Reimann, the body of Henry Winton stiffened. A high-pitched, almost squealing sound came from his throat and forced its way past his tightly clamped lips, causing his sister to whirl toward him on the steps. Winton's eyes had widened and seemed ready to pop from their sockets in a face that was suddenly flushed and dark. Like a marionette on badly handled strings, he straightened from a hunched, nervous posture to starchy erectness.

"You see?" Marcus's voice, less unsteady now, seemed to fill her ears, drowning out all other sounds. "I do not need any help. I can help myself quite well, thank you."

Then Winton, still moving in a series of almost spasmodic jerks, made a deep, flourishing bow, the sort that Jessica was sure he had never seen and would never perform under any circumstances. Even in the fading light, she could see the panic in his bulging eyes as he slowly straightened and turned and began a stiff-legged, shuffling walk toward the wagon and the nervously shifting horses.

"Now go, Jessica. Follow him and do not return! I don't need you here. I don't want you here!"

Terrified, Jessica turned to face what had once been her husband.

"Marcus," she began, but abruptly she cut herself off. Once again, reaching out from somewhere deep behind his eyes, was something of the old Marcus, something that, as eloquently as his words, warned her to flee.

But then, as she listened to her brother's feet shuffling slowly across the gravel of the drive, she saw Marcus's hand. It was raised to the base of his throat. Its fingers moved in a stiff but regular pattern, as if fearfully stroking some tiny poisonous creature that might strike at any second.

Suddenly she knew.

She had not a hint where the knowledge came from, but she knew the source of the terrible power that had done this to Marcus. As suddenly and surely as if God himself had revealed his truth to her, she knew.

The talisman.

The seven-sided pool of darkness that for a brief instant a month before she had seen suspended from its golden chain about his neck. The same object that she had seen at Ben Reimann's throat a half dozen times, the object she had seen him fingering with the same absent intensity that Marcus now seemed lost in.

She also knew, just as suddenly and just as surely, how it could be destroyed, how it *must* be destroyed. It was as if, in that instant of revelation, an ancient memory, buried deep within the hidden caverns of her mind, had suddenly burst free of its age-old prison and now shone before her, hard and bright.

Barely in control of her own movements, Jessica mounted the steps toward what had once been Marcus Reimann. Her hands reached out toward the tiny pool of alien blackness that nestled beneath his trembling fingers. Already the words that would destroy it—guttural and unearthly sounds that were pure gibberish to her rational mind—were forming in her thoughts, bunching in her throat like roiling water behind a weakening dam.

But then, suddenly, she stopped.

She *was* stopped.

It was as if, in an instant, the very air around her had

turned stiff and molasseslike, bringing her to a soft but no less abrupt halt. Even her tongue seemed confined by an impenetrable thickness. The wind still caressed her face coldly and blew stray strands of hair across her forehead, but that was the only touch of normality remaining. Barely inches from her outstretched fingers hung the talisman, but she could not force her hand across that final gap.

And Marcus's face! Jessica had no reference for its anguish, but Elena, still watching helplessly, remembered a photo she had once seen, a close-up of the face of an Olympic weight lifter as he grunted and strained to raise barbells more than twice his own weight that last fraction of an inch necessary to fully straighten his arms and lock his joints in place for the required fraction of a second. Except that here there was no visible weight and no sound from Marcus's straining throat. There was only silence.

But a struggle was going on.

Suddenly, a scream, almost a squeal, erupted from behind her and then cut off. It was, she realized an instant later, the scream that had been imprisoned behind her brother's tightly closed lips, suddenly released and just as suddenly cut off. Then the sound of his feet, no longer shuffling but, after a half dozen staggering lurches, running, first toward the wagon but then, as he realized that his own legs were faster than the lumbering wagon could ever be, past the wagon and toward the distant road.

And then there was blackness, like a muffling shroud being lowered over her head, blotting out sight and sound.

But only for a moment.

And when the shroud unraveled from around her, the first nightmare had returned.

Flames battered back the darkness, but now she knew the source of those flames: the Reimann mansion.

A mob, a dozen or more people, surrounded her, holding her back, not from the flames but from the battered body of what had once been Marcus Reimann. But now, as she looked out through Jessica Reimann's eyes, she knew these people. And holding her most tightly of all, his hands bruising her arms, was her brother, with the odor of whiskey strong on his breath.

He was speaking, his voice clear over the chaos of a dozen other voices and the crackling of the flames: "Jessie! No one meant to kill him!"

And another voice, half defiant, half pleading: "He didn't give us no choice. You saw the devil's power he used."

And another: "That weren't the man you married, Jessie. That were the devil himself."

And yet another, the owner of this voice still dangling a pistol limply from one hand: "He was in my head, Jessie, in my head, daring me to shoot. He was telling me I was dead, we were all dead, if I didn't."

But she did not answer, for she knew—she and her brother both knew—that it was all true. The creature that Marcus had become had purposely goaded them on but had not, inexplicably, used that devil's power to its fullest but instead had let them go through their drunken attempt to rescue her and had, finally, let the one gun among them be aimed and fired.

So, for Marcus, it was over.

But for Jessica . . .

Almost unnoticed in the milling, self-justifying confusion, someone was reaching down, his fingers touching the blood-smeared talisman still around Marcus's neck.

"*No!*" The cry tore from her throat, bansheelike, and with a strength she hadn't thought she possessed, Jessica lunged forward, breaking free from the momentarily shock-weakened hands that held her back.

Knocking the other man sprawling away from the body, Jessica spasmodically closed her fingers around the talisman and yanked it free, giving Marcus's entire body a twitch as the chain snapped.

Then, with the talisman clutched tightly to her breast, she let the senseless, guttural sounds pour from her throat. Neither Jessica nor the watching Elena knew where the sounds originated. They only knew that, like breathing, it must be done if Jessica were to survive.

Except, Elena knew, Jessica would not survive, not in this life.

Then, as the dozen around her stood frozen and gaping in the flame-lit darkness, as her voice grated on, the corpse of Marcus Reimann twitched and began to rise.

But even this did not halt the sounds that rasped from her throat. If anything, it increased the urgency.

Then the body was on its feet, swaying unsteadily, its bloodless face chalky white in the firelight. The shirtfront sagged from the weight of the blood that had soaked through it.

Then, suddenly, the voices of the others broke free of their paralyzed throats and filled the air with screams and curses.

"She's with him," the one who had reached for the talisman shouted. "She's bringing him back. They'll kill us all!"

As the corpse loomed over her, its dead face smeared with grass and dirt, just as it had appeared in that first nightmare, she heard the explosion of the pistol, once and then again.

She felt nothing, only a sudden weakness that stole all strength from her limbs, a weakness that slurred and distorted and finally stopped the sounds as they still tried to escape from her aching throat. A growing horror gripped her as Elena realized—although surely she had known from the start how it would end—that she had failed once again.

She felt herself falling, spinning through the flame-lit darkness, weightless. And the corpse, the blood-soaked thing that had been Marcus Reimann, moved with her, still grasping for the talisman.

Then there was nothing.

Except in the pool of darkness at the heart of the talisman, the face of that same hideous creature, mocking her failure as it had mocked a hundred failures before.

She struck the ground.

And awakened.

Not Elena March, but Jessica Reimann awakened.

She was on her hands and knees. Her fingers were pulling at the cold, wet grass and digging at the unyielding soil beneath. The sounds, the senseless, guttural incantation that seconds before she had not had the strength to continue erupted once more from her throat.

Suddenly, strong hands were gripping her shoulders and lifting her to her feet.

"Miss March? What happened? Are you all right?"

It was a man, a strangely dressed, bearded man, his sleeves rolled up as he stood facing her, holding her erect. Fifty yards behind him, dimly visible in the moonlight through the nearly leafless trees, was the mansion, whole once again, although only moments before flames had been sprouting everywhere.

But it was not the mansion. It was the same shape, but smaller, so much smaller.

"Miss March?" The man was leaning closer, his bearded face anxious in the pale moonlight. "Miss March? This is John Groves. Are you all right?"

Who was this man? And the others—her brother and her would-be rescuers—where were they? And how— For the first time she noticed her own body, clad in some strange two-piece, loose-fitting garment with nothing beneath it. And her feet, bare and freezing on the ground. Suddenly she was shivering uncontrollably, wanting to scream but finding her throat too tight and stiff to allow it.

Then she was falling once again, and the man was catching her, scooping her up in his arms and turning to run, stumbling and catching himself every few steps, through the trees, toward that impossible building that loomed in the background.

Day Three

Henry Winton eased his stiff and aching body from the bed as quietly as he could. It was well after midnight, and no one had stirred for more than an hour. The last sound had been his nephew Donald padding down the hall from the bathroom and closing the bedroom door. There might have been some murmured conversation after that, a continuation of the largely silent battle that had been raging since Donald and Edith had first greeted him in Dr. Edwards's office fifteen hours earlier, but none of it had reached Winton's ears no matter how hard he listened. And his hearing was still good, thank God! And his sight. Despite the stroke, despite the pain and stiffness that made every movement an effort, his eyes and ears were little worse now than twenty years ago.

Switching on the bedside lamp, he looked at the pale, brown-spotted hand, its enlarged knuckles standing out like beads on an abacus. Purposely, he flexed the fingers, forcing the creaking joints to yield to his stringy muscles, forcing muscle and joint alike to yield to the force of his will. There were faint cracking sounds from the joints and brief stabs of pain, but the fingers obeyed. And they would continue to obey, as would the rest of his creaking body, for as long as was necessary. A day, two days, a week—however long it took, he would last.

Slowly, he raised himself from the bed and made his way to the metal wardrobe cabinet that served as his closet. The sound the catch and the hinges made as he pulled open the door seemed clangorous in the midnight silence, and he stood listening for a sign that someone else had heard.

But there was nothing, only the click and whir of the

furnace blower as it cycled on and warm air began to flow from the baseboard register.

Soon he was dressed. His suit, the only one he had owned the last twenty years, smelled of mothballs and was probably decades out of style, but it was the best he could do. No matter how he dressed, anyone as old as he was would attract attention, but the suit might at least give him a look of respectability so that he wouldn't look like what he really was: a demented, probably senile runaway. He even managed to don a tie, a forerunner of the clip-on that was held in place by an elastic band around the neck of his starchy white shirt.

In the bureau drawer, where they had lain unused for at least a year before his stroke, were the extra keys to his car, a mid-1950s model that despite its age still ran at least as well as the last year's model it sat next to in his nephew's garage. Or so Donald had said when Winton had asked during supper: "Edith uses it for all her errands, even when our Buick is right there."

Shutting off the light, he waited for his eyes to adjust ever so slowly to the dim light that filtered in from the streetlamps outside. Finally, he opened the door and made his way into the second-floor hall. Luckily the hallway was carpeted, and so his shuffling steps were almost soundless. Then he went down the stairs, resting his weight on the bannister as much as he could as he eased himself over the step that always creaked.

At last he was at the bottom, and still there was no sound from the floor above.

Edith's black, multicompartmented purse was where she always left it, on a small table in the hall just inside the front door. He was in luck. In her billfold there was almost fifty dollars. Transferring the money to his own cracked and worn wallet—a present from Sarah more than twenty years ago, he remembered with a slight catch in his throat—he returned Edith's to her purse and snapped it shut.

In the kitchen, he was making a sandwich of lunch meat and mustard to take with him when he heard the telltale creak from the stairs. Cursing himself for having dillydallied with the sandwich, he waited in angry resignation. He knew he could never in a month of Sundays come up with a good reason for being down here in the kitchen in the middle of the night, all dressed up like he was ready for church. He thought for a second of putting on some kind of bughouse act, as if he didn't really know what he was doing, but that would only make things worse. Edith would be all the more set on dumping him in another nursing home, and Donald would watch him more closely than ever, maybe even take to locking his door or rigging some kind of alarm.

Footsteps padded through the dining room and stopped in the door to the kitchen. Winton didn't look toward the door but just slumped against the kitchen counter, leaving the half-put-together sandwich on a paper towel in front of him.

"Uncle Henry?"

Relief flooded through Winton as he recognized the childish voice. It was Nickie, eight-year-old Nickie.

"Yes, Nickie, it's me," he said in a whisper even softer than the child's.

"What are you doing in the dark?"

"I didn't want to wake anyone up. Now, what are you doing up at this time of night? You got school tomorrow, don't you?"

"Sure. I always have school. But I heard you. I came down to see what you were doing."

Winton held up the mustard jar in the dim light that filtered through the uncurtained windows over the counter. "Just fixing something to eat. A midnight snack."

"Oh." The boy seemed to consider the answer as he looked more closely at the old man. "But you're all dressed up," he said at last.

Winton looked down at himself in make-believe surprise. "By golly, so I am."

"How come?" The boy sounded worried now, maybe even afraid. "You're not going back to the hospital, are you?"

"No, Nickie, I'm not going back to the hospital."

"But how come you're all dressed up?" the child asked again, almost forgetting to whisper.

Winton was silent as he looked down at the boy in the dim light, his flannel pajamas wrinkled from half a night's sleep. One of the pajama legs was still hitched halfway up the boy's calf.

Leaving Nickie, he knew, was the one thing he was really sorry about. Edith and Donald—well, Edith would probably do a little crying, but she'd be more than happy to be rid of him. Donald would worry and stew and feel guilty, but in the end he'd be relieved, too.

Only Nickie would really be sorry to see him go and would miss him. He would get over it quickly enough, like any healthy eight-year-old, but it would hurt him for a while, just as it hurt Winton. He had more in common with Nickie than he did with the others. They were both honest with each other for one thing, but maybe that was just because of their ages. People could be honest when they were very old or very young but not in between.

"Nickie," he said, lowering himself carefully onto a chair, as much to rest and save his precious strength as to get on eye level with the boy, "can you keep a secret? Just until morning?"

The boy's eyes widened eagerly. "Sure, Uncle Henry. You know that."

Winton held his fingers to his parchment lips in a gesture for the boy to lower his voice. "All right, then," he said, "I'll tell you. Now don't forget, you can tell your folks about it, but not until morning, when they get up. Understand?"

The boy nodded enthusiastically. "What is it? What are you doing?"

"And don't make any noise, not now. If you wake your folks up, I won't be able to tell you."

"I won't, I promise," the boy said, his voice sinking back to a whisper. "And anyway, they never wake up for anything. Dad snores a lot, and Mom puts stuff in her ears so she can't hear him."

"All right," Winton said again, leaning closer to the expectant face. "I have to go somewhere. And if your folks knew about it, they wouldn't let me go."

"Where? Where are you going?"

"A place I used to live, a long time ago."

"Is it very far?"

"Not real far, but far enough."

"Can I go with you?"

Winton shook his head. "I have to meet someone, and we

have to do something. Besides, you've got school tomorrow. You can't go running off just like that."

The boy seemed to think about it for a while. "But you still didn't tell me what you're going to do."

"It's complicated. But I'll tell you all about it when I come back."

"When? When are you coming back?"

"I don't know. A few days probably."

"Will you be back by Sunday?"

"I'll try. But why Sunday?"

"That's when that new movie starts at the Strand. You know, the one—"

"I know. The one your folks said they didn't want you to see. They don't want you to go to scary things like that."

"They don't want me to do anything. But if you took me—"

"We'll see. I may not be able to get back by then, but if I do, we'll see."

"Aw, you sound just like them."

"I'm sorry, Nickie, but that's the best I can do."

Nickie was stubbornly silent for a few seconds, and then he sighed. "Okay," he said. "Besides," he added accusingly, "if you run away like this, they probably won't let either one of us go."

Winton winced at the boy's insight. He was probably right. "I'm sorry, Nickie, but it's something I have to do. I really do. And now that I think about it, maybe you better not tell your folks you saw me leave. I know it's not right to lie, but they would get pretty mad at you. You know that, don't you?"

Nickie nodded. "I know." He looked down at the floor, his eyes avoiding the old man's. "They told me to keep an eye on you. You know, to see if you acted funny. I'm supposed to tell them right away if you do. Act funny, I mean."

"But you're not going to?"

Nickie shook his head. "They might send you away. I heard them when they didn't know I was around. If you start acting funny, they said they'd send you someplace. And I don't want you to go away again."

"And I don't want to go, Nickie. But this time I have to. But I'll come back as soon as I can."

"Okay," the boy said, "I guess I know what you mean. It's like I don't want to go to school, but I have to go, anyway."

"Something like that." Bracing his hands on the table, Winton raised himself to his feet, standing as straight as he could manage. "Now, do you think you could do one more thing for me, Nickie?"

"Sure. What is it?"

"Help me with the garage door. It's pretty heavy, and I don't know if I could get it up by myself."

"You got to go already?" the boy looked up anxiously.

"I'm afraid I do. It's a long drive to where I'm going, and I want to get there before your folks find out I'm gone."

"They might send the cops after you?"

The old man nodded. "They probably would. Couldn't blame them. Only sensible thing to do."

"They wouldn't hurt you, would they?"

"Not on purpose, Nickie. But they'd bring me back if they found me. And I'd be awfully easy to find out there on the highway in that old rattletrap of mine. So I really have to get started." He looked down at the boy, wondering whether Nickie knew that he wouldn't be coming back or only feared it.

Finally Nickie shrugged, but even in the dim light that filtered in through the windows, Winton thought he saw a tear glistening in the corner of the boy's eye. He felt an answering lump in his own throat.

"Okay," Nickie said, his voice unnaturally brusque as he turned away, moving to the door that led to the side of the garage. "I got to get back to bed, anyway. Like you said, I got school in the morning."

The boy hesitated with his hand on the doorknob and turned his face half toward the old man. "Don't forget your sandwich," he said.

The dimly lit numbers on the digital clock showed one-fourteen as the jangling of the phone yanked Dr. Seth Laird from the midst of an uneasy sleep. Despite the lowered nighttime temperature in the bedroom, a film of perspiration covered his broad, lumberjack's face and much of his husky body. Automatically, he started to reach for the receiver, but his large-knuckled hand stopped halfway.

A patient with an emergency, imaginary or otherwise?

Or the police, with another call about his son?

A patient he could deal with easily; he'd had plenty of practice. But if it was another problem with Carl . . . Steeling himself, he brushed the nighttime tangle of lank, gray-streaked hair from his forehead and completed the movement begun two rings earlier.

"Laird," he said tonelessly into the receiver.

"Doctor Laird? This is John Groves."

Relief washed over Laird, followed instantly by annoyance. Groves was the one who had been in his office just that afternoon. He'd badgered Rosie into giving him an appointment when he'd called at noon, and then he'd come in around four, worried sick over some minor behavioral changes, wondering if he might be developing a brain tumor or something else equally horrendous and unlikely. What the hell did the man want now?

"Yes, Mr. Groves," Laird said, trying to keep the sleepy annoyance out of his voice. "What is it?"

"It's a woman who's staying with us here at the lodge."

"Yes? What about her?" Laird prompted him impatiently.

"She, well, I found her out behind the lodge, back in the trees, down on the ground. She may have been walking in her sleep, but she's been acting very strangely since we got her back in. She has to see a doctor."

"My office hours—"

"I know this is an imposition, but I really think it's an emergency. If you could see and hear her . . ."

Laird sighed. It was at times like this that he could understand his ex-wife's reasons for leaving him a dozen years ago and never coming back.

"Very well," he said resignedly. "Bring her in." He was awake now, and he wouldn't be able to get back to sleep no matter what, and so he might as well see her now rather than eight hours from now.

"I was hoping you could come out to the lodge," Groves

said, the apologetic note growing stronger in his voice. "My wife and I tried getting her in the car, but she, well, she just seemed terrified, that's the only way I can describe it. She seems to have calmed down a little now that we have her back inside in one of the rooms. And she has a child with her, a little girl only four or five. We couldn't leave the child alone, and I don't think I can safely drive the mother to your office without help. The car just seems to scare her to death."

Laird frowned. It sounded like something he wasn't equipped to deal with, a sudden onset of some kind of personality disorder, the kind of thing that Groves himself had thought he had. A sedative was probably the best he could do, a sedative and the name of someone who could handle it.

"Very well," Laird said tiredly. "Just do your best to keep her calm. I'll be there in a few minutes."

"You know where—"

"Yes, I know where the lodge is," Laird said, and hung up abruptly.

Grabbing the first items that came to hand— the bulky gray pullover sweater and slacks he had been wearing the evening before in his basement woodworking shop—he was dressed in a minute, pausing only to stretch some of the stiffness from his sturdy, six-foot-three frame. Picking up his bag with its stethoscope and limited range of other necessities, he hesitated and turned back down the hall to push open the door to Carl's room. He was not surprised to find the bed empty, still unmade from the night before.

Shaking his head in tight-lipped, angry frustration, Laird slammed the door and made his way heavily down the stairs and through the seldom-used kitchen to the garage. His son's car—a gift for his sixteenth birthday five months ago, just a month before the leukemia was diagnosed—was of course missing.

Christ, he thought as he dropped the bag on the passenger seat of his car and climbed in. Didn't the boy know that he was killing himself? Literally killing himself? The disease had been in remission since the chemotherapy, but his resistance was still low. It would always be low, remission or no remission. The boy needed extra rest, would always need extra rest. If he took reasonable care of himself, there was an excellent chance he could survive for several years just with today's methods of treatment, and every year new and better treatments were being found. Ten years ago, barring a miracle, he could have expected a year, possibly two, but now the chances for a nearly normal life for many years to come were vastly improved.

If he would simply take care of himself.

Cursing audibly, Laird tried unsuccessfully to turn his thoughts to other things as he pulled out of the garage and onto the street; the car bottomed out as he hit the end of the drive too fast. At this time of night, he had the streets of Wertham to himself. The tiny downtown business district was like a deserted movie set. His headlights glinting off the plate glass in the dozen or two stores was the only sign of life. Even Orville's, for years the only place in town open twenty-four hours a day, was closed and dark, its gas pumps reduced to twelve hours of service by the oil embargo nearly two years ago. The truck stop out on the bypass might be open, but that would be all. Even in the houses, everyone was asleep. In the eight blocks from the center of Wertham to the city limits, he counted only five lighted windows.

So where was the boy? And what the hell did he do all the endless hours he was away? Night after night, what did he do? Sullen silence and angry shouts were all Laird got from him on the rare occasions when he could be found to be questioned. None of last year's friends from school had seen him except in classes, and even his appearances there were becoming more infrequent. From the time he had realized—he had been told early on, but he hadn't believed it—that being on the football team was simply out of the question, he had avoided his former teammates like the plague. The only information Laird had came from the police and well-meaning friends. Twice the boy had been stopped for reckless driving, once while drunk; God knows where he had gotten the liquor. A half dozen times, friends had come to Laird with variations of "I saw your boy last night, out on the road. That car of his zipped around me like I was standing still." Or "I'd swear I saw him down in Brattleboro, either him or his twin brother. He was with some guy, I suppose a few years ago you would've called him a hippie."

But there was nothing Laird could do about it short of locking the boy in the house or permanently sedating him. Laird had tried logic, he had tried punishment, he had tried pleading and bribing, he had tried everything he could think of, but it only seemed to make it worse. The harder he tried, the more the boy avoided him, as if he thought Laird were the cause of his sickness rather than his only hope of surviving it. This fall he had taken to skipping classes, simply vanishing from school and not showing up until evening, if then.

Following the sharp curves and hills of the old highway, Laird reached Groves Lodge not long after one-thirty. As he turned between the columns and their grotesque guardians, the front door burst open, and Groves, wearing a gray cardigan and a distracted expression, ran down the steps. He was waiting on the edge of the gravel drive by the time Laird braked to a crunching stop.

"She's unconscious," Groves said.

"What happened?" Laird asked as he followed Groves at a run up the steps.

"I don't know. My wife and I took her to one of the rooms, as I told you, and she seemed to be calming down. We were trying to reassure her, you know, telling her she would be all right, not to worry about anything, that her daughter was still asleep, things like that. And all of a sudden her eyes just rolled up out of sight, and she fell back on the bed. And that was it."

They were moving through the huge central lobby and down the hall. "She's in here," Groves said, ushering Laird into a room on the left side of the hall.

A slender young woman in a quilted robe— Mrs. Groves, Laird assumed—stood by the bed, looking anxiously at another woman, tall and big-boned, her hair a dark mass of curls against the pillow. She was wearing flowered flannel pajamas, and the bedspread had been pulled over most of her body.

Touching the woman's forehead briefly—no obvious signs of chill or fever—he lowered himself to the bed next to her and felt for the pulse in her throat. Rapid, he thought without consulting his watch, but not running away with itself. A hundred at most, and strong.

He was about to raise an eyelid for a look at her pupils—drugs were always a possibility—when the woman opened her eyes abruptly. For an instant, seeing Laird's hand only inches from her eyes, she cringed back, but then she seemed to relax slightly, although her eyes remained fearful.

"I'm Dr. Laird," he said, taking his hand back and resting it on the black bag next to him on the bed. "How are you feeling?"

Elena March's mind was spinning as she looked at the haggard, square-jawed face looming over her. Fragments of the nightmare—the senseless sounds it had seemed so imperative to scream into the darkness, the mud-smeared face of the risen corpse, the dozen or more one-time friends milling about her in growing fear and frenzy—surfaced briefly, like a dolphin shooting out of the water and vanishing a second later. It was over. Like the others, it was over and could no longer harm her.

But this man—who was he? What was he doing here?

Then her eyes fell on Mattie and her husband, standing worriedly by the foot of the bed. She looked sharply toward the other bed. It was empty.

"Beth! Where is Beth?"

"Beth is fine," Mattie said hastily. "She's still asleep in your room."

"My room?" Her eyes darted about, and only then did she realize that this room, so much like the other, was not hers. Relief and then puzzlement, flowed through her. "How did I get here? What happened?"

"What's the last thing you remember?" The man—a doctor? Had he said he was a doctor? —asked.

"The nightmare," she began, but she realized a moment later that she was wrong. The nightmare was not the last thing she remembered. Or had it just been a new and different nightmare?

"Nightmare?" the man prompted, his eyes darting briefly toward John Groves. "What sort of nightmare, Ms. March?"

"Just a nightmare," she said, shaking her head.

"Do you often have nightmares?"

She grimaced. "Never, at least not before I came here. But Beth—are you sure—"

"I'll look in on her," Mattie said soothingly, and hurried from the room.

"Mr. Groves says you were walking in your sleep. Have you ever done anything like that before?"

She stiffened, a sudden chill raising gooseflesh on her back. "No, never." She looked nervously toward Groves. "I was sleepwalking? Where?"

He hesitated, glancing at the doctor. "Out behind the lodge."

More gooseflesh rose. "I was outside? Tonight?"

Groves nodded with seeming reluctance.

"What was I doing?"

"Nothing, not when I found you. You looked as if you'd fallen. You didn't seem to recognize me or Mattie."

Suddenly she felt out of breath. It hadn't been part of the nightmare. It had really happened. She had somehow left the lodge and walked all that distance barefoot, through the cold, wet grass, through the dark. And when she had awakened, she had been someone else.

She had been Jessica Reimann, a terrified, disoriented Jessica Reimann, with no idea where she was or how she had gotten there.

Jessica Reimann, a creation of Elena's own sleeping mind, had awakened instead of Elena March.

She was going insane. There couldn't be any doubt after an episode like that. And all because of this place. Groves had said that there was something here that caused dreams, and he was right. But he hadn't known the half of it. It was insanity, not dreams, that was bred here.

She had to get out, she knew that now. She had to get out while she still had the chance, before whatever spirit or demon that lurked in the shadows sank its claws so deeply into her that she could never escape.

"Are you all right, Ms. March?" The doctor was leaning closer. The smell of sawdust touched her nostrils.

She took a deep breath, trying vainly to banish the gooseflesh.

"Yes, I'm all right now," she managed to say. She even forced a weak smile. "I was just remembering the nightmare.

It was right out of an old horror movie. Probably something I saw on the late show in some motel the last few days. I've been traveling, you know, just driving around and seeing the country, the last week or so. And in motels—"

She stopped abruptly, realizing that she was chattering pointlessly, the way she often did when she was upset. At the same time, Mattie reappeared in the door.

"Your daughter's doing just fine," Mattie said. "Still sound asleep."

"And you seem quite all right yourself, Ms. March," the doctor said. "However, as long as I'm here, I might as well finish what I was starting when you woke up."

"That won't be necessary," she began, but he cut her off gently.

"No extra charge." He glanced at Groves and his wife. "If you'll excuse us for a few minutes?"

"Oh, of course," Mattie took her husband's arm and led the way from the room. "We'll be in the kitchen if you need anything," she said as she closed the door behind them.

The examination went quickly and seemed quite cursory to Elena, almost as if the doctor's mind was on something else and all the listening and poking and thumping was being done automatically. Even the questions about her mental state—during which the reasons for her "trip" came out—he seemed oddly impersonal, even for a doctor.

"You seem quite healthy, Ms. March," he said when he had finished. "Superficially, at least. If you would like a more thorough examination, however, I could arrange for one tomorrow."

She shook her head. "No, I feel fine now, just a little foolish. Besides, Beth and I will be leaving in the morning."

"Well, I certainly found nothing that would prevent you." He glanced toward the door to the hall and then back at Elena. "Nothing at all. However, I would suggest you see your own doctor when you return home, particularly if you experience any further episodes of somnambulism."

For a moment it seemed as if he were about to speak further, but instead he snapped his bag shut with a brisk, businesslike movement and stood up. "Good night, then, Ms. March."

* * *

It was no wonder the woman was having bad dreams, Laird thought as he climbed into his car and gave a peremptory wave in the general direction of John Groves on the front steps of the lodge. With all the turmoil in her life—an ex-husband recently dead, in-laws bugging her about her daughter—some kind of upset was certainly not unexpected. To top things off, she had ended up here. If what Laird had seen of Groves that afternoon was any indication, the man had very probably been filling her head with accounts of his own nightmarish dreams, which was perhaps all it would take to tip someone with that woman's problems over the edge. He had almost asked her point blank about it but had decided not to. If she was leaving in a few hours, it wouldn't make any difference, and it was too late for a word of warning to Groves to do any good. The man had already done the damage, no matter how unwittingly.

As Laird pulled out onto the narrow blacktop road, he hesitated a moment, twisting around in the seat to look back at the pillars that flanked the entrance to the lodge grounds. The light above the "Groves Lodge" sign had apparently gone out while he was inside, and the dim, red glow from his taillights gave the little monstrosities perched on the pillars an even more sinister look than usual, enough to send a shiver up his spine. Just chunks of stone, he told himself, but unnerving nonetheless and one more thing that could have nudged the March woman in the direction of her nightmares.

Then, to his surprise, an image of his own grandmother, now more than ten years dead, darted through his mind. But of course, he thought an instant later as he released the brakes and accelerated down the winding, hilly road. It was only natural that he should think of her. Stories about the old Reimann place had always been among her favorites, as they were among so many of the town's old-timers. Despite the fact that the last of the Reimanns had vanished when the old mansion burned down and despite the fact that the land itself had gone through a dozen or more owners since then, it was still, to many, the old Reimann place. His grandmother had been a young girl then, no more than fifteen, a solemn, round-faced girl according to the half dozen faded pictures in the family albums. Those stories, though, had been clearer in her mind—perhaps because of the repeated telling—than things that had happened to her only hours or days before.

She had never seen any of the "miracles" actually performed, of course, but "everyone" knew that they had happened. The mother of a friend of hers had even been the recipient of one. The woman had been at death's door when she had been taken to the mansion one winter's day when Ben and Sarah Reimann had just returned from one of their frequent journeys. She had been so weak she could barely walk, and pale and haggard, her appetite totally gone. But when she returned home, although she was still weak, her color was good, and inside two days she was eating like a starving farmhand.

Assuming that there was a grain of truth at the core of the story, Laird had suspected from the first that the woman had simply experienced a spontaneous remission from some form of cancer, and that remission had just happened to coincide with her visit to the Reimanns. Remissions did happen, and even now medicine was often in the dark when it came to reasons. It was little wonder that a host of stories popped up around the Reimanns and were perpetuated. Some told of even more miraculous cures, while still others told of the terrible fates that had befallen those who had been bold enough to cross the Reimanns. When Ben Reimann had died and his only son and his wife had vanished together that same year, at the same time the mansion itself had burned down, the stories were reenforced and embellished. The entire family had been struck down in some mystical or biblical fashion, although no two people had ever agreed on either a reason or an agency for the destruction. And, the old woman had firmly maintained, the very ground the mansion had stood upon was haunted or perhaps cursed ever after. It had been, of course, a classic example of a self-fulfilling prophecy, the first installment of which was the rather bizarre behavior of Jeremiah Coplen around the end of the World War I. Coplen had been one of the Reimanns' servants in the 1890s, and his only son was killed in France in the war. When the body was shipped back in the winter of 1918, Coplen literally stole it and hauled it out to where the mansion used to be. No one knew what he hoped to accomplish, but what he did when he got there was commit suicide. His body was found next to his son's, among the trees behind the rubble that was all that was left of the mansion.

When Laird had been in medical school, he had tried to find out more about the one healing his grandmother seemed most familiar with, that of her friend's mother. He had tried to coax more specific descriptions of the woman's illness from his grandmother, and he had tried to convince her countless times that his own explanation of a spontaneous remission was far more likely than any kind of magical healing, but his success had been minimal. She had believed in that story and others for more than half a century, and she wasn't going to change her mind just because, as she often said, with a certain amount of justification, "my smart aleck grandson went away to school and decided he knows more than God almighty."

Grimacing, Laird thrust away the image of her stubbornly confident face, only to have it replaced by the angrily defiant one of his son. For a moment he wished desperately that the miracles his grandmother had believed in would occasionally prove out, that at least one of the faith healers who seemed to be springing out of the woodwork everywhere these days would turn out to have a little bit of healing to go along with the faith.

None would, of course, but at times like this, Laird could understand their appeal, no matter how irrational it might be. The remedies that doctors offered—such as his son's chemotherapy—were too often uncertain and unpleasant and weighed down with the burden of innumerable side effects. The others—the miracle healers, the layers-on of hands—were both certain and quick and guaranteed no adverse side effects. All you had to do was believe and, as often as not, discontinue conventional treatment.

A painful wave of apprehension twisted at his stomach and then subsided as Laird forced himself into a stiff calmness. Carl couldn't be that foolish, he told himself. He might be going through a stage of rebellion. Laird had seen and heard of similar cases by the dozen. But the boy couldn't possibly put himself totally into the hands of some irresponsible quack.

When the symptoms reappeared, when this period of drug-induced remission drew to a close, the boy would calm down and accept the treatment, no matter how difficult and uncomfortable.

He had to.

Shaking his head sharply, Laird realized that he was almost home. He had already, without being able to remember it, made the turn off Main and was halfway up the hill that was Jefferson. The clinic, only a couple of blocks from his house, was approaching on the right, its square, utilitarian shape contrasting sharply with the houses that surrounded it, mostly two-story brick or frame structures dating from well back in the nineteenth century. Laird had always marveled at old Doc Hoffman, who had been responsible back in the 1950s for not only getting the zoning changed to allow the clinic to be built but successfully pacifying the neighbors. It was an accepted part of the neighborhood now, but a lot of figurative blood had been shed at the time, before Doc Hoffman had stepped in as peacemaker.

As Laird was passing in front of the building, a motion caught the corner of his eye. In the clinic? Impossible at this time of night, of course, unless . . .

Almost relieved at this new diversion from his troubled thoughts, Laird made a right turn at the first cross street past the clinic and made his way around the block. Slowly, he pulled out onto Jefferson again and drove toward the clinic.

There it was again. Still a half block away, he saw the venetian blinds in one of the waiting room windows twitch as they fell back into place. Even in the dim glow from the office night-light, the motion was plainly visible. Someone was definitely in there.

Quickly, he tried to think where the nearest phone was. If there was one near enough for him to keep an eye on the clinic while calling the police, they could catch whoever it was. Someone after drugs, he assumed, though whoever it was would probably be disappointed if he expected to find much. Very few drugs were kept in any of the offices, primarily little more than recent samples that various salesmen left.

But the closest public phone, Laird realized, was back on

Main, three blocks away. It would be quicker to use the phone in his own house, only two blocks in the other direction, but to use either one would require that he be out of sight of the clinic for minutes, more than enough time for—

He was even with the clinic again, considering cruising around the block yet another time while he tried to think, when something caught his eye. In the alley that ran beside the clinic, close in the shadow of the wall, sat a car.

A dark Nova.

No, he thought abruptly, angrily. I won't believe it!

A mixture of despair and anger twisted at his stomach and tightened his throat as he accelerated around the corner once again, this time turning into the alley that went past the back of the clinic and then intersected the alley the car was parked in. Within seconds, he braked to a stop behind the car.

Fearfully, he leaned forward over the wheel and squinted down at the car's license plate, full in the glare of his headlights.

He swore, a single obscenity repeated a dozen times through clenched teeth. As he swore, the anger gave way to a kind of cold fear, not for himself but for his son.

Forcing himself to at least maintain an appearance of calm, he shut the car off and climbed out. Slowly, he walked past his son's dark red car—a pair of the boy's gloves lay in the passenger's seat, he noticed—and around to the waiting room door at the front. There was no motion at the window as he passed.

He inserted his key in the lock and turned it. The door clicked open, but there was no answering scurry from inside. Laird stepped in and closed the door behind him. The thirty-watt night-light above the receptionist's window on the left seemed bright after the dimness of the streetlamps outside. He stood a couple of feet from the door, looking around.

"Carl," he said finally, surprised at the steadiness of his voice, "I know you're in here. I saw your car, and I saw you at the window a minute ago."

More silence, stretching on for an eternity. Outside, another car approached. Nervously, Laird glanced through the window and breathed a mental sigh of relief when he saw that it was simply another late-night traveler, not the police.

The door to the corridor of offices, just to the right of the receptionist's window, opened. Carl Laird stepped out, his hands extended before him, fingers folded, palms down, wrists close together in the classic put-the-cuffs-on-me pose. His expensive sports jacket—another of the innumerable gifts Laird had showered on the boy—was smudged and wrinkled, and one of the pockets was torn. His head, a tangled mass of dark brown curls, hung down.

"You got me, officer, sir," the boy said theatrically.

"Son, this is not a joking matter," Laird heard himself saying, knowing even as he said it that it was the wrong thing to say but not knowing what could possibly be the right thing.

"So who's joking? You nailed me dead to rights, copper."

"You've been drinking again! I warned you last time, when they picked you up for—"

"Mea culpa, mea culpa!" The boy's head lowered even further in mock guilt and then raised as he peered up at his father through upturned eyes. "Or is that *'Nolo con'* something or other? I never could remember all the different Latin ways of saying you're guilty. Incidentally, Dad, you don't have much stuff around here, you know? Hardly worth stealing your extra keys for."

Laird sucked in a breath, fighting to keep from shouting. "Come on, let's get out of here."

The boy's eyes widened disingenuously. "No bracelets?" He waggled his hands, still held out, close together. "Not even after I confessed to breaking and entering? Or doesn't it count, since I'm a relative in good standing? Well, a relative, anyway."

"For Christ's sake, Carl," Laird blurted out. "What do you want? What in God's name do you want me to do?"

The boy shrugged broadly. "For His sake and in His name? Calling in the big guns, aren't you? But who said I wanted you to do anything? What in the world gave you an idea like that? Besides, is there anything you *can* do?"

Laird winced at the last question, during which a trace of bitterness overcame the exaggerated, drunken playfulness in the boy's voice. "I can do as much as you'll let me, that's all. Now let's go home, before we both get picked up."

"The police aren't on their way? I thought the place would

be under siege by the friendly neighborhood SWAT team by now. Or is Wertham big enough to have one of those? Well, the least you could've done was arrange for someone to lob some tear gas through the windows."

"No, the police aren't coming. I haven't called them, and I don't intend to. Now please, Carl, just come home with me."

"And here I thought you were a good law-abiding citizen." The boy shrugged again. "I wouldn't want you to ruin your good standing in the community on my account. There's a phone right there. I'll wait quietly while you call."

"Carl, please! If you won't let me help you—"

"I don't need any special favors just because I'm dying." The boy's words were filled with harsh bitterness.

The same hollow feeling that had gripped Laird when the bone marrow tests had come back the first time clamped down on him again. "You're not dying, damn it."

The boy dropped his arms to his sides and shrugged even more elaborately than before. "You could've fooled me, Dad."

"What you're doing isn't dying. What you're doing is killing yourself! Drinking, not resting, trying to—"

"Drinking? You think I'm drinking? For shame, jumping to unwarranted conclusions like that. For your information, Buck gave me something very nonalcoholic to make me feel good." The boy gestured around the clinic. "I was just looking for something I could give him in trade. You know, the old free enterprise, barter system. The American way."

Laird closed his eyes and held his jaw tightly clenched for a second. When he could speak quietly again, he said, "Who is this Buck?"

"Nobody you'd know, Dr. Laird, sir."

"A pusher?"

"How quaint! A pusher. No, I do not believe I will accept that terminology. If you don't mind, sir."

"All right, whatever you want to call him. But who is he? How did you get mixed up with him?"

"Another quaint turn of phrase, that. How did I get mixed up with him? you ask. Well, it wasn't easy, I'll tell you that. I'd always heard how easy it was to get dope—another quaint little phrase—but it really wasn't. I guess I just didn't know where to look or how to approach people. Would you believe it wasn't until I spent a couple of hours in the slammer, as you would probably call it, that someone showed me the way. A very nice fellow, very helpful. He pointed out how your kind of recreational drugs—beer and whiskey and all that—were really quite harmful. And he was going to save me from all that damage." A harsh laugh. "Little did he know, even if he hooked me for life, he wouldn't have a very long-term customer."

"You met this Buck person in jail?"

"Did I say that? I must be more careful. No, just a friend of a friend, so to speak. I didn't tell him I was already hooked on those other good, healthful, nonrecreational drugs, of course. Prednisone? Isn't that one of the little beauties you were shoveling into me?"

"Yes, that's one of them," Laird said, suddenly mentally exhausted, not knowing what to do or say next.

Nothing seemed to help; everything just made the situation worse. The boy was intelligent, obviously. His grades—until this year, at least— had been almost straight A's. And even now, the elaborately satirical jabs the boy kept making showed that the mind was still keen. But it was apparently expending all its energy in keeping the boy from acting sensibly, from accepting the help he so desperately needed.

"Just give them a chance, Carl," he went on finally, knowing even as he did that it wouldn't help. "Please? Don't fight us. There are new and better drugs coming along every year, every month. You know that as well as anyone."

"Sure, more miracle drugs, like those things you were pumping me full of in that vacuum chamber or whatever the hell you call it."

"A laminar flow room, and all it does is maintain a relatively germ-free atmosphere, which you need during that stage of therapy. Your natural resistance is almost nonexistent then. Almost any bug that got to you would take hold and grow. As for their being miracle drugs, compared with the treatments that were available twenty or even ten years ago, they are miracle drugs."

"Miracle drugs from the miracle doctor, administered in the miraculous laminar flow room. Some miracles. They make me sick as a dog, and the fine print tells me my hair may fall out. It hasn't yet, but that does give me something to look forward to next time, doesn't it? And everyone tells me over and over just how goddamn lucky I am that maybe, just maybe, I'll still be alive a few years from now, when maybe, if my luck goes really sky high, a real cure will show up. Well, Buck's brand of miracle drugs make me feel good, not rotten. After a little of his treatment, I don't give a damn if I last out the year or not. Maybe his treatment can't keep me going any longer than yours, maybe it even makes me go faster—you didn't think I knew that?—but I'll tell you one thing for damned sure. It's one fucking hell of a lot easier going his way than it is yours!"

The boy's voice had grown more intense with each word, and as he finally fell silent, breathing heavily, tears were trickling down his cheeks.

Choking back all the sensible, logical arguments that had already been made and rejected, Laird reached out and took the boy's arm.

"I'm sorry," Laird said in a husky whisper.

"I know that, too," the boy said, his voice now softer than Laird's. He didn't try to pull his arm from his father's grip.

And that arm, Laird could not help but notice, was still trembling. When the boy had first appeared, holding his hands out for the imaginary cuffs, his arms had been trembling, but Laird had thought nothing of it, assuming that it was a result of his emotional state. But now, as the tremors continued even though the boy's breathing was returning to normal, the ever-present hollowness in the pit of his stomach began to grow. Could the remission be ending so soon? Or was it only the effects of whatever drugs the boy was strung out on? Vainly, he tried to remember if there had been anything like this the last time he had seen the boy, but he had trouble remembering when that had been.

"Are we friends, then?" Laird asked, releasing the boy's arm and standing back.

The boy shrugged, his eyes averted. "Might as well be, I guess."

"All right, then," Laird said, forcing an unfelt lightness into his voice. "Now, as long as you're here and I'm going to have to charge you for an office call, anyway, we might as well get your blood test out of the way. You have one due next week, you know."

The boy stiffened, and for a moment Laird could see the anger twisting at his features again as it bubbled to the surface, but then he slumped and shrugged once again. "Why the hell not? I guess it's better than being arrested."

Quickly, nervously, the boy turned and walked down the short hall toward his father's office.

As Laird followed, watching for the slightest unsteadiness in the boy's movements, an image of Laird's grandmother intruded once again, and he found himself wishing blindly and irrationally that the Reimanns and their healing touch still existed and that his own rational, medically trained mind could somehow be tricked into believing that such things were, after all, within the realm of possibility.

It was nearly 3 A.M. when John Groves decided that Mattie was deep enough in sleep for him to begin.

Cautiously, he slid out from under the covers, collected clothes and shoes from the closet, and made his way to the bathroom to dress in the dark. Five minutes later, flashlight, spade, and pick under his arm, he eased himself out the back door of the lodge. Switching the flashlight on, he tried to follow the path he had followed earlier as he had trailed behind Elena March.

It had been after midnight, and he had been getting ready for bed when he heard her footsteps in the hall. The taste of the toothpaste still in his mouth, he peered out of the bathroom and saw her walking unsteadily away from her room and into the lobby. Puzzled, he followed as she crossed the lobby to the back door, slipped the latch, and went out. He had almost tried to stop her, but he only watched, walking a few yards behind her, with the only light coming from the open door behind them both. Across the damp grass in her bare feet she had gone, then into the wilder, weed-grown area beyond, and finally into the thick stand of trees beyond that. Then, suddenly, she fell to her knees and began to claw at the damp soil with her bare hands.

Hurriedly, he awakened her, grasping her shoulders and

pulling her roughly to her feet. Her eyes were glazed and unseeing, her face expressionless. He shook her harshly, and suddenly he found himself facing not Elena March but—he was sure—Jessica Reimann.

That was when, just as suddenly, he had realized what lay waiting beneath the soil she had been digging in.

The talisman.

In her dreams—which were not really dreams, any more than his own visions were dreams—she had lived out the last minutes of Jessica Reimann's life. Jessica Reimann had died with the talisman in her hands, and, through Elena March, she was trying to reclaim it.

But now *he* would claim it. Ever since he had come here, it had been calling to him. He knew that now. Night after night, the dreams that were not dreams had been calling to him, but he had been unable to answer that call.

But now, with that woman's unwitting help . . .

Suddenly, as the beam of Groves's flashlight fell on the spot where Elena March's fingers had earlier gouged at the earth, a wave of unreasoning exultation swept over him. He no longer felt the cold, damp wind that tangled his hair and pierced the coarse weave of the sweater he had thrown on. The angers and frustrations of the last three months—Mattie's constant putdowns, those bastards at school, students and teachers alike—all were engulfed in a surge of euphoric anticipation. Dropping the spade to the ground and stuffing the flashlight in his back pocket, he raised the pick high over his head. It felt light as a feather, and he no longer needed the feeble glow from the flashlight to show him where to strike.

With all his strength, he brought the pick down, driving the blade deep into the ground, and then wrenched it free. He struck again and then a dozen times again, each blow as powerful as the last. Then he took up the spade, jabbing it into the loosened dirt and heaving it onto a rapidly growing pile.

And then, a minute later—or perhaps an hour—he stopped. It was close now, he knew, very close. He could feel its cold glow beneath his feet; he could feel it reaching out, beckoning to him, caressing him. Laying the flashlight, unused until now, on the lip of the hole and dropping to his knees, he took the sharp-pointed tip of the pick in both hands and scraped with it along the ragged surface of wet clay, like a miniature plow turning back a tiny furrow.

It struck something, and he stiffened abruptly. This was it. The exultation reached an unbearable crescendo; his quivering stomach felt as if it were somehow undergoing an orgasm.

Cautiously, his whole body trembling and soaked in sweat from his exertions, he probed delicately with the blade of the pick. Slowly, he scraped another layer of loosened clay away, careful not to let anything, even the smallest pebble, escape his notice.

Then, as he continued to scrape at the loosened dirt, he uncovered what looked, in the faint glow of the flashlight, like a nest of twigs. Laying the pick aside, he brushed and picked more of the wet, slimy dirt aside, and soon the pattern was clear. It was not twigs or even roots but the fragile bones of a human hand.

Jessica Reimann's hand, he was positive.

No longer held together by flesh or tendon, the bones separated easily.

Holding his breath, Groves closed his fingers around the half-buried thing that had been beneath the bones. With a faint sucking noise, it came free.

Groves stood up, the orgasm continuing in what had once been his stomach. He stuffed the object into his already grimy pants pocket and began to refill the hole he had dug.

It seemed like hours or even days, but finally he was finished and ready to make his way back to the lodge. As he stepped inside the back door and into the light, he realized that he would have to burn the clothes he was wearing, they were so covered with grass stains and dirt. He hoped that his pajamas, still on underneath the shirt and pants, were not soiled as well.

Taking off his shoes—they would have to go, too—he walked to the kitchen and then down the narrow stairs to the basement. With the pick and spade wiped relatively clean with his already filth-covered pants, he put them in with the other tools, dumped his unsalvageable clothes into the incinerator, and returned to the kitchen.

The feeling in his stomach had subsided, but he was still

trembling as he lay what still looked like a handful of muck in the sink and carefully turned on the warm water.

Slowly, as he held it under the stream of water and massaged the dirt loose with his fingers, the familiar shape emerged, and a touch of fear began to mix with the remnants of exultation that still inhabited his stomach. The slender chain, corroded and useless, fell away at the first tug, but the rest was exactly as it had been in his dreams. The seven-sided ebony disk seemed untouched by its nearly seventy-year entombment. Once the dirt was rinsed away, its blackly glistening surface was smooth and silky to his touch, as if it had been precision machined and polished only hours before. Only the locketlike frame in which it was mounted showed any signs of deterioration, and even that was minimal, limited to slight discoloration in spots.

Christ, he thought. It really exists, and I've actually got it.

But then, almost instantly, came the second thought, the thought that had been fighting its way to the surface since he had first followed Elena March to the grave: What the hell is it? It exists, true enough, but what the hell is it?

More to the point, what could he really do with it? Even assuming that it did have some mystical qualities—and obviously it did; otherwise, he and Elena March could not have been led to it—what were they? According to the local old wives' tales, the Reimanns had been able to heal people now and then, and some of their enemies had come to a bad end.

He was, he realized with a nervous grin, in the same position a child would be if he suddenly awoke one morning to discover that overnight he had been made king of some mythical country. From the fairy tales he had read or made up, he wouldn't have the faintest idea what a real king should do, how he should act, or anything else about the king business.

And he, John Groves, didn't know a damned thing about the warlock business, if a warlock was indeed what possession of the talisman made him. Until he got the hang of it, so to speak—or at least until he found out whether there was anything to get the hang of—he would have to continue with business as usual. So far, all the talisman had done for him was ruin a pair of pants, a shirt, a sweater, and a pair of shoes.

And keep him up all night. He would be dead tired in about two hours when he had to get up to go to work.

Go to work and face another day of Weber and Cunningham and Gilford and Corman and all the other smartasses and goofoffs, maybe even the Laird kid if he condescended to come to school for a change. Shit!

Now there, Groves thought, would be a damned good way for a harassed warlock to start—by conjuring up a few bad ends for the likes of them. If anyone in Wertham deserved a bad end, it was them. Like that idiot Corman. He had had the stupid gall not only to bitch about the F he had gotten but to put up a pathetic argument that he hadn't lifted most of his so-called report right off the book's jacket.

Unfortunately, Groves didn't have any idea how to go about conjuring up a bad end or anything else. Still, it was fun to think about. He could imagine Corman if—

Suddenly Groves laughed as a particularly appropriate punishment for the blank-faced, blank-brained Corman popped into his head. Probably not fatal, but that didn't matter. A really good scare would be enough to start with. Unfortunately, it wasn't the kind of thing that even a warlock could accomplish, particularly a beginning warlock like himself.

Stifling a yawn, he stood up. He would have to get it all sorted out later. Right now, warlock or no warlock, talisman or no talisman, he needed some sleep.

Scooping up the talisman, now bereft of its rusting chain, he hurried with it into his den, found a plain manila envelope, dropped it in, and slid the envelope as far back in the corner of the center drawer as it would go. Then he locked the drawer and, a minute later, the door to the den, just in case the sleepwalker walked again and was still looking for something. Groves didn't know what he had in the so-called talisman, but whatever it was, he didn't want to lose it through carelessness.

Yawning openly this time, he made his way down the hall and slipped quietly into the bedroom, thoughts of Elena March and Corman and Mattie and the talisman all beginning to jumble senselessly in his mind.

* * *

Without warning, Arthur Corman found himself alone, walking through a dark, shadowy forest. The full moon, appearing now and again through rifts in the clouds, was the only light.

For a time, he continued to walk unquestioningly, picking his way along a virtually unseen path that somehow his feet knew to follow. The air, moist and filled with mossy odors, was warm and still. His own feet swishing through the wet, ankle-high grass made the only sound.

Finally, it occurred to him to wonder where he was going.

But he did not know. He did not even know, he realized, where he was or why he was here.

Still he continued to walk, as if he were on a dark and twisting treadmill. I must be dreaming, he thought, but realized at once how impossible the idea was. People in dreams never think that they might be dreaming.

But if he wasn't dreaming, where was he? How had he gotten here? And why the hell didn't he stop walking?

He tried to stop, but he couldn't.

He tried to look down, to see how he was dressed, hoping that his clothes might give some clue to what was going on. But his eyes would not respond. They remained steadfastly searching the darkness ahead.

He tried to think back, tried to send his mind back along the unmarked trail to see where it led, but there was only a blank.

Fear began then, but only inwardly. Externally, there was no sign of emotion of any kind. He could no more shout or scream for help or shiver in fear than he could stop walking.

Slowly, as the ground began to rise more sharply, he became aware of an odor that didn't fit, that had no business being here in the forest. He wrinkled his nose, surprised that it responded to his will. The odor, he realized, was like rotten eggs.

And a light—a dim, pulsing glow—appeared through the trees ahead, probably near the brow of the hill he was climbing.

Suddenly, he knew what was coming next. Although he still did not have even an inkling about where he had been going or why he was here, walking through some unnamed forest, he knew what was coming next.

An instant later, to his horror, he was proved right. Blocking his path was a huge, featureless creature, easily eight feet tall. Something like a translucent bell jar glimmered faintly in the moonlight where the head should be. The odor of rotten eggs was overpowering.

He was dreaming. He had to be! He recognized the scene being played out. It was right out of that crazy UFO book he had done his book report on a couple of days before, the one that bastard Groves had given him an F on just because he had copied a few words from the back cover.

If the scene continued, he knew that in just a few seconds he would be picked up and carried through the woods. He would barely be able to breathe because of the ever more powerful stench of rotten eggs. He would be taken aboard a UFO, a small and glowing cylinder with a rounded top and no visible windows. Other creatures like the one standing before him would be waiting in an antiseptically white room with a single rectangular slab in the center. He—his body—would be placed on the slab. An instrument, a tiny transparent tube of some kind, would emerge from an opening in the ceiling of the room. Silently, a beam of intense light would shoot out from the tube. He would feel the first stabs of pain across his chest, and then there would be nothing. He would awaken back here, where he had been picked up. Five days would have passed, five days of which he would have no memory whatsoever. There would be scars, seemingly several months old, across his chest and stomach, but that would be all.

Except, he somehow knew, those five days would not be a blank. He would first have to live through them. Only later, when his mind rejected the horrors he had experienced and wiped them from his memory, would the blankness come.

Then, as the clouds closed over the moon and he could see a faint glow like the fading luminescence of the numbers on a clock face coming from the creature itself, the sequence began.

The creature reached down and, not quite touching him with its fingerless hands, picked him up. He tingled all over with the pins-and-needles feeling of a limb that has gone to sleep. The odor was overpowering, and behind the shimmer where the head should be was a hint of grotesque, demonic features.

He screamed. And awakened.

Soaked in sweat, the bed sheets tangled about him, Arthur Corman awakened in his own room on the second floor of the converted farmhouse he and his younger brother and mother and father lived in.

It had been a dream.

Relief flooded over him, leaving him weak. Limply, he flopped flat on the bed from the knees-up half crouch he had been in when his eyes had first snapped open. He could still feel his heart thumping. God, but that had felt real!

But at least he hadn't awakened anyone else. That scream at the last minute must have been just in his head, just in the dream. If he had really made that much noise, everyone in the house would have been in his room by now, particularly Danny, his ten-year-old brother, who would have had a field day with something like this, using it to get back at him for all the times Arthur had poked fun at him.

But it was all right now. It had been a dream, and he hadn't made enough noise to wake anyone else up. He could go back to sleep and—

Frowning, he sniffed the air.

For a moment he couldn't believe it, but then it was so strong that he couldn't ignore it any longer. The odor of rotten eggs, the odor from his nightmare, filled the air around him.

But this wasn't a dream.

The sweat on his bare shoulders and back was suddenly a film of ice. In nervous, twitching motions, he looked around the darkened room. There was nothing, only the faintest smudge of light from where he knew the window was.

But the odor would not go away.

Trembling, he untangled the sheets from around his pajamaed legs and got out of bed. He swayed momentarily, his balance uncertain in the darkness. He started for the light switch by the door, but, not knowing why, he stopped.

Suddenly, it was like the nightmare all over again. He tried to move toward the light switch, but he could not. Instead, he felt himself turning and walking slowly to the window. Parting the curtains, he looked down at the backyard, almost invisible beneath the cloudy sky. But the clouds must have parted just then, letting the moon shine faintly through, because suddenly the entire yard, all the way back to the fence that marked the end of their property, was visible.

There, beyond the fence, at the edge of the stand of trees that extended into the hills beyond, stood the figure from his nightmare. There was no face visible behind the shimmering bell jar where its head should have been, but he knew that it was looking at him.

Slowly, deliberately, it raised one arm, its fingerless hand extended toward him. The odor of rotten eggs was as strong as it had been in the nightmare.

But he was awake. This was real.

Frozen and unable to move, he stood at the window for what seemed like forever but must have been only seconds. Then the figure lowered its arm and slowly turned and disappeared among the trees.

Gradually the odor faded, but a faint glow seemed to pulse somewhere far back among the wooded hills.

And somewhere in Arthur Corman's paralyzed mind, something watched and laughed.

The clock in the courthouse tower a half dozen blocks away solemnly clanged out four o'clock as Dr. Seth Laird let himself into the hospital through the side door nearest the lab. Closing the door quietly behind him, he made his way down the coldly antiseptic corridor, past the darkened and locked doors of the hospital library and the public relations office. Since there were no patients' rooms in the corridor, there was no reason for any doctor or nurse to come this way at this time of night. If he was lucky, he could get into the lab, check the blood, and get out without anyone even knowing he was there and therefore without having to answer the inevitable questions. Anyone who saw him in the lab, particularly at this ungodly hour, would know why he was there, and he didn't feel like talking about it or, worse, accepting the sympathetic noises that he knew would be forthcoming.

In the lab, he switched on only the one bank of fluorescents above the bench he would be using. As he took a pipette and transferred a drop of Wright's stain onto the blood smear, he found that he was trembling almost as badly as his son had been. Taking a deep breath, he steadied himself and continued. Luckily he had made more than one slide; even if he ruined one or two, the test could still be done.

Rinsing the stained slide, he waited impatiently for it to dry, resisting the impulse to pat away some of the excess moisture. In his shaken condition, he would probably just ruin it and have to start over with a second slide.

Nervously, he drummed his fingers on the counter top as he waited. He should not, of course, have lied to Carl, telling him he would not take the blood sample to the hospital until the next day, but he had been afraid to do it any other way. Even though the boy seemed temporarily cooperative, Laird knew that mood would probably not last out the night. The next day, the boy would be tearing off as usual, probably not even bothering to pretend that he was going to school.

If the blood smear showed what Laird feared, he wanted to be able to lay his hands on the boy. He didn't want him disappearing before he even had a chance to explain. Whether he could talk the boy into acting rationally, he didn't know, but he at least wanted the chance to try.

At last the slide was ready. Laird felt his heart pounding rapidly, felt icy sweat trickling down his sides beneath his arms as he switched on the microscope light. Again he sucked in a deep breath, telling himself that he was a physician and to at least try to behave like one.

But he was still trembling as he finally hunched over the eyepiece and began to focus the instrument.

Slowly, the image came clear, and as it did, the ever-present hollow ache in the pit of his stomach was suddenly all he could feel. Weakness gripped every part of his body with a suddenness that almost brought nausea. Somehow he steadied himself, forcing himself to take slow, measured breaths.

There was, he knew, no need to go through the mechanical task of counting the white cells or platelets. The outsized lymphoblasts and a pair of ruptured cells told him at a glance what he had desperately wanted not to know.

The remission had ended.

In less than three months, the remission had ended.

Less then three months, for God's sake!

Cursing softly, continuously, he picked up the little plastic counter from the bench next to the microscope and, after a final, unnecessary adjustment of the focus, began clicking the numbers in.

As Henry Winton drove through the silent darkness of the New England hills, Jessica, his twin, rode with him. Although she could be seen only in his mind, although her physical body had been dead nearly seven decades, she was as real to him as the uneven hum of the motor or the ridged steering wheel he gripped in his gnarled hands.

The call he had followed to her freshly dug grave an eternity ago was once again strong in his mind. Once again her voice kept him company as he made his way to her.

"When we were children, Henry—do you remember the first time?" it asked.

Of course he did, as clearly as if it had been eighty seconds ago rather than eighty years. They had always been close, seeming to share their thoughts as well as a makeshift crib, but it was not until they were nearly seven that they realized how truly linked they were.

It was mid-December, and Henry had been kept in bed the entire day because of a slight fever and sore throat. At seven, he had not minded and had not understood why his parents seemed so worried. In fact, he rather enjoyed being pampered and looked after. His mother's hand, repeatedly touching his forehead, was pleasantly cool, and the hot soup, even if it didn't taste as good as the cocoa he would have liked, warmed his scratchy throat and took away the soreness for a few minutes. Best of all, he didn't have to go to school. He and Jessica had started just three months before, and he did not like it. No matter what his mother and father and Clayton told him, he did not believe that it was really possible for him to learn to read, not the way they did, anyway. He would never get all those words straight in his head.

In the afternoon, about the time when he and the others would normally be getting out of school, he dozed off, as he had been doing off and on most of the day. When, seconds or minutes later, he awoke, no one was in the house. Clayton and his father had probably gone out to milk the cows, and he could hear the clanking as his mother operated the long-handled pump in the side yard not far from the frosted-over bedroom window. She would be starting supper soon, although he would probably get nothing but more of the soup she had been keeping hot on the kitchen range all day.

Then, as the clanking of the pump stopped and there was a moment's silence before the faint sound of the water bucket being lifted from the pump's spout, he realized that there was something he had to do. He didn't question it, didn't wonder how or why he suddenly knew.

He simply acted.

Climbing out of bed, he put on a shirt and faded bib overalls over the heavy flannel nightshirt his mother had kept him in that day and then the heavy, scuffed, faded shoes that he always had so much trouble lacing all the way to the top. But this time it went quickly, as if his hands had gained new skills in the last twenty-four hours. From the hooks behind the kitchen door, he took the mackinaw he had inherited but not quite grown into yet from Clayton and his own brick-red, tasseled stocking cap and the fingerless mittens his mother had knitted for him to wear to school.

As he went out the door, it was starting to snow. Rushing down the steps, he passed his mother, who was so startled at the sight that he was already past her before she reacted, shouting after him and hastily setting the heavy water bucket on the ground. He was down the bank at the front of the house and across the rutted, frozen road and up the opposite bank of winter-brittle weeds and vines before she realized that he was deaf to her cries. As he scooted under the barbed-wire fence, she began shouting for his father.

The cold air hurt his already raw throat, but the boy wasn't thinking about the pain. He was thinking only of where he must go: the pond in the woods nearly half a mile away. The cloud banks ahead of him grew darker by the minute, the snow thicker. He could barely see the edge of the woods now, and if he had looked back, the house and outbuildings would have been fading into the swirling whiteness. He hadn't taken time to buckle on his overshoes, and the snowy cold was starting to seep through the unprotected seams of his shoes.

Then he was across another fence and in the woods, running between the leafless trees, jumping over the bulging roots and fallen limbs. The sound of his mother's voice was faint in the distance. His breath was coming harder, and his throat was scraped more raw with each lungful of wet, icy air. His face, exposed from the pulled-down stocking cap to the pushed-up collar, was pelted by the wind-driven snow.

Then he stopped. He was where he had to be.

The pond, a fifty-foot widening of the narrow creek, was in front of him. It was frozen, had been frozen for more than a week, but the ice was not yet thick. Near the center, where it was thinnest, a jagged patch of open water was dimly visible through the thickening snow.

Reaching out of the water, her mittened hands scrabbling helplessly at the ice around the opening, was Jessica.

He began to shout then, still not feeling the scraping pain in his throat, and a minute later his father stumbled to a halt and looked in sudden horror at the center of the pond where the screaming boy was pointing.

"And the last time, when we were no longer children—do you remember the last time?"

Of course he did. Although he had kept it hidden in the dark corners of his mind for nearly three-quarters of a century, he remembered.

And he remembered that he had failed her.

But now, after nearly seventy years, he was being given a second chance. It was, he was sure, the only reason his stiff and aching body had persisted so far beyond its allotted three score and ten. He was being given a chance to complete the task at which he had so shamefully failed so long ago.

Finally, as the dull and cloudy dawn filtered down from the surrounding hilltops, he found himself in Wertham. He was, he realized, on Main Street. Ghost houses and phantom storefronts shimmered and mixed with the modern reality of plate glass and concrete to form an impossible shifting montage of past and present in his eyes. For an instant, the figure of his brother Clayton, bushy mustache drooping, checkered mackinaw open to an unseen wind, huge clodhopper shoes thumping on invisible wooden planking that had once covered the sidewalks, emerged from a shadowy general store and seemed to wave.

Then Clayton was gone, vanishing along with the spectral buildings that Winton's wandering mind had created. Slowly, trying to keep all his senses in the present, Winton followed the highway out of town, able largely to ignore the fleeting glimpses of rutted dirt and open fields and hillsides that still thrust themselves upon him. Minutes beyond the city limits, a ghost road appeared on Winton's left and, a hundred yards beyond, a more solid but less familiar one.

He lifted his foot from the accelerator and let the car coast and rattle to a stop on the deserted road just short of the intersection. A sign a few feet behind the car had pointed in the direction of the turn he must make, but the words on the sign had not registered. His hands, he realized, were shaking, but not with the helpless palsied motion that had occasionally afflicted him in recent years. It was the same nervous trembling that all those years ago had nearly stopped him before he had even begun. And in his stomach there was the same icy churning he could remember so well even after nearly seven decades.

For a long time he sat silently, looking down the narrow road and imagining himself again and again making the turn and moving on to whatever lay waiting.

Finally, the rumble of a truck approaching somewhere on the hilly road behind him stirred him to action.

When, little more than a minute later, Winton slowed the aged car, he thought for a moment that his mind was once more playing false with him, that it was again dredging up phantoms to haunt him. But as he came closer, as the pillars loomed larger and more solid, he saw that they were real. Equally real were the hideous, snouted stone faces that peered down from the tops of the pillars.

In nearly seventy years, the pillars and their obscene guardians had not changed.

He turned between them, his left rear fender scraping one pillar noisily.

A building loomed up before him.

Again a moment came and went in which he felt sure that

he must have been dragged back in time, regardless of the fact that his car was still solid and real around him, its ridged steering wheel clutched in his knobby fingers like an anchor.

But this time there were differences. The size was barely half that of the mansion that had vanished in flames that night. Its front was a cheap imitation of the original, like the false front of a movie set. Where the carriage house had been, there was now only a graveled-over parking area. Three cars, including one box-shaped blue sedan that looked like a plainer version of his own twenty-year-old car, huddled together at the far end.

The grave, he thought with a sudden burst of new and different apprehension—where would the grave be? And with people here—it seemed to be a hotel of some kind—would he have the freedom, the time he needed?

He looked at the spade he had taken from his nephew's garage. He had had doubts about his own physical ability, but he had been sure that, given the necessary uninterrupted hours, he would eventually have been successful. But if he did not have those hours, if the people who now owned this place . . .

But there was no point thinking about it. The wordless call was as strong as it had ever been. He had no choice.

He parked carefully at the end of the short line of cars, noticing as he did that his headlights were still on. He switched them off and climbed stiffly out of the car.

He stood, bent and gaunt, looking at the building. The damp morning air bit through the aging suit jacket he still wore, but the discomfort was easily ignored. It was nothing compared to what he knew was to come.

He started toward the front door. He would have to rent a room and stay here until he found the chance he needed. He should have brought clean clothes, but he had not imagined any need. He had been prepared for death, not for delay.

While he was still shuffling across the gravel parking area, the door of the building opened. A woman came out, carrying a suitcase and tugging a reluctant child by the hand.

Suddenly he knew why he had once again felt the call. He recognized her.

The recognition was not a physical thing, although there was a faint similarity between Jessica and this tall, big-boned woman who strode toward him. Nor was it even in the way she carried herself with a calm determination, although there, too, there was a similarity.

She simply was Jessie. He had known when to answer the call, and now he knew that this stranger walking rapidly toward him was his long-dead sister.

Elena March breathed a silent sigh of relief as she and a reluctant Beth emerged into the damp morning air. Every minute since the doctor had left had seemed endless. Discovering that those last minutes of her nightmare had been not a nightmare but reality had made her realize that Jessica and all those others whose deaths she had also died were real. They had existed, and somewhere they existed yet.

And that somewhere was not far distant. Jessica Reimann's terrified awakening in Elena's body proved that this world was not yet beyond their reach. They were still there, waiting for another opportunity, waiting for Elena to drift off to sleep, to let down her guard. But she didn't. She didn't dare sleep. If one of them gained control, as the terrified Jessica had for those few minutes, she would not this time be able to shake free.

And she would not be allowed to leave this place. There would be one more death to add to the long list of deaths: her own. Her only chance was to leave, to escape before that happened.

Every sound that broke through the dark silence, even the cat as it dropped softly to the floor from Beth's bed, sent a stiffening shock through Elena. But at least her taut nerves kept her awake until it was time to awaken Beth and break the news that they were going to have to leave her "house." "But why, Mommy?" was repeated a dozen times, grating more harshly on Elena's nerves every time, but finally the child resigned herself to the move.

Now, at last, they were out of the building, and nothing had happened to stop them. She had stayed awake. There had been no more nightmares. Her body still obeyed her own commands rather than those of someone dead since the turn of the century, and she was finally on her way. Assuming that the moisture in the air hadn't incapacitated the car—please, not now—they were going to make it. Her biggest worry once again would be keeping Beth placated and amused over the next few days while waiting for word from Bill that Grantland had come to his senses and that it was safe to return home.

She was nearing the gravel parking area when she saw the old man.

He was over six feet tall but thin as a rail, dressed in a suit that was at least a dozen years out of style and had that distinctive just-taken-out-of-storage look. He had gotten out of a car so old that its body style was almost identical to that of her own Checker; that would make it mid-1950s, which was probably when the suit was from, too. And the man himself, although he stood erect and alert, had to be eighty at the very least.

He was watching Elena, and for a moment, as their eyes met, she half stumbled on the gravel. Then, abruptly, he was moving toward her, his scuffed shoes scraping over the loose gravel. A few yards from her car, he stopped, standing directly in her path.

Elena stopped and looked up at his gaunt, ancient face. Beth looked first at the old man and then, with sudden hope widening her eyes, at her mother.

"Are we going to stay after all, Mommy?"

Elena shook her head uncertainly, and the scarecrow of a man took another step toward them. Slowly, his lips moved.

"Jessie? Jessica?" he whispered.

Elena gasped, her hand tightening convulsively on Beth's, bringing forth a muted, "Ouch, Mommy!"

"Who are you?" Elena asked, feeling the damp, chilly air burrowing into her very bones.

For a long time the man's sunken eyes did not leave her face. Finally he spoke again. "My name is Henry Winton."

And with those words, Elena felt the invisible bonds she had feared close about her. Jessica had not returned, but her brother had. The last chance for escape was gone. Something inside her, something that had suddenly grown immeasurably stronger at the old man's approach, would hold her here. It had, in a weaker, incomplete form, led her here, but now, fully awakened, it would hold her here.

She was joined inextricably to Jessica Reimann and those countless others, and one more battle—one more death?—was about to begin.

When the alarm jerked John Groves awake, his first thought was an angry, Christ, it was just a goddamn dream, after all.

But then, as he forced himself to sit up and felt the stiffness in his muscles and the soreness in his fingers and palms and saw the traces of dirt beneath his nails, he realized that at least part of it had been real.

Ignoring Mattie's sleepy mumbles as she came slowly and blearily awake, he threw back the covers and, in pajamas and bare feet, snatched his keys from the drawer of the bedside stand and hurried from the bedroom to the den. A moment's fumbling with the lock and he was inside, where he lurched to a stop beside the desk, still cluttered with last evening's papers. For a long moment, he stood leaning heavily against it, trembling. He was not sure which possibility frightened him more, having his disjointed memories of the last few hours proved true or having them proved to be nothing but a grotesque dream like all the others.

Then, hearing Mattie yawning past the door on her way to the bathroom, he dropped into the chair behind the desk and jammed the key into the lock.

It opened easily, and as he pulled the center drawer open, he saw that the small manila envelope was still there, pushed far back in the corner, just as he remembered.

For a long time Groves sat motionless, his hands gripping the arms of the chair like a novice speaker who is suddenly catatonic with stage fright just as he is being introduced.

But then a sound—the front door? Who would be coming or going at this time of the morning?—jarred him loose from the block of ice that shrouded him, and he found himself almost involuntarily reaching for the envelope and pulling it from the drawer. He heard an object scraping against the heavy paper as it shifted inside the envelope, sounding for all the world like tiny, clawed hands scrabbling at the insubstantial walls of its prison.

Cautiously, he folded back the flap of the envelope and held it up to the window and the dull morning light that filtered through the curtains. He looked inside and saw that the talisman was still there, just where he had left it.

It was still real.

He was still an apprentice warlock, and he still didn't know what to do about it.

Shivering, Groves shoved the envelope back into the drawer and locked it.

"How did you know?"

Elena March and the old man who had called himself Henry Winton sat, half turned toward each other, on one of the nearly antique high-backed sofas in the huge central lobby. It had been nearly two hours since she had first seen him, and this was the first chance she had had to be alone with him. Mattie and her husband had been getting up when they went inside, and between Mattie's obvious concern over Elena's seemingly erratic behavior and Beth's renewed high spirits at being allowed to stay in her house another day, Elena had had no time to herself until now, several minutes after breakfast. By mutual but unspoken agreement, she and the old man had treated each other as the strangers they were, and she noticed later that the spidery scrawl of his registration spelled out "Wilson" rather than "Winton."

John Groves, after a solicitous but nervous few minutes at breakfast, had left for school, while Mattie, reluctantly abandoning her efforts to hover around Elena like a mother hen, had gotten out the vacuum cleaner and dustcloths and started cleaning out not only Elena's and Winton's rooms but a couple of others. "Just in case someone else loses his or her way," she said. "You never know. With two guests at one time, we're already on a hot streak." Beth was on the floor near the registration desk with B.C., who had come in only a few minutes before and was now doing its fastidious best to wash off all traces of the outdoors from its fur and feet before retiring to the top of the desk for the day.

"How did you know that name from my dreams?" Elena repeated.

The old man shook his head. "They weren't dreams," he said simply.

For a long time she was silent, watching Beth and the cat out of the corner of her eye but hardly seeing them. Finally she slumped in resignation.

"No, I suppose I knew they weren't. I wish they were, but I don't see how they can be." Another silence, and her eyes moved up his scarecrow frame and settled on the nearly translucent skin of his face.

"You're Jessica's brother," she said, trying to find some similarity to the figure from her dream as his head nodded silently. The height was there, still over six feet, and the forehead was broad, the nose slightly flattened and bent from a childhood accident. But that was all. The years had obscured all else.

"Tell me about her," Elena said, although she knew that whatever he said would only tighten the already unbreakable bonds that held her here.

He told her.

In his thin but remarkably steady voice, he told her of their early life together, and it was like having the memories of her dream self replayed. She—Jessica—and Henry had been born in a farmhouse less than two miles from here in 1888. One older brother, Orville, had already died, but Clayton, born in 1885, had still been alive in 1910. Jessica, apparently for no reason other than pure cussedness, had always ignored her parents' admonitions and had gone out of her way to hang around the Reimann estate, although she rarely got past the gates except for the few times the servants, a gardener in particular, took pity on her and let her in. But Marcus Reimann, when he returned from college after four years' absence and realized that she had grown up while he was gone, married her a few months later in 1907, when she was nineteen and he twenty-two. He, of course, took the local superstitions about his family with a massive grain of salt. The so-called healing, he often said, was simply a backwoods version of the royal touch that European kings and queens had been credited with for centuries and that was only now going out of vogue. He dismissed it and all other forms of magic with a good-natured sneer. The Reimann wealth, mostly in the form of real estate and stocks, was simply an inheritance from more adventurous and less ethical ancestors. There was certainly no reason to think that there was anything supernatural about it, any more than there was to think that the Rockefellers or the Morgans were families of witches and warlocks.

But suddenly, a year after the marriage and a week after his mother died, Marcus changed. No one, least of all Jessica and her brother, ever learned what caused the change, but from that day on Marcus cut himself and Jessica off from Ben Reimann totally. It wasn't until Ben's own death two years later that Marcus returned, and then it was only with the avowed purpose of disposing of the estate. But it didn't work out that way, whatever the reason. The servants were sent away on the first day, all with generous allowances, but the next day, when the work of inventorying the estate and looking for buyers was scheduled to begin, Marcus cancelled everything and was not seen again— except by Jessica for those few short minutes— until the night of his death.

"He just shut himself up in that house," Winton said, the memories plain on his parchment face, "alone. He let all the folks go that'd worked for Ben, and he never got anyone else in. I went by a dozen times, but he never answered the door, never even let on he was in there. Except for a light once in a while at night, he could've dropped off the face of the earth for all we knew. And then she—you— came looking for him, trying to find out what happened to him, and he wouldn't even let you in."

Elena nodded, remembering. When the old man seemed hesitant to continue, she said, "Tell me the rest. I think I know what happened, how she was killed, but tell me, anyway. I have to be sure."

Reluctantly, he went on, telling how he had accompanied Jessica to the mansion, how he had been "possessed" for a brief moment and then let go, how he had later managed to round up some of his sister's friends and lead them back to the now-burning mansion in a vain attempt to save her from he knew not what.

"When we got there, he'd already set the place on fire, like he thought maybe if he couldn't bring himself to sell it, he could at least destroy it. And Jessie, she said she'd had some kind of vision. She'd been given some kind of spell that would save Marcus, and when she told me, I knew she was right. It was like I'd got part of her vision myself. But it took a long time. You had to do it over and over, and she didn't get the time. Somebody'd brought a gun; I guess he just carried it with him all the time. And Marcus acted like he wanted to be killed, calling everyone all the names he could think of, daring them to do anything. So he was shot. And then when Jessie tried to use that spell again, they thought she was on his side. I tried to tell them what she was doing, but they wouldn't listen. They were past listening. And when that body started coming back to life and getting up—"

He shivered and stopped for a minute, forcing himself into relative calmness.

"They just went crazy when Jessie was shot," he went on. "All they wanted to do was hide what they'd done and get out of there. So they buried them both, back in the woods behind what was left of the mansion. They covered the grave with leaves and things and went home, scared half to death, afraid someone would find out, afraid they were all cursed because of what they did. And I don't know but what they were. Maybe I was, too. But at least I thought it was all over then, and I guess for the rest of them it was. But for me, maybe it was partly my guilty conscience, but she kept calling to me. I didn't sleep for a week, and finally I couldn't help myself. I went back. And I couldn't finish it then, either. I failed again. Jessie was there, telling me what I had to do, but I still couldn't do it."

Visibly shivering, he told of his efforts to dig up the grave and his ultimate failure as the rotting corpse of Marcus Reimann rose once again.

"I don't know what it was after, but I just ran and kept on running. I never came back, not to the grave, not to Wertham, not even to my family. I knew if I ever came close, I'd hear her again. I made a sort of a life for myself out in Ohio, farming and working at odd jobs for sixty years. I even took me a wife, but Bonnie never had any children, and it's most likely right that she didn't. Every so often I'd almost forget what'd happened back here, but it'd always come back, always. Then Bonnie died, and there wasn't nothing left, nothing at all. I almost came back here, but I couldn't. I guess I was still scared, even after sixty years. But I did find one of my brother Clayton's grandchildren, Donald. He only lived a hundred miles or so from here, and I've been living with him and his family ever since. And then I heard you calling me again."

He fell silent for a moment, with a look of pain flickering across his ancient face. "I guess that's why I stayed alive so long, so I could answer you when the time came."

He was stiffly silent for a full minute, and then he seemed to relax, his bony form bending here and there into a softer posture. He shrugged almost imperceptibly. "Guess you can call the nuthouse now if you want to."

"I probably should," she said, "but they'd have to take me, too, if I did."

"You don't think I'm crazy, then?"

"I wish I did. I really wish I did, but I can't, not now," she said, and rushed on to tell him of her own visions: the same tiny, seven-sided pool of darkness, the demonic caricature of a face that had appeared to her at the moment of death in a hundred lives in a hundred places and times stretching back across countless centuries, the same face that even now sat atop the crumbling pillars that flanked the entrance to the lodge grounds. And the final death, that of Jessica Reimann herself. And the words, the guttural and nonsensical collection of sounds that made up the incantation that Jessica and a hundred others before her had been given, each in his own way, each in his own time. The words—the grating, unearthly sounds—that would cast out the being that had possessed and been possessed by generation after generation in country after country down through the millennia.

"It felt as if her throat were being torn to shreds by the sounds," Elena said. "They were never meant to be spoken by anything human, but somehow she managed to go on. Until she was killed."

She paused then, letting her breath out in a shuddering sigh, her throat aching simply at the memory of those sounds. "That's when I woke up. Except that it wasn't really me who woke up, not at first. It was her, it was Jessica. She was digging at the ground, digging with her bare hands—my bare hands."

"Digging? Where?" Winton's ancient face was suddenly even paler and more drawn.

Elena shook her head. "I don't remember. Out there somewhere." She waved one arm vaguely toward the rear of the building.

"Can you show me?"

"I think so, if I have to. But why?"

But even as she spoke, she knew the answer. Now that Henry Winton had told her the rest of what had happened that night, now that she knew that Marcus and Jessica had been buried almost in the shadow of the mansion, she knew where she—where Jessica—had awakened and what she had been doing. She had been doing the same thing she had been trying to do when she had died. She had been trying desperately to reach that object which her own long-dead body still clasped in its fleshless hands, trying to reach it and complete its destruction.

Slowly, Elena stood up from the sofa. Winton only looked at her, saying nothing but, she was positive, seeing into her thoughts.

"Yes," she said, "I can show you where I was."

He sat for another minute at least, silent, hardly seeming to breathe. Then he raised himself, the sounds of his joints as audible as the rustle of his clothes, and waited.

She spoke briefly to Beth, who was still deeply involved in petting the loudly purring B.C., and then wrapped her cardigan more tightly around herself and led the way out the small door at the back of the central lobby.

The early-morning fog was gone, but the clouds had not lifted and the grass was still damp. The trees started a dozen yards or more behind the lodge. Seventy years ago, she knew, the mansion itself had extended back to within a few feet of the nearest trees, but the lodge was barely half the size of the mansion. There were no fences, just a sharp boundary where the grass was no longer mowed. Beyond that point, it was completely untended. Grass and weeds ranged from calf to knee high, and here and there small trees—mostly oaks and a few birches—were beginning to take hold. From back among the full-grown trees, where the land took off almost vertically into the surrounding hills, came the sound of a running stream.

Her shoes and the legs of her slacks were already wet when she stopped a few feet short of the uneven line of trees. Winton, his feet dragging heavily through the tall grass, looked at her.

"Is something wrong?"

She shook her head as if to clear it. "I don't know." Then she pointed. "It was there, straight ahead, between those two large oaks."

He watched her for another few seconds, as if waiting for her to take the lead again, but she remained motionless, her arm dropping to her side. Then he turned and moved on by himself.

It seemed to take forever, but finally he neared the spot she had indicated. "There," she called, "just a few feet farther."

He moved another step and then stopped. There, in the heavy shade of the trees, the grass was thin, replaced by other, weedier ground cover. He pointed to a spot a few feet in front of himself.

"There?" he called back, his voice barely strong enough to carry.

"Yes, I think so."

He turned and started back toward her. A glassy look was evident in his eyes as he approached, and it seemed that only an effort of pure will kept him from collapsing.

"We're too late," he said in a broken whisper as he came to a faltering stop in front of her. "It's gone."

"What do you mean?" she asked, although she was sure what his answer would be.

"It's been dug up," he said. "The grave has been dug up."

* * *

Dr. Seth Laird, whose red-rimmed eyes had not been closed in sleep since the call from Groves had awakened him nearly eight hours before, sat in his living room, watching as his son came down the stairs from the second floor, yawning. This morning, unlike most mornings, the boy had on jeans and a pullover, which perhaps meant that he was thinking of going to school for a change.

Laird raised himself stiffly to his feet as the boy reached the bottom of the stairs. Carl looked at his father's haggard face and the slump in his broad shoulders and bulky frame, and a frown creased his forehead beneath the dark brown tangle of curls.

"God, Dad, but you look awful. What are you sitting down here for, anyway?"

"I couldn't sleep," Laird said.

"Maybe you should get something from Buck. He's got something for every condition."

"I'll bet he does," Laird snapped, suddenly angry, but then he shook his head. "I'm sorry. I don't want to fight."

The boy shrugged. "That's okay with me. Incidentally, when will the verdict be in?"

"It's already in."

"What? How? That lab isn't even open yet."

"I went in last night by myself, after you were asleep."

The boy swallowed loudly, as it seemed to Laird that he actually, visibly paled. "So, what did you find out? If it's as bad as you look, I'm in big trouble."

"It's not good. The white blood count—"

"Spare me the details, all right?" the boy said sharply, cutting Laird off. "Not good is good enough."

"I can get your treatment started today. I've already talked to Simpson, and he said—"

"So you talked to Simpson, did you?" The sarcasm of the night before was back in the boy's voice. "How about me? Why didn't you talk to me before you made all these neat plans?"

"I'm sorry, Carl. But there is only one treatment, and the sooner it's started, the better your chances are." He forced the faintest of smiles. "Besides, you were sleeping peacefully, and rest is part of the treatment."

The boy snorted angrily. "Sure, only one treatment and only one result. I'm locked up, and things are shoved in me that make me feel like warmed-over puke. And when it's all over, I die, anyway." The boy's voice was shrill and angry now, and Laird knew that he had lost him. But he didn't know what else he could have done.

"Please, we've been over this a hundred times. Your chances are really not that bad if you would only—".

"Fuck my chances! Fuck you! Fuck everything!" the boy almost screamed, and then he was running from the house.

Laird stood silently for several seconds, as much from exhaustion as from indecision. Then the sound of his son's car starting sparked new movement. Running to the kitchen window overlooking the driveway, he saw the car, blocked by his own sedan, bumping back and forth, grating against his car's bumper and fenders until it was angled enough to back off the side of the drive across the lawn. Finally, with a roar, the car shot off the lawn and across the sidewalk, bounced down from the curb, and hit the morning street with screeching tires.

"Christ," Laird muttered fiercely as he balled his fist and pounded it in helpless frustration on the windowsill until the dishes in the cabinets rattled. "Christ! Christ! Christ!"

John Groves stopped at Mort Waldon's jewelry store on Main on the way to school, intending to have a new chain put on the talisman, but as he was about to lay it on the counter, he realized that he did not want to let it out of his hands. More specifically, he did not want to let it into anyone else's hands, even for the minute or two it would take to attach the chain.

Dropping it in his jacket pocket before Mort, just emerging from the back room, saw it, he picked out an inexpensive pendant with a chain that could be easily transferred, paid for it, and left. A few minutes later, borrowing a pair of pliers from an unlocked toolbox in the school's machine shop, he made the change and slipped the chain and its new pendant around his neck inside the collar of his shirt. Hurriedly, before the shop instructor or any of his students showed up,

Groves returned the pliers to the tool box, scooped up his folder of papers, and made his way into the hall just in time for the bell announcing that the first class of the day was three minutes away.

As he walked, jostled at every step by the rushing hordes of students, he wondered whether it was his imagination or whether the spot on his chest beneath the talisman actually felt warm. After last night, he could believe almost anything. His usual morning-after rationalizations with which he had so often and so easily demolished the seeming reality of his dreams could make no headway against the solid reality of the talisman itself, which matched the object from those dreams so perfectly. Such things were simply not explainable in terms of coincidence. However, no matter how real it all was, he still had not made any progress toward getting the hang of the warlock business. Trying to remember how he had felt and what he had done in the dreams hadn't helped, since none of the dreams had ever involved the actual use of the talisman. In each dream that he could remember, he had simply been enjoying what the talisman had already done for its possessor. The women, the money, the power: it was always an accomplished fact, like a millionaire enjoying his wealth without any remembrance of how he had earned or perhaps stolen it.

In fact, Groves thought disconsolately, maybe all the thing really did was generate dreams: nice dreams, but dreams nonetheless. After all, the only evidence that it had ever actually affected reality was in the old wives' tales that were still told about the Reimanns. And whatever the talisman's powers, it certainly hadn't done Jessica or Marcus Reimann any good. Their bones in an unmarked grave had proved that. They had both come to an end as bad as any their family was supposed to have inflicted on anyone else. No, despite the irrational high he had been on last night when he had first found the talisman, he still didn't have the faintest idea what it could really do for him, if it could do anything at all.

Sighing, he entered the classroom. It was, of course, still half empty. No one came to English classes before it was absolutely necessary, and there must have been at least another forty-five seconds until the final bell. Denton and Ascencio were huddled in their usual corner, a pocket chess set between them. At least they weren't rolling dice the way a few had done the year before in Cleveland.

He was barely out of the way when the door burst open and most of the missing herd thundered in and scattered to their desks. Settling behind his own desk at the front of the room, Groves laid out the attendance sheet and began checking off names. Alber, Ascencio, Bailey, Brubaker—missing again, third day in a row; have to check with his parents—Clark, Corman, Denton, Durkes, Enyart—

Groves stopped, frowning. Uncertainly, his eyes moved back to Corman. The boy, tall and muscular with a head of tight blond curls like a bleached Afro, sat quietly, which was in itself unusual. Normally he was quiet only when under direct orders. Maybe the F on the book report yesterday had subdued him. He probably hadn't gotten one before, and he wasn't used to it. Well, if he kept on turning in jacket blurbs or ad copy for book reports, he'd be getting more of them, that was for sure.

Groves started to resume taking attendance, but his eyes came back once again to Corman. The boy was nervous, he realized, even frightened, but he didn't understand how he knew that. The boy was just sitting there quietly, saying nothing, his face a relative blank. It was unusual, but that was all. So how the hell did he know that the boy was frightened?

An image formed fleetingly in Groves's mind, an image of a creature at least eight feet tall, a shape like a softly glowing bell jar where a head should be. And an odor struck at his nostrils, an unmistakable odor of rotten eggs.

Blinking, Groves shook his head in an effort to clear it. What kind of nonsense was this? Was he starting to have dreams even when he was wide awake? Was that what having the talisman was going to do for him?

But then he remembered. The image that had flickered through his mind was the image of the space creature, the UFO monster described in Corman's idiotic book report. And it wasn't the first time the image had been in his mind. Last night, when he had been thinking what he would like to do to some of the dunderheads in his classes, it had occurred to him, logically enough, that an appropriate fate for Corman would be to be picked up by one of the imaginary creatures from that ridiculous book. He remembered thinking the idea quite amusing, although it didn't seem nearly as funny now as it had at five in the morning. And then, as he had been lying half asleep in bed, his mind had played it all out for him: Corman wandering alone through the woods somewhere, coming face to face with the creature, and then—

But it was happening again. His mind was once again filling with those very same images, except now they were not steady and real but flickering and insubstantial, and all were edged with icy terror instead of dry amusement. His own skin, he realized, was developing goose bumps.

Blinking again, he refocused his eyes and brought the Corman boy into the center of his field of vision. The boy was sitting up straighter now, his eyes darting from side to side. His nose was wrinkling as if he smelled something bad.

Then, abruptly, their eyes met.

Just as abruptly, the truth dawned on Groves. Last night he had projected those images into Arthur Corman's sleeping mind, and the boy, still badly shaken by the experience, was remembering it now. And he, Groves, was apparently picking up those garbled memories.

I'll be damned, he thought. I will be damned!

Locking his eyes on Corman's, he tried to sharpen the images, flesh them out with the same kind of reality he had unwittingly given them last night. And apparently he was succeeding. It was all he could do to keep from laughing as Corman's eyes widened and his hands twitched nervously.

Groves allowed himself a smile. "Is something wrong, Mr. Corman? You seem a little edgy."

The boy seemed barely able to blink. He looked like a frightened snake, Groves thought, a very frightened snake facing a mongoose.

"Well?" Groves persisted. "What seems to be the trouble, Mr. Corman?" Everyone had turned to look at the boy.

The boy shook his head, trying unsuccessfully to take his eyes from Groves. "I'm all right," he said, but his voice was weak and unsteady.

"Of course you are," Groves said quietly. "You really should try to relax, however. You look much too tense. You look as if you'd seen a ghost—or perhaps a flying saucer. You haven't seen a flying saucer, have you, Mr. Corman?"

There was scattered, nervous laughter as others in the class remembered Groves's sarcastic comments as he had handed Corman's paper back the day before.

Then, his eyes still locked on Corman's, Groves sharpened the image of the creature again, but now he changed its surroundings. Suddenly, instead of standing waiting on a forest path, it walked slowly down a familiar hallway, the hallway outside the very room they were in. It moved steadily toward the door, its feet scraping like something out of a monster movie. The few people in the hall backed away silently, so overcome by the rotten-egg odor that they could only gasp.

Then it was at the door.

Corman jerked around in his seat, and everyone else, some nervously, some puzzledly, followed suit. When the door opened and a latecomer—Harvey Taylor—burst in, everyone laughed as he scurried to his seat. Everyone but Corman, whose eyes had threatened to pop from his head as the door started to open.

All right, Groves thought, you can relax now.

As best he could, he banished all thoughts of UFO monsters from his mind.

As he watched the Corman boy's face slowly unfreeze and saw the dark patches of nervous perspiration under his arms, Groves laughed silently. The spot on his chest where the talisman rested definitely felt warm.

So this was what being a warlock was like. And it was only the beginning. Now that he had, however accidentally, stumbled across the key, there would be more, much more. This had been amusing, even somewhat gratifying, but it was basically nothing more than a simple, childish trick.

But it was a start.

"All right, class," John Groves said abruptly, "let's get down to business."

* * *

As they made their way back to the lodge, all of Winton's eighty-seven years seemed to have descended on him. Inside the lodge, he lowered himself stiffly onto the same antique sofa they had been sitting on before. He slumped back, his eyes closing.

Beth, apparently taking a break from petting B.C., came over to look at Winton. "Isn't Mr. Wilson feeling good?" she asked her mother.

"He's just tired, honey," Elena said. "Don't bother him."

The words seemed to rouse Winton and give him new energy. He opened his eyes and sat up a little straighter. He even essayed a faint smile for the girl.

"I'm all right," he said. "How are you feeling?"

"Okay, I guess. I like it here. It's a nice house, and B.C. is nice. Are you going to stay in this house, too?"

"I'm afraid not."

"That's too bad," the little girl said solemnly. "You're nice."

"Why, thank you. You're nice, too."

She studied him thoughtfully and then asked, "How old are you?"

"Beth," Elena said, but Winton's ancient face cracked in a grin.

"How old do you think I am?" he asked.

"Really old. Older than Grandma Wilma, I bet."

"And how old is Grandma Wilma?" He leaned forward. He seemed to be enjoying himself, almost as if he had forgotten what he had found outside a few minutes earlier.

"Really old. I bet she's forty. Are you more than forty?"

His smile widened. "A lot more than forty."

Beth looked awestruck. "A lot more?"

He nodded. "A whole lot more."

"Are you fifty?" She sounded as if she couldn't believe that anyone could actually be fifty and still be alive.

"More than that." He paused and then announced dramatically, "I'm eighty-seven."

The girl's eyes widened, and then she frowned. "Nobody's that old."

Winton laughed. "Not very many, that's true. But a few of us are. Don't you believe me?"

"I guess so," she said, but she didn't sound convinced.

"How old are you?"

"I'm over five."

"How much over?"

"Almost two months."

"That's pretty young."

"No, it isn't."

"I didn't think anybody was that young anymore."

"It's almost old enough to go to school. That's pretty old. And I'm old enough to read. Do you want to hear me read?"

"I don't think that's a very good idea, Beth," Elena put in.

"I could read him that 'Little Lulu' you bought me yesterday. There's one story in there about her grandpa, and I bet he's not as old as you are."

"No, Beth," Elena said with a touch of firmness in her voice that the girl recognized. "But if you want to read it to yourself, you could do that. Or did you finish it all in the car yesterday?"

Beth shook her head. "I saved part of it."

"That's good. Then you can go read it now."

"Will you get me another one when I'm done?"

"We'll find something for you."

"Okay." The girl stood back and looked around. "Maybe I'll read something to B.C.," she said as the cat, now on the registration desk, stretched and yawned. Then she was trotting across the lobby toward their room.

When Elena looked back at Winton, the slump and returned to his body, but his eyes followed Beth's retreating back.

"I'm sorry," she said. "She can be a pest sometimes, I'm afraid."

Some of his smile returned. "Not in the least. She reminds me of Nickie."

"Nickie?"

"My brother's great-grandson." He fell silent again, and the smile faded into sadness. "I hope he didn't get into trouble on my account."

"Trouble? How?"

In slow detail, as if to prolong it as long as he could, he

told her about their early-morning meeting. "And he probably ended up telling them the truth," he finished, "and they'll never understand why he didn't wake them up so they could stop me."

"Perhaps you should phone them? So they won't worry about you?"

He shook his head. "It's long distance. They'd sure as shooting be able to find out from the phone company where I called from. Edith used to work there, and a bunch of her cronies still do. Then they'd send the folks in the white coats after me. Not that I'd blame them, mind you."

"Are you going back now?"

He shook his head again and ran knobby fingers through the remaining strands of hair in a motion that suddenly reminded Elena of the same move made by the twenty-year-old in her dream. It brought the whole insane situation back into sharp focus.

"What are you going to do?" she asked. And then, reluctantly, "What are *we* going to do?"

"I don't know. I didn't think that far ahead. I just came." He grinned ruefully. "I don't even have enough money for more than a couple days."

"That's all right. I have enough."

"No, you can't—"

"Of course I can. After all, I did call you here, didn't I? I can't say that I'm glad I did, for either your sake or mine, but your leaving isn't going to help. I have a very strong feeling that I'm stuck here for the duration, no matter what."

"I know," he said quietly. "I guess I am, too." And then, just as quietly, he asked, "What about your daughter?"

She looked at him blankly for a second, but then his meaning penetrated the mental blinders she suddenly realized she had been wearing almost from the first moment Winton had appeared. A wave of weakness swept over her. What had she been thinking of? To let herself become involved in this insanity was one thing, but to endanger Beth was unthinkable.

But what could she do? Until a few hours ago, she had been able to rationalize it all away. Until a few hours ago, she might have been able to simply walk away, as she had been in the process of doing when she had come face to face with Winton.

But now retreat was impossible. Even without Winton, she would have been back, somehow, sometime. Whether or not she was truly the reincarnation of Jessica Reimann and a hundred others no longer mattered. During the time she had spent here, something had sunk its barbed hooks deep within her and would never let go. Throughout her entire life, she now realized, a link had existed, drawing her toward this place of all places, but until now she had had a choice of yielding or resisting. Until now. In a grotesque way, she thought, it was like sex. The urge, the attraction, whether strong or weak, always exists, but normally it can be resisted, is even often ignored or forgotten in the press of other things. It is always there, but it is not all-powerful. Until the sex act itself has begun. Once two bodies are locked together, there is no stopping until the release of orgasm.

And so it was with her now, except that there was no pleasure involved, no promise of orgasmic release. There was only the already unbreakable bond, the irrational magnetic power that Jessica had rationalized into her love for Marcus and a desire to save him. Even had she known how it would end—and perhaps she had—Jessica would not have been able to stay away. For Elena there was no such rationalization, but the bond, like an impossible mixture of an overwhelming curiosity and a massive guilt complex, was no less strong because of that lack.

Abruptly, Elena stood up. "I'll be back in a few minutes," she said. "I have to make a phone call."

"Someone to take care of the girl?"

"Yes. I don't see what else I can do."

He didn't disagree or try to argue.

She was through the area code and half the number itself, when she stopped dialing. Calling the farm wouldn't be a good idea. Her mother would probably answer, unless Charlie Wallace was still there, and in either case they would want to know what was wrong and why was she calling now, in the middle of the day, barely twelve hours since the last time.

Besides, her brother might not be there. Some days, when the regular carrier was sick or on vacation, he drove a mail route, and other times he worked the switchboard and radio at the Greenville police station. She would try the station first. He'd been working there more regularly lately, and even if he wasn't there, they might know whether he was on the mail route. If he was, she would just have to wait until afternoon, when he finished.

But she recognized Bill's distinctive drawl as he answered on the first ring.

"Bill, this is Ellie. Do you have a minute to talk?"

"Sure. We got two lines here, and nothing worthwhile's come in on either one all day. What's up?"

She hesitated, realizing too late that she should have taken the time to think up a logical reason for what she was going to ask. But she doubted whether she could have come up with anything, anyway, at least anything that her brother would fall for.

"Bill," she said at last, "I need a large favor."

"Anything I can do. You know that."

"Good. I'll hold you to that."

"That sounds downright ominous. What is this favor?"

"Don't worry, you'll enjoy it."

"Worse and worse. Out with it, dear sister."

"How would you like to take care of Beth for a few days?"

A brief silence, and then, "Under any other circumstances, I'd jump at the opportunity."

"But? There was very definitely a 'but' in that statement."

"But as I told you last night, I don't think it's a good idea for either one of you to be seen back here for another few days. Or am I jumping to conclusions? When did you want this baby-sitter?"

"As soon as possible. But do you really think Grantland—"

"I do. And so do his wife and lawyer. But look, what's come up that you want to give Beth to me? You're not sick or anything, are you?"

"No, nothing like that."

"Then what?"

"It's hard to explain."

"Obviously, or you would've already explained it. Is it important?"

"It's important."

A thoughtful pause, and then, "What happened? You meet a guy?"

"What?"

"You met a guy, and you want to spend some time together? Alone?"

Why hadn't she thought of that? In a way it was true, although Bill probably didn't have someone like Henry Winton in mind. "As a matter of fact," she said, "I have met someone."

"Where?"

"Right here."

"He must be a fast worker." Thoughtfulness gave way to suspicion in his voice. "Look, Sis, be careful. Okay? Do you know anything about this guy?"

"Quite a bit," she answered, improvising. "Actually, he's not that fast a worker. I knew him a long time ago, before I met Gerald. He's living out here now, and I just happened to bump into him. Really a wild coincidence." She cut herself off sharply, realizing that as always, her nervousness was making her chatter.

"Okay, I understand, Sis. But I don't think, right this minute, it would be the best thing for Beth to come back here, not with Grantland still frothing at the mouth the way he is."

"Actually, that wasn't what I had in mind, anyway."

"No? What, then?"

"I thought maybe you could come out here and take her somewhere for a day or three. You know, down to New York or something like—"

"Now hold on a minute. Hold on. In the first place, I'm not sure I could take the time off, and in the second, that sounds kind of expensive."

"My treat. Don't forget, Grantland is paying for my trip, so he might as well pay for yours, too."

"But you'll need—"

"I'll have plenty of money left when this is over, don't worry. A few hundred for plane fare and car rental isn't going to break me. Besides, you deserve a vacation. When's the last time you had one? You've been working three jobs the last year or two, and that's too much, even if they are only part-time."

"So now it's all for my own good, huh?"

"I didn't say that. Look, to be perfectly honest, traveling with a five-year-old, even a comparative sweetheart like Beth, can be a bit wearing. Besides, you know how she likes you. It'll be good for all of us."

He was silent for several seconds, and when he spoke again, the bantering edge was gone from his voice. "All right," he said, "I'll come out. I suppose I can get a flight out of Indianapolis in the morning. Is that soon enough?"

"Don't be sarcastic. Of course it is."

"All right, in the morning. What's the nearest city with an airport?"

"Probably Albany. At least that's the last large town I remember. Should have pretty good service. It's the state capital. Can't be more than fifty or a hundred miles from here."

"Okay, I can figure all that out later. And I shouldn't have any trouble finding this place you're staying at once I find Wertham, should I?"

"No. You can probably ask anyone in town where Groves Lodge, or the old Reimann place, is. That's what a lot the old-timers still call it."

"Okay. Like I said, I'll be there tomorrow sometime, and we'll work something out. Meanwhile, do you have any suggestions as to what I should tell Mom?"

She grimaced. "None, I'm afraid."

"I didn't think so. Oh, well, I'll come up with something. Seminar for police radio operators or mail carriers or something. See you tomorrow, Sis."

So it's done, she thought as she hung up, but she wasn't out of the woods yet. Although he hadn't said it, part of her brother's reason for agreeing to come was, she was sure, to check up on her and probably on the imaginary boy friend.

Bill was a couple of years younger than Elena's twenty-nine and was still a bachelor, but he was also something of a mother hen to her, and to their mother, for that matter.

For a moment she wished she could tell him the truth or that what she had already told him was the truth. But it wasn't, and there was no way she could tell him or anyone else what was really happening. Sighing resignedly, she raised herself from the sofa next to the phone and made her way back to the lobby and to Henry Winton, the only person to whom she dared speak the whole truth.

John Groves shivered as he stepped out of the high school and stood on the broad concrete steps that led down to the sidewalk. The clouds and fog of the morning had given way to a sky of cobalt blue dotted with high, fast-moving clouds. A cold, dry wind bit through his jacket and stripped the last of the leaves from the trees and sent them whipping along the streets and sidewalks.

But it wasn't entirely the wind that prompted the shiver.

It was the talisman.

Since the encounter with the Corman boy that morning, Groves had gradually developed a sense of what he was and was not able to do, and some of it was more than a little unnerving, far more unsettling than he had thought it would be. For weeks he had dreamed and fantasized about such things, but the reality was vastly different from what the dreams had promised.

The ability he had stumbled onto when he had realized he was looking into the Corman boy's mind, for instance, was one he had literally lusted after, but now that he was actually able to glimpse certain people's surface thoughts and even influence those thoughts, the whole thing made him uneasy. What was worse, he couldn't think of any reason for the uneasiness, and that made him more uneasy. It was as if, in the clichéd tradition of Faust and all the others who had made deals with various devils, Groves feared the future, feared that it did not hold what it logically should hold for someone with the kind of advantage the talisman provided.

Even the thought of healing disturbed him, although for

this there were more logical reasons. For one thing, the thought of meddling with the internal workings of another human body bothered him, which was not surprising, considering his profound lack of knowledge in that area. For another, he didn't have the faintest idea how to go about it, and if it weren't for the fact that the stories about the Reimanns included tales of healings, he would not even have thought of it as being in his warlock repertoire. And finally, the last thing he wanted to do was go public, which he would almost inevitably have to do if he was to heal anyone. His guilty thoughts had gone at least a dozen times to Herb Franklin, the man whose sudden relapse last summer had resulted in the opening that had allowed Groves to be hired at the school, but still he had not been able to convince himself that he should try, despite the fact that the man was in the hospital, constantly on oxygen, his only hope a heart transplant or a miracle.

The most unnerving faculty of all, however, was his apparent ability to literally leave his own body. He hadn't dared try it except for a few brief moments during a free period in the faculty lounge, but even those moments were enough to frighten him thoroughly. For one thing, the sensation it produced was so eerie and unsettling that it almost paralyzed him. The very air around him seemed to thicken and grow cold as he emerged from his body, and the light, although at least as bright as before, seemed utterly different. It was a sourceless and shadowless glow that gave no heat but seemed instead to absorb warmth from its surroundings like a glowing sponge. The outlines of physical objects—except for living things—seemed indistinct, as if photographed through gauze, which only added to the impression of thickness and heaviness in the air. Worse, though, was the subtle but unmistakable feeling that he was not alone, that unseen eyes watched his every move. Perhaps, his paranoid thoughts told him, the beings behind those eyes were waiting for him to move too far from his physical body, leaving it unprotected and vulnerable. But there was also the fear of becoming lost, of wandering into totally unknown areas and being unable to find his way back. For just as he had the feeling that someone or something watched unseen, he had the even stronger feeling that there existed a place—a place outside the normal space-time continuum, a dimension unknown and unseen—from which it watched. A place into which he, divorced as he was from his physical body and the physical world of which it was a part, could stumble unawares at any instant and find himself lost or trapped, unable to find his way back to his own uninhabited body.

For at least a full minute he stood on the steps outside the school. It was after four, and except for Willy Overstreet, the janitor, he was the last to leave; he wondered at the way he seemed to be purposely delaying. He had been impatiently looking forward to the freedom the end of the day would bring, but now that it was here, he was becoming hesitant and unsure.

The reason, he suddenly realized, was that he was afraid, not for himself but for Mattie. Whatever it was that was watching him—and he felt sure that it was frighteningly real and not just the result of his own hyperactive imagination—was not watching him for the first time. It had never been this close before, but it had been nearby ever since they had moved into the lodge.

It had been the closest two nights before, when he had almost attacked his own wife. The incident had seemed at the time to be only the result of his pent-up anger finally being released, but he knew now that it was more than that. And whatever it was, it had influenced him, had prodded and guided his angry thoughts, building and stoking the fire within him until it had exploded. It had influenced him, just as he had influenced the Corman boy and a half dozen others today.

Even his anger at his students and at nearly everyone he had met or worked with the last three months was somehow related to this same thing, to this unseen watcher. It had to be.

And the watcher, in turn, had to be somehow related to the talisman.

The thought that the talisman should simply be destroyed crossed his mind, but he thrust it away instantly. No matter how uncomfortable it made him, it would be sheer idiocy to even try. It would be like throwing away a million dollars he'd found in the street because having that much money made him nervous or because he was afraid that whoever lost it would come looking for him with a gun. No, he would just have to be careful, that was all, careful how he used it and careful not to let it use him.

Besides, he had the distinct feeling that he would never be allowed to destroy it.

Grimacing at his own mental dithering, Groves felt some of the anger he had so often directed against others now turning inward against himself. Cursing silently, he hurried down the steps and around to the parking lot at the side of the building.

His car, a beginning-to-rust, five-year-old Ford, started easily, but as he pulled out onto Fifth and headed east, he noticed with annoyance that the gas gauge read just short of empty. There might be enough to make it to the lodge and back, but there might not, and he was reasonably sure that his warlock repertoire did not include spells to bewitch cars into running without gas. If it did, he might really have something.

At Main, he turned left and headed for Jake Lowman's station at the north edge of Wertham. It was slightly more expensive than the self-service station on South Main, but Jake, something of a rarity these days, always checked everything under the hood and even did a fairly conscientious job with the windshield.

But Jake wasn't there. It was Curt Weber, one of the lesser lights from Wertham High. Weber was not, thank God, in any of Groves's classes, and from what he'd heard, it was unlikely that he'd be in anyone's classes much longer. He had turned sixteen during the summer, and only a lot of pressure from his parents had kept him from dropping out already. The boy looked resentful, of course, when Groves, after telling him to fill the tank with regular, reminded him to check the oil and do the windshield.

Weber had grumped through the services and was taking Groves's money, when a Cadillac drove in and pulled up on the opposite side of the pumps.

Suddenly, from out of nowhere, an intense feeling of elation swept through Groves. It was as if his entire body went through a brief orgasm, but an instant later it was gone, leaving him shaking and unsteady.

He had, he noticed belatedly, dropped some of the change the Weber boy had been handing back to him, and now the boy was glaring at him before stiffly leaning down to retrieve the coins from the ground. Blinking, Groves shook his head and shifted his entire body in the seat, tensing his muscles and working his shoulders in an effort to get rid of the residual tingling that still blanketed his back.

Then he saw the driver of the Cadillac. He was, as far as Groves could tell, a complete stranger. He was middle-aged, probably in his late forties, with light brown hair and a beard speckled with gray. The man scowled impatiently as he watched the attendant reach under Groves's car for some of the errant change.

Then his eyes met Groves's, and the annoyance in the other driver's face vanished. His eyes widened, and his lips parted almost imperceptibly. He drew back, seeming almost to shrink physically. For interminable seconds, their eyes were locked together, and the same senseless feeling of elation began building inside Groves again.

Abruptly, the man looked away, and a second later his engine purred to life. Without a backward glance, he pulled out, tires squealing and the car rocking on its expensive springs.

At the sound, the Weber boy jerked upright and spun toward the departing car, raising his hand in a "wait-a-minute" gesture. When the Cadillac didn't pause, he turned back to Groves, scowled angrily, and slapped the change—not quite all that had been dropped—into his hand.

But Groves did not climb out to look for the missing coins or snap at the boy to find them for him. Instead, he dropped the coins on his lap and found himself reaching for the ignition. He tried to stop the motion, tried to reach for the coins before they slid between his legs and onto the seat or the floor, but he couldn't.

His fingers twisted the key. The engine caught, roaring briefly as his foot twitched down on the accelerator. Out of the corner of his eye he saw the attendant jump backward onto the raised pump island, but his eyes were following the Cadillac as it pulled into the luckily sparse traffic.

Putting the Ford in gear, Groves shot onto the street no more than fifty yards behind the Cadillac, which was already well over the in-town speed limit.

Now just a goddamn minute, Groves thought with a mixture of anger and sudden terror. What the hell is going on? He tried to take one hand from the wheel and reach for the key to shut off the ignition, but he could not.

Swerving erratically, Groves passed a battered pickup truck, and then he was directly behind the Cadillac, pulling rapidly closer. Both cars bounced across the railroad tracks just beyond the city limits and followed the highway as it curved sharply to the right and then back to the left. The intersection with the bypass was a mile or less north, and if the Cadillac was still moving with the same reckless abandon then . . .

Groves shivered and renewed his efforts to stop the car, but still he could not.

Then, as the road twisted and wound and the oncoming traffic thickened, the Cadillac slowed, blocked by a slower-moving car. The Cadillac swerved to the right, as if about to try passing on the shoulder, but when the wheels almost slid off into the deepening ditch, the car lurched back onto the highway, and the horn began to blare as the driver shouted wordlessly for the right of way.

For a moment it seemed that Groves was going to smash into the trunk of the other car, but at the last second his foot jerked from the accelerator to the brake and then, as their speeds matched, back to the accelerator. Only yards now separated the cars, and Groves was bathed in a cold sweat, his heart pounding, a scream bubbling up in his constricted throat.

Suddenly the horn fell silent.

The road made one final curve; ahead lay the intersection with the bypass. Just short of that intersection was a smaller road of pockmarked blacktop. After a mile or two, Groves knew, it changed to gravel as it wound further up into the hills that surrounded Wertham. A hundred years before, there had been a small town somewhere in those hills; it had long since died and been abandoned, but the road remained. It was never used by locals, since it led nowhere that could not be reached more easily by other routes. Its only use was by occasional tourists who liked to explore odd byways. There was nothing left to see of the town but a sea of weeds and trees, unlike the abandoned mining towns in the West, where sections of rotting buildings still stood.

The Cadillac slowed, although its brake lights did not flare on until it was almost even with the other road. It skidded into the turn and, less than a car length behind, the Ford followed.

Once again Groves tried to stop the car, but he could not. This time there was a dull twinge of pain at the back of his head, but it went almost unnoticed as his heart continued pounding so loudly that he could almost hear it. A scream remained locked behind the iron-tense muscles of his throat.

All the while, unbidden and inexplicable, the feeling of an orgasmic elation had been growing once again deep within his body. Despite the terror that held him in its grip, the elation had been growing steadily as well, the two mounting side by side toward some impossible climax. It was, he realized, much like the dreams, but vastly more intense, more real. It was as if he were a passenger in his own body, experiencing both the emotions of whoever or whatever controlled it and the terror of the helpless passenger.

Ahead of him, the Cadillac slowed even more, and then it pulled off to the side of the narrow road, its right wheels slipping into the ditch. With a lurch, it stopped, and its underside scraped the rounded edges of the ditch. Groves coasted to a stop next to it.

The door of the Cadillac opened slowly, and the bearded driver climbed out. His face was pale and his eyes wide. The brisk wind blew his hair and pulled at his unbuttoned suit jacket. Fallen leaves crackled as he took the few slow steps from his car to the Ford. He stood for a good thirty seconds, and Groves could see his hand trembling where it hovered inches from the door handle.

Finally, the man got in, dropping limply into the seat. He looked straight ahead, as if purposely avoiding the sight of Groves.

With a lurch, the Ford pulled away.

Finally, in the relative silence that followed, Groves felt for the first time the almost uncomfortable warmth that was bathing his chest, the warmth that radiated out from the spot on which the talisman rested.

It was nearly six when Elena and Beth returned to the lodge from an afternoon of aimless but scenic driving. Beth, elated but impatient ever since her mother had told her that she would be able to spend a day or two with her Uncle Bill, had been on her best behavior most of the day. Elena had even, on occasion, been able to put out of her mind the reason why her brother was coming. She had talked only briefly with Winton after the phone call to Bill, and they had agreed to wait until Beth was safely away before attempting, or even seriously planning, anything. They would simply get through the next twenty-four hours as quietly as they could and hope that whatever it was that had brought them here would not become impatient.

As Elena and Beth entered the lobby, Mattie appeared at the mouth of the hallway. She slumped slightly when she saw them, but then she straightened and came toward them.

"Mr. Wilson said to tell you he went into town to do a little shopping before the clothing stores closed," she said. "He should be back any minute." A worried frown crossed her face. "I do hope he's going to be all right. He looked so exhausted this morning, and so old. Did he tell you how old he is?"

"Eighty-seven," Elena said.

Mattie pursed her lips in a silent whistle. "I wonder what he's doing here. He didn't tell you, did he? He was awfully closed-mouthed with me."

"He didn't tell me, either," Elena answered, lying.

"Seems kind of strange he didn't have any extra clothes with him or anything." Mattie leaned closer. "You don't suppose he's running away or something like that, do you? I mean, I've heard of old people doing that, just like kids. Did he seem all right to you? You know, in possession of all his faculties?"

Elena nodded. "I'm sure he's all right," she said.

"He's nice," Beth chimed in, and then hurried on once she had gotten a word in. "My Uncle Bill is coming to see me in the morning."

Before anyone was required to answer, the sound of a car on the gravel of the parking area filtered in. Mattie hurried to the window behind the registration desk and peered out. After a second of squinting into the growing twilight, she slumped and turned back.

"It's Mr. Wilson," she said with disappointment in her voice as well as in her posture.

"Is something wrong?" Elena asked.

Mattie shrugged and glanced at her watch. "Just that it's almost time for supper, and John isn't home from school yet."

"What time does he usually get here?"

"Rarely later than five," she said, but then she shrugged again. "Unless there's a faculty meeting. But he always tells me about that, and they've never run this late, anyway."

Something in Elena's stomach twitched. Although neither she nor Winton had spoken of it, she had little doubt that it was Groves who had dug up the grave. He had seemed relatively normal, though a little nervous, that morning, but he had to be the one.

Now he was missing.

Had she missed her chance? Had he simply left this morning, never to come back? For a moment, she couldn't help but feel relieved. If he was gone, then the thing—the talisman— was gone as well, and she would not have to face up to it once again.

She would not have to die as she had, in those insane visions, already died a hundred times before.

But no, it was not going to be that simple. Of that she was sure. She had not been drawn here, to this place, at this time, for it to end so simply.

"Have you called the school?" Elena asked. "Maybe he's been held up."

"I called a half hour ago," Mattie said. "No answer."

"He probably just stopped for a beer or something. Husbands do that I've been told."

Mattie shook her head, but then she sighed. "He never used to, but you could be right." She seemed about to confide something more, but she hesitated, and then it was too late.

"Did I hear something about supper?" A new voice made Elena spin around.

A stranger, a balding man in his fifties, slightly overweight and round-faced, was emerging from the hallway leading to Elena's room and the Groves family's living quarters. He was wearing gray slacks and a dark jacket over a dark, open-collared sport shirt.

"It'll be a few minutes, Mr. Jessup," Mattie said, fastening a hospitable smile on her face. "But as long as you're here, I'll introduce you. Pete, I think you said? Pete Jessup, these are two of our other guests, Elena March and her daughter, Beth. They're in the room two doors down the hall from you."

"Pleased to meet you, Ms. March. Ms. Groves here said you were from Indiana, too. Actually, I spied it out on the register when I signed in myself." His voice had a Southern drawl, more like Kentucky than Indiana, Elena thought. She put out her hand.

"Nice to meet you, too, Mr. Jessup. What part of the state are you from?"

"Indianapolis the last few years. Down around Madison before that," he said, confirming her guess about the drawl being from closer to Kentucky than to Indiana. "That town you're from, Greenville—that's not far from Indianapolis, is it?" He gave her hand a two-handed, slightly sweaty squeeze before releasing it.

"Not far," she said. "Thirty or forty miles."

"Thought so. Been through there a few times myself. Nice little place, real nice. But not as nice as it is around here," he added, bestowing a toothy smile on Mattie. "Lovely place you have here. Used to stay at places like this all the time, years and years ago, but they don't hardly exist anymore, I'm sad to report. So much nicer than all those plastic motels, don't you think?"

Then, before anyone could reply, he turned to Beth and leaned down. "And you, young lady, how do you like it?"

"It's nice," Beth said promptly, happy to be consulted. "It's a house."

Jessup laughed. "You bet it's a house. That's what's so nice about it. You know, Beth, I've got a niece just like you back in Indiana. I bet you'd like her."

"I've got an Uncle Bill back home in Indiana," she said. "Do you know him?"

"I don't think so. What's the rest of his name?"

"The same as mine," she said. "He's coming to see me tomorrow. He's going to take me—" She stopped and looked up at her mother. "Where is Uncle Bill taking me, Mommy?"

"I don't know yet. We'll talk about it when he gets here."

While Beth was thinking that over, Elena heard the outside door of the lodge opening and heard the buzzer announcing it coming distantly from the living quarters in the opposite direction. A moment later, Henry Winton's scarecrowlike figure pushed through the inner door, paper sacks in both hands. Beth ran to greet him.

"I can carry that," she said, pointing at one of the sacks. "What is it?"

The old man smiled. "Mostly clothes."

"What kind? Can I see?"

"Beth!" Elena said, hurrying over apologetically. "I'm sorry, Mr. Win— Wilson, but she's used to helping me take things out of bags whenever we come back from a store."

"That's all right," Winton said, still smiling.

"Is there anything for me?" Beth asked, persisting.

"As a matter of fact, there is," Winton said. Handing her the smaller bag, he reached into the larger and pulled out a comic book. "It's even got another story about the old geezer like me that you like."

"Thank you," Beth said, grabbing the comic book in her free hand.

"You're very welcome," he said, taking the other sack back from her. He looked questioningly at Elena. "You don't mind I got it for her?"

"Not at all. I was going to have to find something new for her fairly soon, anyway." She looked down at the girl. "Now, Beth, why don't you take that to our room. You can look at it later. Supper will be ready in a few minutes, and you have to do a little washing up."

Beth seemed to think about her mother's proposal solemnly for a second or two. "Okay," she said, and, clutching the comic book, headed toward the room at a fast trot.

"Lovely child," Jessup said. "Just lovely. You seem to have quite a rapport with her. Not like a lot of young people today."

"We get along pretty well," Elena said. The man's words made her unaccountably uneasy.

"Yes, Yes, I can see that," Jessup said, his eyes following the girl as she disappeared in the hallway. Abruptly he turned back to the others, but he seemed to be looking past them, not at them. Pushing back his jacket sleeve, he looked at his watch.

"Excuse me," he said, "but I have an errand to run. It won't take long. I'll try to be back in time for supper."

Pete Jessup, sweating despite the dry chill in the air, stopped at the first pay phone he came to, just a block from the courthouse square. Most of the town's retail stores seemed to have closed, and so he had no trouble parking within a few yards of the phone booth.

Doing his best to keep the butterflies in his stomach subdued, he dialed the operator and gave her the name and number for his collect, person-to-person call. Once the operator dialed it, the answer was almost instantaneous.

"Yes, I'll accept the charges," the voice snapped before the operator had finished asking. "Just put him on."

"Mr. Grantland?" Jessup began.

"Of course this is Grantland. Are you deaf? Well? What's the situation?"

"The girl and her mother are at the lodge, just as we thought. I've taken a room there myself."

"Good, good. How soon do you intend to conclude this matter?"

Jessup hesitated, feeling his stomach knot even more tightly. "I don't know," he said. "A day or two if I'm lucky."

"A day or two?" Grantland's voice was a mixture of anger and disbelief.

"It's not going to be easy," Jessup said hastily. "Or legal. Don't forget that!"

"I'm not likely to. You whine about it every time I turn around. But don't you forget who's paying your bills! Now I want you on your way back here tomorrow. With the girl! Do you understand?"

"I'm sorry, but that's impossible. It will take two days at the very least."

"Jessup, you listen to me! You—"

"No, you listen to me for a change! This isn't a piece of furniture I'm stealing for you! This is a child! A human being! I have to get to know her, let her get to know me. If I grabbed her now, she'd be scared to death. Do you want that? Do you want her screaming her head off the whole way back? Do you want her scared to death of me—and of you? Is that what you want?"

There was a brief silence, and then: "All right, Jessup, do it your way. But don't waste any time, and don't let her get away from you again."

"I won't."

"And keep me informed, damn it. Keep me informed."

"Yes, sir."

The line went dead, and the sounds of the town around him began to filter into the silence: a car idling at the stoplight a dozen yards away, a woman's heels clicking as she came down the broad steps of the courthouse, a couple of boys laughing at nothing as they darted across the street in midblock, the dry, chilly wind whistling softly through the narrow opening where the phone booth door didn't quite shut.

Finally, he replaced the metal-cabled receiver and made his way back to his rented car. He had bought some time, but not much. A day, two at the most, and then Grantland would—

Would what? Fire him? If that were all Grantland could do, Jessup would never have made the trip in the first place. But Grantland could do much more. He could very probably drive Jessup out of business, and he could certainly find someone else to do anything Jessup might refuse to do. Someone who wouldn't think twice about snatching the girl, any time and any place, someone who wouldn't worry about the effect on the girl, only about the effect of Grantland's fee on his own pocket.

Grimly, Jessup slid behind the wheel and started the motor. He was going to have to do something and do it soon. But what? He had hoped, before actually seeing the girl and her mother, that Grantland's wild story about the girl being kidnaped and taken out of the state actually had a grain of truth in it, but it was obvious that it didn't. Not only did the girl legally belong with her mother, she obviously wanted to be with her mother. Not all of Grandland's money and stubbornness could change that.

Yes, he was going to have to do something soon, and no matter what it turned out to be, it would be wrong for someone.

With John Groves still missing, supper was an uneasy affair for everyone but Beth, who filled the frequent silences with everything from how many words she could read to how much she liked B.C. and how much fun she had with the animals and everything when she visited Uncle Bill and Gramma Wilma. Since the newcomer Jessup seemed willing, even eager, to listen to everything she had to say, she was wound up even more than she had been with Winton earlier in the day. Mattie probably heard very little, since hardly a minute went by that some sound, whether a car on the road or a plane overhead or an unidentified creak somewhere in the lodge, didn't make her turn her head and listen more carefully or dart to the window to peer hopefully toward the parking area.

Elena found herself hoping more eagerly every minute that Groves would simply stay away, that his disappearance would remain permanent, not only for her own good but, she rationalized, for Mattie's as well. Whatever the talisman did to people who possessed it—or were possessed by it—was not good. What had happened to Marcus Reimann was ample evidence of that, as were the dozens of other nightmarish visions of her own death.

No, if he was gone, taking the talisman with him, it would be better for her and for Mattie, immeasurably better.

Shortly after supper, Mattie began calling the other teachers at the school, but no one had seen John since the end of the last period, nor had anyone heard him mention any plans for after school. Corie Sideman, a freshman math teacher, said that she had seen him in the teachers' lounge not long after lunch, "looking really out of it, if you know what I mean," but he hadn't said anything to her. "Probably just daydreaming," the woman said, "and I can't say that I blame him, not with his lineup of classes."

She even called Dr. Laird, but he had not seen Groves since leaving the lodge after checking Elena over the night before. When she mentioned that Elena had decided to stay over another day or two, he sounded annoyed but said nothing to indicate why.

Then, not long after eight, when she had run out of numbers to call, Mattie contacted the police. From their tone and their questions— "Have you had any arguments with your husband lately?" "Is this the first time he's ever stayed out late without telling you?"—it was obvious that they weren't taking her seriously. At worst, they seemed to be saying, he was out getting drunk or seeing another woman or both.

"We'll put his license number out with our patrols, Mrs. Groves, and pass it on to the sheriff's office and the state patrol," the man said patiently, "but that's really all we can do at this point. Give us another call if he isn't back by morning."

The first thing John Groves did when his body was at last released was become violently ill. In a matter of seconds, cold sweat literally drenched every inch of his body, and his muscles turned to quivering jelly. Staggering backward in the near darkness, he thudded against the rough bark of an oak and was able for a moment to support himself against its trunk. But then even that was impossible, and he slid jerkily down onto the crackling bed of fallen leaves.

All the while, the lump of nausea that was his stomach churned ever more violently until, in a spasm that he thought must tear the lining from his throat, everything gushed out like a burning, putrid fountain. He had fallen on his side, unable even to stay on his hands and knees, and the foul-smelling near liquid hit the ground only inches from his face, soaking the leaves and spattering on his face and clothes. Long after his stomach was empty, it continued to convulse, propelling upward only tiny, fiery specks of acid that burned at his throat and trickled from the corner of his mouth.

Finally, it was over.

Slowly, the chilly night air dried the sweat that had at last stopped forming, and his trembling turned to shivering. Still on his side, he tried to roll backward, away from the smell, but he couldn't. His back was against the trunk of the oak.

Gradually, as he sucked in one open-mouthed breath after another despite the odor, the weakness lessened, and he felt that he might be able to move. His right arm, doubled under him, tingled as he raised himself. Finally he was on his feet, leaning heavily against the tree once again, his legs trembling under his own weight.

But at last they steadied, and he was able to push away and stand unsupported.

For an instant he thought: A nightmare. It had to be another nightmare.

But then, in the faint moonlight that filtered down from a still cloudless sky, he saw the body, or what was left of it.

It had been stripped—had stripped itself—at the start. Hardly an inch of undamaged skin or flesh still existed. Cuts and gouges and tears were everywhere, as if it had been mauled by a wild animal. Nails were torn from fingers and toes. Flaps of flesh were peeled back. Bones were twisted and snapped. Glistening ropes of intestines spilled out of the abdominal cavity onto the ground.

He had seen a photo of an autopsy in progress once, and this was worse.

But what was most horrible of all, what had caused the sudden and violent illness, was the knowledge that until only minutes ago, that body had been alive.

Through it all, it had been alive. And conscious, fully conscious.

It had been kept alive and aware.

Something had kept it alive.

Something had fed on the pain and terror, like a vampire

that took its sustenance not from the blood of living creatures but from their violent emotions, from their impossibly protracted death throes.

Something . . .

Groves's fingers touched the talisman where it still hung, nestled inside his soiled shirt on the slim chain. It was still warm but not as warm as it had been minutes before.

His fingers closed around it. The chain bit into the back of his neck as he tugged.

But then he stopped. The same feeling that had stopped him that morning from handing it over to the jeweler, even for a minute, stopped him again, almost paralyzing him.

He strained to pull the talisman free, but the pressure of the chain against his neck grew lighter rather than heavier.

Finally, he dropped his hands to his sides.

But it was no surprise, this inability to make his hands obey his will. Whatever power had controlled him the last three or four hours still held him in its grip. And stopping him from ripping the talisman from his neck had to be childishly easy compared with forcing him to do what he had already done to that nameless stranger whose body littered the ground before him.

Very, very easy . . .

Taking a handkerchief from his pocket, he wiped the blood and vomit from his hands and face and beard and removed what he could from his clothes. Slowly, he made his way out of the thickly wooded, desolate area and back to his car.

With not one but two grown-ups seemingly willing to listen to whatever she had to say, Beth was in seventh heaven for most of the evening. She seemed to prefer Winton's straightforward, treat-her-as-an-equal manner to Jessup's often forced joviality, however. When Winton, understandably exhausted after his ordeal of the last two days, retired to his room, Beth decided that she was ready for bed, too, provided that she could take B.C. with her and leave the light on for a few minutes so that she could read part of the comic book Winton had given her. After that, Jessup made nervous small talk with Mattie and Elena for a few minutes. He even volunteered to drive around the town looking for Groves's car, but nothing came of his offer, and soon he made his excuses and returned to his room to do a little reading.

Elena, still hoping for the sake of all concerned that John Groves had disappeared for good, did a couple of loads of laundry in the basement washer and dryer and, between dashes to the basement, kept Mattie company while they both pretended to watch a movie on the TV set in the living room. As before, every sound, no matter how faint or unlikely, pulled Mattie from her chair to the window that looked out on the parking area.

Strangely, however, when Groves did finally arrive a few minutes after ten, Mattie didn't seem to notice. She had just returned from her hundredth trip to peer out the window, when the unmistakable sound of a car crunching to a stop on the gravel came through a dozen times louder and clearer than the last vague rumble that had pulled her from her chair.

And yet she didn't move. This one time she remained seated, her eyes watching but probably not seeing the tiny figures go through their motions on the TV screen.

Elena started to rise herself, but instead she remained seated, watching not the screen but Mattie.

First there was the sound of a car door closing, and still Mattie remained motionless. Then, faint and muffled, the front door of the lodge opening and closing, accompanied by the buzzer in some other part of the living quarters. And finally, footsteps in the hall, moving quickly past the room they were in and into another room farther on, presumably the bedroom.

Slowly, as if afraid any sudden motion might break whatever spell Mattie was under, Elena stood up and walked to the window. Parting the curtains and shading her eyes against the reflected light from the table lamp at the end of the couch, she saw that Groves's car was indeed in the parking area, almost out of sight beyond Jessup's much newer rental car.

She turned back to Mattie.

"I think he's back," Elena said as she looked down at the other woman.

There was no response.

Elena thought: He is doing this. If I had the least doubt that he was the one who dug up the grave and found the talisman, this removes that doubt.

And the words, the guttural, throat-wrenching sounds that had filled those nightmare visions of her own recurrent death, began to form in her mind. From somewhere deep within her, like a long-forgotten memory seeping to the surface, the sounds slowly emerged, and she felt her lips parting silently, felt her tongue contorting ghostlike around the alien sounds that bubbled through her mind.

Then the footsteps came again, and without thinking, Elena crossed the room and snatched open the hall door.

In the hall, crossing to the kitchen, was John Groves. He wore hastily donned jeans and a sweatshirt and carried a bundle of other clothes wadded under his arm. Even in the dim light of the hallway, his face looked haggard and pale behind the beard; his blond hair was specked with dirt.

For a moment he stopped, his eyes widening in surprise, and then he hurried on, pushing through the door to the kitchen and disappearing. She heard him cross the linoleum and open the door on the opposite side of the kitchen, the door she had already taken a half dozen times that evening to the basement.

The desire to run, to snatch Beth in her arms and dash to the car, not even taking the time to pack, was almost overwhelming, but she could not do it. It was too late for that. It had been too late to run since the moment her eyes had met those of Henry Winton.

But it was also too soon to begin whatever it was she had been drawn here to do. Although the urge was there, although the senseless sounds of the incantation still strained in her mind, she could not begin, would not begin, until Beth was safely out of harm's way.

Until then, until Bill took her with him tomorrow, she must wait. She must survive and wait.

Closing the door to the living room, she took a last look at Mattie, now slumping back in the chair and beginning to doze, her breathing regular and untroubled, her face expressionless. Shivering, Elena hurried down the hall to her own room before Groves returned from the basement. From Winton's room across the hall, she heard the old man moaning softly in his sleep.

John Groves emerged from the shower after nearly thirty steaming minutes. He felt better, but he didn't think he would ever feel totally clean again. No matter how hard he scrubbed, the feel of the blood and torn flesh on his skin and under his nails would not go away. Like the phantom pain from an amputated limb, it remained long after the cause was removed.

WIth renewed energy, almost in a frenzy, he toweled himself dry, turning the skin on his arms and legs and torso even redder than the near-scalding water had already done.

But it didn't help. Nothing would help except the one thing he was apparently unable to do—rid himself of the talisman.

Moving out of the bathroom and into the bedroom, he found a pair of pajamas in the bureau and put them on. In the next room, he knew, Mattie still sat, dozing. He would have to release her soon. He had intended only to keep her from confronting him until he had a chance to dispose of the soiled clothing and hastily clean his hands and face, a few minutes at the most.

But now it had dragged on for nearly an hour.

Pulling on a robe, the same faded relic Mattie had given him the year they were married, almost a decade before, he walked slowly into the hall. The other rooms were silent. The only light was a sliver from the bedroom door behind him and the indirect glow that filtered back from the bulb over the registration desk in the lobby.

With his hand on the knob to the living room, he stopped.

Faintly, the voice of one of the Albany station weathercasters filtered through, but the individual words were lost. For a minute, then two, he stood motionless, dreading the moment when he must enter and release her. What would she think? Was there any way he could obliterate this entire evening from her memory?

From his own memory?

Shuddering as the bloody images flooded through his mind once again, he clamped his eyes tightly shut in a futile attempt to block them out.

Had it been only this morning that he had been, like a child with a new toy, eagerly but nervously looking forward to getting the hang of the warlock business? It seemed like a thousand years ago, another lifetime altogether, just as that other, normal life before they had come to this place seemed yet another lifetime distant.

A lifetime distant and now totally beyond reach.

Steeling himself, he opened the door and, simultaneously, released his hold on his wife.

But nothing happened. She remained motionless except for the slow rhythm of her breathing. Her head was tilted back and to one side, resting against the back of the chair. Her arms had fallen from the arms of the chair, one lying in her lap and the other dangling toward the floor. Her lips were slightly parted, and with each breath came a faint, whistling whisper of a snore. A few strands of her almost-black hair had come loose from the bun she normally wore and strayed forward across her slender face, which looked younger than ever in this state of total relaxation.

Then a new fear stabbed at him, driving the mental agonies of a moment before from his mind. In controlling her this way, in making use of this power that he couldn't even begin to understand, could he have injured her? Had the simple command to sleep done more than he had intended, interfered with the workings of her mind in some way so that now she was unable to awaken?

Closing the door hastily behind him, he crossed the dozen feet to her chair. Leaning over her, he touched her cheek lightly and tentatively.

"Mattie?"

She stiffened, coming awake abruptly. Her head jerked erect, bringing a grimace of pain as her neck, its muscles cramped from holding one lopsided position for nearly an hour, straightened. For an instant, her blue-green eyes were unfocused, her expression blanker than it had been in sleep.

Then she blinked and gave her head a shake that was a little more than a violent shiver. The hand that dangled over the arm of the chair twitched and jerked up as if pulled by a clumsy puppeteer and then dropped onto the chair arm and closed on it.

Finally, the eyes seemed to focus, first on the TV screen directly in front of her and then, dartingly, on his face.

"John?" Her voice was shaky, too. "What time is it?"

"A little after eleven," he said. He put his hand on her shoulder and felt it twitch beneath his touch. "Are you all right?"

"I think so." She shook her head again in an effort to clear it. "How long have you been here?"

"I came in an hour or so ago," he said. "You were sleeping so peacefully, I didn't want to disturb you."

"Where were you all evening?" Her voice was normal now, beginning to sound angry. "I was worried sick. Why didn't you call?"

Silently, he breathed a sigh of relief. She was all right. "I'm sorry," he said. "I should have called, I know, but I just didn't think."

"But where were you? I called everyone I could think of at school. I even called the police."

He shook his head. "I'm sorry, I really am. I was just driving around, trying to sort things out in my head. You know, all the problems we've been having since we moved here."

"I know, but for half the night?"

He manufactured what he hoped was a sheepish grin. "I stopped at one of those little roadside parks, you know the type. And I fell asleep, like you did just now in front of the TV set. I guess the fact that I got only three or four hours of sleep last night caught up with me. Anyway, the next thing I knew, it was almost ten."

For a long time she sat looking up at him, as if trying to get her thoughts straight but not quite able to manage. Finally, she glanced at the flickering TV set, now droning through the sports news. Gripping the arms of the chair tightly, she stood up.

"It looks like we could both use some rest," she said, snapping off the set.

He watched as she eased past him to the hall.

As she left, as he heard the door to the bedroom a few yards away click shut behind her, the bloody memories of the last few hours surfaced once again, wrenching at his stomach.

He thought: If I did it once, what is to keep me from doing it again? If I can be forced to torture and kill a stranger, someone I never laid eyes on before, then what is there to keep me from doing the same to a friend?

To a wife?

Shivering, fearing that he could never trust himself again, he sat down in the chair Mattie had just left. The warmth of her body remained in its cushions, but that only made the shivering worse.

Day Four

Elena's eyes opened.

For a moment, just a moment, she wondered where she was, but the thought slid quickly away into the darkness and was gone.

Slowly, she rolled back the covers and sat up. The rug felt soft under her bare feet as she turned and lowered them to the floor. Automatically, she reached for the robe she normally laid on the foot of the bed, but she stopped. It wasn't there.

For another moment a puzzled frown began to form on her broad, handsome features, but then it was gone. She had no need for a robe.

As she stood up, there was the sound of someone shifting position in the other bed, and she started to turn toward it.

Again she stopped. There was no one in that bed, a voiceless feeling told her, at least no one that need concern her at this particular moment.

Turning, she walked slowly to the door and out into the dimly lit hall. Quietly, she closed the door behind her.

A dream, she thought. This is just a dream. What else can it be? Why else would I be walking down this strange hallway without the least idea why?

But then even that thought was firmly nudged from her mind as, farther down the hall, she saw a single door standing ajar. A sliver of light slashed across the dark, patterned carpet and touched the opposite wall.

She pushed the door open and stepped inside. She stood motionless for several seconds before closing the door quietly.

A man sat in the chair facing the TV set. His bearded face looked familiar, and some remote corner of her mind knew that he was someone she knew, but the information did not seem important enough for her to make any major effort to retrieve it. The faded robe he wore was belted loosely over flannel pajamas. His head lolled backward and to one side, his blond hair a tangle, his lips parted a fraction of an inch.

She moved to stand in front of the chair, only a couple of feet from him, knowing somehow that he would awaken any second. Slowly, not knowing why she was doing it, except that in this particular dream it was what she must do, she reached for the snaps on her pajama tops and began to unfasten them.

John Groves's eyes opened.

He was, he decided instantly, dreaming. What else could it be? A woman, not beautiful perhaps but more than attractive, almost statuesque, stood before him. As he watched, trying futilely to recognize her, she opened the snaps on her pajama top and shrugged out of it, dropping it to the floor. A moment later, her fingers were closing on the elastic waistband and sliding the bottoms of the pajamas downward. Her breasts, pleasingly full, so unlike the petite firmness of his wife's breasts, swung erotically as she leaned over, lowered the pajama bottoms, and stepped out of them.

Yes, definitely dreaming, he told himself, although he couldn't remember having had a fantasy like this since his high school days, particularly his sophomore year, when an especially sexy math teacher had been, physically at least, his ideal. And he had certainly never, even then, had a dream that was this realistic. It seemed like he could reach out and touch her smooth skin, brush his fingers against her dark pubic hair.

For a moment, just a moment, something dark and frightening floated up from a remote corner of his mind, but before it could be identified, it was gone, and with it went the doubts and the uncertainty it had raised.

He stood up, feeling his erection pressing against the rough material of his pajamas, and he thought once again how incredibly realistic everything seemed. He could even catch the faint scent of the woman's hair, could hear her breathing.

The woman, still tantalizingly familiar, reached out, pulling open his robe and letting him shrug out of it. Then her hands were on his hips, slipping beneath his pajamas, softly caressing and kneading his flesh, sliding his pajamas downward as she moved. His own hands unbuttoned the top, letting it fall to the floor onto the robe.

Her hands slid along the sides of his legs as he stepped out of the pajama bottoms. She was on her knees in front of him now, leaning forward, her curling tangle of hair brushing against his body, his erection touching her cheek.

Slowly, her arms went around him, and her hands pressed against the backs of his thighs. Pressing herself against him, she slowly raised herself. Her breasts, nipples erect, slid along his body. His erection was pressed upward against his stomach by the soft, warm pressure of her body. He felt it pulsing with each heartbeat, felt the slippery beads of moisture as they oozed and spread from its tip. He couldn't remember any sensation in his life that had approached the intensity of this. It was as if the feelings in all his nerve ends had been magnified a hundredfold. He was sure that he would erupt into orgasm any second, bringing it all to a shuddering halt, but he did not. Even as, still slowly rising, the woman swayed her body from side to side, rolling his erection back and forth as she pressed against him even more tightly, her hands and arms caressing his back, the intensity only increased, enveloping every square inch where their bodies touched.

But then, suddenly, all motion stopped. Her moaning body was still pressed against his, her breasts flattened against his chest, his erection sandwiched ecstatically between their bodies, but it was as if, in an instant, her flesh had turned to warm, motionless plastic.

A voice—from somewhere, from that same remote corner of his mind that had intruded briefly and darkly before, came a voice, a harsh, despairing voice, an angry, frightened voice.

"Jessica," it said silently. *"Jessica!"*

In an instant, the unreal euphoria, the blind acquiescence that had smothered Elena vanished.

In that instant, as the voice grated in her mind, she knew that it was not a dream. In the instant that her breasts, moving softly across the man's chest, touched the seven-sided pendant that was suspended from a small chain around his neck, the real world flooded back.

Suddenly freezing cold, she jerked backward, her hands releasing Groves's body and then shoving against him.

He stumbled backward, blinking and shaking his head. The look of orgiastic pleasure on his face vanished, replaced instantly by total confusion. His erection shriveled to nothing in seconds.

"I didn't mean—" he began, but the sound of his voice galvanized Elena into motion. Snatching up her pajamas, she turned and ran from the room.

But even as she ran the few yards down the shadowy hall to her room, even as she shut and locked the door behind her, she knew that she had recognized the voice that had cried out to her, the anguish-laden voice that had, in an instant, stripped away the dreamlike fog that had been shrouding her mind.

It had been the voice of Marcus Reimann.

John Groves, abruptly expelled from his dreamlike cocoon, hastily snatched up his pajamas and fumbled them on, hardly noticing the patch of cold, slippery moisture that still clung to his stomach.

Christ, he thought as his fingers fumbled with the buttons. What the hell is going on?

Finally, throwing his robe on and clutching it around himself, he lunged into the hall after her. But before he had gone a half dozen steps, he stopped. Her door was closed, and not a sound was coming from behind it.

He stood motionless, realizing that charging after her, pounding on her door now, could only make the situation worse. What could he say to her that would do either of them the least bit of good? How could he explain something he didn't understand?

Uncertainly, he turned back to the living room. There was still not a sound from Elena March's room.

Christ, he thought again. What had happened? Had it been some kind of insane shared dream? Now that the talisman had been unearthed, were the orgiastic dreams it had caused before being turned into reality?

Or, the thought came abruptly, could it have been his own

half-sleeping mind that was the culprit? Could it have, unknown to his conscious mind, reached out and controlled her? Brought her to him the same way he had unsuspectingly reached out and controlled the Corman boy's dreams the night before? Could this whole episode have been the result of nothing more than his own subconscious desires?

He swore silently as he closed the living room door behind him. Was that what it had been? His own goddamn subconscious? Was it linked that tightly to this power? So tightly that it could bypass his conscious, rational mind altogether? Was his every whim from now on going to be translated into reality, no matter what his conscious wish might be?

Then, like a solid, physical blow to his stomach, another thought struck him, leaving him shaking and weak.

That other madness, that obscene and nauseating ritual of mutilation and death he had performed only hours before—could that, too, have been prompted by some dark, sick part of his own soul?

Shuddering, he dropped into the large, overstuffed chair, hunching forward and wrapping his arms around himself, his hands clutching at his upper arms until it seemed like the tips of his fingers would puncture the aging material of the robe and stab into his flesh. He had always known that there was a dark side to every personality, certainly to his own. Intellectually, he had always acknowledged that there still existed in all men the remnants of the ancient reptilian brain and that those remnants were capable of most of the thoughts and impulses that civilization called sick and savage. But this kind of sickness, an evil disease that made him literally skin and butcher a man while keeping him alive and conscious through it all, was simply beyond his comprehension.

But then, from that same dark somewhere that had spilled forth the voice only minutes before, something else emerged. There were no words this time or even feelings. John Groves simply realized, without any warning or preliminaries, that there were certain things he knew. It was as if he were remembering something that had until that very moment slipped his mind. It was in a grotesque way not unlike a hundred other times, such as when, back in Cleveland, he had driven home from school and remembered only as he opened the apartment door and saw that Mattie was not there to greet him that he had arranged to meet her at a restaurant in a suburb a dozen miles away.

But the things he remembered now were unlike anything he could possibly have known or learned himself.

He remembered that the source of the power— the power the Reimanns and hundreds before them had wielded over the millennia—was not the talisman itself but a being that was somehow bound to—trapped in?—the talisman like a malevolent genie in some perverted Aladdin's lamp.

And the being, entombed with the bones of Marcus and Jessica Reimann for nearly seventy years, had been able during that time only to reach out and scratch feebly at the sleep-weakened walls that during waking hours shielded rational minds from such intrusions. For those endless years, the longest such period in its seemingly endless memory, the creature had been cut off from all but the faintest trickle of nourishment.

After nearly seventy years of near starvation, it had been ravenous.

And it had fed.

It had sensed the approach of a creature—a human—which, for reasons it could not itself comprehend, promised a lavish feast to end its long decades of fasting. And it had sent its host scurrying after it.

When the creature was snared and safely removed to a place where interruptions were unlikely, it fed. In a sharklike frenzy, it fed on the intolerable pain and terror of the victim's unnaturally prolonged death.

Afterward, not yet sated but at least sustained, it brought a different creature, a creature that would, it knew, satisfy that host's own cravings.

It had attempted to reward him for a job satisfactorily completed.

Revulsion and horror swept through John Groves, swamping all rational thought, and for a long time he sat hunched over in the chair, his legs drawn up fetally against his chest while he shook and sobbed. He could not in that state detect the extra patina of fear that lay over those suddenly acquired memories. It was lost in the maelstrom of other, more violent emotions, and even had he noticed it, he could not have realized that it belonged not to him but to that other being with which he now apparently shared not only his body but his mind. The rational thought that would have been required to make the distinction was beyond him. The only thought he was periodically capable of was a despairing realization that "warlock" was not, after all, the term that best described him.

"Slave" was far closer to the truth.

It seemed to Elena March that morning would never come.

A dozen times she decided to scoop Beth from the bed, place her still-sleeping form in the car, and simply drive away, never to return. A dozen times she changed her mind, knowing that she could not stay away, no matter what the consequences.

She could not stay away any more than Jessica had been able to stay away. The most she could do was wait until Beth had been taken away, and even that would take an almost superhuman effort. Then she would have to try to finish what Jessica and a hundred others had begun.

Although it probably meant her death, she would have to try. There was no longer any room for doubt. Until that moment when she had been drawn to Groves like a helpless automaton, there had existed—in her own mind, at least—the remote possibility that she could, at the last minute, have turned and run despite the compulsion that gripped her. Common sense and logic just might have been enough to convince her of what she desperately wanted to believe—that dreams are just dreams, that the dead do not walk, that evil spirits do not exist and certainly are not capable of controlling living men and women, and most of all that she herself had not already suffered a hundred slow and terrible deaths at the hands of such spirits. Even Winton's confirmation of the truth of one of those deaths could have been rationalized if she had tried hard enough. Bridey Murphy's previous lives, after all, had been turned into dramatized memories of snippets of information glimpsed as a child and then forgotten, only to be dredged up by an eager-to-please subconscious during hypnosis. Although hypnosis was not involved here, the same theory of a pack rat subconscious, filing away every sight and sound ever experienced, could be applied. Her experience could even have been dismissed as some form of trickery, even telepathy, which would be far preferable to what she now knew was the absolute truth.

The truth was that the creature she had seen at each moment of death in those past lives did exist. In some form it existed here and now, and it was controlling John Groves, just as it had tried with limited success to control Marcus Reimann.

And she, like Jessica Reimann, was the only person now alive on earth who possessed the secret of the creature's destruction. Down through the centuries, in life after life, she had been the only one capable of ending the creature's existence, but each time she had failed.

But this time . . .

This time, with Henry Winton's help, perhaps even with Marcus Reimann's help, she would at least be better prepared than poor Jessica had been. Jessica had not known what she was challenging, what she was being forced to challenge. She had thought only in terms of demons and exorcisms. She had not been aware of the dozens of failures stretching back across the millennia, far beyond, Elena was now sure, the beginnings of Christianity, perhaps beyond the beginnings of any religion on earth.

But would that awareness aid her in any way? Was her vision of the creature any more accurate—or any more helpful—than Jessica's conventional demonic image? In some ways, what she faced now was even more frightening. Demons at least were a familiar if terrifying part of human history, whether they were real or imaginary. They could be controlled or exorcised by known rituals in known, if dead, languages.

But this . . .

The ritual, the incantation that would exorcise this creature was in a language—if language it was—that had never been spoken by human tongue, never heard by human ear. Except when she, in dozens of previous failures, had struggled to force the alien sounds from her throat.

Shiveringly alert, she waited for dawn.

* * *

Dr. Seth Laird jerked awake for the tenth or perhaps the hundredth time. Holding himself motionless, he strained to hear a sound, any sound beyond his own breathing and the tick of the clock on the coffee table next to the couch where his outsize form lay, cramped and uncomfortable.

But there was nothing, just as there had been nothing the previous nine, or ninety-nine, times. Raising himself, he winced at the aching stiffness in his joints and reached over the back of the couch to part the filmy curtains. The driveway, clearly visible now in the cloudy dawn, was empty except for his own car, as it had been empty the other nine, or ninety-nine, times he had looked since lying down a little after midnight.

Earlier, around eight the evening before, he had called Simpson and asked him to hold the laminar flow room open for another day. He didn't have to explain to the man what had happened. In one form or another, resistance to treatment was not all that unusual. Carl might be at the extreme end, but objectively, that was all that could be said.

But that didn't help Laird. It didn't help him understand his son. More important, it didn't help him find the boy. Yesterday Laird had cancelled all his appointments for the day and had spent the long hours searching, first haunting the school and anywhere else around Wertham the boy might have gone and then driving aimlessly through nearby towns and cities he knew the boy had driven to in the past.

But he had found nothing, of course.

He had called a friend—a grateful ex-patient, actually—in the state police, and the boy's license number had been circulated and was being watched for. But nothing came of that, either. Whatever the boy was doing, he wasn't out cruising the freeways, which Laird had been reasonably sure of, anyway.

What the boy was doing, most likely, was indulging himself in his own treatment of choice, his own brand of chemotherapy, the kind that his anonymous friend Buck prescribed and peddled. What it was doing to the boy and how he was getting the money for it, Laird didn't even want to think about.

And now it had been—he squinted at the clock on the coffee table—almost twenty-five hours.

Twenty-five hours. How many hours or days did he have until, without treatment and without even commonsense precautions, it would be too late? The rapidity with which the first remission had come to an end was not encouraging. And the state the boy had been in—could he, whether he meant to or not, overdose on Buck's medicine?

Cursing impotently, Laird lurched to his feet. There just wasn't a damned thing he could do. Everything he could do, he had already done, and all he had gotten for his efforts were aching joints and rumpled clothes, first from driving around aimlessly half the day and then from sleeping fitfully on the couch. That and a dozen or so patients irritated at having their appointments cancelled. And if he cancelled another dozen today . . .

Shaking his head violently, he lumbered toward the bathroom to clean up. Sitting around stewing or aimlessly roaming the streets and highways would gain him nothing, and if one of the appointments he had cancelled was with someone like his son, for whom every day without treatment simply raised the odds against him . . .

The least he could do, Laird thought bitterly, was go on trying to help others, even though he was powerless to help his own son.

Mattie hurriedly shut off the alarm and stretched and grimaced herself awake.

It took her a few seconds to realize that she was in bed alone and then another few to come up with a vague reconstruction of the events of the evening before. John had not come home after school, and she had started worrying and had eventually made a total fool of herself by calling the police, and then she had inexplicably dozed off, only to wake up and find him already home.

But where was he now?

For an instant the entire previous evening, particularly her dazed awakening to find John standing over her in the living room, took on an unreal, dreamlike quality. The calmness she had felt then, so in contrast with the nervous near panic she had felt earlier, seemed impossible. There had been a flurry of anger at his apparent thoughtlessness, but when he had explained about falling asleep . . .

Her thoughts slithered away, disintegrating as they went, and she shook her head irritably. She just couldn't concentrate this early in the morning. And anyway, what happened last night was not the question, not right now. The question before the house at the moment was, Where was John? Had he vanished again?

Pulling her utilitarian terrycloth robe over her pale, shortie nightgown and pushing at the early-morning tangle of her long, unfastened hair to get it out of her face, she hurried to the kitchen.

No one.

Glancing out the window into the dull, morning light, she saw that his car was still at the end of the line, next to the new guest's car. What was his name again? Jessup?

Blinking the man out of her mind, she turned and shuffled to the living room.

Silently, she gave a sigh of relief, followed almost instantly by a surge of irritation. John was there, sprawled on the couch, one arm dangling over the edge onto the floor. What the hell was he doing here?

She reached down and gave his shoulder a quick shake and squeeze.

His eyes snapped open with startling suddenness, and his breath was sucked in sharply. His eyes, even before they could focus, darted in all directions, and his entire body twitched as if about to pull itself into a protective ball.

"John? Are you all right?"

His eyes, at last in focus, settled on Mattie's slender face, but for a moment he didn't seem to recognize her. Then, abruptly, the look of panic was turned off.

"Yes," he said, "yes, I'm fine. What about you? Are you okay?"

"I'm all right, considering."

"Considering?" Hurriedly, he sat up, reaching for her hand but then drawing sharply back. "Considering what? Is something wrong?"

"Nothing much," she said. Some of the annoyance she

had felt the night before began to resurface. "I was a little concerned about you for a minute, that's all. You know, waking up and finding you missing. Again. Why did you sleep in here?"

"I'm sorry. I guess I—"

"I know. You just dozed off."

"Yes, I guess I did. Look, I'm sorry, I really am." He glanced at his watch and suddenly stood up. "I have to go in early this morning," he said hastily. "I left some papers at school, and they have to be ready to turn back today."

Frowning, she stood back to let him pass. "I'll get the coffee on," she said. "A couple of eggs won't take long."

"Never mind," he said, barely pausing in the door. "I don't really feel like eating anything right now. I'll pick something up in town later if I get hungry."

Then he was gone, and the door to their bathroom clicked shut a second later.

Puzzled, Mattie looked after him. What the hell had gotten into him? After his visit to Dr. Laird, she had thought that things were well on their way to being under control. John had seemed to accept Laird's diagnosis of nerves without batting an eye, although he hadn't seemed as relieved as she herself had been. "Things will be better now that I've got a real handle on what's wrong," he had said, and at least for a few hours things had been better. For the rest of the evening, he had been in better spirits than he had been in since they had first come here. Even that sleepwalking episode of Elena March's hadn't seemed to upset him very much, despite the fact that he lost half a night's sleep as a result.

But now . . . Staying out last night without calling her and then sleeping on the couch. And running off to school with hardly a word of explanation, as if he couldn't stand to be around her.

Then, abruptly, an explanation occurred to her, an explanation she wished she hadn't thought of. A sinking feeling filled her stomach.

He had said that Dr. Laird had found nothing wrong with him physically.

But had he been telling her the truth?

* * *

Pete Jessup jerked upright in bed as he came awake abruptly. Slowly, the unfamiliar room came into focus around him. The world seemed to spin as he tried to remember where he was. The high ceiling, the huge, draped windows, the tiny writing desk and the black-and-white TV set on the table next to it—none fit into anything he could remember, certainly not any hotel or motel he was familiar with. But—

There was a knock on the door, and an instant later he realized that it had been another knock a few seconds earlier that had awakened him.

"Mr. Jessup?" a woman's voice called through the door. "Telephone for you."

Then, like a small avalanche, everything came back. Where he was and why he was there and possibly the reason he hadn't been able to remember instantly. He simply hadn't wanted to remember.

And he certainly didn't want to answer the phone. It could only be the one person in the world he didn't want to hear from, because that was the only person who knew where he was.

The knock came again, louder. "Mr. Jessup?"

"Yes," he called hastily. "I heard. I'm awake."

"Telephone," the voice repeated. Presumably it was that young woman who ran the place, Mrs. Groves.

"Yes, I heard. Give me a second. Tell him I'll be right there."

"All right. The phone is through the next to last door on the right. I'll leave it open."

As the footsteps receded down the carpeted hall, Jessup forced himself to throw back the covers and put his feet on the floor. He didn't have a robe or slippers; he hadn't thought he would need any. Picking his pants off the chair he'd draped them across the night before, he tugged them on over his pajamas and padded barefoot, into the hall. He half expected the woman to be waiting in the hall to direct him, but she wasn't.

Glancing at his watch as he walked down the hall, he saw that it was a little after seven-thirty. Why the hell was Grantland calling this early? It had been barely twelve hours since he had talked to him last. He certainly couldn't want another progress report this soon. And calling him here! He hoped Grantland hadn't given Mrs. Groves his name. As friendly as she and Elena March were, the cat would be out of the bag before breakfast was over.

The phone was on a small end table by the couch; the receiver lay on the broad arm of the couch. He picked it up as he sat down, but it was several seconds before he put it to his ear.

"Jessup," he said.

"You took your time," Grantland's attenuated voice snapped.

"I'm sorry, but I was still asleep."

"Damn it, man, don't you—"

"What do you want?" Jessup said, talking over Grantland's angry words.

Grantland sputtered to a stop and then resumed. "What I want is results, but that seems too much to ask."

"I told you what the situation was."

"I know. Well, the situation has changed."

"What?"

"I said, the situation has changed. That's simply enough, isn't it? You no longer have the two days you say you need. You have only a few hours."

"Impossible. I am not going to—"

"I said, you have a few hours: perhaps twelve, perhaps less. The woman's brother is flying out sometime today."

"Why?"

"I don't know why. I can only assume that you fouled matters up somehow. She probably knows what you're up to and called him for help."

"What? That doesn't make sense. If she knew who I was, all she had to do was drive away."

"It doesn't matter. Whatever the reason, the fact is, her brother will be there in a few hours. And I intend to have this matter taken care of before he gets there. Do you understand?"

Jessup let out a sigh of exasperation. "I don't think you understand. Look, even if I take my time, it's going to be rough. That child is not going to welcome you with open arms. You will never win that child over, don't you realize that yet? You'll be in jail before that ever happens."

"It may take a little time," Grantland said, suddenly defensive for the first time. "But once she sees everything we can give her, she'll come around. She can have her own room, with everything she could possibly want. As for the mother, she'll come to her senses eventually, don't you worry."

"You're wrong. I've seen them together. You're not going to break them up without destroying them both. And I will not have anything more to do with it."

"Jessup, you know better than that. I—"

"I know, Mr. Grantland. With any kind of luck, you can run me right out of business. I don't care anymore. I will not be a party to this."

"All right, all right." Grantland's voice was suddenly conciliatory. "If you feel that strongly about it, all right. But don't just walk away from there. At least keep an eye on them for another few hours. All right?"

"Why? So you can have time to hire someone else?"

"No, nothing like that. I'm coming out myself. I'll talk to both of them, if that's what you want."

"What I want is for you to leave them alone. And me!"

"I can't do that, not now. I have to at least speak to them. Don't you understand?"

"Honestly, no."

"Then understand this. I'll double your fee and add a bonus."

Jessup's lips were parted, the word "no" forming on them, but he stopped. He recognized the tone of desperation in Grantland's voice, but he knew that Grantland could hire a dozen other detectives if he, Jessup, quit.

"Well, Jessup?" Grantland's voice prompted. "Isn't that enough? You want more?"

Jessup pulled in his breath. "No, that's fine. I'll keep an eye on them until you get here and can talk to them. But all you're going to do is talk, right?"

A brief hesitation, and then, "Of course." And then, in an almost querulous tone that Jessup didn't believe for a second, "Don't you really think it could ever work out?"

"I'm positive it couldn't," Jessup said. "And when you

talk to them, you'll realize the same thing yourself. If you have any sense at all."

Another hesitation, and then: "Very well. I'll be there as soon as I can make it. I haven't checked flight schedules yet. Just don't let them leave until I get there."

"I'll do what I can," Jessup said, and hung up.

He slumped back on the couch, his eyes going to the open hall door. He wondered belatedly whether anyone had heard him.

But it didn't matter, he thought abruptly. In fact, it would be better if someone had. It would make it easier for him to do what he had to do. It would take the choice away from him.

He stood up and walked down the hall to the room Elena March shared with her daughter. He knocked on the door.

He thought he heard a slight movement, a shifting of bedclothes, but that was all. He knocked again.

"Ms. March?" he called softly. "This is Pete Jessup."

Elena March, lying fully dressed in brown slacks and green pullover, freshly laundered the evening before, sat up on the bed abruptly. It seemed like only minutes ago that after seeing John Groves climb into his car and drive away, she had lain down and dozed off. Why had she awakened so soon?

There was a knock on the door, and a quiet voice was calling to her: "Ms. March? This is Pete Jessup."

Frowning, she lowered her feet to the floor and stood up. For a moment she swayed, and the room seemed to spin around her.

But she shouldn't be surprised to be dizzy, she thought as she steadied herself and let the motion of the room slow and halt. She'd had little sleep the last two nights.

"What is it, Mr. Jessup?" she asked, leaning close to the door and speaking softly so as not to wake Beth, who was still sound asleep, with the covers twisted and half pushed off onto the floor. B.C. was curled up at her feet in an untidy yellow ball.

"I have to talk to you," he said. "May I come in?"

"I'm really rather tired," she said, wondering how long she had before Groves returned. "Can't it wait?"

"I'm sorry, but it's very important." He paused and then said in an even softer voice, "It's about your daughter, Beth. And her grandfather, Davis Grantland."

Elena stiffened, her eyes darting to the sleeping child.

"What about them?" she hissed.

"Grantland hired me to find you, and—"

"Then I certainly don't want to talk to you!" Hastily, she checked the latch.

"No, you don't understand," Jessup said urgently. "I want to help you."

"Of course you do. You're working for Grantland, and you want to help me? By relieving me of the burden of having to raise my own daughter, no doubt."

"I'll be honest. That's why Grantland originally hired me, yes. But I quit just a couple of minutes ago. Grantland doesn't know it yet, and I may regret it the rest of my life, but I quit. I just couldn't go along with what he wanted. Now please, let me talk to you."

"You can talk from where you are."

"But—"

"From where you are!"

Reluctantly, nervously, he explained in a voice that was a hoarse whisper, barely audible through the door. He explained about her mother's phone being tapped, about his having been sent to take Beth back, and about the call he had just gotten from Grantland.

As he was finishing, Elena heard another door open in the hall and then Henry Winton's ancient voice: "Something wrong, Mr. Jessup?"

"No. That is, I was just talking to—"

Then the old man was knocking on the door. "Jessie? Are you all right?"

Before she could answer, a third voice was heard. Mattie was coming quickly down the hall. "Is something wrong?" she asked as she approached.

Opening the door, Elena slipped through into the hall and closed the door hastily behind her. Mattie, wearing an apron over a light blouse and slacks, was standing a couple of yards away, looking at the three of them in confusion.

"I think something *is* wrong," Elena said quickly. Then she faced Jessup, who was looking flustered in his pajama tops and hastily donned trousers. "If you meant what you said about having just quit, you won't mind telling these people what you just told me."

He looked for a moment as if he were going to resist, but then he slumped visibly. "All right. I suppose it's just as well. Maybe the rest of you can help."

In the kitchen, while Mattie fried some eggs and bacon, as much to keep herself physically occupied as to feed people, the balding detective went through his story again, this time finishing with, "It's occurred to me while I've been talking that maybe the best thing to do is call the police back in Greenville. If your brother hasn't left, maybe they could get in touch with him. Or they might be able to talk to Grantland if he hasn't left. Maybe they could talk some sense into him. God knows, I haven't had much luck."

When everyone agreed, Jessup made the call. Chief Travers, already familiar with the situation from what Bill had told him, agreed to do what he could. When he called back an hour later, however, it appeared there was little to be done at that end.

"Bill already took off for the airport in Indianapolis at least an hour ago," Travers said to Elena while the others watched her anxiously. "As for Grantland, no one knows where he is. His office just says he's out of town, and the people at the house say he and Mrs. Grantland drove away some time ago. Either they didn't say where they were going or the people I talked to just aren't telling."

"So what do we do now?" Elena asked.

"You could tell your local police there in Wertham," Travers said. "Tell them what you've told me. You and Jessup. Have them give me a call if they have any doubts about your story. Maybe, if Grantland does show up there, they could have a talk with him. At the very least, you can tell him we've got an eye on him and that if he tries something, all the money in the world won't keep him out of jail." Travers's voice hesitated for a moment and then went on.

"That last may not be a hundred percent true, lawyers being what they are, but it ought to at least slow him down. And if his wife is with him—well, from what Bill told me a few days ago, it sounded like she was on your side. So maybe it isn't as bad as it sounds."

"I hope you're right," she said. "I really hope you're right."

She was hanging up and turning to the others, when a small voice came from the door behind them.

"Mommy? Is it breakfast yet?"

For the first half hour, John Groves sat in his five-year-old Ford in the faculty parking lot behind the high school. Then, when some of the early-bird teachers started arriving, enough of his mind was functioning on an everyday level to realize that if he stayed there much longer, they might get suspicious. At the very least, one or two of them would stop to chat and ask him why he was just sitting there, particularly on such a gloomy, overcast day.

He could hardly tell them the truth, that he didn't dare stay home because he was afraid a momentary burst of annoyance at his wife might be taken seriously by some mysterious and incorporeal creature he had acquired by digging up an unmarked grave little more than twenty-four hours ago. But he was almost equally afraid to go into the school for much the same reason. Considering the fits of temper he had been having the last few weeks, his students would be in far greater danger than his wife.

But then, as he made his way along the mist-damp sidewalk and up the steps to the wide front doors of the building, he remembered something. He almost tripped on the top step as the strange memory drifted to the surface of his mind, and for several seconds he stood swaying, his hands not quite touching the door's brass push bar.

He needn't worry about the sort of things he had been worrying about, this newfound memory told him. Except for the feeding, nothing would be done without his consciously willing it to be done.

Except for the feeding . . .

Abruptly, the bloody images filled his mind once again:

real memories this time, not the imaginary ones that were apparently this creature's way of communicating.

Real memories of things he himself had done barely twelve hours before.

He found his stomach turning queasy and his knees almost buckling. Forcing himself to move, he shoved through the door and almost ran to the nearest rest room, his mouth clamped so tightly shut that his lips were thin lines and his teeth grated as they ground together.

Thankfully, the rest room was empty. Going into one of the stalls, Groves dropped onto the seat and lowered his head to his knees.

After a minute, the nausea passed, leaving only cold perspiration coating his face and dripping under his arms.

He sat quietly another minute and then another, until the weakness in his arms and legs lessened, until his ragged breathing became more nearly normal. Then he wiped his face with a handful of toilet paper, flushed it away, and pushed open the stall door.

He looked at himself in the mirror over the line of lavatory bowls. He was still pale, but not the birch-bark white he was sure he had been minutes before. His underarms felt icy and uncomfortable, and for a second he considered stripping off his jacket and shirt and trying to at least rinse some of the sweat away, but he didn't. Someone would be sure to come in, and he didn't feel like trying to explain. It would be easier to put up with the discomfort.

Then there were voices in the hallway, and the door started to open. In an instant, Groves had turned guiltily from the mirror and was walking toward the door before it was fully open. The raucous laughter of the two boys who pushed through was cut short as they practically ran into him.

He stood for a minute in the hallway outside. It was still a half hour till the first period, and the hall was almost deserted. Another teacher—Barlow, physics and math—came in, removing his glasses and wiping them dry with a large white handkerchief he pulled from his trouser pocket. He waved glasses and handkerchief at Groves as he started up the stairs a few yards away.

Groves waved back desultorily and decided that he would

rest for a few minutes in the faculty lounge. He would rest a few minutes, and then he would go to his first class, and somehow he would get through the day.

Somehow he would get through the day.

By ten-thirty, Elena and the others at the lodge had done as much as they reasonably could to prepare for the arrival of Davis Grantland. It was not, unfortunately, all that much, nor was it, Elena was afraid, all that effective. They might even have damaged their case, but there was really nothing they could do as long as the police and sheriff's department thought of them as, at best, slightly paranoid.

The call to the police had gotten them little more than the information that Groves Lodge, being outside Wertham's boundaries, was not really their concern. To make matters worse, the person Elena talked to was apparently familiar with Mattie's call the night before. There was a definite undertone of sarcasm in his voice when he inquired politely as to whether Mr. Groves had ever showed up. Then he explained with exaggerated patience that as long as no crime had been committed by this Mr. Grantland, there was nothing either they or the sheriff's people could do.

"However, if you care to have him stop by our office or even phone us, we will be glad to inform him that kidnaping is indeed against the law," were his final words on the subject.

Elena hoped that Bill would arrive before Grantland and that Miriam, Grantland's wife, would come with Grantland and be as sympathetic to their cause as Bill had said she was. It was only when all the calling and talking coasted to an uneasy stop that thoughts of the talisman and Groves and the rest pushed back to the surface of Elena's mind. Similarly, Mattie's thoughts had been distracted from her worries about John, but now they returned.

Excusing herself from the group—she and Elena and Jessup and Winton had been sitting in the large, central lobby while Beth had been playing with B.C. with a long piece of string with a rolled-up piece of paper tied to one end—Mattie went to the living room and the phone.

Nervously, she dialed Dr. Laird's number, almost hanging

up as the ringing began. She wasn't sure what she expected to find out, if anything, and deep down she wasn't sure that she wanted to find out anything. No answer he could give could reassure her. If John had lied to her, if he really was sick, that would explain his odd behavior, but that was the last thing she wanted to hear. On the other hand, if he wasn't physically sick, his behavior simply became even harder to explain.

Finally, the nurse Laird shared with the other doctors in the clinic answered the phone curtly.

Mattie was silent a moment, unable to get the words started, but finally she said, "This is Mrs. John Groves. May I speak with Dr. Laird?"

"I'm sorry, but he's with a patient. Perhaps I could help you?"

"I don't think so," Mattie said with a nervous gulp. "I'll be glad to wait until he's free."

There was a frosty silence, and then: "Very well, if you wish. It could be quite some time, however."

"That's all right."

Without another word, the nurse put Mattie on hold, and irritatingly bland music filled the receiver. Finally, after nearly ten minutes and a dozen or more abortive moves to hang up, a gruff voice came on the line.

"Laird here. What can I do for you, Mrs. Groves?"

Jolted by the suddenness of the words after the long wait, she blurted out, "My husband came to see you two days ago."

"That's right."

"He said you couldn't find anything wrong with him, anything physical, that is. Is that true?" she asked bluntly.

He hesitated a second but then said, "That is correct. Why do you ask?"

"No reason. I just—"

"No reason?" Laird snapped, suddenly irritable. "I find that difficult to believe, Mrs. Groves."

"I'm sorry, but—" Abruptly, she stopped. Why was she lying? He was a doctor, not a mind reader, and he couldn't help if he didn't have the facts. Hastily, the words stumbling over one another, she outlined her husband's actions over the last two days. She wasn't quite finished when Laird cut in.

"And you thought these actions might indicate what, Mrs. Groves? That I had found something seriously wrong with your husband and that he was lying to you about it?"

Mattie felt herself blushing at his blunt question, but he was right. "I'm afraid so," she admitted. "I'm sorry."

Laird hesitated again, and then, in a slightly more conciliatory tone, he said, "I'm sorry, too. I should have realized you were simply worried. But as I told your husband, I could find nothing physically wrong. As a matter of fact, his blood tests came back from the lab today, and everything is well within normal limits. I was planning to call him soon, but you can tell him yourself, now."

"There's nothing you could have missed?"

She heard the beginnings of a sigh, quickly cut off. "As I told your husband, there are more tests that could be performed, many more, but I don't really see any reason for them. However, if he wishes, if it would set your mind at rest . . ." She could almost hear the shrug as his voice trailed off.

"Very well, Doctor, thank you. I'll tell him about the blood test."

Without waiting for acknowledgment, she hung up. Leaning back on the couch, she looked up at the dark ceiling, trying to think. But the only tought that came was the same one, repeated over and over like a litany:

Whatever is bothering John, it isn't anything physical.

As Seth Laird hung up the phone, he swore at himself silently for having been so sharp, even rude, to the woman. It was no wonder she was concerned. not only with the way her husband had been acting the last couple of days but, from what Groves himself had said when he had come in for his exam, with the way he had been acting the entire time since they had moved here last summer.

But there was nothing he could do about it now. Stewing about it would only make him fall even further behind in his appointments. He had been trying to keep up, but with little success. He should never have had Rosie call all the patients whose appointments he had cancelled yesterday and tell them he would work as many as he could into the schedule before the weekend. A good two-thirds of them had decided on today, and the major result was that everyone, with or without an appointment, had to suffer through unconscionable delays.

To make matters worse, he was afraid he wasn't giving them their money's worth, anyway. No matter how hard he tried, his mind persisted in darting back to the problem of his missing son at every odd moment. Patients repeatedly had to describe a symptom a second or even a third time.

Thoroughly annoyed at himself, he turned from the phone in his office and started toward the examination rooms across the hall. Someone—Al Heywood, he thought—would be sitting uncomfortably in his undershorts, waiting, growing more impatient and uneasy every minute. But before Laird reached the door, the phone buzzed again.

Irritably, he turned and snatched up the receiver. "Yes, Rosie?"

"Sergeant McNaughton is on the line, Doctor. He said it was about your son."

The annoyance vanished, replaced by stomach-wrenching apprehension, the kind his patients often felt as they waited for the results of tests.

"Put him on," Laird said, and as he waited the second or two for Rosie to punch the necessary buttons, he realized that he was holding his breath. Deliberately, he released it and sucked in another.

"Dr. Laird?" McNaughton's Southern drawl—he was originally from Georgia—came through the receiver.

"Yes, this is Seth Laird. Have you found Carl?"

"I'm sorry, no, but we have found his car."

"His car? You know where he is, then?"

"No, I'm afraid not. It—"

"Not an accident!"

"No, it wasn't in an accident."

"But Carl—" Laird began loudly and then cut himself off. Deliberately, he went on. "I'm sorry. Tell me what you've found."

"That's okay," McNaughton said easily. "I know how it is when your kid's missing that way and sick, too. All right, like I said, we found the car, but it isn't your son's anymore. He sold it. We found it on a used-car lot down in Brattleboro."

The apprehension twisting at Laird's stomach turned to a sinking feeling, mixed with a touch of anger. He had been right. The boy was undoubtedly with that Buck person, and Buck would give out his medicine only in return for cash. So the car, with less than five thousand miles on it, had been turned into cash, into drugs.

"How did he look? Did the dealer remember him?"

"He didn't see him. The car was brought in by a middle-aged man with a long, scraggly goatee, wearing a flashy corduroy jacket and an Australian bush hat. From what you told us, I'd guess it was Buck. The title to the car looks like it's been altered. The boy wouldn't have been able to sell it himself without your signature. You know how that is."

"I'm beginning to. Is that all?"

"Not quite. The only good news in this whole thing is that the guy took another car as part of the deal, a real junker, a 1960 Thunderbird. We've got the license number and description, so we at least know what car to look for."

Irrational relief surged through Laird. Maybe there was still a chance to find the boy, although if he remained as stubborn as he had been before, finding him wouldn't do much good.

"Thank you. Could you tell me what the license number is?"

McNaughton hesitated. "I don't think it will do you any good. We've got everyone looking. It's sure to turn up."

"I know," Laird said, "but I'll feel better if I have it."

"All right, I guess you deserve it. Just be damned careful if you do happen to see it. This person he's probably with, well, he could be dangerous, to say the least."

"I realize that," Laird said. "And I'll be careful. Don't worry."

He copied the description—dark blue with several rust spots around the rear wheel wells— and the license number, thanked McNaughton, and hung up.

After an impossibly long minute of stomach-churning inner debate, Laird turned once again toward the examination rooms across the hall. These patients, he told himself with a mixture of anger and bleakness, might not be as sick as his son, but at least they would allow themselves to be helped.

* * *

John Groves's two morning classes went almost normally. Luckily, this was the day set aside for the half dozen or so in each class who exercised their option to give their book reports orally, and so Groves had little to do but listen and occasionally clamp down on hecklers. He soon found, however, that even that was too much for him. The words he heard just would not combine into sentences, and for once it was not totally the fault of the students. After the fourth or fifth time, he caught his mind slipping back to his own problem. He decided that he would give everyone a B and let it go at that. There was no way he could make any objective judgments today.

By the time his second class thundered out into the halls at ten-thirty, Groves had come to a decision.

He would try to heal Herb Franklin.

All the original arguments against it—not knowing if it was possible, not wanting people to know, and all the rest—faded to nothing when set alongside the single overwhelming argument for it. He had to do something to balance the agony he had been forced to inflict in order to feed the creature that now possessed him. And the only way he knew to even begin to do that was to use the healing power.

If the healing power did indeed exist.

Leaving his books and papers untended on his desk, John Groves walked quickly from the classroom, wondering.

Herb Franklin let the paperback book fall onto the blanket on his stomach. The lightest, both in physical weight and intellectual content, of the latest batch his wife, May, had brought in, it was still too much for him. He had been able to manage only a half dozen pages before the effort to hold the book became too much for him. And even those six pages, although he had read each of them at least three times, were already fading from his mind.

It was just as well that he was too tired to hold the book up, he thought bitterly. All the physical strength in the world wouldn't help him keep track of the words long enough to be able to follow the story. Even if someone read it to him, it wouldn't work.

With an effort, he looked up at the TV set high on the wall above the foot of the bed. He pressed the button near his left hand, and the bed hummed a few degrees higher. With another, more prolonged effort, he was able to operate the set's remote control. The set clanked and flickered past a commercial, several empty channels, and a soap opera before it finally settled on a game show.

He watched for a minute and then began to swear silently to himself. He couldn't follow half the clues, couldn't fathom the references, could barely follow even the scoring. It was the same problem he had had with the book. He just couldn't concentrate worth a damn. He couldn't even think.

"Shit!" He jabbed weakly at the remote control, and the picture zipped down to a bright, central point. Then even that was gone.

Like himself, he thought, just like himself. He was shrinking down to a point, though not a very bright one, and pretty soon even that point would fade away.

Again he touched the bed's control, and it hummed downward until his gaze was angled up at the ceiling of the spartan room. The plastic oxygen tube, like a noose that fitted around his head just below his nose instead of around his throat, shifted, and the two extensions that projected up into his nostrils scraped uncomfortably. The plastic bands around his head, holding everything in place, never felt right, anyway.

He lifted his fingers to adjust the tube, but the effort was too much. His hand fell to his side. The feeling of exhaustion worsened daily. Soon it would be an effort just to continue breathing normally.

He wondered whether May would come to see him at noon. She hadn't yesterday. She had said that she had to cover for someone at the store, and so she had barely had time to wolf down the lunch she'd made for herself that morning. But he wondered whether it was true. Or was he just sinking so rapidly, deteriorating so badly that she didn't want to see him any more than she had to? Were the sight and sound of him in this condition simply getting too painful for her to bear? He certainly couldn't blame her for not coming or for staying only a few minutes in the evening, the way she had the night before, instead of the two or three hours she had always stayed before. She had things to do, she said, although he couldn't remember now what they were. But then, he couldn't remember anything lately.

Unless a well-matched heart donor conveniently died in the next few weeks, he was on his way out. Either that or a miracle, and miracles had always been in very short supply. It was a new heart or nothing.

And it would probably be nothing.

To tell the truth, the way he was feeling now, he was just about ready for it.

After the second attack, when they told him that it wasn't the fault of the pacemaker or a clogged artery or anything else they could open up and repair, he had done a lot of complaining and shouting and a lot of regretting and worrying. But not lately. It was partly, he supposed, that he just didn't have the energy.

Then he thought of May again, and he felt an ache forming in his throat, felt tears trickling from the corners of his eyes. She deserved better than this. How much longer would she be forced to exist in this goddamn limbo? How many more times would she have to drag herself in here to watch him die while trying to make pleasant, optimistic conversation?

He lifted his hand to the plastic tube again, touching it with trembling fingers. Would he have the strength to pull it loose? Would someone come in and reattach it in time? Would he simply drift off to sleep without the extra oxygen, or would he—his chest hurt at the very thought—start gasping for breath like a hooked fish?

Did he have the guts to do it?

Or was it the other way around? Did it take guts to do it? Or to keep from doing it?

His hand dropped limply to his side once again, and he let his eyes droop shut.

John Groves was jolted by his first sight of Herb Franklin. If the term "shadow of his former self" ever applied to anyone, it applied to Franklin. Except for the relatively smooth skin, he could have been eighty instead of forty: pale, every visible part of his body limp, as if the bone and muscle had secretly melted under the pallid skin. The only sign of life was the almost invisible rise and fall of the chest.

Groves walked quietly around the foot of Franklin's bed and sat on the edge of the other, unoccupied, bed. The crisp sheets crackled under his weight.

For a long time he sat and watched, reminded of the bustle of activity in the rest of the hospital only by an occasional nurse hurrying past the open door or a convalescing patient shuffling by in slippers and rumpled bathrobe. His own heart, he realized after a minute or two, was pounding more rapidly, and the too-familiar nervous perspiration was beginning once again to soak through his shirt. You'd think, a perverse corner of his mind said acidly, that a goddamn warlock could control his own goddamn *sweaty armpits*.

And they stopped. His armpits stopped sweating, and within seconds he could feel the material of his shirt beginning to dry.

For a moment, the urge to laugh loudly and raucously was almost overwhelming. With an effort, he dragged his mind back from its silent paroxysms of hysteria. And then he wondered whether his no-sweat condition would be permanent. He seemed to remember reading somewhere that if you didn't sweat, you died. Sweating was an essential part of your temperature control system. Stop sweating and your temperature went up, and your brain fried.

It was with relief that he noted, a few seconds later, that he was sweating again.

He looked at the figure on the other bed and realized with a rush of embarrassment that Franklin's eyes were open and that his head was tilted toward Groves. He had been sitting there, holding in an explosion of hysterical laughter, probably grinning like an idiot. The man was dying, and his visitor was sitting there grinning at him.

"Herb, how are you?" he said quickly, inanely.

The man's once-broad shoulders twitched a fraction of an inch in what might have been an attempt at a shrug. "Not quite as good as yesterday," he said, his words slurred. His lips seemed barely to move.

"Any word yet about a donor?" Brilliant, Groves thought as his words littered the air between them, just brilliant.

"Nothing yet, but they haven't given up."

"Is there anything I can get you? Anything I can do?"

A washed-out smile flickered briefly on the pale lips. "Not unless your tissue type matches mine, in which case maybe you might like to walk in front of a truck or something like that. Or call down a miracle. Or maybe you could just tell me how much trouble you're having at school. Make me feel glad I'm out of the rat race for a while."

Franklin seemed to sink back into the pillows even farther, totally exhausted by the long speech. His eyes closed again.

"I've been having my problems," Groves said, "but nothing I can't handle."

He stood up, thinking, Okay, now or never. He took a step toward the other bed, his hand reaching out for Franklin's limp right arm.

But then he remembered. Just the way he had remembered that some kind of creature was linked to the talisman and was now linked to him, he remembered that he didn't have to touch people to heal them.

Why should he have to? He hadn't touched the Corman boy to influence him. He hadn't touched Elena March, yet he had caused her to come to him. Why should he have to touch Herb Franklin in order to heal his fast-fading heart?

A faint ray of hope pricked his mind. Perhaps he wouldn't have to go public in order to do healings. If he didn't have to touch anyone, nobody need know that he had anything to do with it.

If it worked, of course.

Then he remembered that it *would* work, that there was no question about it. It would work.

But he still didn't know how to do it. He couldn't visualize the necessary repair work, since he didn't know what the damage was or what a healthy heart should look like. It wasn't like visualizing an outer space monster and telling someone that he could see it.

But he didn't have to know those things, he remembered. All he had to do was think that he wanted this person before him to be healed, that he wanted the heart to be in good physical condition.

And he did.

He stood looking down at the limp form, wanting it to be healed, seeing it sitting up in bed, seeing the color come back to its cheeks, seeing the muscles tighten and strengthen, seeing the breathing strengthen and become regular.

Then, not waiting to see the final results, he turned and walked quickly into the hall.

Herb Franklin opened his eyes again, wondering whether he had dozed off. Had he gotten so bad that he went to sleep in the middle of a visit from one of the few people, aside from May, who had come to see him in weeks?

He looked around the room, rolling his head from side to side on the pillow. Groves was gone.

But was it any wonder? What was it he had said to him? Some feeble, bad-taste joke. And he had done the same thing, he remembered, with May. Not the same joke but some unfunny bit of gallows humor, something he couldn't even remember now. Could that be why she was cutting her visits short? Why she wasn't coming at noon at all?

He couldn't blame her if it was. Who the hell wanted to visit someone who was not only dying but insisted on reminding you of it all the time? And with unfunny jokes at that.

He remembered when his own grandfather had died. He'd had a stroke, but they hadn't taken him to a hospital. He couldn't remember why. Probably because they didn't have medical insurance the way everyone did now. And they couldn't afford a hospital, even if they had thought it would do some good. Herb had stayed out of the old man's room the entire week it took him to die. Once in a while he would hear what was left of the old man's voice, mumbling or demanding something, and the others—his mother, his grandmother, and an aunt who came to stay and help out—trying desperately to figure out what it was he wanted, wondering whether it still existed or was something he had once owned but had long since lost. Everyone had been miserable. They would emerge from the room, eyes red-rimmed, lips clamped tightly together. Sometimes the old man's garbled words would follow them, sometimes only silence, sometimes a pathetic scratching sound as the one hand that still functioned pulled at the blankets or scraped on the bedside table. No one was ever able to understand what he wanted, no matter how often or in how many ways he repeated it. The words were not words except perhaps to whatever had still lived inside the old man himself. The gestures, without words to accompany them, were meaningless.

But Herb Franklin thought that he finally knew what the old man had been saying. Not the exact words, maybe, but the thought.

He had wanted it all ended. Whether because of his pain or because of the pain of those around him, he had wanted it to end.

And now Herb Franklin wanted it to end. He had no pain himself, only an impossible, never-ending exhaustion, but the pain of those who came to see him—of May, at least—had suddenly become obvious to him. And he had only been making it worse.

She deserved better than this.

The decision made, he lifted his hand to the plastic oxygen tube. So easy, he thought. Who had an easier way out than he did?

As his fingers closed on the tube, he realized that the movement, the lifting of his hand to his face, seemed easier than it had before. A last-second burst of strength? A shot of adrenaline that would enable him to accomplish this one last task?

Smiling faintly, he pulled the tube extensions from his nostrils and then lifted the plastic bands over his head and let the whole nooselike contraption fall to the floor beside the bed.

Again he marveled at the strength that had allowed him to do this, and then he lay back against the pillow to wait.

John Groves was halfway to his car in the hospital parking lot when he stopped.

There are others, he thought abruptly, not just Herb Franklin. He might be the only one Groves knew personally, but there were others. Right here in this hospital, there were others.

He remembered one of the other teachers, after one of her rare visits to Franklin two or three weeks ago, talking about it. He couldn't remember the person's name or much of anything else about the case, except that whoever it was was in his or her thirties and had ALS. "Amyotrophic lateral sclerosis," the teacher had enunciated carefully, "better known as Lou Gehrig's disease."

Slowly, almost as if moving in a dream, Groves turned and walked back to the hospital, wondering whether he could find this other patient without attracting attention.

Then he remembered. He need only ask, and then the people he asked would forget that he had asked. It was so simple.

He stopped at the desk near the entrance. The nurse looked up at him. "What can I do for you?"

He asked for the room number of the patient suffering from ALS. She told him. As he walked away, she looked after him, shrugged, and went back to whatever she had been doing before. She had not asked him whether he was a relative or why he wanted to see the patient, a woman named Greta Tremont. She had simply told him the patient's name and room number.

He opened the door to the private room but didn't go in. The woman was in even worse shape than Franklin. She was connected to a respirator, and there were tiny twitching movements in her otherwise motionless hands. A tall, haggard man sat in the only chair in the room, watching her. When the door opened, he started to turn toward it but stopped halfway through the turn. Then, as if forgetting why he had moved in the first place, he turned back to face the bed.

As he had with Franklin, Groves stood looking at the figure on the bed, wanting it to be healed. He could not even imagine what it was that needed healing since he had almost no idea what ALS was. Some form of progressive deterioration of the nervous system, obviously, but that was the extent of his knowledge. He had read nothing about it, had had no reason to read or learn anything about it. But, as with Franklin, he knew that it would make no difference. He wasn't doing the healing. The creature that lived within him was doing it.

After two or three minutes, Groves turned and left, closing the door softly behind himself. The man in the chair had not looked around, had not even stirred. The woman in the bed opened her eyes briefly, and they had seemed to meet Groves's for a moment, but that was all.

He was tempted to return to Franklin's room, just to reassure himself that what he had remembered—what the creature had told him— was true, that Franklin was indeed improving if not already cured, but he resisted. No matter what was happening, his returning could only make matters worse.

As he walked down the hall, past the desk near the entrance, and out into the parking lot, he was beginning to feel better. His use of the talisman's power in this way seemed to erect the beginnings of a barrier between himself and the memories of the evening before, or perhaps not so much a barrier as a kind of distance. The memory was still there, as sharp as ever but not as large, not as painfully grisly. It had been a horrible experience, but it was past. He had, to some extent, made up for it, and he would, in the future, make up for it even more. There were others like Franklin and the Tremont woman, and if it was always as easy as it had been in those two cases, he could cure them by the dozens.

But then, as he was sliding into his car, he remembered something else.

The optimism that had been gradually asserting itself suddenly vanished, replaced by sheer horror. It was only by a massive effort—an effort aided by the talisman creature?—that he didn't scream out a throat-rending but futile denial. Instead, he only slumped back into the seat, his head lolling backward and his heart pounding as hard as it had in any of his nightmares.

For a long time, he sat silently except for his heavy, uneven breathing, hoping against hope that the newly found memory would vanish or at least be modified in some way.

But it was not. It remained. The creature had spoken to him once again, shattering the unfinished illusion of a warlock healer into a million shivering fragments. To exercise the talisman's power requires energy, the memory said. The mental eavesdropping and the influencing require small bits of energy. But to physically heal another body, to search through that body's patterns and re-form the parts that have departed from those patterns—to do all that requires a great deal of energy.

And that energy must have a source. The talisman—the creature trapped in the talisman— must be supplied with its own form of energy.

It must be fed.

After nearly half an hour of puzzled waiting, Herb Franklin decided that he was not going to pass out, let alone die. In fact, he felt better than he could remember feeling in months. For a moment it occurred to him that the medication, perhaps even the oxygen they had been giving him, had been somehow screwed up so that it had been gradually weakening him rather than keeping him alive. But that, he told himself, was paranoia of the purest kind.

Except that he couldn't think of any other rational explanation.

Gingerly, he put his fingers to his throat and felt for a pulse. The last time he had tried this, not long after he had been put in this infernal bed, he had been hard pressed to find a pulse at all, so weak had it been. But now it was easily located, easily felt. It seemed as strong as it had been before his first attack.

And, damn it, he just plain felt better.

Experimentally, he lifted both his arms and held them straight out in front of himself.

Son of a bitch, he thought. They're perfectly steady.

Slowly at first and then more rapidly, he alternately stretched his arms out as far as he could and then brought them back to touch his shoulders, as if he were doing pushups against the air. After at least thirty repetitions, he stopped. He wasn't even breathing hard.

And he was beginning to believe, really believe, that something totally impossible had happened. Not a miracle, maybe, but he could damned well make do with it until a real miracle showed up.

And, he suddenly realized, he was hungry as hell.

He found the appropriate button by the bedside and buzzed for a nurse, but before one could respond, he grew impatient and, with a muttered "Might as well go for broke," threw back the starchy hospital sheets and slid his legs over the edge of the bed. He was sitting there, wondering whether his slippers were still in the spartan little closet a few feet away, when Angela, one of the regular nurses, looked in.

Her eyes widened as she saw him. "Mr. Franklin!"

In a flash, her squat, sturdy form was next to him. Her capable hands grabbed at his arms and did their best to force him back into the bed. When he resisted, she released one arm and grabbed for the discarded oxygen tube.

"I don't think I need that anymore," he said, fending her off as she tried to slip it over his head. He didn't really believe that it was contaminated oxygen that had been weakening him all these weeks, but he didn't want to take the chance.

"Of course you need it, Mr. Franklin," she said, trying her best to sound soothing but losing the battle and beginning to sound out of breath. When it became obvious that she couldn't force it on him, she dropped it and jabbed at one of the buttons before resuming her efforts.

A few seconds later, running footsteps slapped down the uncarpeted hallway toward the room. A male face appeared in the door. It was one of the orderlies, Franklin realized.

"Help me, Charlie," the nurse said. "Mr. Franklin's gotten his oxygen loose, and he won't let me put it back."

"I told you, Angela, I don't need—" Franklin began, but the male orderly was suddenly at the bedside, trying to hold him still while the nurse struggled with the oxygen noose.

With all his strength, Franklin managed to jerk one arm free from the orderly's grip. With his free hand, he snatched the oxygen tube from the nurse's hands and gave it as hard a jerk as he could manage. Something gave with a snap, and suddenly the nurse and orderly stopped struggling with him. They both looked at the oxygen tube, ripped from its socket in the wall, and then at Franklin.

"I told you," he said in a steady, angry voice, "I don't need that anymore!" He was breathing a little hard, but certainly no harder than either of them. "But I *could* use some food."

* * *

A mixture of puzzlement and annoyance blanketed Dr. Seth Laird's thoughts as he hurried from his car to the hospital entrance. What Dr. Swanson had told him on the phone was obviously impossible, and yet Swanson had sworn that it was true, that he had taken the man's blood pressure himself no less than three times. Such things just didn't happen, couldn't happen. When the atrioventricular node begins to degenerate, particularly as rapidly as Franklin's had, it rarely stops degenerating, and it never repairs itself. All the money and medication and therapy in the world couldn't make it regenerate itself. It was slow death or a heart transplant. There was no third alternative.

But unless Swanson and a half dozen nurses and orderlies had gone completely insane, Herbert Franklin was improving. No, it was more than just improving. He was, they said, acting as if he had never had a heart problem in the first place. They had taken his pulse and blood pressure repeatedly, done an ECG, and, by the time Swanson had called Laird, had started a blood gases test, which the lab was rushing through as quickly as they could.

Angela Dalton came out from behind the hospital reception desk to meet Laird as he entered. His bulky figure towered a good foot over hers as they met.

"What the hell is going on here?" Laird asked abruptly.

"I wish I knew," she said, giving him a fast rundown of what had happened when she answered Franklin's buzzer. They were at Franklin's room before she finished.

Franklin was finishing off a small tray from the hospital kitchen as they entered. Spotting Laird, he said, "Thank God you're here at last. You're my doctor. Tell these people to listen to me. I keep telling them I want real food, not this . . ."

His voice trailed off as he gestured distastefully at the almost empty tray.

"I take it," Laird said, "that you're feeling better."

Franklin laughed. "You're damned right I am. Look, if I can't get any decent food around here, at least let me call May and tell her I'm okay. Or let me out of bed and I'll get dressed and walk over to the damned store and tell her."

Everyone else looked at Laird, who was as stunned as they

had been earlier. It was obviously impossible, but it was equally obviously true. Franklin's usual pallor was totally gone. And the fact that he was talking and moving normally, without oxygen and without any sign of tiring, said more than any blood pressure measurement or ECG could. Even his appetite seemed fully back to normal.

"All right," Laird said, abruptly deciding. "What would you like? This seems like a special occasion, so I guess we can make an exception and send out."

"For real? You're not kidding me?"

"For real. What would you like?"

"A big medium-rare steak for a start. I am really starving, and I haven't tasted anything decent for months."

"All right, medium-rare steak it is. Vegetables? Salad?"

"The works."

Laird turned to Angela, who was standing wide-eyed in the door. "Call Portman's," he said, "and see if they deliver. If they don't, send someone to pick it up."

She blinked, glancing apprehensively at Franklin, but then she nodded. "All right, Dr. Laird."

When she had gone and only Laird and Swanson remained in the room with Franklin, Laird dropped onto the other bed in almost the same spot where Groves had sat earlier.

"What happened, Mr. Franklin? I'll admit right now, whatever it was is way over my head."

Franklin laughed again, more from sheer exuberance than from amusement, Laird suspected. "You probably know more than I do, with all the needles and things you've been sticking into me."

Laird shook his head. "Not yet. All we know is, a few hours ago you were sick, and now you appear to be well. And, like you, we know—well, normally I'd say we know it is impossible."

Another laugh, this time from amusement. "I did receive that impression from all the furor my recovery caused. You should have seen the looks on their faces."

"Probably a lot like mine when Dr. Swanson here called me. But what happened? Tell us about it from, well, from the start, whatever that is."

Franklin shrugged. "Sure, why not? But look, what about May? Can't someone tell her I'm okay?"

Laird thought for a second and then turned to Swanson. "Have Angela or someone call her. Or have her picked up if you have to. Get her over here, and don't scare her to death in the process."

Swanson hurried from the room, and Laird turned back to Franklin. "All right, Mr. Franklin, you were going to tell me what happened."

Franklin did. As well as he could, he reconstructed his every action, his every feeling, even the suspicion about the debilitating oxygen. He was as puzzled as Laird or anyone else, and he hoped that by dredging up every tiny detail, some answer might surface. He was also, to some extent, enjoying testing his newly revitalized memory.

"Actually," he said after a time, "I was thinking of suicide rather than recovery, so I guess positive thinking can't have anything to do with it."

"What about before? Did anyone give you any medication? Do anything at all to you?" Not that any medication, no matter how potent, could have done this, Laird added to himself.

Franklin shook his head. "Nothing at all. I hadn't even seen a nurse or doctor since regular rounds this morning, and all they did then was their usual 'how-are-we-today?' routine. I remember I was trying to read a book May brought me the other day, but I couldn't concentrate on the damned thing, couldn't even hold it up to read it. And then somebody stopped by for a minute to visit, and that's it." He shrugged as he finished.

"A visitor? Who? It wasn't May, was it?"

"No. As a matter of fact, it was that fellow they hired to replace me at school. Groves, his name is. No idea why he was here. Never'd come before."

"Groves? John Groves?"

"That's the name, yes."

"What did he do?"

"Nothing." Franklin grinned ruefully. "I probably made him nervous. You know, my usual gallows humor. And then

I think I dozed off while he was sitting there, right where you are. When I woke up, he was gone."

"And when you woke up you were feeling better?"

Franklin shrugged again. "Not right away. That's when I started thinking about suicide again. I don't remember how my mind wandered around to it, but it seemed perfectly logical at the time. I was even wondering if I had the strength to pull that tube out of my nose."

"But it was after Groves was here—a few minutes after, at any rate—that you started feeling better?"

"I suppose so. Why? You think he made some kind of miracle?"

Laird was saved from answering when Swanson lurched to a halt in the door.

"It's happened again," Swanson said with a puzzled, frustrated emphasis on the last word.

Laird stood up abruptly. "What's happened again?"

"Another—oh, shit! Another miracle, for want of a better word."

"Who?"

"Another one of your patients, Seth. Greta Tremont."

"Tremont?" Suddenly Laird's stomach felt as if someone had turned a Mixmaster loose inside it. "But that can't be. It's impossible!"

"Any more impossible than what happened to me?" Franklin asked, an exuberant grin showing on his face. "What did this Greta Tremont have?"

"ALS," Laird said, forgetting for the moment the fact that he shouldn't be talking about one patient in front of another. "Lou Gehrig's disease."

Franklin whistled. "I've heard of that. Now that is what I would really call a miracle."

Laird blinked, looking again at the impossibly alive and vital man sitting up in bed, grinning and waiting for a steak and a visit from his wife.

"Only slightly more of a miracle than whatever happened to you," Laird said, and then hurried to follow Swanson into the hall.

*   *   *

It was shortly after twelve when Davis Grantland and his wife Miriam left the Albany airport in their rented Buick, looking very much like any other well-to-do middle-aged tourists, though quite different from the way they usually looked, particularly Davis Grantland. His normally perfectly groomed and styled white hair was mussed from the wind at the airport in Indianapolis, and he had not bothered to comb it since. His expensive gray jacket was worn over a dress shirt with an open collar, probably the first open, tieless collar he had subjected himself to outside the privacy of his home in thirty years.

Miriam, a few pounds overweight but not too heavy for the full-cut slacks she wore, pulled off the fur jacket she had snatched up as she had raced to catch her husband that morning when he stormed from the house after the phone call to the detective in Vermont. Her hair, still largely brown with streaks of gray, had been pinned back as well as possible with what she had been able to find in the slim, fashionable purse she had grabbed unceremoniously along with the fur jacket.

She watched her husband silently as he pulled out of the airport, listening as he muttered angrily about the inadequacy of the directions the girl at the rental counter had given him.

Was it time yet to make another try at talking sense into him, she wondered? She had done her best earlier, during the hectic drive to the Indianapolis airport, but it had seemed to have no effect. A derisive snort had been his only response to her insistence that local law officials in Greenville, particularly Chief Travers, would frown on kidnaping, even a supposedly well-intentioned kidnaping. Even pointing out that the child herself would, at best, be resentful and frightened only triggered a vitriolic tirade about the child's mother, "that ungrateful bitch," and how she had "had her chance" and how "*she* was the one who ran away, the one who kidnaped the girl."

Throughout the flight, as long as they were within earshot of others, even during the plane change in Buffalo, he had maintained a stony silence, and he didn't seem ready to break it yet. Finally, however, as they emerged into the open but hilly country northeast of Troy, he lightened the touch of his foot on the accelerator and cast a quick glance in her direction. The anger was still plain on his narrow, clean-shaven face, but now, Miriam noticed with a touch of relief, there was something more. Uncertainty, perhaps? Possibly, during the last four hours of brittle silence, something had been happening in his mind. Perhaps he had actually been thinking about what she had said. He was not, after all, accustomed to having anyone defy him or even disagree with him, least of all his wife. He surrounded himself with too many yes-men for that to happen very often. Miriam had learned long ago that discretion was the better part of valor. Perhaps it had simply taken the entire four hours for the reality of her words to sink in. At least she hoped that was the case.

After another few minutes, as they neared the Vermont border, he sucked in his breath and tightened his hands on the steering wheel as if to get a better grip on the world before he spoke.

"Do you honestly believe those things you said?" he asked, and again she was relieved to hear that the words, though nearly identical to the ones he had used a half dozen times during her initial attempts, now had less of a carved-in-stone tone behind them.

"I do," she said simply.

She didn't repeat her accusations and warnings. Now, when he seemed to be teetering on the brink of reason, they could only nudge him back into the irrational, vindictive mental jungle he had submerged himself in for the last week and a half, ever since he had learned of his ex-daughter-in-law's disappearance. There was no point hammering once again at the fact that he had treated the woman like dirt throughout her marriage to their son, that he had acted like a victorious warlord when he had gotten news of the divorce, and that he had gone to expensive lengths to make sure there would never again be any need for contact between the Grantland family and Elena March. He knew very well what he had done, and he knew equally well that any lawyer or police chief or sheriff would see it the same way Miriam did. He only needed to let that knowledge somehow penetrate the bristling shell of anger and frustration he had built around himself. He wasn't stupid, Miriam told herself, just jackass stubborn and arrogant.

"All right," he said, breaking the silence once again as they emerged from Bennington and began the scenic but tortuous route through the Green Mountains, "what do you think I should do?"

Keeping her heartfelt sigh of relief silently inside, Miriam felt some of the tension melting out of her body. For the first time, she let herself sink back against the luxurious cushions of the car. Perhaps there was hope, after all. But she would not, as one of her cousins often said, bet the farm on it.

Bill March tossed the map onto the pasenger seat as he eased himself carefully into the cramped subcompact rental he had just picked up at Boston's Logan International. Whoever had driven it last—the tiny brunette who had handed him the keys?—must have been at least a foot shorter than his own lanky—or skinny, as his mother always said accusingly at mealtimes—six foot two.

Once the seat was adjusted as far back as it would go, which was of course not quite far enough, he unfolded the map and gave it a closer look. What he saw only confirmed what his earlier cursory glance had told him. It was a long way, through heavy traffic, from Boston to Vermont.

What he should have done, of course, was get moving a little earlier so that he could have caught that flight to Albany. Not only was Albany closer to where he was going, traffic would undoubtedly have been lighter there than here, expressways or no. But then, with the low visibility that according to their chatty captain blanketed most of New England, he supposed he was lucky to have gotten here at all.

And who knows, if the fog cleared up enough during the three- or four-hour drive, he might spot a few places Beth would like to see. He suspected, however, that Disney World in Florida was probably the closest thing to the top of his niece's things-to-see list.

Still, he was looking forward to seeing her, although he was still totally puzzled by the circumstances that had brought him here. Once he'd had a few minutes to think over his sister's call, he had decided that he couldn't buy Ellie's story about wanting to spend time with a suddenly rediscovered old boy friend, not by a long shot. He couldn't remember the exact words, but he knew that he was the one who had first brought up the subject of boy friends. Ellie had just grabbed the ball and run with it. He had supplied the ball unwittingly.

There had even been moments last night, while he was thinking up reasons for his own absence that would satisfy his mother and Charlie, when he had thought of calling Ellie back and either saying that he couldn't make it or demanding that she tell him the truth.

But he hadn't. Ellie wasn't the flighty type, and she wouldn't have called him like that unless she'd had a good reason, a better reason, certainly, than the one he had unintentionally supplied her with. It couldn't have anything to do with Grantland, since the man couldn't possibly have any idea where Ellie and the girl were, but Bill couldn't imagine what else it could be.

But, he supposed, he would find out soon enough. If he survived the Boston traffic.

For over an hour after leaving the hospital, the scene of his healings, John Groves drove aimlessly, barely seeing the mist-shrouded but still spectacular scenery that would, less than six months ago, have been a feast for his eyes. Only once did his mind take complete notice of his surroundings, and that was when he found himself following the road up which he had mindlessly pursued the Cadillac and its terrified occupant the afternoon before. Shuddering, he almost stalled the car in the ditch as he turned around.

A half dozen times the thought of returning to the lodge bobbed to the surface of his mind, but each time it was rejected. Although he was now reasonably confident that he would not inadvertently harm Mattie, there was still an odd repugnance, even fear, that shivered through him whenever he thought of returning. It was a fear that could not be overcome despite the fact that there was, as far as he was aware, no possible reason for the fear to exist.

Finally, he found himself back at school, pulling into his parking slot, but he was not, he knew, any further ahead than he had been when the last memory had bludgeoned into him in the hospital parking lot. The knowledge it had brought still lay in his mind like poisonous pellets of lead. No new memories had surfaced to diminish the impact or to show him any way to escape the situation. A dozen attempts to rip the talisman from around his neck and heave it from the moving car had failed. Even the thought of suicide had crossed his mind, but he feared that it would not work, feared that he would be healed and would awaken to find the creature's hunger even more urgent.

Slowly, hardly noticing the misty drizzle that floated in the air and clung to his face and hair, he climbed out of the car and made his way into the building, wondering whether there was any way he could possibly get through his afternoon classes. Or, worse, the hours of the evening.

Or any of the thousands of evenings and nights to come.

If he continued to feel like this, he thought bleakly, he would somehow find a way out. He would have to. This kind of existence was intolerable.

For a moment the thought of yielding, of blindly accepting the power, as hundreds of others must have done over the centuries, darted around the edges of his mind. Could he turn himself into a total hedonist, drowning himself in sensual pleasures the way a drunk drowns himself in liquor? If the interrupted reward of the night before was any indication of how intensely felt those pleasures could be, of how sensations could be literally amplified until—

Abruptly, guiltily, he thrust the thought away, as if he had suddenly discovered someone looking over his shoulder while he was in the midst of masturbating over a pornographic picture. No, not just a pornographic picture, an errant thought told him, but a pornographic picture of someone he—or the person looking over his shoulder?—loved.

Shaking his head at the sudden confusing welter of thoughts and emotions, he realized that he was in the middle of a bustling school hallway and that someone was speaking to him.

"You ever catch your pal in the Caddie, boss?"

Blinking, Groves looked around. The Weber boy, Curt Weber, stood a couple of yards away, his posture challenging. Groves looked at him blankly, his mind still not fully locked into the real world around him.

"What?" he asked. "What did you say?"

The boy took a step closer, his husky six-foot frame looming over Groves's lighter five foot eight threateningly. "I asked," the boy said, anger clipping his words short, "if you ever caught that guy you chased away from the station yesterday. What'd you do, tell him to get his gas somewhere else? Where the service is better?"

Only then did Groves realize what the boy was talking about: the man he had caught and killed. The talisman's food . . . He had first seen the man at the service station, and the Weber boy had apparently seen him, too. He even remembered what kind of car the man had been driving.

And when that car was found, when the mutilated body was found and linked to the car . . .

A new memory sprouted deep in Groves's mind and bubbled quickly to the surface, as if it had been waiting to be triggered by the boy's appearance.

A memory that said: The boy must die.

Images of the bloody feast of the evening before slammed into Groves's mind, twisting at his stomach, but then another memory appeared, a memory tinged with regret. Although the boy must die, his death would be only that—a death. That other process, the feeding, was separate and different. Those who could properly satisfy the creature's hunger were rare and must be searched out. This death was simply a necessity if Groves was not eventually to fall under suspicion.

But there was more. This death—and there was no doubt that the death would occur, with or without Groves's assent or assistance—might not appease the talisman creature's growing hunger, but it could be useful in another way.

The boy, who would shortly be dead no matter what Groves or anyone else did, could be made to serve a useful purpose before he died.

A useful purpose . . .

In desperation, Groves tried to grasp at that thought, to find what lay behind it, but he could not. There was only, as there had been the night before, a flash of fear. The same fear that had bubbled to the surface a half dozen times this morning, Groves realized, each and every time he had so much as thought of returning to the lodge.

And it was not *his* fear.

It was the talisman creature's fear.

For the first time, Groves felt a ray of hope stab through the despair that blanketed his thoughts. If there was something this creature itself feared, perhaps there was a way out for him.

And there *was* something it feared.

There was someone it feared, someone at the lodge. That was why the very thought of returning to the lodge made him uneasy. It made the talisman creature uneasy and frightened.

But as quickly as hope appeared, it was smashed aside.

He felt the pulsing warmth where the talisman lay against his chest. He felt the energy flowing out of the creature, out through the talisman. At first it was a trickle and then a rushing torrent. He saw the anger on the boy's face gradually change to puzzlement and then to a mindless blankness.

With each passing second that the energy continued to flow, he felt the hunger growing greater.

It was after two o'clock when Seth Laird finally left the hospital, once again having delayed or cancelled most of his office appointments.

The results of Franklin's blood gases test had come from the lab just as he and Swanson were beginning a series of exhaustive tests on Greta Tremont. The balance of gases in Franklin's blood was, to no one's surprise, perfect. With the external symptoms—or lack of symptoms—the man had been displaying, it could hardly have been otherwise.

He was cured. That was all there was to it.

Franklin's heart, which until only three hours ago had been so weak that even with oxygen, it could not beat powerfully enough to give him the energy to sit up by himself, was in perfect shape, doing its job even better than before his first heart attack. The pacemaker inserted after that first attack was now not a lifesaver but a useless electronic lump in his chest. As soon as it became clear that this was not a temporary phenomenon—as if it weren't clear enough already—it would be removed.

And the results of the tests on Greta Tremont, Laird was sure, would be equally positive and equally impossible. Roughly a half hour after Franklin had begun his miraculous recovery, she had awakened, she said, feeling better than she could remember feeling in months. She saw her husband sitting in a chair facing her, looking half asleep. She tried to speak to him but realized that she couldn't talk because there was something blocking her mouth and throat. Not knowing what it was or why it was there—the respirator had been put in only a few days before, and she had been semiconscious ever since—she panicked, almost gagging, and started trying to pull the obstruction out.

Her husband, terrified by her sudden, seemingly demented spurt of activity, had tried to stop her, just as the nurse and orderly had tried to stop Franklin. But she had managed to get the tube out of her throat in time to croak the words, "Stop it! What are you doing to me?"

The very fact that she had been able to speak so clearly and strongly and the fact of the remarkable physical strength in her arms and legs in holding him off had stopped her husband. She hadn't spoken above a murmur in weeks, and her arms and legs had been almost totally lifeless except for sporadic, uncontrolled twitches. Watching her with a mixture of throat-clogging hope and a horrible fear that he was seeing only some terrible, last-minute spasm, he buzzed for the nurse.

Greta Tremont had been talking a blue streak ever since, despite the fact that her throat was more than a little sore from the weeklong presence of the bulky respirator tube. She was filled with the same last-minute-reprieve exuberance and exultation that had filled Franklin, and, also like Franklin, she was ravenously hungry. When Laird had arrived and looked at her, a second dinner was ordered from Portman's.

Laird asked the same questions of Tremont that he had asked of Franklin, with roughly the same results, except that there had been no visitors either of them remembered. Greg Tremont did have a vague impression of the door opening behind him at one point, but he couldn't remember when or even if it had actually happened, certainly not who, if anyone, had looked into the room.

But the recovery had begun only minutes after Franklin's.

And John Groves had visited Franklin.

And John Groves lived on what Laird's grandmother had

called the old Reimann place, where, again according to his grandmother as well as other oldsters, many strange things had happened, not the least of which was an occasional seemingly miraculous healing.

And something had been mightily upsetting both Groves and his wife, not to mention at least one of their guests, in recent days.

To any doctor, to any scientist, the very idea of miraculous healing was, at the very least, absurd. True, there was holistic medicine and psychosomatic medicine and acupuncture and endorphins and a thousand other oddities, but there were limits. There had to be limits or the world would descend into chaos.

The total recovery of terminal patients like Herbert Franklin and Greta Tremont was far, far outside even the most liberal of limits. And yet, in a matter of minutes, they had both staged complete recoveries! Two terminally ill people who could not possibly have recovered were completely healed.

So perhaps, Seth Laird thought, a third could recover as well. Perhaps a third . . .

Climbing into his car, Laird pulled out of the hospital parking lot and turned not in the direction of his office but in the direction of the school and, he hoped, John Groves.

Curt Weber moved as if in a dream. He didn't speak. He didn't respond to greetings or shouts from his friends. He didn't even seem to recognize his closest friend, Phil Harrison, when Phil grabbed his arm and almost yelled into his ear, "Hey, Curt, where the hell do you think you're going? Class starts in a couple of minutes."

Curt Weber kept walking. He had to go home. Before he could do something that would be, he somehow knew, the most important thing he would ever do in this life, he had to go home.

Soon he was home. The dozen blocks he had walked through a misty drizzle were forgotten, if they had ever existed in his mind at all. His mother, watching a soap opera on the tiny black-and-white TV in the kitchen, looked up as he passed the kitchen door on the way to the den.

"Curt? What's the matter? Are you sick?" she called after

him, but he paid no more attention to her than he had to his friends at school or to the slick of moisture that covered him from head to toe.

Then she was standing in the hall, calling more loudly, a little angrily. "What did you do, lose your jacket? You're soaking wet."

She started after him as he pushed into the den. "Now wait a minute! You know your father doesn't want you in there. And I don't either, especially not with muddy shoes."

In the den, he went to his father's desk and gripped the large middle drawer. It wouldn't open.

For a moment he stood motionless, with some small part of him wondering what he was doing but most of him simply knowing that he was doing what must be done, wondering how he could continue if he couldn't get into the locked desk.

He was turning away, starting for the kitchen to get a knife from the silverware drawer, when he saw the metal letter opener on a corner of the desk. He picked it up, jammed it into the crack at the top of the desk drawer above the lock, and popped the drawer.

Dropping the letter opener on the desk, he pulled the drawer open. What he was after lay at the right side of the drawer, positioned so that it would slip easily into a hand that was dropped casually into the drawer.

He hesitated a moment, but only a moment, as that one odd corner of his mind asked again what he was doing. Then he picked up the gun, forced it into the hip pocket of his too-tight jeans, slid the drawer quickly shut, and walked back into the hall where his mother stood waiting, hands on hips, her forehead wrinkled in an angry frown.

She was saying something, but the words, although they filled his ears, didn't work their way through to his mind. He brushed past her and walked out into the drizzly afternoon and began the long walk to Groves Lodge.

By noon, the nervous energy on which Elena March had been running abruptly faded, and exhaustion closed in. She and the others had long since done all that could be done to brace for the arrival of Davis Grantland, and there was nothing she and Winton could do to prepare for whatever they alone knew was coming. The talisman—and the gargoylelike creature it apparently contained—wasn't something that police or private detectives could help with. It was something that they alone must face.

Finally, after a snack of cold cuts and milk that Mattie had nervously prepared, Elena left an increasingly impatient Beth—"Isn't Uncle Bill going to be here pretty soon?" was asked every ten minutes or less—with Winton and the others. She lay down, fully clothed, on the bed in her room. She was asleep almost immediately.

Then, seemingly the same instant her eyes had closed, she was awake again. If not for the chill that had settled over her and the momentary ache in the arm that had been lying cramped beneath her, she would have thought that only seconds had passed, not the more than two hours her watch said had slipped by.

She lay still for a minute, trying to get her thoughts sorted out again, and it was only then that she realized that she had not awakened by herself.

Something had awakened her.

Abruptly, she sat up on the bed. For a moment, the room spun around her and a faint touch of nausea brushed at her stomach. She looked around the room, but there was nothing out of the ordinary. She listened, and again there was nothing that could be considered upsetting, not even the voices of the others that filtered faintly through the open door to the hall.

But no, there was no sound at all. What she thought had been voices had been—what?

Hastily, she got to her feet and hurried into the hall. Still there was no sound, no movement.

Had something happened to the others while she slept? Was she alone in the lodge? She started toward the kitchen, the last place she had seen the others, but before she reached it the living room door opened and the rotund detective leaned out into the hall, holding a finger to his lips in the classic "don't make any noise" gesture.

He stepped the rest of the way into the hall and eased the door shut behind him. "Beth's taking a nap," he said softly as they came together. He smiled. "I guess she figured her Uncle Bill would get here quicker if she went to sleep."

"Where are the others?"

"The old man's in his room. At least that's where he said he was going. Probably taking a nap himself. Mrs. Groves is in there with your daughter, reading something or other."

"Nothing's happened?"

"Not a thing. Everyone's just waiting." His round, middle-aged face twisted in a nervous grimace. "But things should start happening any minute now. I checked the airline schedules, and Grantland could be practically here. Depends on what flight he caught and where to. And how fast he drives."

Was that it? she wondered uneasily. Was her ex-father-in-law's approach the reason she had awakened?

No, it was something else, definitely something else.

Winton? Had something happened to Winton?

She turned to his door, but before she could knock lightly, it opened. The old man, in flannel shirt-sleeves and suspenders, emerged slowly, his limbs moving stiffly. His eyes met Elena's, and she knew that, like her, something had dragged him up from sleep.

He shook his head slowly in answer to her unasked question. He didn't know the reason for their awakening or their uneasiness, either.

Trailing a puzzled Pete Jessup, Elena and the old man went to the living room and peered in at Beth, who was asleep on one end of the couch. Mattie was on the other, leafing distractedly through a play script: *Our Town*, Elena assumed. Mattie had told her about the drama group and the play they were planning. Mattie looked up but said nothing.

A moment later, the buzzer in the living quarters sounded. Someone had come in the front door.

Mattie frowned and got up quickly from the couch. "Did you hear anyone drive in?" she asked as she glanced through the curtained windows toward the parking area.

"Not me," Jessup said, "and I think these two were asleep," he added, nodding at Elena and Winton.

Mattie's frown deepened when she turned back from the window. "There's no car out there," she said, and then shrugged nervously. "Maybe we're getting some walk-in trade."

The others parted to let Mattie past as she hurried from the room. As she came to the end of the hall and entered the huge lobby area, she stopped abruptly.

"What can I do for you?" she asked a second later, her voice uncertain.

There was no answer, and then Mattie spoke again. "You're from high school, aren't you? I'm sure I've seen— Has something happened to my husband? Is that why you're here?"

There was still no reply, and then Mattie was backing from the lobby into the hall. Jessup, hearing the apprehension in Mattie's voice, hurried toward her.

"Trouble, Mrs. Groves?" he asked loudly, making sure that whoever was in the lobby heard him clearly.

"I don't know," Mattie began, but then she cut herself off. She had backed well into the hallway now, still watching whoever was in the lobby.

A moment later, a boy—a young man— appeared. He was a husky six feet, wearing tight jeans and a dark sport shirt but no jacket. His face and hair, his clothes and shoes, were wet. He must have walked a great distance in the light drizzle to get so wet.

And then Elena and Winton knew. This was why they had been awakened.

Elena began to back away, but Winton started forward, his stick-thin arms reaching as far as they could in front of himself.

As the old man approached, the boy reached behind himself, into his back pocket, and brought out a pistol.

He leveled it not at Winton or Mattie or Jessup but at Elena.

Curt Weber's mind was a turmoil, a battleground.

The longer he walked through the steady drizzle and the closer he came to Groves Lodge, the more slowly he walked and the more resistance he felt growing in his mind.

He had the gun, and he had to use it. He knew that. He knew that it was the most important thing he would ever do, perhaps the only important thing he would ever do. The reasons for its importance skittered away like slivers of smoke whenever he tried to grasp them, but it didn't matter. He knew that they were true, whatever they were, and he knew that he was the only one who could possibly do it.

And yet, as he had walked across the fields and finally climbed the last fence and made his way toward the door to the lodge, the resistance had continued to grow. It was as if the very air around him was thickening and holding him back. Something was afraid. Something wanted him to stop.

But he couldn't. He couldn't stop. He had no choice. This was his one and only chance.

He would succeed.

And now the one he had come for was in sight, only yards away, and he had the weapon in his hands. The enemy, the ancient enemy, was there before him. He had only to squeeze the trigger, and it would be over.

It would be over, and he would have succeeded.

But she was moving, backing away, and there were others all around him, coming toward him, leaping for him, but all moving in agonizingly slow motion, as he himself was moving.

Squeeze the trigger, his mind screamed, and he felt the pressure on his finger as it tightened on the trigger. Squeeze the trigger and you will have won.

But then one of the forms struck him, smashing into his stomach, sending him flailing backward, and the sudden explosion of the shot was meaningless noise. He knew, without having to see where the bullet punched a hole in the plaster ceiling above the enemy's head, that he had failed.

The enemy, the ancient enemy, still lived, and he had failed.

An overwhelming fear settled over him even as he was falling backward, grappling with the massive form that had thudded into him. He tried to bring the gun around to fire again, not at the enemy, now escaped, but at himself. He had failed, and now he must die.

But before he could turn the gun, his back struck the floor, smashing against it with not only his own weight but that of the attacker. His head struck an instant later, and the gun went flying. Tiny dots of whirling light speckled the scene before his eyes.

Time speeded up. Objects once again moved at normal

speed. The shouting around him, until then a muffled, distant roar, was suddenly chaos.

"Get the gun," he heard someone shout, while someone else was still yelling, "Stop him! Stop him!"

Then, suddenly, he was himself again. Whatever had been controlling him, tricking him, was gone. In a split second, the memory of what he had done in the last hour crashed into him, but his mind simply couldn't take it all in. It was absolutely crazy. He couldn't have done anything like that. He just couldn't. Stealing his father's gun, walking all the way here in the rain, trying to shoot someone—someone he'd never even seen before!

No, it was crazy. It couldn't have happened.

Then he felt himself being dragged to his feet. The man who had knocked him down a few seconds before was hauling him to his feet. Someone had already grabbed the gun from the floor and was handing it to the man.

Releasing him, the man stood back, leveling the gun at him.

"Call the police," the man said over his shoulder to the woman who had handed him the gun.

"No," Curt blurted out, but the woman was already hurrying away. The other woman, the one he had been trying to kill, had tripped and was only now climbing to her feet. She looked at him with frightened eyes.

"Who are you?" the man, who was fiftyish and balding, snapped. The others stood back.

"Curt Weber," he said in a voice that cracked and shivered. He rushed on, "I don't understand what happened. I didn't mean—"

"You barged in here with this gun," the man said sharply, waggling the gun in emphasis. "And you tried to shoot someone. That's what happened, whether you understand it or not. Why? Why did you do it? You weren't hired by someone named Grantland, were you?"

The boy blinked, so frightened now that he was afraid he was going to lose control of his bladder. "No. I wasn't hired by anyone to do anything. I don't know why I did it. I don't know."

"And you never heard of anyone named Davis Grantland?"

The boy shook his head violently. "No!" Then his eyes found Elena again. "I'm sorry," he said. "It wasn't my fault. Something made me do it."

The man holding the gun pulled in a deep breath. "All right," he said. "We'll let the police sort it out. You just move on out there." He motioned with the gun toward the lobby.

Shaking, the boy obeyed. He turned and started to walk slowly in front of the man.

As he walked, Curt realized that he was short of breath.

Very short of breath.

Until that very second, the growing discomfort had been masked by the adrenaline-pumping panic that had gripped him from the instant he had "awakened" and felt the memory of the insane things he had done smash into him like a hammer blow.

But now it could not be ignored.

He blinked and breathed in as deeply as he could, filling his lungs to their utmost.

But it didn't help, any more than did the second breath or the third. The shortness of breath and the tightness in his chest only grew worse with each passing second. He felt as if instead of breathing deeply, he had been holding his breath, like the time he swam underwater the length of a pool. He had felt like this just as he was forced to surface for air.

"Keep going," the man's voice said, sounding as though it came from dozens of yards away. "Just lie down on the floor, face down, there in front of the registration desk."

But Curt barely heard the words; his ears were beginning to ring, and the tightness in his chest was becoming scrapingly painful. The huge room swayed and then spun like a wobbly merry-go-round.

And his heart! He could feel it pounding like a fist striking his chest, but it was slow, so very slow, like it was still stuck in that world of slow motion he'd been in. A new panic gripped him, wiping from his mind all thoughts of why he was here and what he had done. Only the aching tightness in his chest and the frantic gasping for breath and the impossible slowness of his heart had any meaning to him.

"Is something wrong?" he heard the man's voice ask, distant and indistinct.

"I can't breathe. I can't get any air." The words jarred him with their loudness, but they echoed and faded to nothingness in split seconds.

The man said something else, but Curt wasn't listening. He couldn't listen. His chest still pumped at a frantic rate, but he was getting no air. No air at all!

Then his legs were turning rubbery and weak, and the wobbling of the room grew worse. Specks of light danced ever faster before his eyes.

And his heart. With one last beat that seemed to shake his entire chest, it stopped.

It wasn't beating at all.

A kind of fear he had never thought possible, a feeling of totally helpless fear, settled over him.

Then he was falling, crashing to the floor on his side and rolling onto his back. The man with the gun was leaning over him, his mouth moving, blowing the specks of light in all directions, but no sound could penetrate the increasing ringing and hissing in his ears.

He tried to scream, but he could not.

He tried to suck in more air, but his chest would not respond. The frantic pumping of a few seconds before had faltered to a stop along with his heart. No matter how wide he opened his mouth, no matter how hard he strained, there was almost no result. It was like trying to suck thickening molasses through an ever-narrowing straw.

The weakness was spreading with impossible speed. His arms and legs went from rubbery to numb to dishrag limp. The specks of light multiplied like a silent fireworks display, and then everything—the man leaning over him, the distant beamed ceiling, the walls of the stairway and the narrow catwalks—everything faded but the specks of light and the blackness they swam in.

The numbness spread until the only sensation was the crushing pressure that seemed to be squeezing his chest like a hand squeezing the last drops of moisture from a sponge.

Finally, there was nothing.

* * *

The fear—the fear that was not his own but that of the creature who controlled him—returned to John Groves in a cresting wave.

And with that wave, carried like swirling fragments of ice in a frigid flood sweeping down from a crumbling glacier, came more of the memories.

But these were not memories the creature intended to share. These, Groves somehow knew, were slivers of its very being, chipped away by the fear before it could regain control of its own thoughts.

Countless lives and deaths flashed through Groves's mind. Lords and bandits, castles and barbarians' huts and desert tents, darted through his memories like shrapnel, but beyond them, before them all, was something else. And it was this something else that was, Groves realized, the source of the creature's fear.

It was a darkness, but a different darkness from any he had ever experienced. A darkness that twisted and writhed and pulled, dragging him toward it like a colossal whirlpool. A living darkness, pulsing with a life that was, to Groves's earthly mind, totally alien and incomprehensible.

And yet, for an instant an image appeared, an image out of his darkest nightmares. Not an image of the darkness but of the worst horror that his own limited mind could conjure up to inhabit that darkness. A giant spider the size of a horse loomed over him, its ebony beads of eyes glinting, its hairy legs and grotesque, loathsome body settling over his own, its poison-tipped mandibles touching and tearing. It was real, as real as anything he had ever experienced, yet he knew that the living, squirming darkness that this creature feared was worse, far worse. To escape such horror, he would do anything, go through not one but a hundred of the feedings he had been forced to witness and to participate in.

But then, as quickly as the fear had come, it vanished, as if some massive gate had been slammed shut in a dam. A few dribbles and puddles of terror remained, but only for a moment, and then they, too, drained away.

New memories, purposeful memories, appeared.

The enemy, the ancient enemy, must be faced directly.

Using others, like the Weber boy, would not work, not this time, although it had worked often in the past.

But before such a confrontation could take place, the creature's strength, already squandered and nearly depleted by the healings, must be restored. It must be at its strongest and most alert at such a time.

It must be fed.

Slowly, an awareness of his surroundings returned to Groves: the car, the seat against his back, the wheel in his hands, the mist-covered windshield, the mossy scent of the damp, autumn forest that lined both sides of the deserted dead-end road where he had driven and parked while the creature waited.

Finally, he felt his hand go to the ignition. He heard the engine sputter and catch. He felt and saw the car begin to move.

The search was beginning.

Davis Grantland frowned as he saw the pillars and the grotesque stone creatures atop them. What kind of Mickey Mouse place was this Groves Lodge?

His frown turned to a scowl as he maneuvered the Buick between the pillars and saw a patrol car of some kind parked lengthwise behind three other cars in a gravel parking area on the right of the drive. The lodge itself, an ugly and blocky-looking building, was in the middle of several leafless trees and a few evergreens on the left. Another line of evergreens marked the boundary on one side.

Miriam, apparently noticing his scowl as well as the patrol car, put a hand lightly on his arm. "Don't jump to any conclusions," she said softly.

For a moment he turned his scowl on Miriam, but then, seeing her anxious face, he pulled in a deep breath in a conscious effort to calm himself. She was right. Jumping to hasty conclusions was counterproductive. He never did it in business, and he shouldn't do it now. There were a hundred reasons for a patrol car—a sheriff's department car, he added to himself as he drew close enough to read the gold lettering in the starred circle on the doors— to be here. And unless that incompetent fool Jessup had decided to commit professional suicide by telling the woman who he was and why he was at the lodge, there was no way the presence of the local law could have anything to do with Davis Grantland.

Parking well away from the others, Grantland shut off the car and got out. Miriam, not waiting for him to open the door on her side, quickly followed, hugging the fur jacket tightly around herself.

"Don't worry," he said. "You convinced me. I'm not going to do anything foolish."

She seemed to relax a bit, but not completely. The misty rain had stopped sometime in the last dozen miles, but the air was still damp, the ground still wet.

Pushing through the double set of doors, they found themselves in a huge room with an enclosed central stairway connected to the second floor on both sides by narrow, rail-enclosed walkways. For the first few seconds, the odd architecture held his attention, distracting him from everything else, but then he saw his granddaughter. She was sitting on an old-fashioned couch along one wall nearly at the back of the room, sitting with an emaciated old man who was eighty if he was a day. The old man had been talking quietly to the child when Grantland and his wife had entered, but now they both looked around.

The little girl obviously recognized both the Grantlands, but she made no move toward them. Or away from them, either, Grantland thought to himself. That has to be worth something. Maybe this can be worked out amicably, after all. Maybe Miriam was right.

He walked slowly toward the two. Miriam kept nervous pace with him.

"Hello, Beth," he said when they were still a dozen feet apart. "How are you?"

The girl looked at him. "You're my grandpa, aren't you?"

"That's right." The ancient scarecrow put a hand on the girl's shoulder, Grantland noticed, and the old man's eyes looked hard.

But before anything else could be said, two other figures hurried into the huge room from a hallway on the right: the girl's mother and that incompetent fool of a detective.

"Don't try anything," Jessup said the instant he saw Grantland. "I told Ms. March all about it."

That was all he needed. The man was not only an incompetent fool but a traitor to boot.

But then Grantland felt Miriam's hand on his arm, and, with a massive effort, he forced himself to at least sound calm as he spoke.

"That's just as well, I suppose," Grantland said, lying. "But I've, well, I've been thinking things over on the way out here." He glanced at Miriam. "My wife saw to that. But in any event, I'm sure we can work something out eventually that will be satisfactory to everyone."

"Not if it involves our coming to live with you, Mr. Grantland," the woman said stiffly. "We've been through that a hundred times. I have been, at any rate, with your attorneys."

"No, nothing like that if you don't want to. Though the invitation is always open, of course. Always. To both of you."

She looked at him suspiciously. "You came all the way out here to tell me that?"

He hesitated and then decided that there was no point lying. Jessup would just contradict him, and the woman was obviously more ready to believe the detective than himself. He moved toward Jessup and the woman, out of earshot of the girl.

"No, I didn't," he said, keeping his voice low. "I wasn't sure what I was going to do when I got here, to tell the truth. But, as I said, Miriam talked some sense into me on the way. I don't know what I thought I was going to do, not really, not specifically, but now I know I just want a chance to talk it out with you."

He glanced toward the little girl and the old man. "I don't want to lose my granddaughter completely. Can you understand that?"

She nodded stiffly. "And can you understand that I refuse to sell her? To you or to anyone else." Her voice, held low to keep the words from her daughter, was almost a hiss.

Grantland felt his teeth clenching. The bitch. She hadn't changed. Still talking like she—

He cut the thoughts off sharply, trying to calm himself or at least to retain the appearance of calm. Finally he nodded. "I can understand that," he said. "I'm sure we can work something out."

"We can talk about it."

"That's all I ask," Grantland said, but then he could not help adding, "I'm sure you want what's best for your daughter, the same as I want what's best for my granddaughter. You wouldn't want her to miss out on anything just from a lack of money."

He knew even as he spoke that it was a mistake, but there was no stopping it. The woman's face stiffened, and he could see her fingers twitch as her hands resisted the impulse to clench into fists.

"We can talk about it tomorrow," she said. "Things are a little hectic around here today."

"Yes," Miriam put in, "we saw the police car outside. Has something happened?"

"Yes, something happened," Jessup said. Then he stepped closer. "I suppose you're planning to stay the night?"

Grantland nodded, but Miriam looked at Elena. "If you don't mind?" she said.

Some small part of the stiffness went out of Elena. She shook her head. "Not at all. As long as Mr. Grantland and I understand each other."

"Oh, I'm sure he understands."

"You might as well register, then," Jessup said, gesturing toward the counter near the door.

As Grantland turned toward the counter, Jessup hurried ahead of him. He was holding a pen out when Grantland reached the counter and stood next to him.

"I have to talk to you alone for a minute," Jessup said in a harsh whisper.

Grantland frowned but said nothing. After a moment, he nodded. What did this fool want now? What more damage could he do than he had already done?

John Groves had been in and around Brattleboro for nearly an hour, cruising aimlessly up and down the streets and along nearby roads, when he suddenly remembered that the one he was looking for, the one he needed, was in the small green and white house on the next corner.

This time, the memories said, the feeding would be efficient and orderly. Before, the talisman creature had been caught unaware. It had expected to have to search long and hard, as it had for the one who had now been found, and so it had not been ready.

But now it was ready.

Inside the house on the corner, fifteen-year-old Jimmy Stevens, home from school just a few minutes, looked up from the peanut butter sandwich he was making. For a moment his entire body was enveloped in a chill, the kind he sometimes got when he went to sleep with the bedroom window open and then in the middle of the night the wind shifted and turned cold and poured in on his unprotected body.

For another moment, something deep inside himself told him to run, to drop his sandwich and dash out the back door before it was too late.

But he didn't.

Despite the remnants of the chill, despite a distant corner of his mind that screamed for him to escape, Jimmy Stevens laid the sandwich down, picked up his blue zipper jacket from the back of the chair he had tossed it on, and moved slowly to the front door.

Davis Grantland watched irritably as Jessup closed the door behind them. Miriam, after another warning look, had stayed in the lobby with Beth and her mother and the old man. So far no one had said where the owner of the place was or who belonged to the sheriff's department car outside.

"All right," Grantland said as Jessup turned toward him, "what the hell is going on? What's a sheriff doing here? And what is the idea of hustling me down here this way? Have you screwed up something else?"

"Someone tried to kill Ms. March this afternoon," Jessup said flatly.

Grantland blinked incredulously. "What? Who was it?"

"His name was Curt Weber. He was a local high school student."

"What happened?"

"The boy just walked in and tried to shoot her."

"Shoot— My God! But he obviously didn't hurt her. Or my granddaughter. Did he?"

Jessup shook his head. "No. I managed to knock him down before he could fire more than once. And that one shot missed."

"But even so, what about my granddaughter? Is she all right? She didn't seem very upset."

"She didn't see anything. The shot woke her up, but that's all."

"Thank God for small favors. So that's why the law is here." Grantland glanced toward the door to the hall. "But you said it was someone from the local high school. Why the hell would some local kid take it in his head to shoot her? Did he say why he did it?"

"No."

"Where is he? That hick sheriff doesn't still have him here, does he? Questioning him?"

"No. He's talking to Mr. Groves, the owner of the lodge."

Grantland was silent for several seconds, trying to collect his thoughts, wondering what effect this would have on his effort to talk some kind of sense into Elena March. If the few words he'd spoken with her already were any indication, it hadn't made things any easier. If anything, she seemed more openly hostile than ever, although that was probably due to Jessup's bungling as much as anything.

"How much did you tell the woman?"

"Everything."

"Christ! Did you even tell her you tapped her phone?"

"Yes."

The incompetent fool! "Don't you even realize you could get yourself arrested for that? And have your license taken away?"

"I know. I figured you'd find a way of getting it taken away, anyway."

"I might not have, but I will now, by God! Whatever it costs, I'll put you out of business and see that you never get started in another."

Jessup flinched at the nearly apoplectic outburst. Sweat beaded his face and balding head. But as Grantland turned toward the door, Jessup swallowed hard and said, "Just one more thing before we go back out there."

Scowling, Grantland looked at Jessup. "What is it? You have some last words?"

"I suppose they might be, at that, but I have to ask. Did you have anything to do with the attack on Ms. March?"

Grantland's jaw dropped incredulously. "What? What did you just say?"

"I said, did you have anything to do with the attack on Ms. March?"

"You really are a fool. Or insane. Maybe I won't have you run out of business, I'll just have you committed! How the hell could I have anything to do with some trigger-happy nut out here in Vermont?"

"There are shady detective agencies everywhere, and for the amount of money you can pay, they'd be willing to do anything, even con some kid into what he thought was a practical joke."

"This is crazy. You *are* out of your mind, Jessup! Since when is shooting someone a practical joke?"

"Maybe he didn't know he would be shooting anyone. Maybe whoever gave him the gun told him it was empty or had blanks or something. I don't know. He was acting pretty oddly, like he was almost afraid to pull the trigger."

"All right, that's all I'm going to listen to. Just keep this crap to yourself. And ask the goddamn kid! Ask him if—just ask the goddamn kid!"

"There's nothing I'd like better, Mr. Grantland, but I can't. He's dead."

"Dead? How? What did you do, take the gun away from him and shoot him?"

Jessup shook his head. "No. I knocked him down, and when he got up, he was having trouble breathing. He passed out and was dead in a couple of minutes."

"So that's it. You *did* kill him. And now you're trying to clear your conscience by blaming me. Well, it's not going to work. In fact, with any kind of luck, I won't have to have you run out of business or even get you committed. I can just watch you be convicted for manslaughter."

Furious now at everyone, most of all at the detective and the bitch who was keeping his granddaughter from him, Grantland yanked open the door and stormed into the hall.

A few minutes after Grantland stormed back into the lobby and dragged his wife off to their room in the opposite wing of the lodge, Henry Winton was at last able to draw Elena aside. He had not had a chance to speak to her alone since the shooting, and as he stood looking down at her, searching for the right words to begin with, he could once again see Jessica in this woman's eyes.

Swallowing away the lump that formed in his ancient throat, Winton said finally, "That boy, he didn't come here on his own to do that. He was sent."

Elena let her breath out in a nervous sigh. "I know."

"What are you going to do?"

She shook her head. "I don't know," she said. "I just don't know. I wasn't expecting something like that, not now, not before I had a chance to get Beth away from here."

"Then leave," he said. "Take the little tyke with you and go. When your brother comes, I can tell him where you've gone. You can meet him somewhere else. Then you can come back here if you still have to."

"I've thought about it, believe me. In fact, I haven't thought about much else the last two hours. But I'm very much afraid it wouldn't work." She shivered, and there was a catch in her voice. "The thing knows I'm here, obviously. It probably knows we're both here. I think it would know where I was no matter where I went. And it could reach me or those around me. It could stop me. It sent that boy to kill me, so it can send others. And if it sends someone while I'm driving with Beth in the car . . ."

Winton's gaunt, leathery face twisted in a grimace. Then, hesitantly, he said, "I could take her."

Elena shook her head again and reached out to touch the old man's hand, her brother's hand.

"I don't think it's going to let either of us get away," she said, "even for a little while."

* * *

In a house not far from Brattleboro, the feeding was about to begin.

Fifteen-year-old Jimmy Stevens had shown John Groves how to find the house they were in and had told him in flat, zombielike tones that the owners, a middle-aged, well-to-do couple with only grown children, were out of town for a month, vacationing in California.

Knowing what was to come, Groves was already having trouble fighting back the nausea and dizziness. Tears already streaked his cheeks as he watched the boy, now totally under the talisman creature's control, bring the gleaming knives from the kitchen and drop them on the bedroom floor in front of the full-length mirror that covered the closet door. He remembered what he had seen the night before in the near darkness of the forest, what he had seen and felt and done, and he knew that what was coming, what he would be forced to see in full light, would be worse. He knew, and he wanted more than anything in the world to scream at the top of his lungs, to run screaming from the house and down the long drive and onto the highway, screaming for help if anyone would stop, throwing himself in front of the passing cars and screaming for death if they would not.

But there was nothing he could do, nothing. No matter how hard he tried to shout at the boy to run, not a sound came from his lips beyond an almost inaudible whimper. No matter how hard he strained to break free of the paralysis that gripped him, not a single muscle so much as twitched. He was a slave, as was the boy.

A spectator.

For a moment, a twinge of hysterical relief flickered through the forest of horror that gripped him, the kind of relief a condemned man might feel if he were told he was to be given a quick death by hanging rather than a slow and painful death by being forced to swallow some corrosive poison.

At least, that hysterical relief told him in a shrill voice, he would not be required to do the killing himself, would not be forced to perform the mutilation and torture.

The boy would do that himself.

In that way, a particularly grisly memory told Groves, the feeding was more efficient. The fact that the boy was doing these terrible things to himself while being kept alive and conscious and while being forced to watch his own bloody, disintegrating image in the mirror would provide a feedback that would multiply the intensity of whatever obscene emanations the creature fed upon.

Groves could only hope that he himself would be allowed to pass out, but he doubted that he would. His own horror, he suspected, was yet another factor in the creature's feast.

Dr. Seth Laird slammed the pay phone's receiver onto its hook and stalked across the sidewalk to his car, cursing. Still no sign of his son, and the state police sounded as if their patience was wearing thin from his repeated calls. And Groves had still not been seen since noon by anyone at the school, nor had he shown up at the lodge.

But the tests on Greta Tremont were all perfect, Dr. Swanson had told him during his last call to the hospital. It was, of course, totally impossible, but it was as if the woman had never had ALS in the first place. Swanson was torn between elation at the recovery and a nagging fear that somehow the woman would also realize how impossible her recovery was. She might decide that her problem had been misdiagnosed originally and then decide to sue everyone on the hospital staff, as well as Laird, for malpractice. Laird's only concern, however, was finding his son and then Groves.

Starting the engine, Laird pulled away from the curb, switching on the police-frequency scanner he had had installed after the second or third fruitless call to the police. It crackled, as it had all afternoon, with routine calls about minor disturbances, traffic problems and the like, mostly from the Brattleboro police, although occasionally the state police or others had a word to add.

What next? he wondered bleakly. How could he find the boy when the state and local police hadn't been able to? He had already talked to the increasingly impatient Brattleboro used-car dealer who had bought Carl's auto, and he had found out absolutely nothing beyond what McNaughton had already told him. A middle-aged man with a long, untidy goatee, a flashy corduroy jacket, and an Australian bush hat had brought the car in, had picked out an old junker to take in trade, had signed all the papers "Carl Brandon," and had left with the junker and a thousand in cash. It could have been considerably more except that Brandon had insisted on cash and cash quickly, which had made the dealer slightly suspicious, he admitted, but "not suspicious enough to turn down a deal like that."

Laird had talked to the local police, asking them about Brandon, but had gotten nothing. Nor had he gotten anything from the Brattleboro school officials except a grudging admission that "the drug problem exists, but it's certainly no worse than in any other school system this size."

And he had cruised the streets of Brattleboro looking for the junker and listening to the scanner, growing more nervous and more furious with every passing minute.

At last, John Groves realized, it was over.

For an eternity—although his watch said little more than two hours had passed—every nerve had screamed in agonizing sympathy as the ritual proceeded, until finally, the shredded flesh and organs were too tattered for even the healing power of the talisman creature to maintain life and consciousness in what had been the body of the fifteen-year-old boy.

Through it all, perhaps in an effort to blunt the horror of the reality by blanketing it with elements of fantasy, Groves's mind had repeatedly conjured up a story from an old comic book, a story he thought he had forgotten until then. A story in which, in a cabin in an isolated, wooded area, a man finds the remains of another man. All the essential organs, including brain and eyes, are spread out on a board, interconnected like a bread-boarded electrical circuit. Aliens had done it as part of their research into the intricacies of human anatomy. And the corpse, the "bread-boarded man," is revealed to be alive when, on the last page, it speaks.

The boy hadn't spoken at the end. In fact, he hadn't uttered a single sound throughout the entire process, which only seemed to make it all the more horrible as the boy sat there in seeming calmness, slowly and deliberately carving at himself, with his eyes the only things registering the pain and terror he felt.

And he did feel it, Groves had no doubt. The boy felt

everything. There was no numbing, no blurring of the consciousness. If anything, the boy's senses had been heightened, just as Groves's had been heightened when his reward had been offered to him. Heightened by the creature that hovered silently at the edges of John Groves's mind, soaking up every iota of agony as it gradually rebuilt its depleted strength.

But finally it was over, and Groves was allowed to leave, allowed once again to take control of his body. But this time the aftermath was different. He was not sick as he had been the first time. Apparently the creature was able to control such physical reactions, but it could not control the horror and disgust Groves felt in his mind. But mixed in with the horror and self-loathing was a feeling of satiety, the kind of feeling one gets after a good meal or a good night's sleep. The creature's strength was fully restored, apparently.

And it was ready for whatever was awaiting it at the lodge.

It was after six and the day was fading rapidly when Bill March finally arrived at the lodge. Elena, who had been listening and watching at the windows, reached him while he was still taking his suitcase from the trunk of his rented subcompact.

Hearing her footsteps on the gravel, he turned toward her as he lifted the suitcase out with one hand and slammed the trunk lid down with the other.

"Hi, Sis. Am I in time for supper?"

"Bill," she said, not seeming even to hear his question, "I know this is going to sound strange, but it would be best if you could take Beth and leave right now."

He blinked down at her from his six-foot-plus height. His lean face quickly took on a puzzled frown.

"You're right," he said. "It does sound strange, and that's a downright generous description. Think you could at least take time enough to explain what's going on?"

She pulled in a bracing breath. "As the saying goes, it's a long story. I solemnly promise I'll explain everything when you bring her back."

If I'm still around when you bring her back, she added bleakly to herself.

"This newfound old beau giving you trouble?" he asked.

She shook her head. "Nothing like that. Just—"

"Does he even exist?"

"What—of course he does," she began, but then she shook her head in exasperation. "No, he doesn't, but that isn't important."

"All right, what is important?"

"That you take Beth somewhere quickly."

"Now wait a minute. I've been doing a lot of thinking about this. I've had a lot of time to think, driving all the way from Boston. Anyway, I got to wondering if you were in some kind of trouble, and now, the way you're acting, I'm pretty darned sure you are. So before I go running off, with or without Beth, you're going to tell me what's going on. All right?"

"Damn it, Bill! Can't you trust me just this once?"

"I trusted you enough to come all the way out here, didn't I?"

She grimaced. "Then trust me enough to—" She stopped, her eyes falling on the Grantlands' rental car. "For one thing," she said, "Grantland and his wife showed up here this afternoon. And you remember what you told me about keeping Beth out of his sight."

"Grantland? Here? How did he know where to find you?"

"Your phone was tapped," she said. "And the one who did the tapping is here, too. A private detective named Jessup. Grantland hired him about the time I left town, apparently."

"Who does Grantland think he is?" Bill started toward the lodge. "Where's a phone? I'll call Chief Travers and—"

"You better listen to the rest first," she said, interrupting and grabbing his arm to hold him back. While he fumed, she hastily outlined Jessup's confession, including the fact that he had been hired specifically to find and snatch Beth. "Now, is it any wonder," she finished, "that I want you to get Beth out of here as soon as you can?"

"They're the ones who should leave," he snapped, and pulled free of her hand. Leaving his suitcase on the ground behind the car, he stalked toward the lodge.

"Wait, Bill, please," she called, hurrying after him. But before she caught him, the door of the lodge swung open.

"Uncle Bill."

Beth ran down the steps to meet him. Faltering in his angry stride, he stopped and assembled a hasty smile. As she ran across the lawn to him, he leaned down and scooped her up in his deceptively strong arms and held her at arm's length in front of him.

"Where are we going?" she wanted to know instantly.

Bill kept his smile, but he looked sideways at Elena, who had just caught up with him.

"I told her you'd be taking her somewhere this evening."

The smile remained on his face, but it looked strained. Beth didn't seem to notice, however.

"I don't know where we're going," he said to the girl as he set her on the ground. "I saw a couple of places between here and Boston that looked kind of interesting. Can't see them too well at night, though," he added, glancing at Elena again.

Hurriedly, Elena took Beth's hand. "You go inside. I have to talk to Uncle Bill some more."

"I want to talk to him, too."

"I know, honey. You can in just a couple of minutes. Okay?"

The child hesitated, looking annoyed, but then she shrugged. "Okay."

As she disappeared back inside the lodge, Bill turned to Elena again. "What is going on here? If you really think Grantland and that detective are going to try to kidnap Beth—"

"There's more than that."

"More?" he prompted angrily when she hesitated. "More what?"

"You'll hear when you get inside, anyway. Some nut with a gun was here this afternoon."

"A gun?" He swore briefly, something he rarely did. "Someone Grantland hired or what?"

She shook her head. "No, just a nut."

"And?" he prompted. "What happened? Are you afraid he's coming back? Is that it? Damn it, Sis, if there's someone like that running around loose, you're both leaving!"

Suddenly, Elena realized that he had given her a possible solution. "She's already packed. I am, too, for that matter.

You wait here, and I'll get her bag. She can go with you, and the two of you can fly back. It's a long trip by car for a five-year-old, and she's never had a chance to fly before. She can stay with you and Mom a couple of days till I make it back with the car."

"I'll carry some of the bags," he said, starting up the steps.

"No, I'll get them," she said hastily, trying to block him, but even as she did, she realized that it was too late.

Over her brother's shoulder, she saw John Groves turn into the parking area. Although she couldn't see it, she could almost feel the talisman resting against his chest.

At the eighteenth service station he tried, Seth Laird found someone who seemed to recognize his description of the man who had traded in Carl's car at the used-car lot. The attendant, answering offhandedly as he moved a trouble light back and forth and peered at the bottom of the car above him on the grease rack, said that he remembered seeing someone like that a couple of times.

"Never driving either one of those cars you're talking about, though. Something big and expensive, I remember."

"Do you know his name?" Laird asked anxiously.

The attendant, a middle-aged balding man in grease-smeared coveralls, shook his head. "No idea. Except I think some girl he had with him one time called him Buck or something odd like that."

So it was the same man. Elation at the discovery was mixed with stomach-twisting anxiety as Laird's guess that the boy had sold the car to get money for more drugs was apparently confirmed.

"What kind of car? What about the license?"

Again the attendant shook his head. "Sorry, no idea about the license. Car was one of those ritzy foreign jobs. You know, Mercedes or Jaguar or something like that. I didn't work on it, you know. Just gave him some gas."

"When was that? When did you see him?"

A shrug. "Two, maybe three weeks ago. Hard to say."

"If you see him again, take the license number. And call the police."

The attendant's eyes widened, and he turned from his inspection of the underside of the car to look at Laird. "Call the cops? What for? What's this guy done?" Then a suspicious frown. "Are you a cop? You didn't say so, you know."

"I'm not with the police, but they would be interested in the man. They think he's a drug dealer. Selling to kids."

A whistle. "So that's how he can afford a jalopy like that. No wonder. But if you're not a cop, who—"

"I'm a doctor from Wertham. And I'm reasonably sure this man has been selling drugs to my son."

"I'm sorry, but I don't know any more than I already told you. I really don't."

"That's all right. It's more than I've gotten anywhere else today." Laird took one of his business cards from his wallet and handed it to the attendant. "Here. If you do see him again, get the license number and the make of the car and anything else you can. Tell the police, but call me, too, the minute you see him. All right?"

"I suppose," the attendant said, although he sounded dubious now. "You out gunning for the guy for doing that to your kid? Is that it?"

Laird shook his head. "No. At least not now. I think my son is with him, or at least he knows where my son is. And I have to find my son. I have to."

The attendant's face shifted to sympathy. "How old's your kid?"

"Sixteen. Look, will you do this? Call the police if he comes back? And call me?" As he spoke, Laird pulled a twenty from his wallet and held it out. "It's worth a hell of a lot more than this to me if you will."

The man started to reach for it, but then he stopped and shook his head. "No, that's not something you should have to pay for. A couple of my kids will be that age in a few years, and I hope this guy gets put away before then. I'll call if I see him, don't worry."

Laird thanked him and got back in his car to drive to the next service station listed in the Brattleboro Yellow Pages. Another dozen and that would be it. He would stop at the police station with whatever information he'd managed to find, and then he would go home on the forlorn hope that

Carl might have decided to come back. Or perhaps he should spend the night at the clinic. He didn't know how long the money from the car sale would last, but when it ran out, the boy would be looking for something else to sell or trade, and he might take another look through the clinic for drugs. He had been interrupted the first time and hadn't had a chance to make a thorough search.

But what, Laird wondered, would he do when—if—he found the boy? He hadn't yet been able even to talk to John Groves, and each time he thought of what any such conversation would be like, he cringed.

"I beg your pardon, Mr. Groves, but I have reason to believe you are capable of performing miraculous healings, and my son is in need of such a healing."

He could vividly imagine Groves's reaction, since it would, under any other circumstances, be his own reaction. If he were wrong or if Groves chose to deny his ability, Laird could receive anything from a stony silence to sarcastic ridicule.

And in any case, how could he get the two of them together when he couldn't even find them?

As he neared the next service station, four blocks away and near the city limits, the scanner crackled into life once again. There was some static, and then a voice asked: "Brock, you still listening in?" Laird snapped to attention instantly. The only Brock he knew was Brock McNaughton, the state patrol sergeant who had brought him the news about the sale of the car that morning.

"Right here," came the reply a couple of seconds later. The Southern drawl was still there, but the words came out rapidly and sharply. "What do you have?"

"That 1960 Thunderbird you were looking for," the first voice said, and then read off the license number.

"Where?" McNaughton's voice snapped.

"Ten miles south of Wertham on 30, headed north."

So he was going home. Making a U turn that sent one wheel bouncing over the curb and drew an angry horn blast from the driver he cut off, Laird jammed the accelerator to the floor and raced toward the expressway entrance a mile away. As he drove, the distant conversation continued to emerge from the scanner.

"Don't do anything to scare him off," McNaughton's voice said. "But don't lose him, either."

"Sure thing. He might be suspicious, though, if he saw me turn around in the middle of the highway. I was heading south when I spotted him."

"Don't worry about it. Just keep him in sight. I'm on 91 not far from Wertham. I'll head for there, and you let me know if he detours."

"Will do. So far, so good. Nobody got between us, and I can see his taillights up the road. Incidentally, so I don't go into this too blind, what do we want this guy for?"

"Medical," McNaughton said. "Needs treatment at a hospital."

"Yeah? What's wrong with him?"

"Just follow him," McNaughton said briskly. "All I know is what the kid's doctor said."

Laird cut to the right onto the expressway ramp and floored the accelerator again.

Bill March turned to see what his sister had seen over his shoulder. A car—he couldn't see the make in the near darkness—was pulling into the lodge grounds and parking next to his own rental car.

Looking back at his sister, he asked sharply, "Is that the one you were talking about? The one with the gun?"

She shook her head, but it seemed to Bill that there was a certain resignation in the movement. "It's John Groves. He and his wife own the lodge. Now, you just wait here, and I'll get Beth and the bags."

Turning, she hurried through the door, but before she could close it, a slender, athletic-looking woman with almost-black hair pulled back in a loose bun darted past her and Bill with barely a glance.

"Who's that?" Bill asked.

"Mrs. Groves."

"Ellie, look—" Bill began, but she had already closed the door behind her.

All right, he thought abruptly, something is going on here, and it's not what she said. It was just like yesterday. He had asked if that nut with a gun was still running around loose, and she had agreed. Just like when he had asked last night if she had found a boy friend and she had agreed.

Well, this time she wasn't going to get away with it. He was going to find out what the hell was going on.

Irritably, he snatched the huge door open and went into the lodge.

But Ellie and Beth were nowhere in sight. The only person in the outlandishly huge room—which he assumed must be the lobby—was an overweight, balding man, probably in his fifties. He was standing near what looked like an enclosed spiral staircase, looking uneasily toward the ground-floor hallway on the right. As Bill entered and stood looking around for his sister, the man turned toward him.

As the man looked at Bill, he seemed to grow even more uneasy. "You're Bill March," the man said, but he didn't come forward.

"That's right. And you?"

"Pete Jessup. I—"

"You're the SOB that works for Grantland. I've got half a mind to—"

Jessup shrank back. "I'm on your side now," he said hastily. "I told your sister what happened and why. You know what Grantland can do to you if you don't go along with him."

"I know what he can try to do!" Forcing himself to stop, Bill March sucked in a deep, calming breath before he went on. "I'm sorry. I'm just trying to find out what's going on around here, and—" He paused, eyeing Jessup more closely. "You're sure you've dropped Grantland? Completely?"

"Completely. More's the pity for my wallet and career." The man forced a small smile, but it wouldn't stick.

Bill nodded but said nothing.

"Well, Grantland does seem to be acting more reasonably now. I think Mrs. Grantland had a long talk with him." A smile returned, this one rueful. "It looks like he's transferred all his hostility, as the shrinks say, to me. I really think your niece is safe now."

"Ellie said something else, that some kind of gunman was here this afternoon. Do you know anything about that? She sounded like she was afraid he'd be back, whoever it was."

Jessup's face, already dotted with perspiration, lengthened as he grimaced. "Someone was here, but there's no chance he'll be back. You must've misunderstood."

"I suppose I could've. But why? What happened?"

"Some local high school kid came busting in here, oh, around two or so. He didn't say a damned thing, just pulled a gun the second he spotted your sister."

"He was after her? But if he was local—"

"You think I haven't wondered about that already? I even thought for a minute that Grantland might've been crazy enough to hire someone to con the kid into it. But it wasn't Grantland." Jessup waved his hands dismissively in the air. "I'm sure of that now. Even he wouldn't be that dumb. This was just some local wacko, I'm sure; he was probably on drugs or something. Glassy stare, the whole bit. And slow, which was damned lucky for all of us. He had your sister right in his sights for a second or two before I managed to plow into him; he missed by three or four feet."

"You mean he actually shot at her?"

"The gun went off, yes. Bullet hit the ceiling. Then he dropped dead a couple minutes after it happened." Jessup shook his head. "Grantland was trying to tell me I killed him just by knocking him down, but I've been thinking. It was drugs, it had to be. You know how they work. They can do anything."

The man was talking rapidly now, as if trying to convince himself of the truth of what he was saying, but Bill had hardly heard the last two or three sentences.

"He's dead?" Bill finally asked.

Jessup stumbled to a halt. "That's right. That's why you must've misunderstood what your sister said about being afraid the guy might be back."

"Where is she?" Bill asked abruptly. "Where is my sister now?"

Silently, Jessup pointed down the hall toward Elena's room.

Davis Grantland blinked awake, automatically lifting his arm and squinting at his watch.

Christ, he thought angrily. He had just lain down on the bed to rest for a minute and he'd gone to sleep, and here it was six-thirty. Not that he could have accomplished anything worthwhile even if he'd stayed awake, not with that March bitch, especially not in the frame of mind he had been in after that scene with Jessup. God, what an idiot the man was. First he goes over to the enemy, and then he starts throwing insane accusations around. If he thinks he's going to get away with that, he—

"Feeling any better, dear?"

Miriam's voice came from somewhere out of sight to his left, and he turned his head to look at her. She was in the armchair next to a lamp by the window. A paperback she'd picked up while they'd been shopping for overnight necessities in Wertham a couple of hours before lay closed on her lap. Some damned romance, he thought irritably. It was the usual kind of crap she indulged in.

He swung his legs off the bed and sat up, wincing at the stiffness in his back. "I thought they served meals in this place. Did they forget we were here?"

Miriam stood up abruptly, laying the book on the chair seat. "I'll check."

Then she was gone, gliding across the room with quick steps and clicking the door softly shut behind her.

Angry at her sudden departure, he started to call after her, but he stopped with a grimace. Taking out his feelings on Miriam wouldn't help. None of it was her fault, not really. If anyone was to blame, it was that March woman.

March, he thought, his anger suddenly boiling over. Not Grantland. Her gall was incredible, not only taking back her maiden name but changing his granddaughter's, too. He didn't know how they had found a judge addled enough to grant such a thing, but they had. If only he had known in time. But he hadn't. There was no way he could have known that his only son would be dead within months, and then it was too late. He could have fought the change if he'd known that the child was the only grandchild he'd ever have. He could have gotten to the judge somehow, kept the change from going through, but he hadn't. He hadn't thought it important. Good riddance, he had thought at the time. The last connection with his son's folly would be gone, and the boy could start building a new, sensible life.

But it was too late now for recriminations, too late for might-have-beens. His son was gone, his life empty. Miriam was right. Unless he was careful, he could totally lose his granddaughter as well.

Or had he already lost her? Was it already too late for that, too? He tried to remember what the woman had said this afternoon, but he couldn't. He could only remember that she had been cold and distant, even angry.

Something twisted at his stomach as he remembered that anger. As if she had any reason to be angry. She was like some animal, mindlessly defending its young against everyone and everything. Never mind that he could give the child a thousand times the advantages she could. Never mind that she had taken advantage of his son, somehow tricking him into a marriage she must have known could never work. Never mind that she had taken the settlement he had offered—and a generous settlement it had been, too. Damned generous—and simply walked away. Never mind that she had literally kidnaped his granddaughter, hauling her from state to state like a gypsy.

What had his son ever seen in that bitch? How could he have defied his own father and plunged into such an ill-advised, foolish marriage? Somehow she had blinded him to common sense and reason. She had tricked him, lured him into wasting more than four years of his life, had even gotten him to pull out of the family business and go back to school. To become a teacher! Where he thought he would get a job, Grantland couldn't imagine then and couldn't imagine now, or why he would want to.

But he had. He had wanted to. Somehow she had lured him into it, the same way she had lured him into marriage. He would never have done anything so foolish on his own. If he had never met that woman, he would have remained sane and sensible, would have heeded Grantland's advice, would have married a suitable wife who would have fit into the family and given Grantland the grandchildren he so desperately wanted.

And he would have still been alive.

The thought came crashing in with the force of a tidal wave. His son would still be alive if it weren't for that woman. Not only was his wasted life her fault but his death as well.

And just as forcefully, just as logically, came the corollary: She must pay. She had killed his son, and she must pay.

His son had died, and so she, too, must die.

Unaware that his thoughts were no longer fully his own, Davis Grantland stood up from the bed, barely feeling the painful stiffness in his back. He stood silently for a moment, as if considering his next action. Then he picked up the paper sack containing the toilet articles he had purchased at the local drug store. How fortunate, he thought, that he had never switched over to electric razors and that the store had happened to have in stock an old-fashioned straight razor, almost as if they had known that he was coming.

It was just what he needed.

Bill March had crossed the lobby and was entering the hallway when his sister and niece emerged from a room on the right of the hall a dozen yards away. Ellie was carrying two suitcases, while Beth was clutching a rolled-up comic book. Ellie lurched to a halt when she saw Bill. At the same time, a door on the opposite side of the hall opened, and a man, even taller than Bill and thinner and at least eighty years old, stepped out stiffly. He appeared slightly dazed as he looked around, and then his eyes fell on Ellie.

"Jessie," he said in a thin voice, "it's starting again."

For a moment it seemed she was going to reply, but then she hurried Beth forward, handing one of the suitcases to Bill. "Here," she said. "I'll leave in just a few minutes. You and Beth go ahead."

"Can we eat pretty soon?" Beth asked, looking up at Bill. "I'm hungry."

"Pretty soon," he said hurriedly. "I'm getting hungry, too, but we can't leave right this minute."

"You have to," Elena said tensely.

He shook his head. "Sorry, but not until you tell me what's really going on here." He glanced down the hall in the direction of the kitchen. "Besides, we're both getting hungry, and it smells like supper is about ready. Didn't you say that meals were included here?"

Beth, who had started to look worried as Bill and her mother began to sound like they were mad at each other, perked up instantly. "Can we eat here?" she asked, and then added what she had been repeating almost every day, "This is a house. And I haven't showed you the cat yet."

"See?" Bill said. "It's settled."

Hearing footsteps behind him, he turned. Miriam Grantland was approaching hesitantly; her gray slacks and dark-blue, loosely fitting sweater were still slightly rumpled on her stocky body from the hours of traveling.

"Mrs. Grantland," Bill said, acknowledging her approach with a touch of stiffness.

"I'm sorry about all this, Mr. March," she said, obviously uneasy. "But I don't think you'll have any more trouble, I really don't."

Bill seemed to relax slightly. "I'm sure we won't. And it's not your fault, anyway."

Miriam Grantland relaxed in turn but was still not fully at ease. "Thank you," she said, and then looked around. "I was going to ask Mrs. Groves about dinner."

"It smells done," Bill said. "And Mr. Groves just drove in a couple of minutes ago, so it shouldn't be long. His wife just ran out to the parking lot to meet him."

As he was speaking, the buzzer sounded, indicating that someone had come through the front door.

"That's probably them now," Bill said.

John Groves followed his wife dully along the walk to the lodge. He couldn't blame her for being upset and angry; he couldn't blame her at all. And he certainly couldn't explain why he had been missing from school all afternoon and where he had been until almost six-thirty.

The truth, he thought with the only touch of humor he'd been able to muster recently, would hardly put her at ease.

What was worse, it was far from over. He didn't know when it would come or what form it would take, but it was coming. The memories that shimmered through his mind ever more frequently told him that, and they also told him that there was absolutely nothing he could do about it. At this point, as in the ghastly ritual he had been forced to witness this afternoon, he was only a spectator. The creature, whatever it was, was in charge.

And the woman, Elena March, was the target. He didn't know why, any more than he knew the nature of the talisman and the creature that inhabited it. He only knew that the creature existed, that it feared Elena March, and that it was determined that she must die.

It had already tried to kill her once. It had sent Curt Weber after her, and now Curt Weber was dead. Mattie had told him when she had come rushing out, but he had already known. He had even known what she didn't know, what no one would ever know—that the boy's heart had simply slowed and finally stopped because the creature had told it to. He even knew— remembered—that such methods would not work with Elena March. She was somehow different, immune to such direct manipulation. Since that first night, when she had been brought to him as a reward, she had been immune. She had touched the talisman, and something slumbering within her had been awakened. She had become untouchable, and the talisman creature had become vulnerable.

But there were other ways, Groves's memories told him. There were other ways, just as there had been in the past. He had half expected to be forced to kill her himself, but that had not happened. He doubted whether he could have resisted, any more than he had been able to resist preparing the creature's meals, but he had not been put to the test. Perhaps, he thought, the creature did not want to endanger its host any more than necessary. As the creature's host, he had to participate in the feedings, but he did not have to participate in Elena March's killing. It might even be easier making use of others who were not keyed up to resist and could therefore be more easily controlled.

If only she would leave!

But she wouldn't. She had been drawn here, and so had the old man in some strange way. She had been drawn here, and now she was as much a prisoner as Groves himself. The creature feared her and could not control her, yet she was a prisoner.

At the front of the lodge, Mattie pulled open the door and waited for him to mount the steps. Would she, too, be destroyed by this creature? he wondered. By what he himself had become? During the months of prelude, while the creature had been reaching into his mind more deeply than he realized, he had practically destroyed their relationship. And it would have been better, he thought, if that relationship had been destroyed totally. She might have left, then. She wouldn't have stayed to be witness to what was to come.

He resisted the impulse to kiss her, knowing that it would only draw her closer, draw her further into his own destruction. He might somehow still be able to cut her free, drive her out so that she would not be destroyed along with him.

He might, but he doubted it.

He doubted his ability to do anything beyond what the creature forced him to do.

But still, he had to try. The fact that it feared anything at all gave him some small hope, although he doubted that it would last.

Entering the lobby behind Mattie, he saw a man emerging from the left-hand hall. He was tall and solidly built, probably in his late fifties, with silvery white hair, mussed as if he had just awakened. His shirt, an expensive dress shirt open at the collar, was mussed as well, billowing out slightly around the waist where it had been partially pulled from his trousers. And his face, set in an angry scowl, was betrayed by a peculiar blankness in the eyes.

It was a blankness Groves had seen before.

It's beginning already, he thought helplessly. It's beginning already.

Seth Laird had been on the expressway five minutes, covering nearly eight miles, when the scanner crackled to life again, this time with something other than the routine calls his ears automatically rejected.

"Brock," came the voice of the one who was following Carl's car, "I think he spotted me. He really floored it a couple of seconds ago."

"You can keep up with a fifteen-year-old car, I hope."

"Maybe. You want me to hit the lights and siren?"

"No, that'd only spook him worse. Just keep him in sight. I'm almost at Wertham."

Cursing aloud, Laird gripped the wheel more tightly. You can't lose him now, damn it, he thought desperately. You can't lose him now!

As Davis Grantland emerged from the hall into the huge lobby, he saw the Groves woman and someone else entering from outside. That pea-brained detective, Jessup, was hovering ineffectually near the entrance to the other hall, and he could hear the March woman and her brother arguing in the hall beyond.

A feeling of grim amusement settled over him, and he lightly touched the rear trouser pocket where the folded straight razor lay. How appropriate. Everyone was assembled for the final act of his little morality play: that treacherous detective, who himself deserved death for his traitorous actions; the March woman's brother, who had conspired with her every step of the way; Miriam, his own wife, who had, in these last hours, proved as treacherous as any of the others. Her case, he thought, was even more reprehensible. She, after all, owed him loyalty for nearly forty years together.

Yes, he thought as he crossed the lobby with a purposeful stride, it was good that they were all here, that they would all witness his action. And it was good that he was able to end it this way, in the open, aboveboard, It would never be said that he did not take responsibility for his actions. He was not the kind to sneak around in the dead of night as if ashamed of what he was doing. He had never been that kind, either in his business dealings or in his personal life. Everyone, friends and enemies alike, had always known where Davis Grantland stood and what he meant to do.

This time would be no different.

Jessup stood back nervously as Grantland approached. The detective looked as if he were working up the nerve to speak, but Grantland gave him no encouragement as he brushed past.

Similarly, Miriam looked at him uneasily as he strode toward her and the others grouped in the hall. Bill March, the slut's brother, looked at him defiantly.

"Mr. Grantland," he said.

Grantland paused, looking at the gangling, ill-dressed form. "It's good that you're here, March," he said brusquely.

"I'm sorry I can't say the same about you," March said with equal brusqueness.

Then the Groves woman was in the hall, making her way past them. She was obviously agitated about something, but her voice was steady. "Everyone that wants can eat in a couple of minutes," she said. "The dining room's right in there," she added, pointing to a door near the end of the hall.

Grantland moved a step closer to the March woman, who stood hovering nervously over his granddaughter. She was saying something to the girl and then to her brother, but he couldn't hear what it was. But it wasn't important.

What was important was what he was about to do.

Again he touched the pocket with the folded razor inside. It would be simple enough. He could get behind her without anyone becoming suspicious. He could have his left arm around her shoulders in a second, pinning her arms and holding her helpless while his right hand took the razor from his pocket and flipped it open. It would be over in a second. She would have paid for her . . .

Grantland blinked. For just a moment, the people grouped around him seemed to shift and change. Their faces melted into other faces; their clothes twisted like blobs of paint being mixed on an artist's palette and became the costumes of a turn-of-the-century drama. The old man suddenly filled out, his parchment skin losing its pallor and becoming young and ruddy, his white hair turning dishwater blond.

And the March woman, too, shimmered like a ghost and became another, younger woman, dressed in a long skirt and heavily bloused sleeves, an outfit that had gone out of style years before he was born.

The walls around them faded into wisps of smoke. Trees, massive oaks and elms and birches, sprang up on all sides, lit only by the flickering of a distant flame.

Then it was over. The momentary delusion passed, and everything was as before.

Almost everything.

For the first time since he had come to his decision, a

doubt appeared in Davis Grantland's mind. Not a doubt that it was the right decision but a doubt that he could carry it out.

While the others milled around him and the Groves woman moved toward the kitchen, Grantland took another step toward his ex-daughter-in-law. But it was hard, as if he were moving through molasses, not air.

A name shimmered in his mind, a name he could not consciously remember ever having heard before: Jessica.

He tried to take another step, but now it was impossible. Everyone was moving away. He reached out a hand, but it fell inches short of her shoulders.

Silently, he swore. Was he going to be denied his victory, his vengeance for his son's life?

Strangely, although it didn't seem at all strange to Grantland, he did not even stop to wonder what was hindering him or what had caused the hallucination of a moment before. He only wondered frantically whether there was anything he could do to avoid the failure that now seemed almost a certainty.

Then he heard a faint and tiny voice.

"Grandpa? Are you all right?"

He saw the little girl looking up at him.

As he looked down at the child, he didn't think of her as his granddaughter except for the briefest of moments. He could almost feel his thoughts being rearranged, but even that did not strike him as strange.

One plan had failed, his thoughts told him, and so another would be tried. It would take a moment for it to come to him in its entirety, but it would come, just as plans had always come to him if he only gave them the time.

"Yes, I'm fine, Beth," he said, and as he spoke, he found that he could once again move without hindrance.

In a few minutes he would be fine, just as soon as the new course of action his subconscious was working out became clear to him.

Elena March had never felt more helpless or frightened in her life. Everything was going wrong. First Grantland had showed up to cause trouble, and then Bill hadn't shown up until minutes before Groves had returned. And finally Bill, slipping into one of his rare obstinate moods, simply refused to take Beth anywhere until he got the truth from Elena. And she couldn't for the life of her—or for the life of her daughter—think of any truth he would accept.

She should have, she realized belatedly, taken Winton up on his offer to take Beth away. It might not have been successful, but at least it would have given the child a better chance than she had now. Even a few scant miles of separation would have been better than this.

But it was too late for second thoughts. She could only hope desperately that Bill would relent or that something brilliant would occur to her. But it would have to be soon, she knew. Something inside her—the same something, she suspected, that had drawn her here and had haunted her dreams with visions of past lives—told her that it was all coming to a head soon.

As if to reinforce that conviction, she felt that stream of guttural nonsense syllables that had poured again and again from Jessica's dying lips and from the lips of a hundred others, felt them inching closer to the surface, straining ever more energetically to force their way from her throat. Again and again they replayed themselves in her mind like some grotesque commercial jingle that just wouldn't let go of her thoughts. With each repetition, the urge to give them physical reality, the compulsion to let the dam break and let them flood out into the world, grew harder to resist.

But until Beth was away, she must resist. She didn't know how the creature would strike back, only that it would. In all those other lives, it had somehow won out, leaving its enemy dead or dying. She was willing to take that chance. Or, more accurately, she had no choice but to take that chance. Whatever lived within her compelled her to take that chance.

But it could not compel her to take that same chance with her daughter's life.

It simply could not.

She told herself that over and over, but with every passing minute she came closer to doubting her ability to continue her resistance.

* * *

The Wertham exit signs glinted in Seth Laird's headlights when the scanner came to life once more.

"Brock," the first voice said, "he just turned off the highway. Went to the right on Douglas Road."

The last half of a curse came through as McNaughton clicked his transmitter on. "What's he doing there?"

"I don't know, but if he doesn't slow down, he won't be doing it for long. That's not one of your better roads. I just hope he doesn't meet anyone."

"I know. Don't push him. If he sticks on it, I know about where he'll have to come out on the old highway. I can get there before he does."

"If you're thinking about turning your car into a roadblock, I wouldn't advise it, not unless you can set it up so this guy can see you for a half mile ahead. He's really moving!"

"I know. I know."

"Look, Brock, what is this guy wanted for? You said he needed medical treatment, but if you ask me, he's acting more like he just robbed a bank and shot the teller. He's—oh, shit!"

"What? What is it?"

There was a second of silence, and then a suddenly shaky voice said, "Get an ambulance out here fast, Brock. That goddamn idiot just missed a curve!"

Laird, just coming off the Wertham exit ramp onto the old highway, gasped as his stomach went into icy spasms. The car wavered and almost went into the ditch as the world seemed to sway around him like a ship on a stormy ocean. His arms suddenly lost all their strength, and although he didn't hear the sound himself, a high-pitched moan began to leak from his throat.

For a moment, as he saw Grantland hesitate and then draw back from Elena March, relief flooded through John Groves. Something had gone wrong. He didn't know what; he didn't even know specifically what Grantland had been instructed to do any more than he knew specifically what Curt Weber had been instructed to do. But he did know that something had gone wrong. Elena March was not going to die, at least not within the next few seconds.

Then, as the group began to straggle toward the dining room in compliance with Mattie's invitation to supper, more memories bobbed to the surface of Groves's mind. He didn't welcome them, but neither did he flinch or make any other outward indication. They had come to him so often now, particularly since the Weber boy's failure and death, that he had ceased to marvel at them or even wonder at their source. He had, he suspected, learned as much as he was going to about the creature, more, perhaps, than the creature had wanted him to learn. The only thing Groves had not ceased to do was try to think of a way out.

But of course he had not been able to think of anything. The creature was apparently afraid of Elena March or of something *within* Elena March. Another nightmarish, parasitic creature like the one that controlled Groves himself? His first thought had been to try to talk to her, but if the creature could force him to participate in the feedings, it could certainly prevent him from speaking to Elena March or anyone else.

But now there had been another reprieve, or failure, just as there had been earlier in the afternoon. And the memories that this creature somehow used as its method of communication with its host were once again bobbing to the surface of his mind.

Abruptly, Groves stiffened. He blinked, thinking that surely he was mistaken or that a further memory would soon surface, altering or negating the first.

But none did. The memory remained and, if anything, grew stronger and more vivid, more compelling.

Not only was he being allowed to speak to Elena March about the talisman, he was virtually being commanded to do so. Immediately.

Grantland and his wife and Jessup had already vanished into the dining room, while Mattie had gone to the kitchen. Elena March and her brother and daughter and the old man still stood in a group in the hall.

"I have to talk to you, Ms. March," Groves said quietly.

Elena's first impulse on hearing Groves speaking practically in her ear was to bolt, but she could not. She could no more run from him now than she had been able to run from this place before.

Was this it? she wondered. Had she delayed the confrontation as long as she could?

But no, she suddenly realized, this was something else. Groves had not approached her as an antagonist, as that boy had this afternoon.

Or was that just illusion? It was growing harder by the second to keep silent, to keep those guttural, nightmarish sounds from breaking free from their prison within her mind and throat.

"It means you no harm," Groves said softly.

"What means her no harm?" Bill March snapped, turning angrily on Groves. He towered several inches over the smaller, bearded man.

"It's all right, Bill," Elena said quickly.

"No, it is not all right. Damn it, Ellie, tell me what's going on and we can be on our way out of here in thirty seconds."

"Don't fight with Mommy, Uncle Bill," Beth's plaintive voice broke in. "That's what Daddy did before he went away."

Anger and concern fought for Bill's features as Elena dropped to her knees and took the girl in her arms. "It's all right, honey, it really is. Uncle Bill's not angry; he's just worried about me."

Standing up, still holding Beth's shoulder with one hand, Elena spoke quietly to her brother. "I'll explain everything as soon as I can, I promise," she said, hoping she would survive to keep the promise, wondering what would happen if she released her iron grip on her tongue and vocal chords and let the pent-up sounds gush out.

"But right now I have to talk to Mr. Groves," she went on. "Why don't you look after Beth for a minute? You and Mr. Winton," she added, looking at the old man standing anxiously by. "He and Beth have been getting along famously."

Bill looked reluctant, but he didn't refuse. For a moment, Elena wondered whether his uncharacteristic stubbornness was entirely his own or whether he, too, was being affected by the talisman and whatever had been released from the grave with it.

Then she was following Groves back down the hall to the lobby. He ran nervous fingers through his blond hair as he walked, a motion that only added to the tension that permeated the air.

For the first time, Elena realized the truth.

John Groves was afraid. Like herself, he was afraid.

And like Marcus Reimann had been afraid?

For a moment, the last hours of Jessica Reimann's life flashed through Elena's mind, and she wondered whether that was how it was going to end once again. One more futile effort to destroy something that could not be destroyed? It had survived the centuries, and it had survived seventy years in the grave of Marcus and Jessica Reimann. How could it fail to survive now?

But she herself—or something within her—had survived equally long. As long as the talisman had existed, she had existed. If her nightmares meant anything at all, they meant that. And if she failed now, she—or something in her—would try again, in some other place, in some other time, in some other life. Somehow the possibility seemed acceptable to her.

All the while, the pressure of the sounds—she could not bring herself to think of them as words—grew stronger, more nearly irresistible, until it became a physical thing, an ache in her throat and a trembling in the muscles of her jaw.

Groves came to a stop near the registration desk, out of sight of the people they had left behind in the hall. As he turned to face her, he lifted the talisman from his chest, held it for a second, and let it fall back on the front of his open-collared shirt.

The thin gold chain, she saw, was new, far lighter than the one that had held it around Marcus Reimann's neck. The setting, actually a simple seven-sided metallic frame into which the talisman fit perfectly, was the same. It had been cleaned, but it still retained the marks of its burial, the streaks of corrosion.

But the talisman itself, a pool of impenetrable blackness, was untouched, as if it were not a material object but a frozen vortex of malignant energies.

"You know what this is," he said expressionlessly, "and where I found it."

She nodded. "In the grave of Jessica and Marcus Reimann."

"Let me tell you what it enabled me to do this morning," he said, and then hurried on to describe his encounters with Herb Franklin and Greta Tremont.

"Check with the hospital if you don't believe me," he insisted. "Before this morning, there was no hope for either of them, and now they are in perfect health."

She believed him, yet there was no lessening of the pressure within her to scream out the sounds that could, if she were allowed enough time, destroy the talisman.

"Why are you telling me this?" she asked.

He swallowed and was silent a moment, as if some internal struggle were going on.

"I know," he said, "that you would destroy it if you could. *It* knows. I simply want you to know what it is you would be attempting to destroy."

"All right," she said, "what is it? It has killed me a hundred times over, and it—"

"You remember?"

"I remember. My dreams were as vivid as yours."

"But it acted only because you were trying to destroy it."

"And the boy who came here this afternoon? When he wasn't able to kill me, that thing killed him."

"An accident, just an accident. It was terrified. I know. I felt its fear myself. It never intended any death but yours, and that only to defend itself."

"And now?"

Another uneasy silence, and then: "It's up to you. Try to think of the good it could do, the good it has done. Because of it, two people are alive and well who would otherwise be dead in days or weeks. And when the Reimanns—I've gone through the local newspaper files, and the same thing happened then. Ben Reimann saved a score of lives that I know about, probably more."

"And you're saying that's how you would use it? Only for good?"

"As much as I can, yes."

"And two nights ago, when you used it to make me come to you?"

He averted his eyes, and a flush spread up his neck. "I'm sorry. I didn't know what was happening. I was dreaming; my subconscious was getting away from me. I'm really very sorry." He swallowed, looking at her once again. "It could never happen again. I'm learning how to control it and how to control myself, too, I guess."

"Supper, you two."

It was Mattie's voice, and as they turned sharply, they saw her standing at the end of the hallway, watching them.

"Coming," Elena said, leaving Groves standing.

As she made her way to the dining room, she knew that Groves's explanation—plea?—had changed nothing. Even if it were true, every word and every implication, it would change nothing.

The pressure within her, screaming to be freed, was not subject to logic. It seemed a miracle that, because of Beth's continued presence, she had been able to withstand that pressure as long as she had.

Seth Laird saw the flashing lights of the ambulance and two police cars a quarter of a mile away as he topped a hill. The scanner, except for unrelated and routine business, had remained silent since the call for an ambulance had gone out and the ambulance had responded. Laird, risking accident and arrest himself, had raced around the outskirts of Wertham and along the old highway to Douglas Road, and now he was on a hill overlooking the road where the accident had happened.

For a moment, as the road dipped and curved and the flashing lights vanished beyond another hill, his foot lifted from the accelerator. Fear of what he would find made the trembling, which he thought he had gotten under control, begin again. At the speed the boy had apparently been going, only a miracle would have saved him from serious injury, and in his condition, any injury was serious. The slow healing, the necessity for renewed chemotherapy, the weakness resulting from the injury—everything conspired against him.

Even the boy himself.

And this last, frantic race through the night— had that

simply been the boy's equivalent of putting a gun to his head and pulling the trigger?

Shivering, Laird topped the last hill and saw the flashing lights once again. They were at a sharp curve near the bottom of the hill. In the glare of the spotlights and headlights, he could see where a section of wire fence had been ripped out. The boy's car was out of sight down a wooded slope beyond the jagged opening in the fence.

Two white-coated men were climbing the slope, nearing the fence as Laird coasted to a frightened stop a hundred yards from the ambulance. They were carrying a stretcher.

The body on the stretcher was totally covered.

Davis Grantland stood in the dining room door, watching his granddaughter still in the hall with March and that old man as the Groves woman hurried past to announce that the meal was ready.

As he watched, he knew what he must do.

Killing the woman, that March bitch, would not be enough, he thought calmly. Death would be too easy for her. No, she must be made to suffer, really suffer, the way he had suffered.

She had taken his son from him.

Justice demanded that her punishment be the same, that she suffer the same loss.

She must have her daughter taken from her.

For a moment he hesitated, blinking. Something seemed wrong with his thinking, but he couldn't, in the brief moment he was allowed, see what it was. He could only see that he must act, that he dared hesitate no longer.

For an instant, as the ambulance attendants brought his son's body up the hill, the image of Laird's grandmother flashed before his eyes in time with the ambulance lights.

In that instant, he decided.

Flooring the accelerator, he covered the last hundred yards with screaming tires and then slammed on the brakes, bringing the car to a skidding, sideways stop only yards from the rear of the ambulance just as the attendants finished sliding the stretcher in. At the sound of Laird's protesting tires, they looked around sharply, appearing ready to dive for the ditch if necessary.

Slamming the transmission into park, Laird leaped out, breathlessly. He recognized the two attendants, Joe Dahlbert and Maurie Jenkins, both men in their twenties.

"Thank God you're here," Laird blurted out. "I was afraid I was going to have to break someone's door in to get to a phone. Follow me."

"Doc Laird? What—" One of them began, but Laird cut him off sharply.

"No time!" He glanced at the sheet-covered figure of his son. "Looks like you were too late for that one, but if you hurry— There was an accident a mile or two back. I couldn't do anything. He's got to get to a hospital fast. Needs blood. Now come on."

Without waiting for any further reply, he leaped back in his car and, tires alternately squealing and spitting gravel, made a U turn. Stopping again, he leaned out the window and yelled back at the attendants, who were only now climbing into the ambulance after having hastily slammed its back doors shut. He waved at them frantically. "Hurry up."

Luckily, during Laird's performance, McNaughton was nowhere in sight. He must have been down with the car, Laird thought as he saw the other officer climb out of his patrol car a dozen yards past the ambulance and look puzzledly in Laird's direction.

Flooring the accelerator again, Laird sped off. Over the first hill, he located an intersecting road and, as soon as he was sure the ambulance driver saw him, turned onto it.

Four or five hundred yards down the tar-patched blacktop, he skidded to a stop and leaped out. The ambulance, its lights still flashing, did the same, the larger machine slewing dangerously. Laird was pointing into a thickly wooded area on the left when the two attendants clambered out of the ambulance.

"In there," Laird said. "Shot. Hurry."

The two attendants looked confused, but they were apparently willing to accept a doctor at his word. In a rush, they pulled another stretcher from the back of the ambulance.

"There," Laird repeated, pointing, "just beyond that large pine tree. About thirty or forty yards. You see it?"

"Why don't you show—" one of them began, but Laird cut him off again.

"Just go! There isn't much time."

They obeyed. Laird called after them, "That's right, straight ahead. About thirty yards. That big tree. Yes, that's the one. You're headed right for it."

As he spoke, he quickly moved back to the ambulance, climbed into the driver's seat, and tried to find the switch that would shut off the flashing lights. But he couldn't. With a last shout at the attendants, he slammed the door of the ambulance, put it in gear, and accelerated around his own car where, its keys in Laird's pocket, it half blocked the road.

As Elena left Groves and his protestations of the talisman's essential goodness and crossed the lobby toward the hall where Beth and the others were waiting, there was a sudden scream and then a shouted curse. At the sounds, her heart seemed to leap into her throat, and she raced the last few yards to the hall.

"Grantland! What the hell—" her brother's furious voice reached her ears just as she skidded into the hall.

"Stay back, damn it! Stay back!" It was Grantland's voice, and as she heard his rasping shout, her horrified eyes took in the tableau.

Grantland had snatched Beth up from behind and was now holding her clamped tightly against his chest with his left arm while his right hand brandished an open straight razor only inches from the child's throat. Everyone else was standing helplessly by, afraid to make a move for fear that Grantland, obviously insane, would be triggered into harming the girl. All it would take would be a split second, a slight twitch of the razor, and her life would be gushing irretrievably out.

"Davis!"

Miriam Grantland's shocked and trembling voice came from the door to the dining room, and Grantland darted a glance toward her.

"Stay out of this, Miriam," he snapped. "It's too late for

that sweetness-and-light crap you've been trying to feed me, too late!"

Miriam Grantland swallowed hard as she looked pleadingly at the others, particularly at Elena and her brother. Then, turning back to her husband, she took an unsteady step toward him.

"Keep back, Miriam. Keep away!" Grantland's back was against the wall, and he moved a step sideways toward the lobby, keeping the razor poised and ready. Elena, standing in the lobby end of the hall, took a step backward. Her heart was pounding; every muscle was piano-wire tense. For the moment, the pressure of the sounds that still boiled within her was almost forgotten.

Then Miriam Grantland took another hesitant step toward her husband.

"Please, Davis," she said, her voice still trembling, "this won't help. Don't you remember what we talked about this morning? Don't you remember?"

Grantland's eyes met his wife's, and for a second he seemed to falter. The razor drooped a fraction, and a puzzled look twisted at his features, but then it was over. He tightened his grip on the girl, and the razor snapped once more to attention.

He swiveled toward Elena. "Stand back, bitch," he snapped. "This is your doing from start to finish!"

She said nothing, nor did anyone else. It was as if no one even breathed.

Then, as Grantland moved warily past Elena and into the lobby, Beth, who had been totally silent until now, blurted out, "Mommy, what's Grandpa doing?"

"It's all right," Elena answered, lying automatically. "Just don't move, and everything will be all right."

Grantland snorted. "Everything's going to be all right," he said derisively. "Of course it is, just the way everything's going to be all right for my son."

His fingers twitched, and the blade came within a fraction of an inch of Beth's throat, but something seemed to stop it. Again that look of confusion clouded Grantland's eyes, but again it was gone in a second.

Shaking his head and ignoring the strands of silvery hair

that fell across his sweat-beaded forehead, Grantland continued to back across the lobby. His breathing seemed heavier and more labored, and his eyes darted from face to face as if looking for some hint of understanding for what he was doing.

As he backed slowly toward the door, his mouth began working silently, as if he were trying to say something but couldn't find the words or the strength to speak. He looked down at the girl, her arms pinned to her sides by his grip, her eyes straining upward to see his face.

"Mommy, I'm scared," she said. Tears were beginning to streak her cheeks.

Once again the hand with the razor twitched, and once again the blade fell short of touching the tiny throat. Grantland grimaced, and new beads of sweat popped out on his forehead.

"It's only justice," his voice grated, barely audible. "I lost my son because of you. It's only justice that you lose your daughter."

"She's your granddaughter," Elena said. "She's your son's daughter. You wanted to adopt her, remember?"

Another, more painful grimace, and Grantland seemed to be blinking back tears of his own.

"Just let her go, Mr. Grantland," Elena went on, and everyone else was deathly silent, listening, waiting. "Just let her go now, and you can see her whenever you want. Whenever you want."

When Elena fell silent, Miriam Grantland took it up. "She's right, Davis. Please, let her go. You don't want to harm your own granddaughter, your own flesh and blood. You want to help her, not hurt her. Don't you remember? You've always told me how much you wanted to help her."

Grantland was almost at the door now, and his face was a twisted mask of pain and confusion, but the razor still hovered barely an inch from the girl's throat.

"You don't understand," he cried. "I have to do it! It's only fair. She took my son. I must take her daughter. It's only fair!"

Then, in a sudden flurry of movement, he whirled and, using the hand still gripping the razor, jerked open the door and dashed out with a wordless cry, as if he were trying to escape not only Elena and the others but himself as well.

An instant later, as the outer door slammed shut, there was a brief scream and then a dull thud.

For a second, everyone was frozen, but then, as if their bonds had all been cut simultaneously, they raced to the door. Groves reached it first and rushed through in front of Elena.

Lurching to a stop at the top of the steps, Elena looked down at the ground as the others clustered behind her like water behind a dam.

On the walkway a yard from the bottom of the steps lay Davis Grantland. His right arm was bent at an odd angle, and there was blood on the hand that had held the razor.

Half underneath him, where he had fallen, was Beth.

She wasn't moving, wasn't making a sound.

It seemed to Seth Laird that it took forever to reach the next crossroad where he could turn the ambulance toward the old highway, but he knew that he couldn't have been driving more than a minute. And the lights, the goddamn lights! With those things flashing enough to light up the whole county, those patrol cars could spot him a mile away. And if they caught him, it would only mean another delay.

And he couldn't afford it! It was still at least three miles to Groves Lodge. He prayed that John Groves would be there.

At last, as the ambulance skidded from the side road onto the old highway and accelerated toward Groves Lodge, he found the switch that turned the flashing lights off. And there were no police cars in sight.

As John Groves rolled Grantland's still-breathing but unconscious form off the child, her mother, momentarily frozen at the top of the steps, leaped down next to him and dropped to her hands and knees.

"Beth!" She touched the child's tear-stained face, but there was no response, and now the others were clogging the door above them. A second later, her brother forced his way roughly through.

"Beth, it's all right," Elena said, stroking the child's brow. "You can move now. It's all over."

Then Bill was there, nudging her aside and leaning close, putting his ear to Beth's mouth. He stayed like that for no more than a couple of seconds. Then he raised himself and yelled back at the people in the door, "Call an ambulance. Fast! She's not breathing!"

With those words, the plan became clear to Groves. The words he had been forced to say to Elena March only minutes before now made perfect sense. A second later, when he found that he was not only able to lift the talisman from around his neck but was compelled to do so, he knew that he was right.

Grasping a frantic Elena March by one arm, he lifted her to her feet.

"Here," he heard himself saying as he held the talisman out to her, "take this. Save her. With this, you can do it!"

The signs pointing to Groves Lodge appeared with startling suddenness as the ambulance rocketed along at nearly seventy. Tires screamed, and the vehicle lurched on its heavy springs as Laird hit the brakes and fought the suddenly balky steering wheel.

The talisman dropping into Elena's hand was like an electrical shock. Physically, her entire body quivered and stiffened and was instantly shrouded in a deadening numbness, as if she had been doused in Novocain except for the one burning spot where the talisman touched her palm.

In her mind, the pressure to speak, to shout those impossible, guttural sounds at the top of her voice, was suddenly almost unbearable, like the urge to scream when an oncoming car looms up on the highway in front of you and you realize that there is no way to avoid it. For just an instant, her own daughter lying at her feet was forgotten. Her lips parted, and she could feel the muscles in her throat tightening and twisting to start forming the sounds.

But then Groves's voice penetrated the dead zone that had sprung up around her.

"Use it. Don't destroy it, use it! Save your daughter. It's the only way. Without it, she is dead."

Somehow, feeling as if she were trying to hold back a raging tiger with her bare hands, she forced the sounds back into her throat, forced her tongue to be silent.

"Use it," Groves pleaded in a harsh whisper, his blond-bearded face only inches from her own. "Only you can save her. Use the power this talisman gives you."

"How?" she hissed between clenched teeth. "For God's sake, how?"

"Accept it," Groves said, his voice urgent and pleading, like a priest urging a dying man to accept Christ. "That's all there is to it. Accept the talisman, and it will work for you. Accept it and believe in it, and it will save your child."

But then another voice lanced through the agony of her thoughts.

"Jessica," it said. "Jessica," it repeated, the name echoing as if there were two voices, not one, a fraction of a beat apart. "Do not be taken in by its trickery. It will destroy you. If you give yourself to it, it will destroy you."

Then one of those voices, one that seemed to touch both her ears and her mind, a faltering and ancient voice, began croaking out those senseless, guttural sounds that she still somehow held imprisoned within herself.

As the gateposts with their grotesque stone guardians loomed up in the ambulance headlights, Seth Laird hit the brakes and made a careening turn between them. Several cars were in the lot, and he hoped desperately that one of them belonged to Groves.

Seconds later, the ambulance skidded to a crunching stop on the gravel, and Laird leaped out. Without a glance toward the lodge, he raced around to the back of the ambulance and jerked open the doors.

As if he had crashed headlong into a brick wall, Laird stopped and stood motionless as his eyes fell on the interior of the ambulance.

The light from the bare bulb on the post a dozen yards away slanted over his shoulder and through the parted ambulance doors. For the first time, Laird saw his son.

The body of his son.

The attendants had slipped the stretcher properly into the brackets that held it to the ambulance wall, but in the confusion that Laird's arrival had caused, they had not strapped the body to the stretcher.

The body lay twisted on the floor of the ambulance. The sheet that had covered it now lay mostly under the body. A smear of blood was on the opposite wall near the floor where, at some point during Laird's frantic drive, the body had struck before bouncing back to the center where it now lay.

There was blood on the boy's shirtfront where something—the steering column?—had smashed into the chest. One side of the forehead and one temple were depressed and bloody. Here and there fragments of bone jutted out. And one eye dangled from the wrecked socket like a bloody marble on a ragged, slippery piece of twine.

All hope drained out of him. In the last few hours he had brought himself to believe that miracles were still possible in this world, but this thing that had been his son was beyond even miracles.

Then, suddenly, someone was grasping his arm and pulling at him, jerking him out of the near trance the sight of his son's mangled body had trapped him in. It was a woman, he saw dimly, John Groves's wife. But what was wrong with her? Why was she pulling at him the way she was? Why was she shouting? Couldn't she see Carl's body a half dozen feet away?

But then, finally, her urgent words began to slice through the haze of his grief and anger.

"The little girl, Beth March," she was saying. "Something happened to her. She's not breathing. Please, hurry. Hurry!"

For another moment his mind refused to shift gears completely, and he couldn't imagine what his son's death could have to do with some little girl he had seen only once in his life. He couldn't imagine what this woman wanted him to do about it. His son was dead, and there was no longer anything he could do about it.

"Please, Doctor," the woman's voice persisted, and her tugs on his sleeve threatened to rip the seams of his jacket. "I don't know why you're here, but please hurry. She's not breathing. We can't find a pulse."

Then, at last, the scene at the front of the lodge fifty yards away forced its way into his mind and connected with the woman and her frantic pleas. People were crowded in the door, while others stood on the steps, and still others were on the walkway below the steps. Two figures lay on the ground, one a man, the other a girl no more than five.

Beth March.

Elena March's daughter, the woman he had been dragged out here to see in the middle of the night, the woman who, somehow, was tied in with Groves and the Reimanns and—

Abruptly, Laird sprinted toward the group.

Elena March was almost literally paralyzed by the two forces warring within her. One was simply her frantic desire to save her daughter, while the other was a mindless, sourceless compulsion to destroy the talisman. It came not from within her or even from those other countless lives she had glimpsed in her nightmares but from something beyond even them, from some ancient, unknowable abyss. And its strength had been growing, becoming a physical force that plucked at her vocal cords, that parted her lips in an excruciating effort to make her join what she now recognized as Henry Winton's ancient voice in rasping out the incantation that was still dammed up within her own throat.

But all logic, all emotion came together in her daughter's pale, lifeless face, blocking out Winton's straining voice. And then Groves was grating in her ear once again.

"Use it. It's your daughter's life you're throwing away if you don't. Your daughter's life!"

Groves's hands closed around hers, folding her fingers around the talisman and squeezing until, through the tingling heat that still pulsed from it, she could feel the edges biting into her palm. Just as, her mind shouted at her, it had bitten into the hands of Jessica Reimann.

The first nightmare was upon her once again. The people standing around her became the screaming mob that had surrounded Jessica Reimann. The building looming over her became the towering Reimann mansion with flames licking against the sky. And on the ground, the body of her husband, the body of Marcus Reimann, began to move.

But it was not the body of Marcus Reimann.

It was not.

It was the body of her daughter.

And it was not moving. It would never move again unless she accepted this thing, this talisman that pulsed in her bleeding palm.

She knew that she had to accept it.

As that conviction flowed over her, the sound of Winton's ancient voice faded, and one corner of her mind saw him crumple slowly to the ground, gasping for breath for a second and then lying still.

She knelt over her daughter, pushing her brother aside and holding the talisman before her. The child's small face was chalky pale in the dim light, and she wondered frantically whether she had delayed too long, whether she was too late.

No. Twin voices suddenly filled her mind, and images of Marcus Reimann and the young Henry Winton swirled in the air before her, blotting out the lifeless face of her daughter.

In that same instant, she was thrust aside by a heavy hand, knocked sprawling on the grass, and then someone else was kneeling over the child, two outstretched fingers repeatedly pressing against the fragile rib cage, forcing the heart to pump.

"Breathing," the man snapped, and Elena recognized the doctor who had come to see her two nights before, Dr. Laird. "Someone get down here and help me with her breathing."

And then, as Mattie, who had been hovering at the doctor's side, leaned down and placed her mouth over Beth's, Elena suddenly knew the truth. In the same wordless way she had recognized Winton as her brother in that other life the moment she had come face to face with the old man, she now knew the truth of what was happening. The link between herself and Winton—her twin—still existed, and through that link, from his dying mind or persistent spirit, came the knowledge that could yet save her.

The creature that had appeared at the moment of her death

in those countless other lives was causing Beth to die. It was keeping her heart from beating, keeping her lungs from breathing. If Elena would accept the talisman and the creature bound to it, it would allow the child to live.

And she would be its slave forever.

It would have won not just in this single lifetime but forever. There were no others to oppose it. There had been no others in past millennia, and there would be no others in future millennia if she became its slave now.

But there was another way. She did not have to accept the creature.

She could destroy it instead, as she had tried to do countless times before.

She could destroy it, and the hold on Beth and herself would be broken, and the child would live.

Those impossible sounds, that guttural, rasping incantation that Winton had begun, would defeat and destroy the creature.

Slowly, but picking up speed and momentum like a growing storm, the incantation began to emerge from her throat.

A mixture of elation and fear flooded through John Groves as Elena March's lips parted and the sounds began, sounds that he hadn't thought a human throat and tongue could produce. The creature was failing, and soon it would be gone, but what could it still do in the seconds or minutes that remained to it?

He felt it reaching out, pulling at his own mind like a magnet, forcing him to move, forcing him to drop to his knees on the grass and search for the razor Grantland had dropped, forcing him to take it in his hand and turn back to Elena March, forcing him to—

But there it stopped. Unlike those other nightmarish times, his resistance was suddenly bolstered. This time he was not alone. It was as if someone put a hand on his shoulder, helping him to hold back, giving him strength he had not possessed before.

With an effort that made him feel as if he were straining against gigantic elastic bands with each move, he turned and, with all his drained strength, threw the razor onto the ground beneath the leafless trees.

Suddenly he was released, as if the bands restraining him had suddenly been cut. His entire body jerked spasmodically as the muscles were freed to follow the dictates of his own mind. Lurching the dozen yards to where his feeble throw had taken the razor, he snatched it up and threw it again, this time far into the shadowy darkness of the evergreens that lined the grounds.

Then the others, one after the other, felt the creature's desperate, momentary touch. First the detective, Jessup, who was just emerging from the lodge after needlessly phoning for a doctor, blinked and lurched forward, almost falling down the steps, his eyes glazing over for a second. But as quickly as the touch came, it moved on, leaving Jessup shaking and limp.

Then Bill March was jerked erect from where he still leaned over the doctor and Mattie, watching their continued methodical work on Beth. March's seizure was even briefer than Jessup's, and Miriam Grantland's was briefer yet. The creature, casting about in desperation, had tried them all and found that their resistance, coupled with that other force—the protectively hovering spirit of Marcus Reimann? of Henry Winton?—that seemed determined to protect Elena was too much for it to overcome in the brief moments left to it.

But there was another way, one last desperate chance . . .

In the ambulance, even as the mind-wrenching words of the incantation were repeated again and again, the physical processes that had begun at Carl Laird's death slowed and stopped.

The conversion of glycogen to lactic acid in those muscles which were still whole halted, although it could not be reversed. The chemical changes in the fluid of the remaining usable eye halted and established a new balance. The clouded cornea cleared as tear ducts secreted the last of their contents and the single eyelid slipped down and remained closed, husbanding those few precious drops. Dozens of cut and torn veins and arteries went shut spasmodically, sealing in what blood remained, and the sludging of the blood itself stopped. In the brief time left, the clumped blood cells could not all be separated and restored to full efficiency, nor could the detached sections of veins be reattached. Vital sections of the body would remain starved and bloodless, but there were enough intact routes to supply a few moments' nourishment to enough muscles to provide a brief spurt of mobility. It would not last long, but it did not have to. Without the resistance of a still-living brain to overcome, the remnants of the body did not have to function long.

Inside the crushed chest, behind the shattered ribs and torn flesh, one lung expanded spasmodically, and the heart began a powerful but erratic beat.

To Bill March, the world seemed to have gone totally mad in a matter of minutes. Grantland and Beth lay on the ground. The old man, Wilson or Winton, had started babbling, and then he collapsed. An ambulance, obviously not in response to any call they had made, came careening in, and someone—a doctor, apparently, if what Mrs. Groves had been shouting was right—came dashing up to start some kind of resuscitation procedure.

But Elena, instead of helping, left that to Mrs. Groves and just continued those insane noises. John Groves was thrashing around like a spastic, and then a brief, jerking dizziness struck Bill March himself.

Just as the momentary dizziness seemed to have cleared completely, a new sound came from behind him, from the direction of the ambulance.

When he turned toward the sound, he knew that the world had gone mad, taking him along with it.

Outlined in the fading glare of the ambulance's still-burning headlights, something out of a cheap horror movie was lurching toward him at breakneck pace. Once it might have been a young boy, but now it was a monstrosity. One shoeless foot dragged like Lon Chaney's in all those Mummy pictures on the "Late Show." The front of the shirt, becoming visible in the light from the bare bulb above the lodge door as the thing approached, was soaked with blood, as was two-thirds of the face.

On the face itself the makeup man had outdone himself.

One side of the forehead and the entire temple were concave as if struck by a sledgehammer. Fragments of bone poked whitely through the blood, and the eye on that side dangled and bounced obscenely against the remnants of the cheek.

Frozen, Bill March watched the grisly apparition lurch past him, raising both arms and stretching them out before itself even though one arm appeared to bend in one too many spots.

There were screams then as others saw what was shambling through their midst, and they fell back helplessly.

Bill saw where the monstrosity was heading.

It was bearing down unwaveringly on Elena. In another second, its bloody hands would close on her throat.

In an action not unlike the instinctive lashing out at a snake or spider, Bill March leaped at the creature's back.

To Elena, nothing existed beyond the talisman that still burned in her clenched, bleeding fist and the sounds that threatened to tear her vocal cords from her throat. If she could continue the incantation that still boiled through her mind, she would be free and her daughter would live.

It was beginning to work.

Although she could not know it, the process had begun when the first sounds had emerged from Henry Winton's throat, just as it had begun that other time nearly seven decades earlier.

But this time the incantation continued.

Deep within the frozen energy that was the talisman, a change was taking place. Triggered by the complex vibrations set up by her twisting, grating voice, something that had not been touched for millennia began to stir. Like a lock that could be keyed only by one person's voice speaking a specific sequence of words, something began to move and expand and grow stronger.

In her hand, the talisman no longer burned but pulsed with a chilling coldness that spread and engulfed her and soaked deep within her, driving out the numbness and replacing it with the feeling that her veins were filled not with blood but with a frigid slush of half-melted ice.

The wind began. It was the same wind she had felt in

Jessica Reimann's body, a wind that poured in on her from all directions as if she were at the center of a vortex, a wind that rushed through her body as it was drawn to the talisman.

As the ethereal wind grew stronger, as it was sucked into the depths of the talisman, a gate began to open. The barriers between dimensions weakened and grew thin, and the darkness, the living darkness of which the talisman itself was an extension, began to flow through.

Questing, reaching blindly like the tentacle of some formless sea creature, it flowed through the expanding gate.

The wind became real, a physical movement of the air itself as it was sucked into that lightless void.

Beyond that gate, hovering helplessly in that other, alien universe, a million eyes watched and waited to see if, at last, the creature they had unwittingly created and then loosed on a world they could not themselves reach could be drawn back. A creature that, a distant and still-rational corner of Elena's frenzied thoughts realized, was not a creature of flesh and blood despite the gargoylelike images that still flared in her mind but an incorporeal being of the same dark, unearthly energies that were compressed into the seeming solidity of the talisman.

Had the message, the single desperate message they had been able to force through the barriers that had inexorably re-formed all those millennia ago—had that message retained its power, its potency? Or had it, as it passed from body to body, through incarnation after incarnation, faded to an impotent shadow, able only to scratch helplessly at the barriers but never to breach them?

As the wind, both the real and the unreal, grew stronger, Elena began to feel the terror of the creature itself as it fought with increasing desperation to retain its hold on this world that had served and fed it so well and so long.

The mangled husk of Carl Laird was only yards from Elena when Bill March lunged and caught its shoulders. One of its legs gave way, the ankle bending at a complete right angle, and the creature twisted and toppled facedown to the ground beneath him.

"Help me," Bill shouted, his voice little more than a falsetto shriek. "Somebody help me!"

But Jessup, his face pasty pale, stumbled backward against the steps. Grantland's wife, now kneeling over her husband, didn't seem to hear. And Groves, still standing a dozen feet away, seemed frozen and incapable of motion or sound.

Then the thing was struggling to rise, twisting and writhing beneath Bill. He could hear the muffled grating sounds as the splintered ends of bone scraped together, could hear the bubblings as air was forced through a throat still awash with blood, could hear the unhuman moaning from vocal cords responding to random impulses from a shattered brain.

Then the body managed to turn itself, and the ruined face was only inches from his own. The blood and splintered fragments of bone were now mixed with grass and dirt, and the dangling eye had been crushed as the creature fell. Its mouth opened with a cracking, grating sound, and then it snapped at his throat like a maddened dog, its teeth catching one side of his unbuttoned collar as he jerked instinctively backward.

But that flinching movement was all it needed. Bill felt himself being heaved to one side, and then the creature was lurching to its feet.

The mangled body staggering across the lawn had shocked John Groves into immobility, not so much because of its grotesque appearance but because of the other images it conjured up so forcibly: the youngster in Brattleboro that very afternoon and that other, anonymous man barely half a dozen miles from here the day before.

But then, as the creature managed to thrust March aside and tried to struggle to its feet once again, Groves's muscles unfroze, and he lunged forward. If the creature succeeded in stopping Elena March, in killing her, Groves would be back where he started, a slave to the talisman forever, forced to live one waking nightmare after another with even death denied him.

As Groves charged, the Laird boy's body fell to its hands and knees as the one ravaged leg gave way again, but one outstretched hand was only inches from Elena, who seemed oblivious to everything that was happening around her as the bizarre sounds continued to boil from her lips. At the same time, Bill March's hands reached out and grasped at the creature's foot but found themselves holding only an empty, bloody shoe.

In an uncontrolled lunge, Groves crashed on top of the body, knocking it flat, its arms and legs spread-eagling grotesquely.

But he couldn't hold it. Its physical strength was obviously failing, but his own arms and legs were suddenly receiving conflicting messages, and he began to twitch and jerk like someone undergoing a grand mal seizure. No matter how hard he willed his hands to pin the creature's arms to the ground, they fluttered like tissue paper in the wind, and the creature twisted beneath him, twisting and bucking and turning to the accompaniment of an obscene cacophony of mindless moans and raspings and bubblings that emerged from the interior of the shattered body.

But still, despite the uncontrolled flopping of his arms and legs, Groves somehow kept his body on top of the thing that had once been Carl Laird. It managed to turn until it faced up at him, and its arms tore at his hair and his clothes and pounded at his head, but still he kept his weight on the thing beneath him.

Just a few more moments, the thought raced through his mind, just a few more seconds and it will be over. A few more moments and the creature would be finished, and he would have made up in some small way for having set it free in the first place. Just a few more moments . . .

But as those desperate thoughts careened through his mind, he felt himself growing weaker, and then he felt the pain, and finally he realized that almost from the instant the creature had twisted itself onto its back, while its arms and legs had been flailing ineffectively, its teeth had been systematically ripping at his throat.

His last thought as blackness closed in was one of sharp relief as his dying mind realized that at least his own term of slavery was over.

A moment later, his still-twitching corpse was thrust aside.

* * *

The wind grew ever stronger, and that other world of alien darkness and unseen eyes drew ever closer as the talisman in Elena's hand continued its unearthly pulsing. The coldness that enveloped her body was a physical thing that sucked at her remaining strength and threatened to send her crashing to the ground, but still the sounds of the incantation continued to gush raggedly from her throat, repeating and repeating themselves like a grotesque litany.

But its work was nearly completed. The barriers between the worlds were fading rapidly now, and where the worlds touched, the gate was completing itself. The creature could not maintain its increasingly precarious hold on this world much longer. The timeless forces that had kept it locked to that other world through the talisman were strengthening their hold like the grasping field of an electromagnet as the current builds. Soon it would be torn free and sucked through the vortex that swirled around Elena.

Just a few seconds more, and a recurrent struggle a dozen millennia old would be ended. Just a few seconds more, and she would not die in defeat as she had died hundreds of times before. Just a few seconds more—

Suddenly the physical world, from which the incantation seemed to have totally isolated her, intruded with brutal force as she felt something slam into the back of her legs. She felt herself falling, and then she struck the ground with a jarring thud that knocked the breath from her lungs and forced the incantation to a gasping halt.

And in that same instant, before she had a chance to painfully suck in a new breath and continue, she felt hands clutching at her own hands and then at her shoulders, and she felt a dead weight pressing down on her hips and legs. Something was trying to drag itself upward, toward her face, toward her throat.

Looking down in shock, she saw first the top of a head, a mass of dark, curly hair matted with bits of grass and leaves and dirt and something that glistened wetly in the dim light. But then the pressure of the hands on her shoulders increased spasmodically, and the head raised itself as the body hitched itself up.

She saw the blood and bone and the remnants of the gouged-out eye and the clouding cornea of the other and the shreds of flesh still gripped in the clenched teeth, and she heard the sounds from within the mangled body as she felt and saw it inching its way inexorably upward.

But she didn't scream, no matter how much her instincts cried out for such release. She wasn't allowed to scream or even to struggle. Whatever it was that had driven her this far continued to drive with unrelenting force. Her lips parted, and her lungs filled with air that was rank with the smell of the dead thing upon her. The throat-rending sounds of the incantation flooded out into the night one last time.

The last taut membrane of resistance ripped and parted, and the worlds met and coalesced.

As she fell silent, exhausted, the world seemed to slow to an inchworm's pace. The screams and shouts that battered at her senses dropped to a thundering bass. The light from the bulb above the lodge door faded into the deepest red and beyond. The spasmodic motion of the thing that pulled itself across her body slowed and stopped, its bared teeth inches from her throat.

But the talisman, still clutched tightly in her bleeding hand, began to move. The pulsing cold was submerged in an actual physical motion, a sinuous, writhing motion like a balled snake uncoiling. As it moved, it expanded. It didn't force Elena's hands open but moved out through them to engulf her in the swirling blackness that was an extension of that other world. Like the cold and the wind that had preceded it, the darkness swallowed her up.

And as it did, she saw motion.

From all sides, riding the invisible wind that still funneled through her and into the talisman, a thousand shapes flickered through the edges of her vision, a thousand blots of even deeper darkness that her eyes could not bring into focus. Inward, ever inward, they spiraled, and as they did, countless shards of memory pierced her mind, the shards that were all that remained of the countless minds and souls trapped in the same vortex of blind forces that had held the creature itself prisoner down through the millennia.

There was Marcus Reimann, who, alone of them all, had possessed the strength to resist and had retained enough of that strength, enough of a sense of a separate identity to continue to struggle long after his death.

There was Ben Reimann, who had fought the power less successfully.

There were the hundreds who had fought it not at all, who had quietly used it, leaving swaths of terror in country after country, century after century.

There were the scores who suspected that the power came from Satan and gloried in it.

There were the self-important few who, knowing beyond doubt that the power to heal came from God, used that power and forced themselves to accept the secret horror that inevitably followed as God's way of meting out justice to an unworthy servant and a sinful world.

And there were the thousands upon thousands who knew nothing, who were simply victims, fodder for that irresistible appetite, thousands from every spot on the globe, from every time in history and beyond.

Then, suddenly, it was over.

The seven-sided, corroded metal frame that held the talisman collapsed and crumpled under the pressure of Elena's hands. The pool of blackness that had been the talisman was gone, as was everything that had grown from it.

The worlds separated, and the rift in the barrier flowed together and sealed itself.

Light shifted back to its normal hues.

Voices returned to their normal pitches.

The body of Carl Laird collapsed on Elena's breast like a flaccid hunk of meat and began spilling blood from its suddenly unsealed veins.

But the only thing Elena heard was the sound of a small girl, a five-year-old girl, pulling in a gasping breath and beginning to cough with life.

In those first seconds, it was Bill March who saved the day, at least as far as Beth was concerned. Acting almost instinctively, he answered her plaintive cry of "Mommy!" by elbowing the doctor and Mrs. Groves aside and scooping up the child and letting her bury her face in his welcome and familiar shoulder. Then, carefully shielding her from the hellish scene that surrounded them both, murmuring comfortingly in her ear, he rushed with her into the lodge. Mattie, either not seeing or not allowing herself to see her husband sprawled on the ground, followed close on Bill's heels and, once inside, spent the next half hour holding and reassuring the child and resolutely avoiding listening to the distant voices that occasionally filtered through the closed windows of the living room.

Outside, it was Bill also who suggested that Grantland and his wife and Jessup leave once Laird attended to Grantland's gashed hand and twisted arm. By then, the others had taken in the full extent of what had happened in those few minutes, and when an almost slobberingly terrified and contrite Davis Grantland agreed, no one objected. Grantland, oblivious to his own injuries, couldn't understand what had happened to him, what had made him act as insanely as he had, and his relief that both Elena and her brother and even the doctor seemed willing to believe his protestations of innocence and bafflement was overwhelming. Even the slightest hint from Elena that he might someday be allowed to see Beth again was greeted with a flood of gratitude that no one who knew Grantland would have believed possible. Jessup, too, was overwhelmed, but in his case it was simply with relief that he was being allowed to leave this place without having to explain anything to anyone but himself. He suspected—hoped— that he would soon be able to convince himself that it had all been a series of nightmarish fever dreams.

Finally, after the Grantlands and Jessup had left and Elena, hastily scrubbed and dressed in fresh sweater and slacks, had put a curious but oddly sleepy Beth to bed with an equally sleepy B.C. for company, and after Mattie had tearfully accepted the death of her husband, a story was agreed upon.

Then the bodies were moved to locations that would support that story, and then the sheriff was called.

Telling the truth, they all had realized from the start, would be pointless and foolish. In the first place, it would never be believed. In the second, whatever it was that had caused these things to happen was gone. There was virtually no discussion of what that cause was, simply an unspoken agreement that something had existed. Elena knew that it had, Laird believed that it had, and the others were more than willing to accept that it had, since nothing else could possibly explain the events of those few minutes.

His son, Laird said—and they all reluctantly agreed—had been high on the drugs he had gotten in Brattleboro. He had waited at the lodge for Groves, a teacher he had recently taken a dislike to, had attacked him like a wild animal and killed him. That was why the boy had turned tail when the police had started to follow him. Laird, who police knew had been desperately trying to track the terminally ill boy down, arrived moments too late. Seeing what his son had done and then, minutes later, hearing of the accident, Laird had rushed to the scene. Realizing that his son was dead and that the marks on Groves's throat could be matched to the boy's teeth, Laird had gone temporarily out of his head. He had stolen the body in an irrational effort to keep the grisly truth from ever coming out. Winton, meanwhile, had stumbled on Groves's body when he went for a walk on the lodge grounds a few minutes after the killing. He had died of a heart attack on the spot.

It was weak, they all knew, and it would leave Laird vulnerable to public opinion if not legal action, but no one could think of anything better. And it was certainly not as weak or damaging as the truth would have been.

When the last of the men from the sheriff's department left shortly before midnight, the four of them stood exhausted in the huge lobby of the lodge. Laird had taken the brunt of the questioning, as he had expected to, although the sheriff had obviously tried to soft-pedal it as much as possible out of consideration for his loss. Even so, and even if no formal charges were ever issued, there was no way the affair could be kept out of the papers, and Laird suspected that his practice in Wertham, except for patients who had a morbid curiosity, was all but ended. Even earlier, however, he had begun to consider the possibility—probability— of setting up a practice somewhere else.

Mattie, after those few early tears, had remained resolutely dry-eyed through it all, but now, as the departing sheriff's car faded to silence, it was becoming harder. She turned to Elena.

"I know it's asking a lot," she said, her voice still controlled, "and there's no reason in the world why you should, but could you stay on? At least for a day or two?"

Until after the funeral, she thought, but kept the words inside.

"These last few days," Mattie went on instead, "you and your daughter have been almost like family."

The only family I've got out here, her thoughts insisted on continuing maudlinly, but again she kept the thoughts to herself.

Elena hesitated a second, but Bill spoke up instantly. "Of course. We can both stay. And Beth, too, of course. I saw how the two of you—"

He stopped, embarrassed, cursing himself inwardly. The woman's husband had been killed only hours ago, and here he was making excuses to be around her, to stay longer. Of all the goddamn inappropriate—

But no, damn it! It wasn't inappropriate, and it certainly wasn't selfish. She was alone out here, and she needed friends, and that was all he was offering, friendship. His and Ellie's and Beth's, although she already obviously had the friendship of his sister and her daughter. Besides, he had seen—or felt, at least—a similar bond growing between Ellie and the doctor. The way they had supported each other while they had been getting their stories straight for the sheriff showed that. They just seemed to need each other, at least for the moment, or so Bill was convinced. The doctor had lost a son, and Ellie had, in that strange old man, lost someone who apparently meant a great deal to her and then had almost lost her daughter. She and the doctor had shared something they could never share with anyone else outside this small group.

"I wasn't going to ask," Laird said then, "but it would be good if you could stay. For one thing, I'd like to try to learn a little more about what really happened here this evening. And before."

Then, as if just remembering, he turned to Mattie. "Whatever it was that happened to your husband, it wasn't all bad," he said, and then went on to tell her about the two healings.

But as Laird spoke, one of the fragments of memory that had embedded itself in Elena's mind in those last seconds bobbed to the surface, the fragment that encompassed the pain and horror of the last minutes of the life of a fifteen-year-old boy named Jimmy Stevens.

And she knew. Just as dozens of other bits of unbidden knowledge—like the incantation itself—had come to her, one more forced itself upon her now.

There was a connection between that death and others like it and the healings. Groves, or the thing that had controlled Groves, was responsible for both. One made the other possible.

But Elena said nothing. There was no point, no reason to speak. The knowledge would only hurt Mattie, who had already been hurt more than enough. It would help no one, certainly not the parents of the boy. They would be far better off if they were able to believe, once the mutilated body was found, that the mutilation had been done after death, not before.

She might someday share it with Laird if he were anywhere that would allow her to share things with him, but not with anyone else. If she were lucky, the knowledge might even fade away and be forgotten, the way the incantation had faded from her mind once its purpose had, after all those millennia and all those lost lives, finally been accomplished.

And then, even as the thought occurred to her, it began to happen.

Or perhaps it had been happening all along, gradually, but she had only then noticed it.

For a moment, as memory after memory faded into nothingness, she felt relief at the lifting of a horror-filled burden. But just as quickly as it had come, the relief changed to fear and anger. Memories she knew she had possessed only seconds before were gone, leaving only the knowledge that they had existed, that she had known something that she didn't know now.

Would it stop? Or would the fading continue, eating away not only the memories of the talisman but her own memories as well? Was this some vicious form of self-destruction built into whatever it was that had skipped down through the ages from mind to mind, from century to century? Now that it had accomplished its purpose, would it destroy not only itself but its host as well?

No, she screamed silently in her mind. No! Stop! Stop! I don't want to forget!

Then, suddenly, the terror vanished, replaced by a sourceless warmth, almost a euphoria, and then that, too, was gone like a parting word of praise lost in a summer breeze.

Her memory was whole once again.

Even the impossible, unearthly sounds of the incantation were there. But there was no compulsion to shout them out. They were simply there, along with the hundreds—thousands— of other fragments of memory, waiting.

Waiting . . .

Abruptly, a voice penetrated her thoughts, and then another.

"Elena? Is something wrong?"

"Ellie? Are you all right?"

Seth Laird stood before her, leaning close, and beside him was her brother. Mattie was looking anxiously over Bill's shoulder. Somehow, although she had no idea how it was possible, any more than she had really understood the events of the last four days, she sensed Beth stirring faintly in her sleep, somehow feeling her mother's reassurance, and drifting back to sleep.

"Yes," Elena said, "I think I'm going to be—*we're* going to be—all right."

PLAYBOY NOVELS OF HORROR AND THE OCCULT
ABSOLUTELY CHILLING

_____ 16920	THE BANISHED J. N. Williamson	$2.75
_____ 16778	BLOOD WRATH Chester Krone	$2.50
_____ 16918	DARK DREAMING Gene Snyder	$2.95
_____ 21107	DEATH Stuart David Schiff, editor	$2.50
_____ 16802	THE DESECRATION OF SUSAN BROWNING Russell Martin	$2.50
_____ 21032	THE DEVIL AND LISA BLACK Russell Martin	$2.95
_____ 16768	HELLSTONE Steven Spruill	$2.50
_____ 16651	HEX Robert Curry Ford	$2.25
_____ 16832	HORROR HOUSE J. N. Williamson	$2.95
_____ 16905	HORRORS Charles L. Grant, editor	$2.25
_____ 16949	INDECENT RELATIONS Kenneth McKay	$2.95
_____ 16766	MESSAGES FROM MICHAEL Chelsea Quinn Yarbro	$2.50
_____ 16612	MIND WAR Gene Snyder	$2.50
_____ 16948	THE NAUGHTY GIRLS Arthur Wise	$2.95
_____ 16868	NIGHTMARES Charles L. Grant, editor	$2.25
_____ 21077	NURSERY TALE T. M. Wright	$2.95
		582-25

PLAYBOY NOVELS OF HORROR AND THE OCCULT
ABSOLUTELY CHILLING

___	16683	RHEA Russ Martin	$2.50
___	16751	SHADOWS Charles L. Grant, editor	$2.25
___	16947	THE SHAMAN Frank Coffey	$2.95
___	21058	THE SIBLING Adam Hall	$2.95
___	21062	SIREN Linda Crockett Gray	$2.50
___	21135	STRANGE SEED T. M. Wright	$2.50
___	21138	TERRORS Charles L. Grant, editor	$2.50
___	16940	THE TRANSFERENCE Ella Smith	$2.95
___	21116	THE TRANSFORMATION Joy Fielding	$2.95
___	16693	THE WANTING FACTOR Gene DeWeese	$2.50
___	16912	THE WOMAN NEXT DOOR T. M. Wright	$2.50

582-26

PBJ BOOKS, INC.
Book Mailing Service
P.O. Box 690 Rockville Centre, New York 11571

NAME_____

ADDRESS_____

CITY_____STATE_____ZIP_____

Please enclose 50¢ for postage and handling if one book is ordered; 25¢ for each additional book. $1.50 maximum postage and handling charge. No cash, CODs or stamps. Send check or money order.

Total amount enclosed: $_____